I0673955

RISE OF THE FAE

USA TODAY BESTSELLING AUTHOR

REBEKAH R. GANIERE

FALLEN ANGEL PRESS

Rise of the Fae © 2014 Rebekah R. Ganiere

All rights reserved. No part of this publication may be reproduced, distributed, or transmitted in any form or by any means, including photocopying, recording, or other electronic or mechanical methods, without the prior written permission of the publisher, except in the case of brief quotations embodied in critical reviews and certain other noncommercial uses permitted by copyright law.

This book is a work of fiction. The names, characters, places and incidents are fictitious and are not to be construed as real in any way. Any resemblance to persons, living or dead, actual events, locales or organizations is entirely coincidental.

ISBN: 978-1-63300-048-3
ISBN: 978-1-63300-054-4

Cover art by Rebekah R. Ganiere
vwzdesigns.com

DEDICATION

For all the Creatures who Hide in the Shadows

Newsletter

To claim your Two FREE Books and find out more about Rebekah R. Ganiere and her other Upcoming Releases You can Go Here:
www.RebekahGaniere.com/Newsletter

GLOSSARY

Coven Lord – The ruling governor over a given area.

Human – Anyone person born of two human parents who wasn't mutated by the V2000 virus. Those of pure human blood who were born human and have not been turned into vampyr.

Minion – A Vampire servant, assistant or companion, who has both rights and a salary.

Rogue Syndrome – A degrading disease similar to syphilis that causes vamps to go insane with bloodlust.

Slave – A human in the service of a Vampire or vampyr who is not paid and is bought and sold like property.

Slavers – Vampires and vampyr who hunt down humans and sell them to the highest bidder.

The High Council – The Society governing body. Made up of the Salvatori family, the High Council is the law. Members of the High Council are over 1000 years of age and rule from their place of power in Romania. Lucian Salvatori is the Venerable King and head of the High Council.

Three Kings – The Three Kings of America govern all of the Coven Lords and answer only to The High Council.

Tracking Squad – The police of the Vampire World. The Trackers are the highest trained Vampires and vampyr available for hire.

Vamp – Once human, now mutated by the V2000 virus, they are a vampire subspecies and the grunt workers of the Vampire Society. Gray of skin and black blooded they eat human food and can walk during the daylight.

Vampire (vamp—ire) – A pureblooded Vampire who is born a Vampire. They are the royalty of The Society that now run the world.

Vampyr (vamp—eer) – A lesser member of the Vampire Society. Vampyr are not born Vampires. They were once humans that have been bitten, or are the offspring of one human parent and one Vampire parent.

CHAPTER ONE

S elene stared into the luminescent void, her breathing
short, eyes watering from the glow. The surface rippled
with light and dark swirling together, waiting to
swallow her. Her heartbeat drummed like a hummingbird's.
It'd been over two decades since she'd seen one. How long had
it been here without her noticing? So many years she'd
searched for one, and now one awaited just within her grasp.

She glanced around the glade. The sickly—sweet scent of
the blossoms growing next to the cherished altar churned her
stomach. Her blood still stained the massive alabaster stone
she'd spent weeks tied to, despite her being ordered to scrub it
till it shone.

Hushed footsteps swished behind her. The Council of
Elders had chosen her for this mission, but not because they
liked her, let alone trusted her. No, they chose her because no
one else who could do what they needed done.

"Selene. Are you ready, daughter?" Her mother's smooth
voice floated over Selene's neck, making her body tingle.

Mother had never sounded so passive and distant when they'd lived on the Earth realm. Her hand fell like a feather upon Selene's shoulder.

Selene nodded mutely, her gaze never leaving the portal, not daring to give away her desire to race through the rift and disappear. Afraid that if she blinked she would find it had been another test she'd failed and be punished for.

"We're all counting on you, Selene. This is your chance to prove to everyone whose side you're on. To avenge what's been done and return honor to me, as well as give you what you've always wanted— a place to belong."

Her mother brushed the hair from Selene's shoulder with thin, light fingers.

Selene balled her fists to keep from swatting them away.

"Don't let your feelings for Maelstrom get in the way of your mission. And don't be distracted by the pleasures of that hedonistic place. It's different now. Worse. The temptations are greater than ever now that the Vampires rule."

Selene's throat dried like it had been scrubbed with sandpaper. She tried to conjure enough saliva to swallow. Ever since she'd left the Earth realm, she'd been trying to fit in, trying to prove herself, while secretly praying for a way out. Excitement and terror clenched her gut and made her palms sweat.

"I won't succumb." Was that too much glee in her voice? She turned her gaze from her means of escape to her mother's beautiful face. Selene donned the placid expression that the High Elder had tried so hard to beat into her and lowered her eyes in the most demure of fashions. "I will do my best, mother."

"Be well, my daughter, and bring me honor." Her mother pushed something into her palm. "There's one of us on the other side. He'll be your contact. When you've gotten close enough, and you're ready for us to prepare the trap, he'll contact us."

"Move already!"

Selene's body lurched, and she took a step forward. Her gaze darted around to see if anyone had noticed, but all eyes remained on their feet.

Selene ran her fingers over the smooth amulet around her neck. Her heart tightened, and her skin tingled as she stepped up to the portal. The hairs rose on her arms as the surface snapped with magic. The desire to dive into the portal, to leap to freedom, caused her limbs to shake. Holding back was torture almost worse than the ones that had scarred her skin. She needed to be careful, patient.

"Don't blow it."

"And remember, my daughter, to wear your amulet always. It will keep you grounded."

Selene nodded, but the lilt of her mother's voice made her want to cut her own ears off. She could hold back no longer. Smiling, she sucked in her last gulp of air and pressed her body into the portal.

The surface sucked her in like quicksand. Every molecule of her body shredded apart. She spun in a vortex, every piece of her moving faster than light, pulling to and fro; whirling, twisting, churning. She wanted to scream but had no voice. Propelled forward by the magic of the rift, Selene fought to stay conscious. Nausea and vertigo mixed in her separate pieces like a tornado through her atoms. To get anywhere close to Chicago, America, she had to focus her thoughts on something she remembered. She pictured Mason, tall and strong, the set of his jaw, the flex of his arms, his laugh, his smile, his rage. Every part of him came into clear, crisp focus.

Pressure built on her form, squeezing and reshaping her.

Every part of her slammed together, and she fell. Head over ankles, she spun until she landed with a thud. Her skull struck solid ground, and she groaned. The smell of decay and grease filled her. Though she'd been away for more years than she cared to remember, the familiar scent made her laugh out loud.

Memories surfaced of the last time she'd been in the earthly realm and then she rolled on her stomach and retched. Her body trembled with exhaustion. Nausea tumbled through her, making her heave again. She wiped at her mouth with the back of her hand and laughed again.

She'd made it. She was free. Free of her mother, free of the elders, free of the boredom.

The sounds of rock music played in the distance. Her eyes teared, and her eyelids spasmed as a flash of light struck her. Selene rolled away. The sharp pain in her knees and the gravel and pebbles grinding into the rest of her skin told her she was naked. Not to mention the breeze on her bare—

"Hey! Are you okay?" a man called from the right.

Selene turned her head and tried to focus. A blurry figure moved closer. "Hey." Heavy, cool fingers landed on her shoulder. "What happened? Are you okay? You're naked."

Someone wrapped a warm piece of clothing around her. The blurriness faded as she continued to blink.

"Where's your master? Who did this to you?" asked the gray—skinned man.

Selene stumbled shakily to her feet and shoved her sore arms through a faded cardinal red flannel shirt. The man put his arm out to steady her, and she got a good look at where she'd ended up. She stood on a city sidewalk. Boarded up businesses scattered the road. Down the block, a customer exited a flashy convenience store.

Selene's gaze lit on the older man next to her. His face held a soft quality, and wrinkles cut the corners of his eyes. His white, like salt hair, stood out all the more due to the dull bluish—gray color of his skin.

"You're... You're a vamp."

He chuckled. "Yup. Haven't been a human like you in almost twenty years now."

She'd not seen any humans mutated by the V2000 virus before her mom had forced her into the Fae realm. It amazed her how different from Vampires and vampyr they were. Vamps looked more like the undead from old movies and books than any pure—blooded Vampire or turned vampyr she'd ever seen.

Her stomach roiled again, and her knees shook as the after-effects of portal travel bombarded her. Her head lightened, and she gripped the older man by his dirty undershirt. She needed to keep it together, needed to focus.

"Where am I?" Her words came out slow and slurred.

His brows furrowed. "You're in the Middle American Territory."

Selene's entire body throbbed. Every remade particle burned like her body continued to restitch itself from the travel. She shook her head, trying to remember where she'd been going.

"Chicago?" She gulped in air.

"This is Chicago."

She'd made it. She planted a hard kiss on the old vamp and then backed up, taking in her home city. Laughing, she spun in a circle. I'm free!

She reached for her amulet and gasped. Like everything else, including the coin her mother had given her to help iden-tify her contact on this side – it had disappeared.

The coin she didn't care about. She had no intention of contacting her mother or those like her ever again. But the amulet... She spun in a circle, scanning the ground. No, no, no! Panic lit within her.

"Dammit."

"Are you all right, miss? Can I help you get somewhere?" The old man's face held concern.

Selene scanned the area and memories rushed back to her and the pain lessened. "I'm looking for Mael— Mason."

"Is he your master?"

Selene straightened. "My master? Of course not. Why would he be my master?" How could this man possibly think someone like her would have a master?

The old vamp looked Selene over. "Well, you're human, so..."

Selene nodded, understanding. Her mother had told her the remaining humans were either slaves to the Vampires or had gone into hiding.

"Come on, girl. Let me get you somewhere safe where they can figure out what to do with you."

"Find Maelstrom."

Selene's head whipped up, and she grabbed the man's saggy wrist. "Do you know Mason?"

The vamp's eyes widened. "Are you sure you're all right?"

Her heart sank. "So, you don't know him then."

"The only Mason I know of is the new mate of Lord Danika—"

"Yes, that's him." Selene gripped him tighter. She needed to get to Mason.

"You... you don't just go to see Lord Danika. But if you'll come with me, I can make a couple of calls..."

"Take his money," said a familiar, commanding voice.

Selene shook her head to rid herself of the voice. "Give me your money."

The man stepped back. Selene glanced around and spotted an alley a few yards away. Quick as the wind, she grabbed the man around the neck, covered his mouth, and dragged him into the alley.

"*Sopor*," she whispered into his ear.

The vamp fell unconscious, and Selene laid him on the ground. She rifled through his pockets and found his wallet.

She'd made it through the toughest part, the rift. Now all she needed was clothing and a ride. So, when her mother's people came to cleanse Earth, Mason would wipe *them* away instead.

Selene buttoned the flannel shirt, raced out of the alley and down the street. She stopped at the first intersection and looked up at the street sign. It took only a minute to orient herself and then she took off again toward the address programmed in her head.

More than once, a vamp called out to her and told her to stop. Twice, a vamp chased her, but she outmaneuvered them easily. Running at top speed, she tried not to linger in the depression cloaking Chicago like a death shroud.

The destruction the Vampires had wreaked on the human world went beyond what she'd envisioned. Stores boarded up. Whole blocks dark and desolate. Not that she could blame the Vampires solely. The humans were to blame as well.

She wondered if they'd ever figured out who had unleashed the V2000 virus that had mutated the majority of the human population into vamps. In truth, she was glad the V2000 virus hadn't worked as designed. If it had, and the Vampires and vampyr had turned into daywalkers, who knew what Earth would have become.

After twenty minutes, Selene reached her destination. She rounded a corner, and the faded yet familiar awning came into view. Her chest tightened, and she choked out a sob. She didn't move for several minutes. Staring at the building, memories of happier times washed over her, reminding her of who her mother had been before they'd run to the Fae.

She darted across the street and pulled on the front door, but a padlock and chain bound it closed.

Selene laid her palm on the padlock. *"Recludo."*

The padlock clicked open. She yanked both it and the chain off and stepped through the door. Setting her hand on the frosted glass of the entrance, she peered out at the street to see if she'd been followed. *"Securus."*

The door locks clicked, and Selene looked around the lobby. She let the silence of the building sooth her. She couldn't remember the last time she'd been alone. In the Fae realm, she'd always been with her mother, or guarded, or watched. Like a prisoner they feared might escape, the Fae had never let her out of someone's sight.

The cream, dust—covered, plush chairs waited in the same places she remembered them. The guard's desk sat vacant and unsecured for the first time she could remember. The chandelier swayed ominously overhead. Her feet peppered the marble floor in silent steps heading for the elevator. The brass doors still gleamed, and she caught a glimpse of herself, disheveled and dirty. She depressed the button, and to her surprise, the elevator opened.

Outside, a large vehicle pulled up to the building and stopped. Selene hurried into the elevator as two tall men in black fatigues approached the front door.

Her heart thundered as the men yanked on the doors. The elevator door rolled closed too slowly, but the lock spell held. The men knocked on the door and pulled on them again. Finally, the elevator closed and pulled upward with a grinding of the gears. Selene sank back against the mirrored wall and blew out a breath. So... looking like a human really did raise the alarm in the city.

The bell rang, and she sprinted from the elevator, rushed to the end of the hall, and spelled the apartment door open.

Once inside, she moved to the window and peeled back the curtain an inch.

The sun had set, but the sky wasn't completely murky yet.

Down below, the two men spoke and pointed. Eventually, they shrugged and drove away.

Selene dropped the chain and lock to the floor and plopped onto the plush, plum—colored sectional.

Home sweet home.

CHAPTER TWO

The music from inside Club Midnight pounded against Neeman's SUV as he pulled up to the curb. The vamp valet rushed to get the door, but he stepped out before the valet could open it.

"Evening, Mr. Colter." The valet bowed.

"It's Neeman."

The valet bowed again. "Of course, Neeman."

Neeman sighed. "Stop bowing. I'm not one of the Three Kings. I'm a soldier."

"Soldiers deserve the highest respect," said the valet. "You're the ones who keep us safe."

Neeman stared at the young vamp for a minute. People usually feared him, not worshipped him. At a loss for words, he nodded, and the valet hopped into the SUV.

The queue to get into Midnight wrapped around the outer wall of the building. Vamps and vampyr lined up for hours waiting to get in. A young female vampyr eyed Neeman and smiled, thrusting out her chest. Neeman chewed the gum in his mouth once before swallowing it and heading for the entrance. Why did women feel the need to throw their bodies around to get what they wanted?

Riley slid from the vehicle. "You want me to call the others and tell them where we are?"

"Why? It's none of their business what I do."

A good Vampire, Riley hadn't been with the Tracking Squad for more than a year. His lesser Vampire parents had nothing to offer him except a place in their technology company, so he'd asked to join the squad— to better his position within the Vampire society.

The Vampire bouncer who guarded the door didn't even glance at Neeman before unlatching the rope and opening the door. "Enjoy."

The music floating out of the bar assaulted him along with the sights and smells of the city night. Blood, sweat, and perfume wafted out to greet him. Neeman stepped into the establishment and pushed his way through the crowded bar. The vamp bartender caught his eye and nodded, his dreadlocks shaking over his shoulders.

Neeman slid through the multitude of bodies pressing against him and headed for the VIP section. Bright colored lights illuminated the dance floor and sent multicolored hues floating around the entire club. Suspended above the floor on platforms, vamp and vampyr females shook and writhed to the music for the enjoyment of the patrons— but Neeman barely spared them a glance.

A female vampyr slid up to him, pressing her mostly revealed flesh against him. Her wise, pale blue eyes scoured his body as she ran her fingers over his chest.

"You're Neeman." She smiled.

The girl's long brown hair hung loosely around her, silhouetting her oval—shaped face and overly pouty lips.

"Can I buy you a drink?" Her short fangs gleamed in the dim light of the dance floor, illuminating the small teardrop rubies she'd inserted into them.

"No. Thank you." Her face fell, and he swallowed hard at the disappointment in her eyes. Why couldn't he say yes? A girl full of curvy loveliness any vampyr would die to have pressed underneath him didn't even stir a flutter in his gut. Neeman reached around and grabbed Riley by the arm, yanking him forward. "This is Riley. He's one of the best trackers in my squad. I'm sure he'd be more than happy for a beautiful woman to buy him a drink."

"I'm Lana," the female said, sidling up to Riley.

Neeman ground his nails into his palms and cracked his knuckles. He slid around the girl, making a beeline for his table. In the past months, he'd taken more females to bed than he had in the whole of his long life. Since Danika had chosen Mason as her mate, Neeman had done anything and anyone to drown her memory. The fact that he was in a bar once more testified to the fact that he wasn't succeeding. Why couldn't he let the girl buy him a drink, screwed her in the bathroom, and then let her go? He'd done it a million times in the last months. The answer was simple; it didn't help the pain.

Neeman reached his booth as the waitress showed up with a Savor and vodka. "Keep 'em coming."

The air held a heady scent, which set him on edge. The heightened energy of the patrons had everyone moving more frenzied than usual. He scanned the room for signs of trouble but couldn't find anything amiss.

He reached for the glass and took a long sip. The synthetic O negative went down smooth with the burn of the vodka. It had been decades since Neeman had used alcohol to dull his pain, but somehow it had become a common occurrence of late. Images of the night he'd been turned flashed into his memory, drowning out the sights and sounds of the bar. *The smell of death, the cold chill of a tight grip on his shoulder, the blood-shot eyes and long, gleaming fangs.*

Neeman shook his head and downed the rest of his drink. A whoop and holler from the dance floor pulled his attention. His gaze swept the area again, but too many bodies made him unable to see anything.

"Your drink, sir." The waitress set a second glass on the table. Neeman nodded, and she picked up the first glass and carried it away.

He scratched at his growing scruff. How long had it been since he'd shaved? Or cut his hair for that matter? Danika had always liked him clean—shaven, hair short.

The years they'd been together had been the happiest in his new existence. When she'd broken it off, he'd thrown himself into the Tracking Squad, making it more efficient than it had ever been, even better than when Roth had run it. His eye for detail and obsession for order had the group running with precision.

So much had changed in the past year. From Danika decreeing, humans no longer being slaves to humans being made into trackers. He barely recognized the woman Danika had become.

When she had returned to his life a year ago, he realized his feelings hadn't changed. And he'd been so close this time to having her for good. But within a matter of days, he'd gone from being hopeful to devastated. He didn't blame Mason or Danika. They were a formidable couple and, as dangerous as Mason's Demon nature was, Danika couldn't have a better protector from those who threatened her.

Danika's uncle Chase remained out there somewhere, hiding in the shadows. He'd tried to kill Danika twice, and he'd try again, no doubt.

Neeman had all of his connections searching for Chase. It would be his pleasure to rip the pompous, self—righteous bastard limb from limb before serving him up to Danika and Mason.

Shouting emanated from the dance floor again and the crowd shifted. Females moved to the edge of the arena, and males migrated to the center. Neeman glanced at the bar for Riley but couldn't spot him. Damn. He only wanted a few minutes to himself to unwind outside the barracks. Looked like he'd be breaking up a stupid vamp fight instead. After another shout, he downed his drink and headed for the upheaval. For a moment he wished he'd bought the smiling vampyr girl a drink instead of letting Riley have her.

The crowd parted around him as he stomped out to investigate the commotion. He stepped through a ring of vamps and vampyr and stopped short. His breath sucked in, and his chest tightened. A female, wearing little more than a bikini top covered in a flannel shirt and a pair of bootie shorts, danced in the center of the floor. Men ground and gyrated all around her, touching her in inappropriate places.

Neeman's gut clenched. Her shoulder—length black hair swished around her neck as she swayed her hips in a sensuality rhythm that few possessed. For minutes, he did no more than stare. Then her scent hit him with force. She smelled of vanilla and cinnamon.

A young vamp bumped into another vamp. Without a word, the second lashed out and punched the first one in the face. Before Neeman could react, the males broke into an all—out brawl.

He moved like light into the fray, pulling the males apart and shoving them to the sides. The female barely took notice, continuing to sway to the music, with her back to him. Her scent grew stronger the closer he got, making his fangs ache and his arousal grow. The sensation shocked him. In all of his years as a vampyr, he'd never once desired to take someone's blood from the vein.

The two vamps ran at him, pulling him back to the problem at hand. Neeman brought the first to his knees with a quick uppercut to the jaw. The second he grabbed by the throat and bared his fangs.

"Do you know who I am? I could kill you right here for looking my direction if I wanted."

The vamp's eyes went wide. He blinked several times and seemed to come to his senses. "Sorry."

Neeman squeezed the vamp's throat tighter, pulling him close. "I didn't catch that."

"I'm sorry." The vamp's already bluish—colored face grew ashen.

Neeman dropped him as a bouncer pushed through the crowd.

"Is there a problem?" He looked at the vamp on the ground.

"Not anymore." Neeman's gaze swept to the female who still danced within a throng of male vamps, her slender hands raised high above her head. He blinked twice as the lights turned from blue to pink on the dance floor and the hairs on his neck stood up. Her skin no longer held the bluish tint of a vamp. In the pink lights, she looked positively rosy. He stalked forward, shoving the vamps aside. Grabbing the female by the wrist, he turned her to face him.

"Hands off." She shoved Neeman in the chest, and his gaze met a pair of brilliant, purple eyes. She stopped moving and sucked in a breath at the sight of him.

She's human.

The two stared at each other for several seconds. Her heart —shaped face sported high cheekbones flushed a light shade of peach. Her exotic beauty and lovely eyes held a strength he'd rarely seen, mesmerizing him.

"What are you doing in here?" He shook his head. "Where's your master?"

A slight smile played upon her lush lips. "I have no master, Loverboy, but would be happy to allow you to take me home if you wish."

Her raspy, husky voice stirred desire within him. She was the walking, talking fantasy every man dreamed of. She slid her hand up his chest and encircled her arms around his neck.

"It's been a long, long time since I've had a man. Especially a vampyr. Why don't you take me to your place, and we can dance there? In private."

Neeman's senses lit up like firecrackers. Her fragrance swirled around him, teasing his resolve. Her eyes held him captive and refused to let him go. She pressed her body against his, and the softness of her flesh rubbed against him. For a moment, Neeman forgot everything. Where he was. Who he was. What he was supposed to be doing. She brought her face close to his and inhaled.

"I love the smell of your cologne."

"I don't wear cologne," he managed.

Her eyebrows knit together again, and she stood on her

tiptoes to reach his neck. Neeman held still as she sniffed him again.

"Mmm... I think it might be you, Loverboy."

Her eyes flashed, and a shiver trickled down his neck. Something wasn't right. Without pretense, he grabbed her around the waist and hoisted her over his shoulder.

"Hey!" she said. "I like it rough, but this is a bit barbaric. Put me down."

The males suddenly turned on him at the removal of their object of obsession. Neeman backed away, and the group followed. He glanced behind, but he still couldn't spot Riley.

"Stay where you are, and I won't take any of you into custody," he shouted.

The vamps and vampyr slowed but didn't stop. Neeman unholstered his weapon.

The female squirmed in his arms and beat upon his back.

"Put me down, you arrogant prick. Trust me; you won't like me when I'm angered."

"Shut up, and I might let you live." Neeman jostled her on his shoulder. He scanned the advancing males. "Stop, or die. Your choice. Is getting offed over a stupid human worth it?"

"A stupid human?" the female shrieked. "You son of a—"

A sudden jolt of electricity coursed up Neeman's spine, making his muscles tense and his back arch. His knees buckled, and he almost went down. Using his gun hand, he slapped the female on the rear. "Stop zapping me with that Taser, before we both get hurt!"

"Oh, I'll show you who's gonna get hurt around here!" She beat on his back.

He leveled his gun at the group of vamps in a last attempt to stop them. He didn't want to shoot. Doing so in the middle of the club would cause problems for Danika, but he refused to let himself get hurt or the girl— no matter how little she valued her safety.

Suddenly another person appeared beside him, and he glanced over at Riley with his untucked shirt and mussed hair.

"Nice of you to show up."

"Sorry, boss. That girl Lana was really... Yeah, well, sorry."

The crowd halted as Riley drew his weapon. Three bouncers joined them, and finally, the vamps backed away.

Neeman swallowed hard, and without a word, holstered his gun, and strode from the bar. Adrenaline shot through him like a bullet. It would take only minutes before the shakes started. He stomped outside and took a deep breath, letting the pounding rain slap his face. The perfume of damp earth and metal filled his nostrils, clearing the female's scent from his head.

The valet moved swiftly to open the door of his SUV. Neeman threw the girl inside while keeping a firm grip on her arm. Riley slid in the driver's seat and started the engine.

"Where to, boss?"

Neeman eyed the female in the backseat. "What's your name?"

"What's it to you?" She smirked.

All sweet innocence and allure vanished from her eyes. She crossed her arms over her open shirt, pushing out her ample breasts and glared at him.

"Where do you live?"

"You don't want to go where I came from."

Neeman ground his teeth together. Her beauty began to fade the more of a pain in the ass she became.

"You're from a survivor camp then. Why the hell would you come into Chicago? You had to know you'd get caught."

"I'm not from a camp," she sneered.

He held out his hand. "Give me the Taser."

"What?"

"The Taser you zapped me with."

She laughed. "The only Taser I have is me."

Neeman growled and tried to keep his temper in check.

"Fine. Keep it. But if you zap me with that thing again, I'm gonna knock you out."

She smiled. "I'd like to see you try, lover."

Neeman examined her. She wasn't dirty, and her bikini and plaid shirt weren't either. But she couldn't belong to someone in town. He'd have gotten a call about her going missing. Maybe she hadn't chosen a master yet.

"Did you get out of Coven House?"

She stared at him for a minute. "I belong to Mason."

All air sucked out of him like a vacuum. Mason had a slave?

"Do you know him?" she asked.

"I'm sure there are many Masons in Chicago." Neeman's mouth felt as if it had been swabbed with cotton and his tongue clung to the roof of his mouth.

She shrugged. "Possibly, but this one is the biggest male you'll ever see, and he's mated to a Coven Lord named Danika."

The blood and vodka burned back up Neeman's throat.

"You do know him. I can see it on your face," she said.

"To Coven House?" asked Riley.

"No," said Neeman. "To the compound."

The female sat up quickly. "But I told you—"

"I heard what you said." Neeman faced forward. "To the compound." He reached into his pocket for a smoke but gripped the pack of gum instead. He pulled out a piece and stuck it in his mouth.

He stared out the rain—soaked window as buildings flashed by.

Mason. Mason had a slave?

If she spoke the truth, then he was pretty sure the shit was about to hit the fan. Probably for him, definitely for Mason. But either way, Neeman knew one thing for sure. Danika did not know about the girl. And if he took her to Coven House, she'd be dead within the hour.

CHAPTER THREE

Selene sat on the small white bed and stared at the door, trying to piece together what had happened in the last hours. She remembered going to her apartment and lying down on the couch. Then she'd gotten up and gone out and... She'd awoken in the barren room with the sexy blond vampyr thrusting a set of clothes fit for a drill sergeant at her and telling her to stay put. A worrisome sense of foreboding rumbled in her stomach. It had been decades since she'd woken up somewhere without remembering how she'd gotten there... and that had only been because of—

She leapt from the bed.

No. It couldn't be happening again.

She reached for her amulet and cursed, remembering it had disappeared. Taking a deep breath, she tried to retrace her steps from the night to figure out the series of events that had ended with her in... prison? She pounded her fists on her temples and focused.

She started at the last thing she remembered, getting

flashes of places she'd gone. After getting up, she'd gone north of her apartment building to the park where she and Mason had found each other years before.

Keeping to the shadows so as not to be seen she'd walked a for hours taking in the devastation of Chicago, the buildings, the smells, the cars, the phones that had no wires, and the closed businesses. Different. All so different.

Going to the club had been a whim. With fifty bucks in her pocket and no idea what to do, she'd gone to get a drink. Margaritas were the one thing she'd missed most in the Fae realm.

That's where things got fuzzy. She'd used her magic, and the Vampire at the door had let her in. The bartender had given her a margarita without asking for money, and the vamps and vampyr had flocked to her like bears to fresh salmon.

She'd been dancing, by herself, when the blond male had shown up and carried her out. She got the vague sense she'd tried to charm him, but it hadn't worked, because she sat in a tiny, windowless room.

Great way to spend her first day back in Chicago. It hadn't even been twelve hours, and already she'd gotten into trouble.

The door to the room opened, and the blond male vampyr stood holding a tray of food.

His shoulder—length hair and a stubbly chin gave him a ruggedly handsome appearance. Memories of pressing up against him in the club and the feel of his sinewy muscles, bunched and coiled beneath his clothing—

"I thought you might be hungry." He stepped into the room and set the tray on a wooden table.

"I'm not." She crossed her arms over her stomach to hold back a growl.

He looked at her and his brows furrowed.

"What?" She eyed the tray of food.

He shook his head. "Nothing, I just thought your eyes were a different color. At the club, they looked amethyst, but they're not. They're jade."

Dammit. It *had* happened again. "Where am I?"

"In the tracker's compound."

Tracker's compound? A million questions swirled through her mind, but only one question mattered. "Do you know Mason?"

"Yes." He crossed his arms over his broad chest and leaned against the wall, giving her the sexiest of glimpses of his firm, toned physique.

"Can you call him?"

He looked at her quizzically. "I already did. We've had this conversation, remember?"

Crap. Selene crossed her legs and put on her best annoyed face. "Well?" she finally asked. "What did he say?"

He threw her a sexy, cocky smile. "He said he didn't own any slaves."

Selene jumped to her feet. "Slave! I'm not a slave, I'm—" She stopped short. Telling people her identity didn't seem like the best idea considering the new state of the world.

"So, you're not his slave?"

"Did you tell him my name?"

"Yup." He watched her closely.

Sheesh! Sexy but infuriating. "And?"

"He said he'd come down and take a look at you."

"Take a look at me?" Selene's cheeks flushed with heat, and she rubbed at them in annoyance. "You'd think I was a dog at the pound." She turned from him and his icy stare.

It didn't matter. Only Mason coming to see her mattered.

That and taking her to his house. Then they'd take up where they'd left off. She knew it... she counted on it.

"Why did you lie?" the vampyr asked.

"What?" She spun to face him.

"Why did you say you were his slave when you aren't?"

"Because..." She didn't even know his name.

"Neeman. For the fourth time."

"What kind of name is Neeman?"

"What kind of name is Selene?"

She liked her name.

"It's not your real name."

Shut it! She blew out a breath. "Anyway, *Neeman*, I said I was his slave because I'd hoped you'd take me to him."

"How'd that work out for you?" He cocked his head to the side and chewed on a piece of gum.

Selene had to squelch a flutter in her stomach at the sight. She wondered if he'd been bitten or if he had been born a half Vampire. He bore the air of one born of a Vampire father and a human mother, but the physique that usually came only through the change of human to vampyr.

"Usually it works out fine." She gave him her most beautiful smile.

His expression darkened. The gum snapped and popped in his mouth. "Not with me. I don't like being lied to, or manipulated. If you want my help, you should remember that."

She let her smile drop. "Well, you won't have to worry about it after tonight. As soon as Mason comes, I'll be out of your hair."

"I wouldn't be so sure about that," he muttered.

"You think I'm lying again?"

Neeman shook his head. "No. Just mistaken."

"How so?"

Neeman chuckled and snapped his gum again. "You really aren't from around here, are you?"

"What does that mean?"

"Things aren't how they used to be when humans ran the country. Not in the encampment you came from and especially not here in the cities. Unless Mason is prepared to take you on as a slave, you aren't going anywhere. And believe me when I say, I know his mate, and it isn't going to happen."

Anger flushed Selene's skin. He had no idea. When Mason saw her, there would be no doubt. Mated or not didn't matter one whit. They shared a bond that couldn't be broken by mating, years apart or anything.

"You're different," he said.

"What do you mean?" She walked to the tray, picked up the lid, and scanned the food. A giant cookie caught her eye, and she sniffed it. Peanut butter with nuts. Yuck. She dropped it back on the tray.

"I don't know. In the bar, you weren't so..."

"So what?" She looked up at him.

He shrugged. "Bitchy."

She slammed the lid down on the tray. "You think *I'm* bitchy? Me? I'm not the bitchy one. I'm the nice one!"

Neeman opened his mouth to speak, but there was a knock behind him.

He snapped his gum and pulled open the door.

The years melted away as Mason entered. Selene's head went fuzzy as wave upon wave of unexpected emotions bubbled over. Her heartbeat wildly, but her stomach turned to gelatin as anxiety knotted her chest.

He shook hands with Neeman before turning to her. He stared for a long time, looking her up and down. He'd gotten older and his hair shaggier but other than that, he remained the same. He didn't move, and her surety that he would take her with him ebbed away. The anxiety in her chest wound tighter, and she feared she might pass out.

"Seraphine." He crossed the room in one significant stride and lifted her off the floor.

Crushed against his giant chest, she let out a sob and clung to him. "Mael." The feel of his hug waxed familiar as if she'd never been away from him. He shuddered, and warm tears fell on her cheek. Memories long since buried rushed back to her. Long walks at night. The park they'd gone to visit that was no longer there. So many things. Years and years and years together. Times when they only had each other to lean on. And now all the bad memories from the Fae realm melted away like they'd never been separated.

They held each other for several minutes before he finally set her on the floor and pushed her to arm's length to look at her again.

"I thought you were dead." He brushed the tears from her eye. "Where have you been?"

"With my mother."

He twirled a lock of her hair and tugged on it. "You cut your hair and went natural."

"There's no such thing as hair color where I went."

Mason nodded and his brows knit together. "Don't get me wrong, I'm so glad to see you I can barely contain myself, but, why are you here? How are you here?"

The truth bottled up inside her like a shaken soda can. The pressure built and built, and she wanted to release it before she exploded. She didn't want to lie to him. It didn't matter what her mother said, or what the elder Fae wanted her to do to him. Let them come and try to wipe out the Earth, at the end both she and Mason would still be standing. Together.

26

She opened her mouth to tell him the awful truth. To tell him about her mission to ensnare him and what would happen if she didn't succeed. To tell about the Fae and the Demons and everything coming for him. All of it. But the words that tumbled out of her mouth were not her own.

"I escaped. I couldn't stand it anymore. You have no idea how they treated me. I was no better than a curlumon. Only at least curlumons get patted down and brushed by their owners and a nice place to sleep after a hard day's work. I had to get away. To get here. Back to you."

She resisted the urge to cover her mouth. Her voice had been too husky. Hopefully, he would attribute it to her being emotional and not to her not being able to control herself.

The words that rushed out weren't far from the truth. In a way, she had escaped, and it was true about the things that had been done to her... She sucked in a deep breath and closed her eyes to force away the images.

When she opened her eyes again, his golden stare pleaded with her. He wanted it to be the truth. But she read the wariness in his gaze. She'd seen that look before. She couldn't blame him. She'd been gone for over twenty years, not a word, not a whisper, nothing. She held his stare. If she showed one ounce of nervousness, he'd know she'd lied.

Finally, he nodded, pulled her close, and kissed her atop her head. "I missed you," he whispered.

"I missed you too." She hugged him tighter.

NEEMAN'S MUSCLES WOUND SO TIGHT HE THOUGHT HE MIGHT SHRED apart. It took every ounce of restraint he had to keep his mouth shut as he watched Mason with Selene. Mason loved the human. That wouldn't work with Danika though. She wasn't known for her ability to share.

Danika had never been the jealous type, but she was fiercely protective of what belonged to her. And Mason was hers.

Mason turned to him. "Thank you for calling me."

Neeman nodded.

"Can we leave now?" Selene looked at Neeman, and for a split second, he didn't want her to leave.

How had an irritating female with black hair and eyes the color of jade gotten to him? Her scent. It had to be her scent. It swirled in his head, mixing him up because he'd never drunk from the vein and he'd finally met a human who tempted him.

He would not let that happen, though.

Mason looked down at Selene and squeezed her hand. "I'm afraid not."

She pulled away. "What?"

"Selene, please. You must understand. I am mated now, to my soul bound mate. I need to tell her you're here. I need to explain. Things are tense in the Vampire society. Between me, and all the humans we've found. Trying to make things better for the slaves and—"

"I can't stay here." Selene's gaze moved to Neeman.

He stiffened under the weight of her green gaze. What had he done?

"I need to talk to you. There are rumors." She lowered her voice as if Neeman couldn't hear her. "Demons are returning."

"What do you mean returning?" Neeman asked.

Her gaze stayed glued on Mason. "They've sensed you, and they're coming. Some are most likely already here, and my mother said—"

"Where's your amulet?" Mason's voice held a hard edge.

She reached up and clutched at her throat. "It didn't make it through the rift."

"Selene, you need your amulet."

She pulled free of his grip. "I'll be fine. I am fine. It was more for mental stability anyway."

"Wait." Neeman's mind moved a mile a minute. If more like Mason were on this plane, it could mean the end of all of them. "How do you know more Demons are coming?"

"She's Fae," Mason said.

"She's what?" *Fae? How were the Fae involved?* They'd gone to their plane years ago, Mason had said.

The phone rang in Mason's pocket. He pulled it out and looked at it before pushing the button.

"Danika, what's the matter, my love?" Mason continued to look at Neeman. "No, I just ran out to see Neeman, to explain why we weren't able to meet with him earlier... Yes, I could have called him, but you were resting, and I wanted to get some fresh air anyway... Yes, I'm on my way, I'll be back shortly... You, too." He ended the call. "I have to go. Neeman, walk me out so I can let you know what's going on."

"What about me?" Selene thrust her hands on her hips.

Mason looked back at her. "I told you. You need to stay here. It's only for a little while. I'll come as soon as I can. There is no one else I'd entrust your safety to other than Neeman. He's the most honorable man I know."

Mason's words were a compliment of the highest degree. And despite Neeman's reluctance to keep Selene in such a confined space, and so close, he wouldn't be able to deny Mason.

"Besides, without your amulet, you need to stay inside." Mason gave Neeman a knowing look.

Selene's gaze burned into Neeman, making his gut twist.

He snapped his gum.

"All right. But I refuse to be a prisoner here. I won't be locked in like an animal."

"But you won't leave," Mason said. It wasn't a question.

There could be only one reason Mason had sway over her so completely.

"I won't leave." She looked at Neeman again. "You have my word."

Mason turned to him. "Is it all right if she stays?"

"As long as she doesn't disrupt our routine, and she stays away from my men."

"No worries there." She rolled her eyes.

Neeman's reasons for wanting her to stay away from his men weren't purely for her safety. He didn't need a riot on his hands when his men smelled her.

"She can stay. But she has to help out."

"In what way?" Selene pursed her lips.

"Do you cook?" Neeman smirked.

Her mouth gaped open. "No!"

"Do you file paperwork?"

"Do I look like a secretary?" She glared at him.

"Well, then I guess you can clean."

CHAPTER FOUR

Selene had never been so humiliated. Even as an outcast in the Fae world she'd never been degraded to scrubbing toilets. She swished a brush around the bowl, giving as much effort to cleaning it as she twirled her fingers through her hair.

Why had Mason left her there? Why hadn't he explained who she was and taken her with him? All these years, she'd missed him more than anything— more than milkshakes, more than burgers, even more than Oreos. No one knew her the way he did.

Instead, she'd been reduced to scrubbing bowls that were already as sanitary as the plates they ate off. She flushed down the bleach and blue water, tapped the wet brush on the side of the bowl, and stuck it in the bucket of cleaning supplies Neeman had brought her that evening.

Selene growled at the thought of him. All of her memories had finally returned from the previous evening. A good day's rest and a hearty meal had been what her mind needed to recover and what her spirit needed to recharge her magical stores.

In the club, she'd been sure she'd felt Neeman's desire as she pressed up against him, but he'd shown no more interest in her in the past eighteen hours than she had to the old man whose money she'd stolen. Even so, something about him attracted her. Possibly his icy stare, which seemed to look right through her. Or maybe his tight, hard body, so different from the Fae males.

Most likely though it was because she hadn't been with a real male since she'd left America after the outbreak. Not that she hadn't wanted a man, but she liked her men hard—bodied and dripping with sweat. Not soft—skinned and naïve like the Fae.

There had been only one Fae she'd bedded. One who had lived on Earth for years, traveling between the realms before the rift had shut.

At first, she'd thought him to be pleasant enough, but alone with him in his home, she'd experience his malevolent nature first hand. His bed had been one of pleasure, but only for him, and once she'd rejected his proposal of marriage, she'd been labeled an outcast. After that, the torture had started.

Thoughts of Neeman ran through Selene's mind, and she found herself heating into a frenzy of desire. Her body throbbed with need. *Stop it. Stop that right now.*

The last thing she needed was cleaning toilets, covered in chemicals, in a compound full of men she couldn't have— and horny.

Selene walked out of the all—white bathroom and into the small bedroom. The room had been furnished the same as the one she stayed in, but someone had personalized it. She stepped up to the desk in the corner and ran her fingers over a small electronic device she'd never seen before. The white rectangle with the apple on the back was no bigger than a pack of cigarettes.

Next to it sat a similar device, only slenderer and the size of a magazine. She set the first device down and pried open another device. Inside it looked like a flat television screen with a flat keyboard attached to it. A door closed down the hall, making her jump. She stepped away from the desk and grabbed her cleaning bucket. She peered into the empty hallway, exited, and closed the room door.

In the Tracking Squad's living quarter wing of the compound, room after room lined the long hall, like her college dorm, only cleaner and silent as a meadow. Neeman had told her to clean all the bathrooms on the floor. But after seeing how clean the first few were, she decided to skip to the last. No one would notice if she didn't do them all.

At the end of the hallway, she pushed the last door open and stepped inside. Unlike the first three she'd been in, this room looked exactly like hers, utterly bare of personal effects.

White bed, white desk, white rug, white walls. For a moment, she almost closed the door and left, but something caught her eye. The closet stood ajar, and clothing peeked out. Setting down her cleaning supplies, she walked to the door and opened it.

Neeman's scent floated out to meet her. She ran her fingers over the black T—shirts, hung neatly and pressed into crisp submission. Black cargo pants also hung in the same manner.

Below them, three pairs of highly polished boots stood at attention.

She laughed and shook her head. She'd rarely seen such order. Just seeing Neeman's room and clothes told her everything she needed to know about him. Orderly, obsessive, no—nonsense. Which also meant no fun.

Bending, she picked up one of the boots. The bottom had not a spot on it.

She set the boot back, and a large wooden box pulled her attention. She crouched on the floor and removed the chest from the closet. A mighty willow tree had been carved into the top, with thousands of tiny branches all reaching toward the ground. The sides were inlaid with woods of every color and set in a pattern that resembled bamboo. The front sported an intricate combination lock. Strange, since anyone who wanted into the box could break the wood.

"Open it."

No! She shouldn't. It didn't belong to her.

"Chicken."

"Shut up," she muttered.

Selene glanced at the open door and then laid her hand on the lock and whispered, *"Recludo."*

The lock dials whirled and clicked. Finally, they stopped, and the lid popped open. She stared at the box for a moment, again telling herself to put it back in the closet and forget about it. But something about the box intrigued her. Neeman had not one personal possession adorning his room, yet he kept a box in his closet full of... who knew what!

She removed it and lifted the lid to the box. Inside, as neat at the rest of the room, lay a stack of photographs, ornate goblet, knife, and a lock of hair. She lifted the pictures and thumbed through them. The black and white, faded or scratched photos were of Neeman and other people. He'd been younger, happy, carefree. In some, his hair hung long, in others, a bit shorter. There were photos of him at the beach, surfing. Images of him skiing. One of skydiving, another climbing a mountain. And in every happy photograph, he was human. So he had been bitten and turned.

"What are you doing?"

The deep voice startled her. She turned, dropping the photos into the box, closing the lid.

Neeman stared at her, his gaze intense. He took several steps toward her. She spun the lock on the box.

When he reached the corner of the bed, his eyes widened. He moved to her in one stride and pulled her to her feet. The box clattered to the plush rug.

"Hey!" She tried to wiggle free.

"I asked what the hell you think you're doing in my closet with my things."

A trickle of fear skittered over her and Selene rubbed her fingertips together. She took a deep breath and sucked in his fresh, manly, ever so enticing scent.

"It's your fault. You're the one who put me on toilet duty. And I haven't been on this plane for so long I wanted to know what's happened since I left."

"You have no right to go through my things." He bared his teeth.

Selene swallowed and kept up her calm facade, though she wanted to run from his anger.

"Sue me. I never said I wouldn't snoop." She wrenched her arm free and crossed it over her chest. "You don't like it, give me something else to do."

Neeman stared at her hard for a minute, his fists clenching and unclenching. Finally, he blew out a large breath and turned from her, running his fingers through his hair.

His broad shoulders tapered to a slim waist and tight buttocks. She couldn't help but stare at the round firmness beneath his pants. Buttocks you could grab onto. A flutter stirred in her stomach. What she wouldn't give to be able to grab onto his firm backside as he— The room compressed around her like a vise, gripping her tight and overheating her body.

She coughed, and fanned herself, trying to get her thoughts under control. Her mother had been right in being concerned that the draw of Earth's pleasures might sidetrack her. And Neeman was definitely a distraction.

NEEMAN PULLED ON HIS HAIR AND TRIED TO CONTROL HIS ANGER. Why had he agreed to let her stay? He had trainees to look after and Demons to hunt. Vampires to protect and a million other things. He didn't have time to babysit Mason's... Fae girlfriend.

He spun around and retrieved the box from the floor. Inspecting it, he caught the faint scent of ozone, but the lock remained intact. She'd not gotten it open before he'd arrived. He had that at least.

He placed the box in the closet and closed the door. It was the only thing he owned that meant something to him, his past, present, and future all wrapped into a single eighteen—inch by twelve—inch by twenty—four— inch box.

She stood defiantly a few steps away. Her cheeks had flushed a beautiful, deep shade of rose, and though she tried to mask it, her arousal wafted off her and made his head spin once more.

"I don't want you in here again."

She shrugged. "Fine with me. One less room I'm subjected to cleaning like a common house slave."

"You aren't a slave. You're a guest."

She cocked an eyebrow. "Do all your house guests clean the bathrooms?"

"They do if they want a bed and food."

Her beautiful face twisted into a sarcastic smile, and he suppressed a sudden urge to laugh.

He blew out a long breath and set his fists on his waist. "Look, Selene. I know you didn't ask to be here, and trust me, neither did I, but this world is different from the last time you were here."

"I noticed."

"What I mean is..." He tried to put into words the last several decades. "When was the last time you were here?"

"The nineties. My mother insisted we leave with the first wave of Fae returning home."

"You didn't see the Awakening, or the Outbreak, or the war?"

"We left after The Awakening."

Neeman nodded. He remembered that time all too well. "So, you never saw the vamps. You didn't witness the human beings slaughtered in the streets. The rogues, the encampments, the destruction."

She shook her head.

How could he put it delicately? He took a deep breath, and her sweet scent hit him. "You're here because humans are food," he blurted. Subtle.

"I'm not human."

"No, you're worse. You're Fae."

Her jaw dropped, and he was pretty sure if he'd slapped her, she couldn't look more shocked. "Worse?"

"Yes, worse. Your scent is like Mason's, alluring beyond a normal human. Remember the vamps? How even they were attracted to you at the bar?"

"Are you saying I'm unattractive?"

Grrr... Why did she take everything as an insult? "I'm saying if you're attractive to even them, think of how you are to the rest of us. Any vampyr or Vampire you meet will have to use great restraint to stop from draining you. And there are those out there, many out there, who won't use restraint. They don't care about you or your life. They only care about the blood."

"It's always been that way. That's no different from when I lived here before." She rubbed her throat with her fingers.

"True. But what is different is now there are only a tenth the humans left to feed on. In a starving world, people don't curb their appetites as well."

They stared at each other for a minute as she processed the information. He tried not to see her beauty, not to feel the urge to kiss her, not to run his fingers through her silky hair.

"I can take care of myself," she finally said.

"I'm sure you think you can." He nodded. "But not in this world. Not now. As much as you don't want to be in this compound, you need to be. Out there you wouldn't last a week."

"I'd be—"

"There's no hotel that would take you. Why? You look human, and you need a master to go in. There's no restaurant that'll serve you without a collar or a bracelet monitor. Why? Because you look human and you need a master. There's no store you could go into, on your own, to buy supplies without someone calling me to let me know that there's a lone human out in the city. Why?"

"I get it! Because I look human." She huffed. "I got into the bar though, didn't I?"

"You did. You got into the bar. But trust me, you were seen well before that. When I got back here last night, I had over two dozen messages on my phone about you, running through the streets, darting into a locked high—rise apartment building. The only reason I didn't get the messages earlier was because of my phone being off during a meeting. But my men got calls as well, and they went searching for you. You've been quite a hassle in the last two days."

"Yeah, well I would've been fine without you, thank you very much."

"You were lucky. Extremely lucky, because at least half a dozen vamps tried to run you down to cash you in. The slaver they called is named Roth, who happens to be my old boss and a good friend. He got in touch with me as well before heading up here to find you. Do you know what would've happened if Roth or his men had caught you? You'd have been chained, caged, and sold to the highest bidder. And a female with your looks? Well... let's say you wouldn't be cleaning toilets."

She threw her hands in the air. "Okay! Fine. I get it. I'm lucky you found me and lucky to be here. Blah... blah... blah. Thank you so much, your highness, for letting me clean your commodes!"

Neeman sighed. She didn't get it.

He stared at her. Really looked at her. With her delicate cheekbones and almond—shaped eyes, she held the air of... royalty. Maybe that was it.

"What did you do when you were here before?" he asked.

"What?"

"When you lived here before. What did you do? For work."

"I didn't work." She looked at him as if he were crazy. "I went to school and studied art. Then I went to school and studied music. Next, I went to school and studied history. And finally—"

"All you did was go to college?"

"All? What do you mean 'all'? Isn't that what people do here? Go to college and learn stuff?"

"Yes. And then they move on and get a job."

"Not Fae. The Fae were here to learn about human culture. My mother said my job was to go to school. Even though she hadn't been to the Fae plane in over a hundred years, she was steeped in their traditions."

"So how did you pay for anything?"

She glanced away. "Mother got us everything we needed."

"What do you mean 'got'?"

She stared at the wall and didn't answer. Her body posture tensed. She bit the inside of her cheek. He watched the emotions play over her features.

It explained a lot. A spoiled rich girl who spent her life studying and getting what she wanted without ever having to work for it. But for some reason, the look on her face... He felt for her. Though spoiled, and high and mighty, she hid a deep pain. Compassion brewed inside him.

"Look." He gentled his voice. "I've explained to you why you can't go near the other trackers. It's like putting an irresistible buffet in front of them. They have been taught to control their wants and desires, but you are a whole different ballgame."

Her gaze met his, and a slight smile played on her lips. She dropped her hands and cocked her hip to one side.

"I'm a buffet then?"

The sensuality she exuded made Neeman swallow hard. How did she do that? She went from spoiled rich girl to sexy siren within seconds. Her scent wafted toward him, making his fangs ache. He clenched his jaw and let his incisors press into his lower gums.

She stepped closer, her lithe body making graceful motions. She trailed her fingers lightly over her collarbone as she moved.

Neeman held still as she drew closer to him until she stood only inches away.

"You know, Neeman. I feel so alone in this new world. And you're right. It is different out there. I can't just go out like I used to and do anything I want. I need help. I need protection."

She reached up and laid her palm on his chest. Her scent surrounded him, making him want to taste her. Her bright eyes pleaded with him.

She licked her bottom lip. "Can you help me, Loverboy? Will you keep me safe?"

Yes!

She lifted on her tiptoes and leaned in close. His body tensed with need. Her petal—soft lips caressed his. He wanted to crush her body into his— instead he took a step back.

Her eyes flew open and flashed with anger. "What?" she demanded.

"Your seduction tricks won't work on me."

She grumbled and dropped her hands. "Well, can I at least get something to eat then? I'm starving."

CHAPTER FIVE

The enormous industrial kitchen reminded Selene of a school cafeteria. She took another bite of the sandwich Neeman had prepared for her and savored the tuna fish, her favorite.

Neeman leaned back against the counter, his arms crossed, ankles crossed in front of him. He watched her eat while popping and chewing his gum.

She took a sip of orange juice, replaying her actions in his room. She'd done everything right. She'd sauntered, touched, bit her lip, and had done everything her mother had taught her to do and say to get a man under her spell. But with Neeman, it hadn't worked. He's resisted her a second time.

"You sure do like gum," she said.

"I quit smoking a few months back."

She cocked an eyebrow. "Why? You're a vampyr. It won't kill you."

"True. But I hated being a slave to it."

She snickered. "I bet that's how the humans feel right about now."

"What does that mean?"

"I used to smoke." She bit into her sandwich. "Mother hated it, that's why I did it."

"I did it to help curb my appetite."

"Heavy blood drinker?"

He popped his gum and looked away.

"What were those things I saw on the desks in everyone's room? The silver things with the apples on them?" She finished the first half of her sandwich.

"Probably a phone and a laptop."

"What's a laptop?"

"A portable computer."

She went to bite into her sandwich and stopped. "How could that be a phone? That thing was tiny and flat."

He pulled a device out of his pocket and clipped it to his ear. "This is a Bluetooth." He shook a silver rectangle with an apple on it. "This is my cellphone. I don't even have to put it to my ear anymore because I can use this wireless speaker." He tapped on the Bluetooth.

She stared, amazed. The Fae didn't have technology like the kind on Earth. Theirs remained completely organic. Not surprising though since they were allergic to several types of metal.

"Can I see?" She put down the sandwich and held out her hand.

Neeman set the Bluetooth and the phone down on the counter. She picked up the phone, smooth like glass, and turned it over, trying to locate the 'on' button.

He took it from her, tapped a small spot on the bottom, and punched in a code, then handed the phone back to her.

All kinds of squares with different colors and logos filled the screen. She slid her finger over the surface of the phone, and it changed to new squares with new logos. She tapped on one shaped like a piece of candy. An orange screen pulled up, followed by a picture of different candies. She turned the phone to him.

He shrugged. "I like games."

"It's a game?"

"Yeah. Look."

She gave the phone back. He swiped the screen, and the candies fell. He did it over and over until he won.

"It's a video game you play on your phone."

She shook her head. "You're kidding."

He smiled, and her heart leapt. She looked down to the phone. Why had that happened? She hadn't seen him smile since she'd arrived, but it amazed her that for a brief second his entire face changed, and she glimpsed the man from the photos in the box, once more.

"When I was younger Mason, and I used to go to an arcade at the mall sometimes and play video games. I always won."

"Look." He pointed to the phone, tapped on the screen and another picture popped up. He hit a button and music poured out of the phone.

"I know this song. This is AC/DC!" She bobbed her head to the music, struck by nostalgia.

He chuckled and turned the music off. "I like the classics."

"Turn that back on." She reached for the phone.

He hit another square. "Do you know the internet?"

"The what?"

"The internet. The web?"

She stared at him.

"You know how a computer can hold information?

Imagine a way to access all the information out there. Books, magazines, news, music, buying products, anything. That's the internet. It connects you with things all over the world. It used to be bigger before the Outbreak, but most of the websites are still there, they just aren't updated anymore. And shopping isn't what it used to be. Not since Amazon went down."

"Amazon?"

"The virtual megastore of the world."

"Megastore?"

"A store that sells everything from groceries to beds to shoes."

She wrinkled her nose. Her mother would never have been caught in such a store.

"Never mind. Anyway. You can access a lot of things on a cell phone now. It's like a computer, radio, phone all in one."

She took the phone and flipped through it again. "So, when do I get one?"

He popped his gum and then nodded. "I'll get you one."

"Can you put all the music in there that you have?" She'd forgotten how much she loved human music. "Fae music is all about the reeds in the wind and the sound of sunshine."

"That doesn't make sense." His brows furrowed.

She nodded. "Exactly! Real music is Motley Crue, AC/DC, Metallica, Def Leppard, Led Zeppelin—"

"Pink Floyd, Van Halen, The Stones, The Eagles—"

"REO Speedwagon!"

His face broke into a wide grin, and he laughed. "REO Speedwagon? Really?"

"What?"

He shook his head and chuckled.

"Air Supply? Chicago? Scorpions?"

He held up a hand. "Okay Scorpions. That one I concede to. I'll get you some good music."

He smiled again, and her stomach fluttered. She broke eye contact, picked up the other half of her sandwich, and bit into it. She needed out of the compound and to find a one—night stand to sate her hormones.

"Party till it's over."

Stop that! She rubbed the side of her head. She'd heard the voice over a half dozen times in the past twenty—four hours. Ignoring it wasn't the best policy, but at the moment, she wasn't sure what else to do.

"Are you all right?"

"What? Yes. I'm fine. So, what do you do for fun?" she asked, looking around.

"Fun?"

"You know, things you do to relax and take the edge off. Besides playing games on your phone and listening to great music."

He looked at her, perplexed. "I... Nothing really. I haven't thought about having fun since—"

"Since what?" She took a bite. Man, she'd missed mayo.

"Nothing." He straightened from the counter and shoved his phone in his pocket.

She stopped chewing. He'd shut down right before her eyes. One minute he might have opened up to her, and the next, nothing. He'd gone back to being the hard—ass.

"Why do you do that?" she asked before she could stop herself.

"What?" His eyes narrowed, and his jaw set in a hard line.

"Shut down like that. For a minute there I thought I might have seen the real you."

His gaze locked on hers, conflicted. "Finish eating. I have stuff to do."

Neeman deposited Selene in the human wing to clean and headed down to the training arena. He'd opened up to her, though he had no clue why. He'd shown her inside the wall he'd built. A wall he didn't let anyone see past. Not even Danika. But then, with them, things had been mostly physical.

His heart hurt thinking about her. He swallowed his gum and headed for the elevator. He couldn't let Selene get to him. He had things to do, and getting involved with someone like her was like playing with a brushfire. No matter how much it fascinated, in the end, it left nothing but destruction in its wake. Besides, the thing between her and Mason wasn't something he wanted to get in the middle of.

Neeman hit the button and waited for the elevator, trying to concentrate on going down and training the humans. He had little patience for the humans, at least when it came to training. They were slower, weaker, and more susceptible to pain than Vampires and vampyr. It had become an interesting battle within him.

He had to admit they were better trained than any humans or vamps on the planet. He instructed them using better techniques than most vampyr and Vampires ever learned. But he wasn't sure how much that would do for them in an all—out war. And it still concerned him that he'd taught them all of a vampyr's and Vampire's weaknesses.

He'd not asked to be made a vampyr. He hated being a

bloodsucking nightcrawler who used humans for food. There wasn't much worse.

But in working closely with the humans for the first time in over a decade, he'd realized how much he liked what being a vampyr did for him. The strength, speed, looks. All of it made him more than he'd been as a human. Except for happy. He'd not experienced more than fleeting moments of happiness since turning. Even with Danika, he'd never been able to truly let himself go.

The elevator opened, and he stepped in. The machine moved downward to the training floor. In an underground compound, with that elevator as one of the only two exits, Neeman wondered what would ever happen if there were an earthquake in Chicago.

He walked down the silent corridor to the end, pushed the door open, and stepped up to the arena viewing window. Riley had a human on the ground showing him how to get out of a hold.

Riley, though still a reasonably new tracker, had a natural ability for teaching for the humans. He had more patience than Neeman, as well as more compassion.

"What are you watching?"

Neeman whipped around to find Selene standing in the doorway. He crossed to her. "I thought I told you to clean the other wing of rooms."

"You did. But it's already clean, so I decided to follow you instead."

Neeman clenched his jaw. "Are you making bugging me your new hobby?"

She flashed him a brilliant smile. "Why not? There's nothing else to do." She pushed past him to the observation window and looked below.

Neeman followed her. She leaned on the desk, her eyes tracking the simulated fight. She watched in silence for several minutes before shaking her head.

"What?" he asked.

"Is that what you guys are teaching humans to help them fight?"

"Is there a problem with it?"

She turned. "Nothing. Except that it won't work."

"And why is that?" He shifted his stance as his trousers became strangely uncomfortable, talking to her about fighting.

"Because soon you will have to do more than fight each other. Have you ever seen a Demon?"

"I've seen Mason."

"Wow. You saw Maelstrom and survived? Mason must really like you guys. Okay, did anything you tried hurt him?"

Neeman worked his jaw several times.

"Yeah. That's because Demons are about as fragile as they sound. Instead of teaching this stuff, you should teach them how to run and hide."

"You think you can do better?"

She laughed. "I know I can."

"Oh?" He gave her a hollow laugh. She really was a Miss Know—it—all. "Show me."

"What?" Her brows knit together.

"If you're so good. I challenge you."

She rolled her eyes. "What, like to a duel?"

"Afraid you might break a nail?"

She held up her hands. "Have you seen my nails? I can't grow these things to save my life." She bit the inside of her cheek, and her eyes flashed purple. "Okay. Let's go."

She pulled the door open.

Neeman watched her hips swish in her black camo pants as

she stomped down to the arena. Below, the training had stopped, and all eyes went to her. He massaged his forehead. What was he thinking? If she got hurt, he would have to take the blame... and explain to Mason.

How did she keep getting him so riled up? He shook his head and followed her down the ramp.

This is a bad idea. A terrible idea.

SELENE SMIRKED AS SHE HEADED TO THE ARENA. NEEMAN HAD NO IDEA what he'd agreed to.

"Clear the floor," Neeman called.

The humans and trackers eyed her as they left through the back door, whispering amongst themselves. She waved to them and smiled. *Toodaloo, boys!*

Neeman stripped to his tank top, revealing pale skin stretched taut over bulging muscles. She sucked in a breath and wished for him to take off the tank as well so she could see the washboard abs that had to be camouflaged beneath.

"I'm not going to take it easy on you," he said.

"Good." Her voice came out strangled.

"This is going to be fun."

"Shut up," she mumbled.

"What was that?"

"Nothing." She waved him off, trying to gain control of herself.

Neeman advanced on her, crouched, and swept at her legs with his. She dropped to the ground, knocking the wind out of her. He jumped on top of her and pressed his forearm to her throat.

"I thought you were going to show me something." The feel of his hard body pressed on top of hers made her tingle.

"I am." She smiled and ran her hand down his chest to his abs. Eight packs, just like she'd thought.

"Procul."

Neeman flew backward and landed several feet away, and she flipped to her feet. He ran at her, eyes glittering with anger. She darted sideways to the wall and jumped. Bouncing off it, she twirled in the air and landed behind him as he smacked into the wall. She reached out with her hands and placed them on his back, ready for another spell. He spun and struck out at her before she could speak. She bent backward and rolled out of the way, and he barely missed.

The inner voice laughed.

He rushed her again, and she kicked out with her legs, flipped backward, and hit him in the chest with her feet. She back—handspringed several times until they stood at opposite ends of the arena. Neeman breathed heavily.

"Can you do anything without using magic?" he yelled.

"Fae won't hesitate to use theirs. Why shouldn't I use mine?" She chuckled.

"I thought you said it was Demons who were coming."

Damn. "Well, yes. It is Demons. They have magic, too, is what I mean."

"All right. Then tell me how to beat them."

She planted her hands on her hips. "Find their weakness."

He strode toward her. "What are they?"

She shrugged. "Every species has a different weakness. Like your weaknesses are different from your friends down here."

He stopped. "Really? What's my weakness?"

"Motus." Selene appeared directly in front of him, used his

51

own foot swipe, and had him flat on his back in an instant. She climbed on top of him and straddled him.

"Your weakness is you don't want to hurt me. You're too kind to the fairer sex."

He wrapped his legs around her torso and flipped her on her back before sitting on her hips and squeezing her throat. The pressure made her nether regions pulse with need. He squeezed just enough that she could breathe but couldn't swallow or speak. He bent down close to her and put his ear to her lips.

"What was that? I couldn't hear you." His cool, minty breath tickled her skin.

"Take him."

Grabbing his head in her hands, she bit his ear softly and flicked out her tongue, licking the inner rim of it.

He reared back and roared. "What the hell?"

She placed her hand on his arm. *"Incapacitans."*

Neeman's eyes widened, and he fell flat on his back, stiff and immovable.

She climbed on top of him and ran her fingers under his tank top.

"What did you do to me?" he yelled.

She cocked a grin. "It's an incapacitation spell so you won't move." She lifted his tank top and took in the sight of his hard body.

"What are you doing?" His eyes held panic.

She leaned in close and gave her most seductive smile while running a finger down his throat.

"Whatever you want me to." She dipped her head till her lips hung an inch from his. Her skin cooled as her breasts smashed against his hard chest. Desire stirred within her. She wanted to kiss him. To have him wrap his fists in her hair and give it a good, hard yank as he took her.

"Let me go," he said.

All thoughts vanished, and she sat up. "What?"

"You've proven your point. Let me go now." His arousal pressed into her core, but his eyes remained cold and remote, causing all sexy sensations to cease flowing.

"Fine." She sighed. *"Finio."*

He bucked her off and hopped to his feet.

What was wrong with him? "You don't like domination games?"

His eyes hardened, and his voice soured. "No."

All desire washed out of her at his distress. She'd never had a male who didn't like her to play games. They all enjoyed her sexy siren side. And when she'd tried her immobilization spell in bed, they'd been enthralled and exhilarated by it. Why was he so different? He didn't like anything she tried.

"If you want to stay here under my protection, you must promise never to do that again," he said.

The emotions racing over his face made her gut clenched, and a sudden pang of guilt struck her. He didn't just not appreciate the game it was more than that. He was afraid. "Neeman, I'm sorry, I was only playing. I didn't mean to—"

He advanced a step. "Promise."

She swallowed and nodded. "I promise," she whispered.

He brushed past her and started up the ramp. Emotions stirred inside her. She definitely wasn't used to this new world.

Neeman's phone buzzed in his pocket as he walked down the hall to the elevator.

"Neeman."

"It's Mason."

Neeman tensed. "What can I do for you?"

"I called to see how it was going with Selene."

"She hasn't run away yet." *Unfortunately.*

"That means she won't. If she stayed the night, she'll stay put."

Neeman clenched his fists and ground his jaw together. He didn't want to know how Mason knew that.

"Is there anything else you need?" he asked.

"Reports have come in that a monster has been spotted down south. I'd like you to go take a look."

"Demon?"

"Probably so."

"Anything I should know?"

"Not much intel at this point. All I can tell you is it would be a lesser Demon— a scout of sorts. You shouldn't need more than a couple of men. The higher Demons won't show until they know for sure I'm here. I can't go myself, and we need to keep them from coming any further north."

"Got it."

"I'll send you the coordinates. This is a capture only deal. I need him alive so we can question him."

"We'll bag him and bring him. It's what we do. Anything else?"

"I just... About Selene... there are things about her. Things you don't know. She means a lot to me and—"

"Don't worry, Mason. I'm not going to tell anyone about your connection. But I suggest you tell your mate. I've known Danika a long time, and if there's one thing she likes worse than bad news, it's finding out that that particular bad news was withheld from her."

"I'm going to tell her, but with the Russians here and now the Demons... I need to find the right moment. And this isn't it."

"The Russians?"

"Distant cousins, I guess. They want an audience with her."

"Well, tell her soon. I can't keep Selene here forever. I'm not a babysitter." Thinking about Selene's spell made his skin itch.

"Understood. I'll send you the information as to where to go."

Neeman shut off his phone and stepped into the elevator. He needed to get Selene out of his hair, if for nothing else, for his sanity. The woman was downright maddening, dangerous as hell, and if she was indicative of the monsters to come in the future, she was right— they weren't equipped to handle beings like that.

SELENE PLOPPED ONTO HER BED, EXHAUSTED FROM HER WORKOUT WITH Neeman. It had been decades since she'd sparred with someone. She looked over to find her cleaning bucket and supplies sitting by the closet door. She groaned. She had a degree from Yale in Anthropological Studies, a degree from Harvard in Art History, a degree from Northwestern in Musical Theater, and a degree from USC in History. Not to mention the various degrees she'd obtained from smaller colleges. As far as she knew, she could be the most highly educated person left in America. Yet she'd been reduced to cleaning toilets.

"Leave. Get out and party."

"Shut up." She pounded on her head. Her inner voice had been caged too long by the amulet her mother had given her. Now free of its cage, the voice's ever—present commentary irritated Selene to the point of insanity.

She sat up. She needed a plan, something that would force Mason to keep her at Coven House.

"So we can party or shop, or whatever. It's obvious loverboy won't pretend to be your master and take us out."

Selene lay back, threw her pillow over her face, and screamed.

"Not used to being so bored, are you?"

She uncovered her head. In her doorway stood a handsome, young faced Vampire. He had a large muscular build and short, dark, umber hair. She recognized him.

"You're the one who drove me here from the club."

"Yeah, I'm Riley." He crossed to her in two strides and held out his hand. His boyishly handsome face showcased a dimple on his left cheek.

"Selene." She shook his hand, letting it linger, and flashed him a smile.

His cheeks tinged pinked ever so slightly.

"Is there anything else to do around here besides clean toilets, *Riley*?"

He gave a nervous chuckle. "Train, meditate, go on runs. Sometimes we go clubbing to blow off steam. But mostly we're supposed to be focusing on our training. Neeman goes out more than the rest of us. Perks of being the boss, I suppose."

"Where does he go?"

"He likes to go to Midnight. The club we picked you up at."

"You go out nightly?" She hoped he said yes.

"Not so much now that your kind are here."

"My kind?" There were Fae in the compound?

"Humans. Did you not hear about the huge cache of them we found in one of Lord Danika's warehouses? They were blood mules. Danika freed them and is training them to be minions."

"Minions?"

His brows furrowed. "Where did you come from? I thought all humans knew the difference between slaves and minions."

She smiled again. "Right, sorry. I thought you were talking about something else. I misunderstood." She laid her hand on his arm and laughed.

He glanced down at her hand. "Has anyone ever told you that for a human, your scent is amazing?"

She feigned a demure downward glance. "Really?"

"Yeah." He leaned in and sniffed her. When he looked at her again, his eyes sparkled. "You smell like vanilla and cinnamon."

Okay. Too close for comfort. She had no intention of becoming dinner.

"So how many humans did you find in Danika's warehouse?" She pulled her hand away and took a step back.

He blinked several times and cleared his throat. "A lot. I don't know exactly how many, but right now we have about a dozen here. They're training to become guardian minions for Vampires."

"Interesting. Humans guarding Vampires?"

"Yeah. It is a bit odd sounding, but Neeman has taught them every one of our weakness and how to use their strengths to their advantage. Surprisingly, the ones here are doing well."

Selene murmured and pretended to listen to him. If she could find out more about Danika and Mason, she might be able to find a way in. "So, these humans you found, Danika didn't know about them?"

"No. It happened behind her back. Her uncle Chase and a lord named Garon who runs Las Vegas were in charge."

"What happened to her uncle and Lord Garon?"

"Garon is back in Las Vegas, probably hiding out while awaiting his sentence from the Three Kings. Chase disappeared the night we raided the warehouse and hasn't been seen since."

"Riley!"

Riley whipped around. Neeman stood in the doorway.

"You should ready yourself. We leave in ten."

Riley glanced at Selene, then nodded to Neeman and strode out.

Neeman's gaze stayed on Selene.

"What?" she asked.

"I told you to stay away from my men."

"He came to me. Are you telling me I can't even talk to anyone if they come in my room?"

"No."

"No, that's not what you're saying? Or no, I can't talk to anyone?"

"No, you can't talk to anyone."

"Are you serious?"

His expression told her the answer.

He stepped into the room and closed the door. "Look. You shouldn't be here. Here in the compound. Here in Chicago. Here on this plane. You affect men, and you're very good at it. So, I want you to keep away from my trackers, got it?"

She stepped up nose to nose with him. "Let me get this straight. I have an 'effect' on you, and you don't like it, so I can't talk to anyone?"

His jaw clenched.

She threw her hands in the air. "Hey, I'm sorry I stir you in the nether regions, and you can't handle it. But you have no right to tell me I can't be friendly because you can't control yourself. Or is it that our little sparring session scared you into realizing you aren't the strongest beings on this plane anymore?"

His muscles bunched, and his expression hardened. A shiver ran through her. She might have actually crossed the line. Her heartbeat quickened, and her gut twisted. What was wrong with her? Being cooped up— that and the voice in her head. She needed to get out, to reenergize and be with people. Real people. Being in the compound reminded her too much of being shut up in the Fae realm.

She closed her eyes and blew out a long breath. "I'm sorry, okay? I... I didn't mean that. Okay, I did mean it. And I'm sorry about in the arena. Most guys like it when I— I'm sorry. How many times do I have to say it?"

He stared at her.

How did she explain? How did she tell him the truth? "Look. I've been cooped up for the past twenty—five years in a world that shunned me. You don't know what it's like there with the Fae. Sure, it's beautiful and peaceful and nice, but do I look like the kind of girl who wants peaceful and nice? Coming back here is a godsend. The music, the lights, the food, the people, I love it all. But I get here, and everything is different, and I can't even go outside to see it! I'm stuck underground, being kept from view like I have been forever. I thought it would be fun being back here. I was wrong, and I'm sorry." Wow! She hadn't meant to spew out that load of feelings.

His stance relaxed, and he kneaded his forehead with his fingers. "I can see where that would be frustrating."

"Frustrating? I feel—"

"Do you ever shut up?" His intense gaze made her close her mouth. He sighed. "I was going to say, I understand how frustrating it is to have to hide away. To not be able to do what you want, be who you want. I get it. I live it and have lived it for fifty plus years. I'm a vampyr, not a Vampire. I wasn't born this way, I was bitten and not by choice, so I get it. But I don't like games. That little stunt you pulled in the arena, immobilizing me. That was all fun and games to you, but in the future, you should know, if you ever plan on using that on someone else, you better plan on killing them. Because if not, as soon as you let them go, they're going to kill you. That feeling of complete helplessness is not something other Vampires or vampyr are going to take lightly."

His phone buzzed, and he turned to leave. "I have to go."

"Where?" She took a step after him, not meaning to sound so desperate. The only person she could talk to was leaving as well?

"I have a run to make, but I'll be back in a few hours at the most. When I get back, we'll do something... fun."

She smiled and then frowned. "What's the catch?"

"You have to stay here." He pointed to the floor. "In here. This room, while I'm gone."

She bit her cheek. That wasn't a tall order at all. "What kind of fun?"

"You decide. We'll do whatever you want."

She clapped her hand. "Seriously? Okay, this is going to be awesome."

He shook his head and chuckled.

"What now?" She huffed.

"No one says 'awesome' anymore."

"What do they say?"

"Sick."

"Sick?" Strange word. "Okay then it's going to be 'sick.'"

"Here." He pulled something from his pocket and tossed it to her.

"A phone! Sick! Now I need to find someone to call." She turned the smooth object over in her hands.

"My number is programmed in there. Hit the green phone button and go to contacts and then hit the phone button again and it'll call me. I also put music and games on there for you so you can waste some time."

"Is Mason's number in here?"

His expression hardened again. What had she said?

"Until he gives me permission, only mine is in there."

Damn. If she could just talk to him.

He tossed her a cord. "You'll need to charge it, so the batteries don't run out. I'll be back soon."

"Neeman?" A flutter ran through her. She hadn't been given a gift in years. "Thank you," she finally said.

He looked at her for another minute, then nodded and closed the door.

NEEMAN HEADED TO HIS ROOM. HE'D GOTTEN THE ADDRESS FOR THE area of the sighting and told Riley and Stephos to prepare to leave. He needed to prepare, as well.

A door opened to his right. "Neeman. A moment?" asked Riley.

He halted.

"I wondered if maybe we could bring a couple of the humans along."

It had been months since their training started, but they were still unable to take down more than a few Vampires at a time. If there were a real attack by Demons, they'd be mostly useless.

No! They weren't ready.

"No."

"Hear me out. I know you think they aren't ready, but I've heard them talk. They want to get out of here. They want to test their skills in a real environment. This should be an easy mission with three of us there. Let me pick two, just two. I'll keep them out of the way and make sure they don't bother you."

Riley had a point. They needed to test their skills, and he needed to see what they could do. But he didn't even know what they were heading into or what they might face.

"You take one of them, only one, in a separate vehicle. I don't want him with me."

Riley smiled. "Great. I'll keep him out of the way. I promise."

"No. You need to treat him like he's one of us. I can't afford to have you splitting your attention. They can either hack it, or they can't."

"He can. And I'll be all there for the squad."

Neeman nodded. "We leave in five."

Riley jogged down the hall toward the human wing.

Neeman continued to his room and opened the door. The sweet smell of lavender hit him. He stiffened briefly and then relaxed at the familiar scent.

"Hello." The female rose from the bed and turned to face him.

"I don't have much time this evening. I have to go on a run."

"We can be quick." Her starched white shirt and black skirt looked clean as ever. Her brown eyes matched her brown hair.

He'd never asked her name. He didn't need to know. "Sit." He gestured to the chair at his desk.

She sat where told.

She'd been coming to him for close to a decade— an arrangement he'd set up with Clive, the owner of the now closed slave auction house. Clive sent a slave to the compound twice a week for Neeman's use. In return, Neeman paid him well and had taken care of more than a couple problems for him. Clive would be having no further business in Chicago though and would be leaving for Europe within a month. Meaning Neeman would need to make other arrangements.

Neeman crossed to his closet and pulled out his old wooden box. He ran his fingers over the design on the lid of the chest, which he'd stolen from the Vampire who'd turned him. Killing the Vampire hadn't been as cathartic as Neeman had spent years anticipating it would be.

Entering the combination, Neeman then removed the lock and set it on the floor. He opened the lid and grabbed the goblet and knife from inside. They'd been gifts from his mentor and the former head of the Tracking Squad, Roth. Roth had been a true friend. Still was, though since he'd become a slaver, they hadn't had much time to speak.

Neeman stood and handed the goblet and knife to the girl. She set them on the desk, pulled out a bandage from her purse, and sat it alongside.

She never questioned Neeman about his methods, never asked for more, never resisted. And Neeman appreciated that.

When she'd arranged the items the way she wanted them, she looked up at Neeman and nodded. He returned the nod, headed into the bathroom, and closed the door.

He glanced in the mirror at his reflection, disgusted by what he saw. His ice—blue eyes weren't his own. He'd been born with deep blue eyes. Sapphire suns, his mother had called them. The bumps under his top lip where his ever—present canines hung low in his mouth, the classic distinction of a vampyr, had yet to become familiar to him.

How could he be what he was, he asked himself for the millionth time. Every evening, he rose and told himself tonight would be the night he'd end it all. But every night passed, and he remained living without living. Like a coward.

Neeman took a deep breath and shook his head. He looked at the time on his phone. He wanted to open the door to see if she'd finished, but couldn't take the chance of slipping. This was his ritual. How he had to do it. He owed it to the humans still living.

The memory consumed him. *Sneaking into the mansion where Brodrick, the Vampire who'd turned him, stayed— waiting for the monster in the gentlemen's study, which smelled of expensive cigars. Bloodlust slamming into him, weakening him, leaving him heavy and dull because he'd refused to feed. The agony in his limbs, like being stabbed with a thousand needles.*

But then the door had opened, and Brodrick had entered, talking on the phone. The texture of the wooden knife handle cut into Neeman's palm, his hands shaking as he waited to strike. Brodrick's brown eyes widened in terror when he saw Neeman and recognition dawned on his face before—

A soft knock on the bathroom door pulled Neeman from his memories. He blew out a breath and scrubbed his hands over his face.

Composing himself, he stepped back into his room. The girl had disappeared, but the goblet and cleaned knife sat on the desk.

He crossed to the goblet, his body humming with need. He picked it up and sniffed. The scent of lavender wafted off the rich crimson liquid. His fangs throbbed for the taste. The pain shot up the nerve endings in his face and over his scalp. He held back, refusing to give in to his baser nature. Control, he needed control. He was in charge, not the appetite.

His gut clenched like a dried piece of lumber. His head throbbed and his eyesight blurred. He took a sip. The taste lingered on his tongue, bold and beautiful. He savored the flavor, letting it pool and roll across his tongue like a fine wine.

Who was he kidding?

Gripping the goblet so tight he feared he'd break it, he drained the glass in two gulps. Strength rushed through him at the influx of nutrients. Like electricity flowing through wires, the blood rushed through him, replenishing his sapped energy stores. He tipped the goblet and sucked down the last drops before rinsing it in the sink and heading to his wooden box.

He weighed the familiar knife in his hand before setting it in the box. Sensations ran through him. The slide of the knife as he stabbed Brodrick so many times he'd lost count. He set the goblet next to the blade, and his gaze traveled to his treasured photographs.

That wasn't the photo that should have been on top.

He took out the pictures and thumbed through them. The top three were out of order. He tried to remember when he'd last looked through them.

"Neeman, are you ready?" Riley called, from outside his door.

He organized the photos before locking the box and setting it back in his closet.

"Coming."

CHAPTER SIX

Neeman pulled out of the remains of the Navy Pier onto Streeterville and headed south toward Chicago Heights. The southernmost part of Chicago city now, but not even close to being the edge of Chicago territory.

The territory Danika lorded over stretched from North Dakota to Oklahoma, over to Kentucky and up to Michigan. Of all the areas, in what was left of the United States, it had become the smallest, population wise. No Vampires lived in most of the states unless they were trying to keep under the radar. And a lot of the hottest and coldest places in the world housed only small encampments of human refugees still fleeing from Vampire rule.

Even though it had been years since the Awakening— when Vampires and vampyr had come out of hiding— he still hadn't become used to driving around in the open. But with the wars and then the outbreak turning the majority of humans into vamps, he became a leader of sorts in the country. That afforded him certain luxuries, not all members of the Society were privileged to have. He went where he wanted, only answering to Danika and the Kings. He'd never been that powerful before.

Driving past the half—vacant businesses reminded Neeman of his firefighter days. For every three or four intact buildings, a burned one slumped in between. A bakery's open sign blared in the dark. Next to it, a flower shop had closed down. The outbreak of the V2000 virus had wiped out over half the world's population. The rest now lived as the blue—collar servants of the Vampire society, subservient to Vampire and vampyr alike.

He passed the stadium. No longer used, the building still stood as a testament to the America that had once been.

"Do we know what we're looking for?" asked Stephos from the passenger seat.

"A Demon."

"That could look like anything. Mason's a Demon, and he looks like a human."

"Then I guess we look for a human. There aren't many Vampire down south, so a human would be as out of place as a bright orange Demon with a tail," Neeman replied.

Going on a run without much of description made Neeman's gut coil. On his missions, he insisted on knowing where they headed, what to look for, and the outcome required. Not having enough intel got people killed.

Neeman hadn't meant to be so flippant with Stephos. He didn't like being harsh to his men. They needed to know he was in charge, but being an ass didn't garner camaraderie. But all of the upheaval in his life in the last months had left him tenser than ever.

Murderous beasts had begun descending on their area.

Chase had disappeared without a trace. Russians had come to Chicago without invitation. He was on a mission with no idea what to expect. Even worse, a reckless female stayed in his house with no regard for either boundaries or rules. One he'd fantasized about sleeping with, but she most likely belonged to the same man who Danika loved. And that man, Mason, he wanted to hate more than anything, but he couldn't. It wasn't Mason's fault he'd been dragged to this plane. He hadn't asked to be caught by slavers and sold to Danika at auction. In many ways, Mason had more in common with Neeman than anyone knew. Even Mason. But above all the outward pressures were Neeman's cravings for blood. They grew nightly, and resisting had become harder and harder.

He turned on some music and tried to focus on the task at hand, but all that popped into his head was a beautiful, ebony—haired, green—eyed girl, with a tongue like a whip and a smile like razor blades cutting straight to his heart.

Thirty minutes later, Neeman pulled the vehicle into a gas station near Chicago Heights and got out. A group of young vamps stood by the entrance. He headed toward them, and they spotted him and stopped talking.

"You from around here?" he asked.

"Down the road." One of them pointed.

"You hear or see anything strange lately?"

The boys looked at each other and then at Neeman. "There's some big party down off 16th and Aberdeen."

"A party isn't exactly what I was thinking of."

"This one might be. It's in one of the abandoned houses. A human took up residence there a few days ago, and all the female vamps in the area have been flocking to it. Parties there every night this week."

A human, alone, in an abandoned house. Sounded like the place.

"16th and Aberdeen? Have any of you gone down there to check it out?"

The boys shook their heads.

"A girl from work went yesterday and didn't show up for her shift today, though," said one.

"Thanks." Neeman walked back to the car. "A human has taken up residence in an abandoned house a few miles from here. Probably our guy."

Stephos cracked his knuckles. "Then let's go knock on his door."

BOREDOM PRESSED DOWN ON SELENE SO VIOLENTLY SHE THOUGHT HER brain might explode. After sitting in her room for over half an hour with the voice in her head incessantly bugging her to leave, she'd decided to explore her 'would—be' jail. After all, Neeman had told her not to go, but that didn't specifically mean her room.

Jumping from her bed, she opened her door and looked into the hallway. She stood in the doorway for a minute listening.

"Neeman?" she called.

But no one replied.

"Helllloooooooo," she called louder.

Again silence.

She smiled and strolled down the hall heading the way Neeman had taken her to get something to eat.

"Helllooooo? Anybody home?"

She continued down the hall and turned to the right at the

end. She followed the corridor around and then took another right and stopped. The whole floor was no more than a large square. Like a hotel configuration. With rooms on both sides. A door led to the kitchen and beyond lay a common room with nothing of interest besides a stereo, some music discs, and a few comfortable couches. What the hell did the trackers do all night? Where was the television? A pool table? Hell, she'd settle for ping pong. Anything.

She shook her head. Neeman did need to learn to relax. If he did, maybe he wouldn't be as dull as her eighty—nine—year—old Oxford professor of biblical literature.

After locating the elevator, she went down a level and ended up above the large training arena. A few Vampires and humans practiced below. She watched them for a long time, shaking her head and laughing. They continued practicing the same moves she'd seen them work on earlier. The temptation to go down and teach them herself almost overtook her, but Neeman's disapproving gaze flashed into her mind. She left before she did something she regretted.

Next, she headed up to another wing of bedrooms that she assumed housed the humans from the smell of it. Unlike the other trackers' rooms, these rooms remained mostly devoid of personal items like Neeman's room. Her get clenched at the thought. She never thought she'd have so much in common with humans. But there they were. Both displaced. Both unwanted. Both homeless.

Leaving the human area, she rode the elevator to the first floor right below the exit. Offices stocked with anything they might need for several months lined one wall. A padded room with a table in the middle sat beyond. Thick straps hung from the table in all four corners. Kinky.

She meandered down the hall, opening doors and looking

inside. Finally, she pushed open the door to a room with several computers turned on. She walked to one, and it showed a location in lower Chicago. She moved the mouse around, and the screen changed to a page called "Google." Intrigued, she pulled out a seat and typed into the search bar, Lord Danika. Several pages pulled up, and she clicked on one. The front page of the Savor Blood Company popped up on the screen. Selene grinned. She wanted to learn everything about the woman who had won Mason's heart... especially if they were going to end up living together at some point— which inevitably they would.

It wasn't hard to figure out which house the boys had mentioned. They followed the stream of female vamps approaching the front of a boarded up house. From behind the wooden slats, multicolored light and loud music emanated. A group of male vamps had gathered on the lawn. Several pulled on the females, trying to stop them from going into the house, but the females screamed and beat on them until the males released them.

Neeman stopped the car, and he and Stephos got out. Riley pulled up behind them and both he and a human, John, exited their car as well.

"I'll take Stephos and get a feel for what's going on. Riley, you and John head around the back and see if the door is accessible. If it is, cover it. I'll call if we need you. I'm hoping this will be an easy one."

Stephos snorted. "That would be a trick."

Neeman shot him a look, and Stephos shut his mouth.

"Do we know what we're looking for?" asked John.

Neeman clenched his jaw. "A human male."

"A human?" John's eyes widened.

"Come on." Riley tugged John away. "I told you not to bug Neeman," he whispered.

Neeman and Stephos retrieved their weapons and headed for the front. They passed the group of male vamps that stood huddled together shooting fearful, angry glances at the house.

"Go home," Neeman said.

"My wife's been in there for two days," said a flabby, balding vamp.

Neeman tried to keep his temper in check. "We'll take care of this."

The vamps watched him and Stephos for a minute and then dispersed. He made sure they were halfway down the block before he continued. The scent of blood hit Neeman as he stepped onto the crumbling porch. His stomach lurched. The sour almost rotten stench of vamp blood threatened to bowl him over.

"That's not a little blood." Stephos covered his nose.

The music pounded out the front door. "Stayin'Alive" played loud enough that he'd have thought the band performed in the living room.

Neeman unholstered his gun, readying himself for what-ever he might see. He took a breath, nodded to Stephos, and burst through the door. His significant booted steps pounded on the creaking wood, but not another soul beside himself and Stephos stood in the room. Neeman motioned for Stephos to go left into a different room and he continued right. Neeman turned off the blaring stereo that sang on a table in the corner. He shook his head at the suddenness of the silence that made his ears buzz.

Giggling drifted down the staircase. Stephos came around from the back of the house, followed by Riley and John.

Neeman pointed upstairs. Stephos nodded.

"The stench is coming from the basement," Stephos mouthed.

Neeman locked eyes on Riley and motioned. Riley nodded, and he and John headed to the back of the house once more.

Neeman followed Stephos to the staircase. They reached the bottom stair at the same moment a female vamp walked out of a bathroom wearing a sheer nightie. She smiled automatically as if she'd been programmed to be nice. Her glassy gaze traveled over them.

"You're not supposed to be in here. Master Rex will be most displeased." She turned to leave her heavy bosom bouncing underneath the pink fabric.

Neeman grabbed her by the arm. "Leave."

She laughed. "Of course not. Master Rex likes me. I'm his favorite."

Neeman gripped her tighter. "Get. Out."

Her brows furrowed, but she kept smiling.

The hairs on Neeman's neck prickled. Something wasn't right. Before she could move, he backhanded her. Her head rocked to the side. She blinked twice, her smile fell, and her eyes widened.

"Where am I? Get me out of here," she whispered. She looked up the stairs, and her frame shook. "Get me away from him. Please. He's a monster."

John and Riley ran to meet them.

"Bodies," said Riley. "The basement. It's full of dead female vamps."

"Take her outside." Neeman thrust the curvy female at Riley.

Riley took her hand and helped her to the door.

"I don't hear my music!" A male voice called from upstairs.

"That's him." Neeman and Stephos took the steps two at a time, trying to keep the creaks to a minimum.

Peeling faded green—striped wallpaper, and yellowing photos of a human family lined the walls. The threadbare, matted carpeting barely covered a scratched wooden floor. At the top of the stairs, light shone from inside several open doors. They passed the first. A dozen naked females giggled on a sagging bed braiding each other's hair. Neeman blinked several times. Then he motioned to Stephos and nodded. Stephos stepped into the room.

Neeman passed other rooms full of equally saggy and worn furniture with naked women in them, all doing innocuous, female things— fixing their hair, putting on makeup, laughing, talking.

"Wife number one, where is my music?" called the male voice again from the end of the hall.

Neeman stopped outside the room. Riley joined him, with John behind.

"Get the females out." Neeman's finger twitched on his gun, and he pushed open the door. He stepped back and covered his nose with his arm to keep from vomiting. Bile gagged him, forcing him to get a hold of himself before stepping in the doorway again.

A wooden chair and a small broken table slept in the dirty, crumbling room, with an enormous, old claw—foot tub looming in the middle of the worn wooden floor. Neeman blinked twice trying to process the scene. In the tub lay a man covered in a dark foamy liquid. Two female vamps held a third over the side of the tub, her throat slit and bleeding out. Neeman's stomach lurched again.

The man held a cup in his hand, and he dipped it into the liquid, filling the tub. His smile fell at the sight of Neeman. He looked Neeman up and down for a minute but said nothing.

"It's not as good as human, I'm afraid," the Demon finally said. "But it's better than what we get where I'm from." He took a long drink from the cup, spilling the ooze back down over himself. He gulped and then burped. "I'm assuming you were sent to fetch me."

"Get out of the tub," Neeman ordered.

The two females noticed him for the first time. They looked between Neeman and the man in the tub.

"I'm Rexius," said the man. "But my friends call me Rex."

Neeman cocked his gun, wanting nothing more in the moment than to blow the son of a bitch away. But Mason had said they needed him alive.

"I said, Get. Out," Neeman repeated.

Rex laughed. "Put the gun away, it'll do very little against me."

Stephos and Riley entered the room.

"Take them out," Neeman commanded.

They holstered their weapons, took the dead female from the other two vamps, and set her on the floor. Then Stephos grabbed both women by the arm and dragged them screaming from the room.

"No need to be rude," said Rex. "If you'd asked, I would have told them to go. My wives are entirely obedient."

"I'm not going to tell you a third time," Neeman growled. With every passing moment, his agitation and nausea increased. He needed to get out of there and sanitize every particle of his body.

Rex shrugged and stood. Dark blood oiled his body and matted his dark hair to his skull. He licked his lips and then his fingers, making Neeman's stomach churn. He stepped out, dripping onto the floor, tossed his cup in the tub, and raised his hands over his head in a dramatic fashion.

"Well, now, you've got me. What are you going to do with me? Beat me into telling you what I'm doing here?"

"Where are your clothes?" Neeman demanded.

"Sorry, haven't gotten any. The portal doesn't let you bring anything through."

Son of a—

"Move." Neeman gestured toward the door, backing up, his gun still trained on the Demon. He stepped in the doorway of the adjoining room and waited. How the hell would he get Rex in the car without ruining the interior? He could send Riley to get some clothes from a neighbor, but he didn't want to stir up the vamps any more than they already had been.

With Rex in front of him, Neeman maneuvered down the stairs toward the entrance. Riley, Stephos, and John waited on the lawn. The female vamps clung to each other, naked and stumbling down the street, crying and screaming.

Neeman stepped out the front door, grateful for the fresh air. He closed his eyes for no more than a single breath, sucking in the crisp air. When he opened his eyes again, Rex no longer stood in front of him. Riley and Stephos looked around, but Neeman who spotted him first. Rex had John on the ground, tearing at his throat. John's eyes widened, and he looked to Riley. He gurgled once, and then his eyes went dead. The whole process had taken seconds.

Rex stood from John's limp body and turned, a huge smile on his face. His eyes had gone pitch black and row upon row of razor—sharp teeth peppered his mouth. He stretched and howled into the night. "That was amazing. I haven't had human in I can't tell you how long!"

Neeman crossed the yard in a blink and knocked Rex upside the head with the butt of his gun.

The monster swayed on his feet. "Ow. That hurt, you—"

Neeman bashed him in the head again, and Rex dropped to his knees. He hit him again, and Rex fell to the ground. Riley rushed to John and felt for a pulse. Eye clouded in disbelief, he looked at Neeman and shook his head.

Neeman cursed a blue streak. He reached down and smashed the unconscious Rex in the face several times. He'd never wanted the humans to be trackers. He'd never wanted to train them. He'd told Danika it was a bad idea. Simple assignment, his ass. Stephos finally grabbed him and pulled him off the bloodied mess of a Demon.

"Boss. Stop. We need him alive."

Neeman kicked the Demon in the balls. "Get me a collar from the car," he barked. "And strip off John's pants and put them on this bastard."

Stephos and Riley exchanged a look.

"Did I stutter?"

They both shook their heads. Stephos went for the collar as Riley removed John's cargo pants.

Neeman kicked at the grass before yelling into the night. He shook his head and stared up into the night sky. He tried to concentrate on finding the constellation Orion, but couldn't locate it. He looked back at Rex. The bastard didn't deserve pants. He didn't deserve to live. He deserved a lifetime of torture and misery for what he'd done.

Neeman reached for a cigarette and pulled out a pack of gum instead. Why had he chosen to give up smoking?

One thing was for sure. The tactics they'd learned, to fight Vampire, vampyr, vamp, and human, were not going to work on Demons. If this was a lesser Demon, they were screwed. All of them. Screwed.

NEEMAN PULLED THE CAR UP TO THE SIDE OF THE COMPOUND AND pushed the button to open the bay door. John's death weighed on him. He'd told Riley they weren't ready and now he had a human's blood on his hands. Something he'd never wanted.

He rolled the vehicle inside and waited for Riley to pull his in before closing the garage door. Stephos opened the back—passenger side door and yanked Rex out. The still unconscious Demon flopped to the floor, his head smacking the cement.

"Owww!" Rex grabbed the back of his skull.

Stephos slammed the door. "Get up, scum."

Dazed, Rex sat up and looked around, still rubbing his head. "Scum? That hurts coming from a Vampire."

Stephos yanked Rex to his feet and punched him in the gut. "If you speak to me again, you're going to wish I'd killed you back on that lawn."

Rex laughed heartily. "Oh, please, do you know where I came from? This is nothing." He smiled, and his lips moved silently.

"Don't!" Neeman raised the remote. The collar lit up. Rex cried out and fell to his knees. Neeman continued to hold down the button on the remote until he was satisfied, with Rex curled in a ball on the floor. He released the button. "This is the collar we use for slaves. If you get far enough from me, your head will explode, and I don't think even you could survive that."

Rex gagged and then vomited all over the cement. Blood splattered the ground. Neeman covered his nose and choked down his own bile. He hadn't thought that there could be anything that smelled worse than the house they'd grabbed Rex from, but he'd been mistaken.

"Get him up," he said. "And hose down the garage. I don't want that sinking in."

Stephos covered his nose. "Come on." He dragged Rex along by the arm to the elevator.

"What should I do with John?" Riley asked, his voice subdued.

Neeman locked gazes with him. "Wrap him in a sheet, and we'll bury him."

Riley nodded and started toward the elevator. Neeman grabbed him by the arm. He wanted to reassure Riley it wasn't his fault, but that wasn't entirely true. Riley was at least partially responsible, Neeman as well.

Neeman patted Riley on the shoulder, gave him a grim smile, and nodded once.

Riley nodded back.

Neeman couldn't manage more than that. The group squeezed into the small elevator, the smell of blood, vomit, and worse permeating the air. The doors opened to the first floor, which housed offices and interrogation rooms.

"Bring him." Neeman motioned Stephos forward. He headed for the interrogation room when the scent of cinnamon and vanilla hit him, and Selene rounded the corner. Dammit, really? "What are you doing up here?" He strode toward her. "I told you to stay put."

Selene came out of the computer room. Heading to the elevator, it opened, and Neeman stepped out. They locked gazes for several seconds. Oh crap.

He glanced at someone behind him and then back at her. "Get back to your room."

"Are we still going out?" She skipped up to him.

"Maybe."

She clenched her jaw. *Liar.*

He sighed. "This isn't the time." The veins in his forehead stood out, and his muscles bunched. "Go."

Anger rolled off his body, enticing her, but the hardness in his eyes told her something had gone wrong.

"What's the matter?" She wanted to reach for him, but her gaze traveled past him to the elevator, and she sucked in a sharp breath. "Shred."

Neeman looked over his shoulder. "You know him?"

Selene swallowed and nodded. The dark—haired, pitch—eyed Demon stared at her, covered in blood and filth.

"Kill it. Kill it now!"

Selene's hands shook. A wave of nausea hit her, and her head pounded.

The voice screamed for her to kill it, over and over.

"His name is Shred," she managed. "He's a shredder Demon."

"My name is Rex!" he yelled.

Selene stepped to the side, but Neeman caught her by the arm.

"Your name is Shred. Like the rest of your kind." Anger and fear pulsed in her veins. Her insides felt like she'd swallowed razor wire as her inner voice clamored to get out.

The Demon elbowed the Vampire behind him in the stomach and rushed toward her. "Do you know what it feels like to have the same name as hundreds of your brethren? To not have an identity? Of course, you don't, *Seraphine Hianag di wer ith di Bekilip.*"

She sucked in a breath.

"He knows. Strike now!"

Neeman's gaze bore into her. "What did he say to you?"

She shook her arm free of his grip and marched to stand directly in front of Rex. From the smell of him, he'd been doing what he loved best, bathing in blood.

Quick as light, she placed her palm in the middle of his chest.

"Si meage wux persvek wer ominak di sia opsola ti ekess utter sia identity ekess tikilvi shafaer nomeno togofor." She hadn't spoken in her native tongue in close to a century, but the command to not reveal her identity flowed from her like water. He gasped, and his eyes went wide. Moments passed, and his skin took on a purple hue as the air refused to enter his lungs.

"Stop," Neeman commanded. "We need him alive."

Selene kept her stare level on the Demon. The revealing of her identity wasn't an option. She'd rather deal with Neeman's anger than what would happen if she were found out.

"Si nymuer vur tyrtrol," he swore finally through gritted teeth, throwing daggers at her with his gaze. His mouth opened and closed several times, and she cocked an eyebrow.

With a flick of her fingers, she released him from his hold. The Demon coughed and sputtered several times.

"Was there else something you wanted to say to me, Rex?"

His eyes flickered, and he licked his lips. She'd commanded him to do something but then had respected him by calling him by his chosen name.

Rex cracked a smile and inclined his head. "No. But I do wonder why you are here. Could it be we seek the same male?"

Selene lunged at him, and Neeman grabbed her arm and ushered her toward the elevator as the others moved Rex around them and down the hallway.

"Don't worry." Rex laughed. "I'll be sure to give your regards to *Dout Opsola.*"

"Fool! You've endangered us all. Kill him."

Selene ripped from Neeman's grasp and ran at the Demon. Rex laughed as she neared him, but Neeman hoisted her up around the waist and threw her over his shoulder.

"If you utter a word, I'll gut you like a fish. You know what I am capable of, and you know what I can do. I am my father's daughter, don't you doubt that for a second," she screamed in the ancient language.

"I look forward to the torture." Rex chuckled.

Neeman tossed her into the elevator and stepped in. "Get him on the table," he yelled over his shoulder, his eyes never leaving her.

The doors closed and she hopped to her feet, pounding on the elevator wall. She couldn't afford for anyone to know she was here. It would endanger Mason as well as herself. Her inner voice cursed and yelled at her so vehemently that banging her head on the wall seemed like it might be the only way to stop it.

"What the hell was that?"

"What?" She pushed her hair from her eyes.

"You know what. What did you say to him?"

"Nothing." She turned away from his prying gaze, rubbing at her head.

"Don't give me that. You said something. What was it?"

"I said nothing." She continued to rub her temples. Why the hell did all elevators have to move so freakin' slow?

"What language was that? Fae? I've never heard it before."

"Something like that."

She stopped rubbing her temples and looked up at him. His jaw worked hard, and his gaze steeled.

Dammit. She'd blown it. Her shoulders slumped. "You're not going to take me out, are you?"

He crossed his arms over his chest.

Suck. "I didn't think so."

Pissed didn't begin to describe the look he shot her, but that wasn't her problem at the moment. Her current problem became the fact that the anger in his eyes and stern set of his jaw held a sensual masculine quality that hit her to the core. Desire pooled inside her. She hated that she needed to be with a male. And she hated it even more that the male she wanted most remained immune to her advances. Sure, sleeping with Neeman might make things complicated, but she was pretty sure that if she didn't have sex soon, she would burst into flames and die.

"Let's go out. Find someone else."

In the Fae world, her hormones had been suppressed. The lack of virile males, and her time strapped to the stone altar, stripped any desire right out of her. But here there were so many strong, lean, sexy men. Vampires, vampyr, and human alike in the compound.

"And even more outside the compound."

Hell, if she waited too long and Rex took a shower, she might even be persuaded to stoop to using him for release.

She had to get away. The elevator stopped, and she pushed past Neeman, gulping in air and trying to clear the incessant taunting voice in her head.

"Hey!"

"Hey what?" She didn't turn.

"I'm talking to you."

She raised her hand and continued to her room. Selene threw the door open with a huff, strode to the bed and flopped onto it. Neeman's boots pounded down the hallway toward her.

"Tsk, tsk, stupid girl."

Selene growled and pushed her palms over her ears. *Shut up! Shut up!*

Anger rolled off Neeman in waves. Obviously, he wasn't used to being disobeyed.

"Don't you have a Demon to hurt?" she shouted.

She threw her arm over her eyes, blocking him out. The room pressed down on her, the walls closing in. Her inner voice's demands to leave the compound had her on the brink of shoving a spike through her brain. She needed to calm down. She couldn't afford to lose control.

Minutes passed before his footsteps headed away from her door. "Don't take that collar off him," she yelled after him. "No matter what you do, don't take it off."

She lay on her bed, and the voice suddenly quieted. She sighed in relief, but a sudden buzzing sound took its place, and the throbbing in her temples grew steadily stronger. Her stomach rolled, and she pressed her palms into her temples. *No, no, no!* She couldn't let this happen.

"Neeman," she cried weakly.

The elevator bell rang, and she sat up. She needed to get to him. To tell him to lock her in. To tell him to take her to the padded room and shackle her.

The room spun, and she swallowed down a moan and blinked several times, trying to focus.

"Neeman, wait." Lunging for the door, she rammed the wall with her shoulder and grunted. She looked out, as the elevator closed and Neeman disappeared.

Her legs gave out, and she slumped to the floor. The light around her dimmed, and a sultry chuckle bounced around in her mind.

"Stop," she moaned.

The room fell out of focus, and like a movie projector in her mind, everything shrunk to a pinpoint of light.

"Don't do this," she whispered.

"Time for some fun."

CHAPTER SEVEN

Seraphine ascended in the elevator to the top floor, which opened into the warehouse. She jogged to the far end and located two SUVs sitting by the exit. She hopped into one before noticing a different vehicle a few yards away.

"No way!" She jumped out of the SUV and headed for the sports car. She ran her hand over the canary yellow hood. Sliding into the driver's seat, she ran her fingertips over the leather steering wheel. Nice!

She pulled down the visor. No keys. No matter. Setting her palm over the ignition, she took a deep breath and concentrated.

"Ignis."

The engine roared to life, and she whooped. The purr of power that enveloped her made shivers of delight travel up her spine. She hit the remote button, and the garage door opened. Shifting the car into reverse, she looked over her shoulder and then rolled onto an open parking lot.

She pushed the radio button, and a female voice said, "Hello, Neeman."

She looked around, but couldn't locate anyone. On a screen in the front of the car, it said Max.

"Max?"

"Hello. You're not Neeman."

Seraphine stared at the dashboard. "Uh... No, I'm not. What are you?"

"I am Max."

A computer? "Do you know where the nearest clothing store is?"

"The nearest clothing store is ten point three miles away. You can choose from—"

Seraphine stopped listening. "Tell me how to get there."

"Go one hundred yards and then turn left at the fork."

She was overdue for some fun.

SERAPHINE MADE IT TO THE FIRST BOUTIQUE CLOTHING STORE, WHERE she charmed the male store clerk into giving her several dresses, a week's worth of bras and panties, three pairs of pants, ten blouses, a myriad of T—shirts, and six new pairs of shoes. Happy her abilities still worked after years of being dormant, she pulled away from the curb and asked Max for the next store's location.

By the time she finished with the third shop, the backseat of the car looked like a clown car ready to explode clothes, pajamas, shoes, purses, jewelry, hair products, body products, and all the other human luxuries she'd missed over the years.

"Where would you like to go?" Max asked.

"A club." She laughed. "What's the hottest night club around here?"

"Midnight is a hot club."

Seraphine groaned. Done that. "What about something with salsa music?"

"The Pink Gypsy."

"Great, take me there."

Seraphine drove south into the heart of Chicago. Gods, how she'd missed Earth. Missed being herself. Being free. She rolled down the windows and let the wind whip through her hair. She turned up the heavy metal music and smiled.

Seraphine stopped in front of a bright pink neon sign with twinkling lights, hanging over a black building. A vamp ran to her car door and opened it. She smiled from ear to ear. The thrum of the bongos ignited in her veins.

"May I help you with your car?" he asked.

"Leave her here and take good care of her, and I might take care of you." She ran her arm down the length of the vamp's arm and muttered, *"Influentiam."*

The vamp nodded; his eyes glassy.

She slid around the front of the car in a dress that fit her like she'd painted it on. She passed the waiting line to the front and approached a statuesque, oak—colored vampyr barred the way.

"Hi," she said in her most seductive voice.

"Where's your master?" He glanced past her to the car.

"He told me he'd meet me here. He's running a bit late."

"His name?"

"Neeman." She flashed him a bright smile.

He stared at her for a minute, then nodded and let her pass.

Music thumped and pounded against her body, and she swayed her hips. Horns chirped, and maracas hissed. The energy in the air snapped and rolled over her skin, making her tingle. The magic she had expended over the past hours recharged with every body she rubbed up against. She purred at the energy that melted into her skin like warm massage oil.

Seraphine cha—chaed through the throng. Males stopped left and right to admire her. She pushed out her chest and swished her hips a bit more, soaking in their attention. At the bar, she leaned into the wood and waited for the bartender.

"What's a beautiful human like you doing here alone?" he yelled over the noise.

"Getting a drink while I wait for my master." She set her breasts on the bar.

He looked her over for a moment and then nodded. "What can I get you?"

"A margarita. And keep them flowing."

He nodded. "That'll be eight bucks."

She reached out and touched his arm. *"Influentiam,"* she whispered.

He blinked twice and smiled. "They're on the house tonight."

She nodded. *Too easy.*

The wooden bar bit into her shoulder blades as she leaned back on it, surveying the club. A mariachi band complete with bright, puffy—sleeved shirts and tight pants played on a stage opposite her. Out on the floor, couples danced and shimmied together, twirling in a sensual, colorful rhythm.

She looked for anyone who might be vampyr or Vampire that she could use to get what she needed.

A male vamp sidled up next to her. "Hey beautiful, can I buy you a drink?"

His graying skin and sour scent made her wrinkle her nose. "No, thanks. I already have one coming."

"What's a fine human like yourself doing in here?" His gaze raked her up and down.

Why did they all keep asking her that? It had gotten old faster than a McDonald's hamburger in a hot car. Couldn't she just go out and have some fun without everyone wondering why she was there? Neeman's words replayed in her head, and it became apparent he was right– for once. Humans really were out of place in the new world.

"My master will be here soon," she said. "And I don't think he'd take too kindly to me talking to someone else." She turned back to the bar, looking for her drink.

"Come on, sweetie, don't be like that." The guy put his arm around her shoulders. "I'm just being friendly. You have the most amazing purple eyes."

Rage flared through her. She whipped around on him and hit him square in the chest.

"*Dolor.*" Pain.

The vamp let out a scream then doubled over and crumpled to the floor, writhing and convulsing. A curvy female vamp with short spiky hair and a nose ring ran over and knelt by his side. She looked up at Seraphine.

"What the hell did you do to him?"

"*Stop. Let him go!*"

Seraphine shook her head. "He hit on me, and I didn't appreciate it."

A group of vamps gathered around. The female stood nose to nose with her.

"Listen, bitch. My boyfriend would never hit on a painted— up Vampire whore like you."

The flames of rage heated Seraphine's blood. She stared at the female hard, and the other woman's eyes went wide, and she backed away.

"Now you listen, you vamp scum. I am no one's whore, and

your boyfriend did hit on me. I suggest you take him and leave before I lose my patience."

The female backed into her boyfriend on the ground. Her eyes never leaving Seraphine's face, she bent down and grabbed him by the arm, trying to lift him off the floor, but he only writhed and moaned.

A larger group gathered around, dousing her anger. She shouldn't draw so much attention to herself.

Seraphine closed her eyes and took a deep breath. "*Absolutus.*"

The moaning vamp stopped, and the couple scrambled away as the bartender showed up.

Seraphine stared at the greenish—yellow drink, her mood to party gone. Her hand quaked, and she breathed in deep. Trying to take in the now diminished buzz in the air. She downed the drink so quickly, her back teeth ached, and her throat burned.

Hurting the vamp had felt good. Too good. She needed to stay in control. She couldn't afford an incident. Not here. It wasn't safe.

The bartender arrived again.

"Tequila," she said without looking up.

CHAPTER EIGHT

Neeman's fist cracked across Rex's nose for the fifth time.

Rex laughed and spat out blood. "You do realize that tickles, right?"

Neeman punched him again. He'd never enjoyed this part as much as he was in that moment. "Tell me what you're doing on this plane."

"Didn't you see? I was bathing in blood. It's my favorite pastime, and I don't get to do it enough, so when given the opportunity to take advantage of a timeshare here in Chicago, I jumped at the chance."

Neeman cocked his fist back to punch him again. "How did you get through?"

Rex laughed, his broken nose gushing onto his bare chest.

Neeman's phone buzzed, and he swore. Only Mason would be able to get anything out of the POS.

He pressed the button on his Bluetooth. "Neeman."

"It's Jonah from The Pink Gypsy."

"I'm a bit busy at the moment."

"I'm sorry to bother you, but I thought you might want to know your slave is here and she's causing a bit of a stir."

"My slave?"

"Human, black hair, purple eyes. She's driving your Ferrari."

"She's driving my—" Neeman cursed so loud the window in the door rattled. Could that woman be any more of a pain in his ass? He looked at Rex. "I'll be right there. Make sure she doesn't leave. Wait. Did you say her eyes were purple?"

"Yeah."

What was the deal with that? "Keep her there."

Neeman hung up the phone and pinched the bridge of his nose. He wasn't sure which pissed him off more— the fact that she'd left or the fact that she had his car.

The car. Definitely the car.

"Seraphine's a handful, isn't she?" Rex said.

Neeman looked up. "Seraphine?"

"Yeah, that's her name. Well, not her full name—" Rex cut off suddenly.

"How do you know her?"

Rex opened his mouth and tried to speak but closed it. He tried again and ended up letting out a string of profanity. It looked like an invisible someone physically held him back from speaking.

"Everyone knows her." Rex panted, his eyes glittering with mischief.

"From when she lived here?"

Rex shook his head. "Nope. Everyone knows—" His body arched and convulsed. He screamed in pain, and his muscles strained so hard against the restraints Neeman thought Rex might actually dislocate his joints.

A chill raced through Neeman, and the scent of ozone hit him again.

After a few seconds, Rex dropped back on the table, laughing and panting at the same time.

"Oh baby, that girl sure does know where to hit a guy."

"What the hell is wrong with you?" Neeman asked.

Rex smiled and gulped down air. "Talk to your girlfriend."

"She's not my girlfriend."

"Really? Because from what I saw of you two... Honestly, I wouldn't mind getting a piece of that for myself. I've heard she is quite—"

Neeman punched him in the gut. He didn't have time for games.

"I'll meet you back at the compound," he told Stephos. "Make sure no one disturbs the Demon till I return."

Stephos nodded. "You got it."

They stopped by Pink Gypsy, and Neeman gritted his teeth at the sight of Max, his Ferrari.

He stepped out of the car and walked to his baby. He ran his hand over it, making sure it remained undamaged, and then looked in the window.

The ignition didn't have a key— if she'd hotwired his car... He took a deep breath and blew it out again. He gazed in the backseat. What the—

He couldn't even see out the back window, so many bags and boxes had been piled and shoved in there.

Neeman growled and stormed to the entrance of the club. Jonah opened the door for him.

"She's on the floor."

Neeman nodded. He pushed his way through the bar and scanned the area.

He didn't have time for this crap. A Demon lay chained in

his compound, and a dead human tracker waited to be buried. The smell of vamps, sweat, and alcohol filled him. He spotted her dancing alone as if a strange void surrounded her where people steered clear.

Unlike at Midnight, the patrons eyed Selene warily and kept their distance. He wondered what she'd done to elicit that response.

The tight dress she wore barely covered her swishing rear. Desire washed over him at the sight of her short, plum dress, which cut to the small of her back and clung to her form. Her hips gyrated with the music in a sensual dance, making his imagination kick into overdrive. Why her? Of all the females he could be attracted to, why did it have to be her?

He stalked out to the middle of the floor and set his hand on her shoulder. She turned, her eyes ablaze, but as soon as she recognized him, her eyes softened, and she smiled.

"Took you long enough, Loverboy."

"Time to go home."

The other patrons looked on. She wobbled slightly, drunk. Great.

"No." She wrenched free. "We want to dance." She moved back and forth in front of him. He reached for her, but she shimmied out of the way.

"We're not dancing. We're leaving."

She grabbed his hand and used it to twirl in a circle. He yanked her close, and her back hit his chest. Rubbing her body up and down his, she made his arousal ratchet even higher, grinding her backside into his front as she bent at the waist. He gripped her by the hips and spun her to face him.

Selene threw her arms around his neck, continuing to writhe and wriggle. "You promised to take us out, but you lied."

"In case you didn't notice, I'm a little busy." He removed her arms from his neck, and she backed up a step, never missing a beat in the music. She kicked out her slender legs and raised her arms over her head, her hands in her hair.

It was one of the most erotic things Neeman had ever witnessed. She ground her hips in circles and turned from him once more. His arousal hit a fevered pitch watching her dress move higher and higher up her legs till the hem of her black panties became visible.

She glanced over her shoulder and his gut clenched. She flashed him a seductive smile and stepped closer, beckoning him forward with her finger. He refused to play her game. Her smile widened, and she sidled up to him and laid her palm in the middle of his chest. Tracing a soft circle through his shirt, she continued to dance and rub against him.

His fangs burned to taste her, and his hands itched to feel her supple flesh. She pressed her body against his, her soft curves melting into him.

"Please," she begged. "Dance with me. Just one dance." The smile fell from her lips, revealing nothing but sincerity. Her eyes were an alluring mix of green—rimmed in purple.

The pleading in her voice tugged at his heart. For the first time, he witnessed a longing inside her. Loneliness and pain oozed off her that he'd not seen before.

Without thinking, he raised his hand and entwined his fingers in the short hair at the base of her neck. "All right."

She led him to the center of the floor and wrapped her arms around his neck, pulling him close. He slid his hands down her soft skin and rested them on the small of her back. Though the song was fast, their movements were a slow caress.

She stared into his eyes and held his gaze. Their bodies swayed to the music, in perfect rhythm. Hip to hip, their bodies began their own intimate tango. Her tempting scent swirled around him and made his throat burn. As she inched impossibly closer, her ample breasts smashed into his chest.

She was so beautiful. *But infuriating*, he reminded himself. A handful. A complication he didn't need. And worst of all, her heart belonged to someone else. He was nothing more than a distraction— a toy.

Without warning, she reached up on her tiptoes and pressed her lips to his. The taste of tequila lingered on her mouth.

Without thinking, he wrapped his hand around her neck, coaxed her lips apart, and his tongue mingled with hers. She let out a soft moan. He crushed his mouth on hers, and his fangs grazed her lip. A thrill raced through him as a drop of her blood hit his tongue. Desire rushed through him like wildfire, spreading to every fiber of his body and threatening to burn him alive.

Her sweet and salty blood warmed his tongue. Bloodlust plundered his body, stronger than it had since he'd first turned. He wanted more of her. Needed more of her. All of her.

He grazed her lip again, on purpose, savoring the sweet taste of her blood. She grabbed his rear. His arousal rubbed against her, and the friction made him almost explode.

No! He couldn't have this. He needed to regain control. Mustering all his training to keep his head straight, he pushed her away.

She peered at him, her eyes glassy, confusion playing on her features.

It took every ounce of restraint to keep from tackling her to the floor right there and sinking his fangs deep into her neck, amongst other things. Sure, she may be Fae, but who said she couldn't be turned if he accidentally lost control? He couldn't risk it. He'd gone his entire vampyr life without biting anyone, and he intended to keep it that way.

"We should get you home."

"But—"

"No 'but.'" Without another word, he dragged her off the dance floor and out the door.

SELENE RUSHED INTO THE COOL NIGHT AIR, HER HEAD AND VISION clearing at a rapid pace. She looked around in panic. How had she gotten there?

Neeman's hand clamped down on hers, dragging her from a bright pink bar. She wracked her brain for the answers, and the memories flooded back in a rush, overwhelming her as she tried to organize them.

She groaned. It had happened again.

She processed the memories faster this time. Up to the last moment on the dance floor when she'd kissed Neeman. *Holy* — She'd kissed Neeman.

Neeman slipped her in the passenger seat of the Ferrari, and she glanced in the backseat. *Double Holy!* She looked down at the tiny, tight dress and tried in vain to cover herself. Mortification drenched her skin like a rainstorm.

She fought to keep the shakes at bay and herself from succumbing to the tears threatening to flow. She needed to find a solution— fast. She couldn't let this start happening again. The last time she'd lost control it had almost gotten her, as well as an entire college fraternity killed. Which was the exact reason her mother had made her the amulet in the first place.

The electric sexual energy of the people in the bar wound

her up, filling her cup to the brim. Her body hummed with magic. She needed a release.

They drove in silence to the compound, Neeman keeping his eyes firmly rooted in the dark blacktop and her keeping her arms firmly planted over her legs in a show of modesty.

Neeman had barely pulled the car into the warehouse when she opened the door and raced for the elevator.

"Selene!"

Humiliated, she refused to turn, hitting the button at the elevator. The doors opened immediately. She stepped in and pushed the button before he could reach her.

"What about all the stuff in the—" His words cut off by the door closing.

"Return it!" she yelled.

Anger and shame stewed inside her. Her emotions mixed until she couldn't think of anything more than reaching her room. She'd come on to Neeman, and he'd rejected her, again. But this time it was different. She'd opened up to let him see inside her, and he'd pushed her away. If she'd been in her right frame of mind, she never would have done that— but that was beyond the point. What must he think? How could she ever face him again?

Adrenaline coursed through her, making her head pound and her limbs shake.

"Oh, hell. Not now," she moaned.

She needed help. A spell to keep herself from blacking out again. She needed her amulet. With her magic at full capacity, it got easier and easier for her the voice in her head to take over.

The elevator doors opened, and she stared into the hallway. With a whisper, she could level the entire floor and drain her powers.

"Yes, do that. That'll be fun. Then we can watch the place burn."

"No."

The elevator began to close, and she jumped out. She sprinted to her room and flung the door open. Her body heated and throbbed like a water balloon overfilled and ready to pop. She needed to cleanse.

She stripped off her dress and flung it to the floor in disgust. "How could you put that thing on me? I looked like a common whore. I am not a whore."

The voice gave a hearty laugh. *"Oh? I think you deceive yourself."*

Sliding out of her heels, she stood topless in the middle of her room, realizing she had nothing else to wear. She'd dropped the black clothes in the dressing room of the first store, and everything else remained in the car. Not that she'd be caught dead in such trashy, pricey clothes.

A cough in the doorway pulled her attention. Neeman stood laden with packages and bags. His eyes devoured her body though his face remained impassive. And since she stood in nothing but her lacy black panties, there wasn't much he couldn't see.

"Are you going to set them down, or keep staring?"

He cleared his throat and stepped into the room, half setting down, half dropping the load. Several bags tipped over, spilling their contents all over the floor. His expression changed. Softened. He straightened and opened his mouth.

Nope! She didn't want to hear it. Couldn't hear it. If he even tried to say one nice thing to her, she'd lose it in front of him, sealing her in her humiliation forever. Selene strode to him and planted her hand in the middle of his chest.

"Selene, let me explain."

Embarrassment quivered her chin.

"Selene, please. I wanted to. I did, but—"

She shoved him hard, and he stumbled back before grabbing onto her waist. "Selene, if you will listen to me."

She used both hands and all of her weight to push him out the door before slamming it in his face.

Once closed, she slid to the floor and sobbed into her hands. His last expression burned into her mind, his brilliant eyes sad and pleading. She shivered and curled into a ball.

She needed Mason.

SELENE AWOKE IN A COLD SWEAT. HER SKIN FELT TOO TIGHT, AND HER heart thundered. She tossed in her bed and tried to sit up. A strange, faint, yet familiar high—pitched ringing sounded in her ears. She stuck her fingers in her ears and then pulled on them, but the ringing continued.

"Wakey, wakey. Hear that noise?"

A familiar sense of foreboding washed over her. She groaned and looked at the clock. Four in the afternoon. She threw her legs over the side of the bed and got to her feet shakily. The energies and appetites of Earth had woken her long slumbering need to cause chaos, pain, and pleasure.

She leaned against the wall as the ringing continued, and she pounded on the sides of her head. *Stop. Stop. Stop.*

Again, the voice echoed through her head. *"Better find that sound."*

Stumbling over the bags and boxes on the floor, she tripped over a T—shirt and stopped. Selene leaned over and picked up the Metallica shirt— *perfect.* She slid the soft cotton over her naked body and ripped the tag from the collar.

Stumbling into the hall, she looked in both directions, but not a soul stirred at the early hour. The ringing grew louder, and she tugged on her ears again. She should find Neeman.

No. No Neeman. She didn't want to see him. She wanted release.

"Neeman could help with that too."

"Not on your life." She needed to cleanse before she did irreparable damage— but how... Leaning on the wall for support, she made her way down the hall, the piercing ringing growing louder the further she got from her room.

She stopped halfway down and whimpered. What the hell was that noise, and how did she make it stop?

Her head snapped up as recognition finally struck her. She peered at the elevator. Rex.

She rode the elevator to the upper floor, fighting to keep on her feet at the almost deafening ringing.

She shuffled out as the doors opened, and the Vampire guard stood and shoved his phone in his pocket.

"What are you doing down here?" He stepped toward her.

She waved her hand at him, barely able to form words. *"Sopor."*

His eyes fluttered closed, and he dropped to the floor, asleep. She propelled herself onward, stumbling over his body. The ringing had surpassed the level of deafening to the point of excruciating pain. She tried the door handle, but it didn't move. Her hand fell on the computerized locking system next to the door. Her vision blurred, and her knees almost buckled.

"Recludo."

The computer screen blinked and went out.

The door swung open, and she fell to her knees. Rex lay on a table, strapped down with a slave collar around his neck and his body vibrating. His puffy and bruised face appeared to be sleeping, but his eyes flew open and raked her. He gave a lopsided grin through a split lip, and the ringing stopped.

So, it had been him. She sucked air into her lungs and struggled to her feet. That couldn't be good.

"Aaaaahhhh. There you are. I wondered if you were really still in there." His chuckle turned into a coughing fit that ended with him trying to suck in breath. He winced as he did so. "I do so love your natural—colored eyes, Seraphine. I can't wait till I can see them again. The green ones you sport playing as Selene are so bland."

She staggered to him and ripped his shirt open. Bruises covered his torso as if every rib had been broken.

She stared at Rex. He'd been calling, signaling to any Demons within the region like a beacon. But they were so far underground it wasn't possible anyone had heard— hopefully. Either way she needed to silence him.

"If you help me, I'll let you go. Tell me where the rift is."

"Let me loose, and I'll take you there, Princess."

She shook her head. It was no use. He wouldn't tell her. He'd already been through hell, and he hadn't told Neeman.

"Let me have him."

The voice crawled closer to the surface, making her stomach lurch.

Selene covered her mouth with her hand and burped. She shouldn't. She needed to release. To cleanse. But hurting someone, even another Demon...

"I'll do it gladly."

Selene laid her hands on Rex's chest. She opened her mouth, but no words came out.

"Missing the old days? Wanting to have a bit of fun, are you?" He smiled. "Hurting isn't as easy when you haven't done it in a while, huh, Princess?"

"Shut up." She tried again. Remembering every spell that

had been used on her. Every whip. Every cut. Every bruise. She couldn't do it.

"But I can."

Rex snorted. "Weak. You've grown so weak. You father would be so disappointed in you."

"Shut up. Shut up. Shut. Up!" she screamed.

"Let me out. Let me do it. You need to cleanse, but you're too weak. I'm not, though. I was made for this."

Selene didn't want to listen to the voice. Didn't want to give in. Didn't want to lose control. "What were you doing when they caught you?" she asked.

"What?"

"Tell me what you were doing." Her skin felt ready to shred apart. Too thin, like a belt sander had removed her outer layer. "I command you to tell me."

His gaze intensified, and he locked eyes with her. "I stripped them of their will, and then I stripped them of their clothes. Finally, I stripped them of their lives. I let their blood flow over me and into me. I bathed in it, relished it."

Horror brought bile to her throat. Good. "How many?"

"Dozens and dozens. And I would've done more, hundreds more, thousands more. I killed the human the Vampires brought with them. That was the best of all. His blood flowed so much faster. So much sweeter. When I get off this table, my brothers and I will shred this world of humanity."

The desire to destroy him ran so deep she shook with the effort of holding back. He was a monster who deserved death.

"Yes. Finally."

She laid her palm on his abdomen and everything inside her quieted. The deafening silence before the firework explosion. She needed this, she told herself over and over. If she didn't do it, she would continue to deteriorate until she did something she'd regret. A soft glow emanated under her skin. Blue and gold swirled in her veins, ready to be unleashed.

"Come on. It's what you came for, isn't it? To kill me. To let loose. I can see it on your face. The way you're trying to rein in your sanity. To keep it under control. That's the Fae way. Control. Did Mommy teach you that, Princess? Did she tell you to control your urges? 'Don't give in. Be a good little Fae?' Did she?"

Memories of the elders testing her, pushing her to the brink, popped into her mind. She pounded on her head, forcing the voice out.

"What did they do to you, Princess? The Fae? What did they do? Anything worse than I would have?"

Memories bombarded her and Selene ran for the exit.

"Wait till Daddy hears where you are. What do you think he'll give me if I tell him?"

She stopped dead in her tracks and whipped back to him. "Why are you here? Why are you in Chicago?"

"I'm here for Maelstrom. Since I found you, I can only assume he isn't too far away. The two of you were always ever so close."

Her heart pounded. The Demons had come for Mason, but they'd found her as well. They'd come in droves now that they'd found them both. She should've stayed put. If Rex hadn't seen her, maybe he wouldn't have found Mason. This was her fault.

"When I get out of here I'm going to parade you back to our plane with Maelstrom in tow. And then I'm going to beg for the pleasure of being your mate."

Seraphine surged through her limbs, so fast Selene didn't have time to stop her.

Quick as sound, she moved to him. "I'd rather eat my face

off. *Annullo!*" She jammed her palm onto his fleshy stomach, and the glow that had built beneath her skin flowed out.

Rex let out a shriek of terror.

"You'll never have Maelstrom. You'll never have me!" Magic, forceful and primal, poured from her hands and into his body. Threads of molten light wove over his chest and wrapped around him in a cocoon of magic. The strands spun 'round and 'round until they closed over him. His eyes popped open wide, and his lips pulled back in a soundless scream. His teeth fell from his mouth, and his eyes sunk into their sockets. His skin blackened and cracked until he charred to a pile of ash.

Her hands hit the table he'd been lying on. The glowing cleared from under her skin, and a boulder lifted off her shoulders. Selene stared down at her palms and Seraphine retreated.

"You're welcome."

Her hands shook, and her entire frame quaked. She'd killed someone. A bad someone, an evil someone, but someone.

"We did it to save Mason. To save us both."

Weakness tore at her limbs, and she dropped to the ground like a forgotten rag doll. Her head lay on the cold tile floor that smelled of bleach and blood. Her eyes opened and closed slowly.

She needed to hide. She needed to sleep.

A SHARP KNOCK ON NEEMAN'S DOOR PULLED HIM STRAIGHT OUT OF HIS slumber. He peered at his clock— quarter to five in the evening. He jumped from his bed in nothing but his pajama bottoms and opened the door.

Ford waited in the hall.

"What are you doing? You're supposed to be guarding the Demon."

"He's gone."

"Gone? He has a collar."

"The collar's there, and a pile of ash is there, but he is not."

"What the hell happened?" Neeman demanded, heading for the elevator.

"The girl. The female, she came down about an hour ago and waved her hand at me and said something. The next thing I knew, I woke up on the floor. She's gone and the Demon's gone."

Neeman cursed under his breath. He raced to the interrogation room. Sure enough, it was bare. He stepped up to the table where the Demon had been tethered and scanned it. His gaze stopped at a set of handprints in the middle of the ash. He placed his palm up to the prints. They were considerably smaller, delicate even.

He sucked in a deep breath. The scent of ozone hit him. That smell. The smell from his room, and earlier when Rex had tried to talk about— Without a word, he turned and ran for the elevator.

The carriage stopped on the bedroom level. He raced toward her room. The shopping bags still lay strewn on the floor, but her bed stood empty.

Neeman's gut clenched. She'd fled. She'd killed his prisoner and fled.

Anger flared his nostrils. He'd find her. He'd find her and make her pay.

He turned to leave when a whimper caught his attention. He glanced around and found the closet door ajar. He walked to it and pulled it open.

She lay on the floor in a ball— eyes shut tight.

He grabbed her, dragging her out and onto her feet. "What the hell did you do?"

Her head lolled back and forth.

"You killed him, didn't you? The Demon. You killed him."

Her eyes barely opened. She clutched his upper arms, trying to hang on.

"Answer me. You used Fae magic to kill him, and to start my car, and in my room. Didn't you?"

She moaned but didn't answer. His anger took a back seat as he examined her. Her unusually pale skin held a waxen pallor, and a subtle sheen of sweat glistened on her body and dampened her T—shirt.

Her eyes opened and closed, but the blank look on her face had him wondering if she was even awake. Her nails dug into his arms, and his grip tightened on her.

"What's wrong with you?" he asked in a softer voice.

The words had barely left his mouth when her legs buckled, and she crumpled to a heap.

His anger extinguished in an instant. He dropped to his knees, pulled her head into his lap and brushed her hair from her face. Her skin temperature plummeted, and she began to shiver.

"Selene? Selene, can you hear me?"

She moaned again and whispered something he couldn't hear. Fear gripped him in its tight fist and made his skin pebble.

"What? What do you need?"

"Mason," she whispered.

CHAPTER NINE

S trapped to an upright stone altar, the ropes on her wrists and legs bit into her already raw skin. How many days had she been tied up this time? Her back spasmed in agony, making her cry out. She looked down at her protruding ribs. How long had it been since she'd eaten?

The caked blood on her stomach had dried, itching, and pulling with every breath. She ran her tongue over her cracked lips, but her tongue felt like a dry cheese grater.

Where was her mother? Not that she would ever show weakness and call for her mother, she just wondered where the woman was. Was she arranging flowers? Eating a meal? Sleeping with an elder to ensure herself a secure place in the kingdom?

Her inner voice whimpered. The sound so unnatural it woke her from her groggy state.

"Let me out."

"No. You're the reason I'm in this mess."

"If you let me out, I can end this suffering."

She snorted. "Yes, but when you burn out, they'll kill us."

She opened her gluey eyes. The grove held no sound, but the sense of being watched skittered over her skin. Animals kept their distance from the horror that permeated the place. Even the trees and bushes bent away.

She turned her head as her mother's father and several other elders wordlessly entered the grove.

"Oh, hell. Let me out. Let me out!"

The observers stood just inside the circle of trees, palms pressed together, eyes on her.

The High Elder broke from the group and moved fluidly across the grass, his robes swishing around his bare feet as if he floated. Which, she was sure, he wanted everyone to believe he did. But she knew the truth about him.

He stopped at her side and held a water skin to her lips. Humiliation soured her stomach, but she was unable to resist the much needed refreshment. The liquid flowed down her throat, pushing its way through the parched tissues that barely clung together. She coughed and spluttered, and he stopped pouring the water too soon. Her stomach growled for the first time in days.

"This will be the last time, daughter of Yelena. If you do well, we will let you go home."

"Back to Chicago?"

His eyes darkened.

Wrong answer.

"Back to your mother's home."

She nodded vigorously. "Yes, of course. That's what I meant. I got confused."

"Don't grovel," her inner voice roared.

"I'm sure." He raised a small obsidian instrument above Selene's stomach. His piercing, aqua—colored eyes glittered with glee.

"Remember," he whispered. "To love your family is to honor your family."

He lowered the instrument slowly, letting it hover over her skin. Her breathing became shallow and rapid, but she refused to shy away. Not from him. Never from him.

"Let me take it. Fade away and sleep. Let me take the pain," said her inner voice.

She wanted to be brave. She didn't want to succumb, but at the first touch of the Demon stick she wailed, and everything went black.

NEEMAN STOOD, WEARING ONLY HIS PAJAMA BOTTOMS, WATCHING Selene rock back and forth, moaning in bed.

He had gotten her to eat a few crackers, and she'd downed three bottles of Gatorade, but she was still weak and refused to speak.

He'd called Mason, who had said it wasn't a good time, but Neeman had explained Selene's condition, and after a volley of swearing, Mason had promised to come.

Neeman ran his fingers through his hair. Anger over the Demon still coiled within him, but concern tugged at him as well. When had his life come into such upheaval? He didn't like it. He needed order, control— two things he wasn't able to get with Selene around.

The door swung inward, and Mason stepped into the room. He nodded to Neeman and went straight to the bed. The box spring creaked and sagged under his tremendous weight.

"Selene." He turned her to face him. A small cry escaped her, and her eyes flew open and locked on him.

Her chin quivered, and then she flung her arms around his neck. "Mael."

He hugged her tight. "It's all right. It's okay."

"I didn't mean to. I swear I didn't. I tried to control her, but I couldn't. I just couldn't. I had to drain my magic, and he recognized me. Searching for you and..." She broke into sobs that wracked her body.

Mason pulled her closer and stroked her hair. "It's okay. It's okay. You had to know this would happen sooner or later."

The sight of Mason holding Selene threw Neeman's jealousy into overdrive. He ground his teeth together in an effort to hold back the words he wanted to spew.

The two sat on the bed and clung to each other for several minutes before Mason's grip slacked.

"You're cold," he said. "Too cold. You need energy. You've spent too much. You're lucky you didn't kill yourself."

"It's not my fault. In the Fae plane, I can control it better. My Fae becomes stronger. I haven't had a problem in so long. But the voice. Her voice. I lost the amulet, and I thought I'd be okay..."

"We'll fix it. You need to recharge. Stay strong. Keep her caged. You need life force magic. It's the only kind that will keep her at bay. Do you understand?"

She nodded and looked at Neeman. Her eyes rimmed with deep shadows.

Mason's gaze traveled to Neeman as well. "You have to help her. Please."

"Help her what?"

"Her magic is depleted, and she needs life force to make her better."

"Why can't you help her? Afraid Danika might catch a whiff of her on you?"

Mason frowned.

Neeman didn't care. To have Danika at home and now

Selene here, in hiding, more than angered him, and he didn't want any part of it.

Mason stood from the bed and walked to Neeman. "You have something to say?"

"What do you want me to say? You're mated to the Coven Lord of Chicago, but your old girlfriend shows up, and you ask me to keep her hidden?"

Mason's brows knit together. "Girlfriend? Selene's not my girlfriend."

"Lover. Whatever you want to call it."

Mason looked over his shoulder at Selene. "You didn't tell him?"

"It never came up." She shivered and pulled up the covers.

Mason turned back to Neeman and sighed. "She isn't my lover, Neeman. She's my sister."

"Sister?"

"Our mothers were sisters, but we have the same father."

"But... you said she was Fae."

"I don't have time to explain. I need to get back before Danika rises. Danika already has so much on her plate, me telling her about Selene right now... I honestly don't know what she will do. I'm torn between them right now but Danika is my top priority. I need your help. Please." Mason stared at him. "I know I'm asking a lot, far more than I have a right to ask, but will you do this favor for me? I..." Mason looked back at Selene and then to Neeman again. "I can't lose her again. But I can't help her with this."

Neeman swallowed hard and nodded, not knowing what he was getting himself into.

Mason turned to Selene. "I'll call later to make sure you're better. I'll return if I can."

"When?" she asked.

"You know how this works. Only now it's even more complicated. A few days at the most, I promise."

She nodded, and her teeth chattered.

Mason headed into the hallway, and Neeman stepped out after him. "Mason. What's going on?"

"The Russians are getting more insistent on seeing Danika. The Kings are as well. You know how they are about diplomacy."

"Does she know what they want?"

"Not yet, but she has a feeling the Russians want to stay. Did you get anything out of the Demon?"

Neeman shook his head.

"That's too bad. It would've been helpful to know where the rift is so we can close it. But at least he's dead and can't talk." Mason's phone buzzed, and he pulled it out. "That's William. Danika's up. I need to leave."

"Mason, Selene can't stay here forever."

"I know. I know. But there are things about Selene that you don't understand. I need to make sure she's safe. Just for a few more days till I can talk to Danika. If I tell her right now, the stress might throw her over the edge. I've never seen her under so much strain. Rumors that the High Council might be showing up has her wound tight enough to snap. I don't want to keep this from her but..." Mason looked at the door. "I don't even know what to do with her. She's so..."

"Annoying?"

Mason laughed. "I was going to go with unpredictable, but yes, she can be a handful as well. It's not her fault; it's in our blood. And she has a hard time controlling her... impulses." He clasped hands with Neeman. "I am forever in your debt for this. My little sister may be a pain, but she's my sister, and I love her. I would do anything for her. Anything... but I have other responsibilities too. To Danika... the coven... I'm sorry to put this on you. I am. Whatever you need. Whatever she needs. Please call."

Mason left, and Neeman walked back into Selene's room and closed the door. They stared at each other for a moment.

His emotions jumbled together. He didn't know which way was up with her looking so defeated. But one thing he knew for sure, he would do whatever it took to help her, and that knowledge terrified him.

He crossed to her and sat on the bed. "What do you need?"

Selene shivered in her bed, a bra and pair of matching panties the only covering she had besides the sheet. She stared at Neeman, his face a mask. What she needed and what she wanted were two different things. She wanted him to hold her and make love to her. But that wasn't what she needed.

"I... I need your energy," she chattered.

"What does that mean?"

Embarrassment flushed her. She'd never had to ask for it before. Men had always been more then willing to bed her, and when they did, she took what she needed.

Neeman stared at her for a minute and then relaxed. "Scoot over," he ordered.

She did as she was told, and he slid in next to her. She waited until he got comfortable and then pushed her body up next to his. She waited for the cooling tingle of his skin, but soon realized they were the same temperature. She pressed into him, but he remained rigid. It was like hugging stone.

One of his arms wrapped around her, but she could tell it took great effort.

This wasn't going to work. His energy was all wrong. There was nothing comforting or protective about him at all.

"You know what?" she said. "That's okay. I'll be fine. You can go." She turned from him, tears welling in her eyes. Damn her frailty. Damn her weakness. She'd rather let the High Elder torture her again then face Neeman after showing him this part of her. Fatigue weighed down her body as if she'd gained a hundred pounds in the last hours.

She pressed her face into her pillow and stifled a cry. Why had she thought she could do this? Control her other half? So many years she hadn't had to deal with it. She'd forgotten what a struggle it had been on this plane. Only finding Mason had kept her sane. That and her mother's amulet. But she had neither.

"What did I do?" Neeman asked. "I was holding you."

She sighed, pushing the pain at bay. "You can't just lie next to me. I could do that with a dog."

"Then what?"

She rolled over to face him. "You're mad at me for killing Rex and stealing your car, and bringing home bags and bags of stuff. I get it. It's okay. You don't have what I need."

"What do you need?" His voice rose with tension. Anger played across his features, but anger could often become something else.

Her inner voice growled. "You can't do this. You're not good at it. This is my job."

She reached out the palm of her hand and stroked his cheek.

He stiffened under her touch.

She ran her hand down his muscular chest and hard—

packed abs. "This," she whispered. She leaned in, letting her lips linger near his. "I need tenderness. Caring." She ran her fingers through his soft hair.

His hand slid up her bare arm, and goosebumps rose on her skin. Warmth pooled in her belly, and her limbs tingled.

He pulled her to him with his rough hands, and her body smashed against his. Every inch of them connected as they lay side by side. He wrapped her leg around his hip, his arousal pressing into her most sensitive spot. One arm snaked under her head, cradling her against him. The other ran up and down the length of her body, sparking her skin with electricity.

"No. Stop. You can't." The voice chanted. Selene blocked the shouts out and reveled in the feel of Neeman– but this part wasn't for her. She needed to keep her wits about her and concentrate.

She planted a hand in his chest, pushed him back on the pillow, and slid on top of him. His eyes widened, and his lips drew back from his fangs. She wondered if he'd bite her. If he did, he did. Whatever got him hot. She unclasped her bra and slid it slowly from her shoulders. He sucked in a breath, his eyes worshiping her every curve. She picked up his hand, and he cupped her flesh, rolling her nipple with his thumb. A thrill of pleasure ran up her body, making her want to kiss him more than anything. No. She needed his chi and to get it, he had to be in utter bliss. She needed to give him what he wanted, not what she wanted.

She allowed him to caress and knead her skin. His arousal grew even more and pulsed beneath her. He sat up and kissed her breasts in turn, suckling them while using his hands to move her hips against him.

"I want you," he growled deep in his throat.

Good.

The voice in her head pleaded with her to stop. But she couldn't afford to. It was too dangerous not having enough magic to keep the voice at bay. She couldn't slip again. She needed to take control.

He gave her panties a yank and flung them to the floor. She hooked her fingers in the waistband of his pajama bottoms and slowly pulled them down over his hips. With every inch she pulled them down, she dragged her tongue down his body as well. His hands fisted in her hair as she removed his bottoms and then licked up the inside of his thigh. She licked over his hip bone and paused to give herself a moment of pleasure, tasting each of his individual, packed abs.

His grip grew tighter on her hair, and his hips thrust toward her, as he moaned her name. The sound of it on his lips had her almost breaking her own rules and kissing him. She never kissed the men she took from. The intimacy tended to... complicate things.

For a moment, she contemplated not going through with it, knowing what would come afterward, but she had to. She had no choice. She needed to regain control of herself.

She sat up, and he ran his fingers up her body to her throat. His eyes and thumb focused on the vein that pulsed there. He then ran his other hand up her body to her mouth. He stuck his thumb into her mouth, and she swirled her tongue around it and sucked hard.

She gripped his length, rubbing his head against her core.

He squeezed her throat and moaned. "You're going to kill me."

Not quite yet. She teased him. Sucking his finger and squeezing him in her firm grasp. His grip grew tighter on her throat, and he bucked his hips closer to her core. He wanted her. And more than anything, she wanted him, but it wasn't the time.

"Selene." He ground out her name through gritted teeth.

"What do you want, Neeman?" she teased.

He sat up in a flash, and his lips moved to hers, but before he could kiss her, she slid down the length of his shaft. He moaned and fell back on the pillows again, his fingers digging into her hips. Her head snapped back at the feel of him inside her. She gasped and clawed at his chest. Too long. It had been too long.

He guided her hips. The friction between their bodies heated her center and made her throb with need.

"Neeman," she said on a gasp.

He growled and sat up against the headboard. He pulled her hips forward and thrust at the same time, causing her to grab his shoulder with one hand and the headboard with the other. The power of his thrusts told her what he needed. Over and over she rocked her hips, sliding down on him, bringing herself closer to the release she had always craved but had never once obtained.

"Selene." He groaned. "You are so beautiful." He caught her breast in his mouth once more, and waves of ecstasy shot through her.

His arms moved faster, pulling her to him forcefully. She watched his expression, waiting for the right moment. His face tightened, and his eyes closed. She no longer felt him inside her. Instead, she concentrated on his energy.

It started as a minute, red, passionate flame behind his ribcage. Flowing and swirling around inside him, growing like a lightbulb slowly illuminating. As his muscles coiled tighter the bulb of chi both illuminated and tightened, ready to snap. She moved her hand up his body, resting it on his cold chest.

His breathing grew labored, and he arched toward her.

Wait. Wait.

At the moment right before he climaxed, she moved her palm over his heart.

He groaned, and his body snapped tight.

Now!

She dug her fingers into his chest and tugged. He cried out, reaching climax, and his ball of energy snapped. Wisps flew in every direction. She uttered the magic words of gathering, and the wisps slithered to her chest, burning through her skin and warming her instantly.

"I bind the one that hides within. I cage her deep and bid her sleep, till her name is called by me," she chanted in the ancient language.

The voice howled in rage and backed away, gnashing and clawing at the magic that dragged her back into her cage.

Selene smiled as her head emptied of any trace of the voice like a radio turning off. She breathed out a relieved sigh and opened her eyes.

Neeman stared at her, clearly stunned. Her body continued to warm as her energy renewed itself.

"Thank you." She slid off him and waited.

Neeman's eyes grew wary, and his skin paled more than usual.

She wanted to explain. "Neeman—"

He leaped up and ran to the bathroom. Hitting the toilet, he retched violently.

Selene swallowed hard. How many men had she taken from in the past? Fed off their chi, leaving them in their bathrooms, confused and weakened. Dozens? More?

But she couldn't walk away this time. Not just because she had nowhere else to go, but also because... she cared. The idea struck her for the first time. She cared about Neeman. Somehow in the last few days, he'd managed to do the one thing no other man had been able to do in her long existence. Make her genuinely feel for him. She wanted to go to him, to apologize.

Instead, she pulled the sheet around herself. Minutes passed, and finally, he stumbled out of the bathroom.

"What the hell did you do to me?" he demanded.

NEEMAN HADN'T FELT SO WEAK SINCE THE FIRST MONTHS OF HIS turning when he'd refused to drink blood. His limbs seared as if every fiber had been torn apart. His throat burned like dry ice had been forced down it and his head spun so violently he couldn't see straight.

Selene sat on the bed in a dizzying spell of health— color restored and skin no longer waxy.

"I asked what you did to me." He swallowed down the nausea that threatened to send him back to the toilet.

"I... I took your chi."

"My what?" He leaned against the doorframe, trying to get his vision to focus.

"Your chi, your energy. It's strongest right before the climax of a sexual act. I'm sorry I didn't explain better."

"Explain? Explain what? That you were going to steal from me?"

"I didn't steal it, Neeman. You gave yourself to me willingly. You said you'd help me. Besides, isn't that what all Vampires and vampyr do? Steal life force from humans? It's blood instead of chi, but it's the same concept."

Rage ripped through him. Though his head thundered like a bass drum, and his vision continued to make him feel like a dreidel, he let go of the door jamb and stood straight.

"That's not what *all* Vampires and vampyr do." Taking massive, deliberate strides, he moved to his pajama bottoms and tugged them on, refusing to fall over and be degraded further.

How could he have been so stupid as to think having sex would be anything more than a means to an end? Another way for her to get what she wanted.

"Neeman, I'm sorry. I didn't mean to—"

"To what? To steal from me or to steal from the Demon upstairs?"

Her eyes narrowed. "I stole nothing from the Demon upstairs."

"But you did kill him."

She folded her arms over her chest. "He deserved to die."

Neeman wanted to be angry with her, but if she'd been truthful earlier when she said the Demons were coming for Mason, then they were coming for her as well.

They stared at each other for a long time, with him trying to get his bearings enough to leave the room without crashing into a wall and knocking himself unconscious.

"Is that how you treat all men? Toy with them? Take from them? Satisfy yourself and leave them in pain?"

"It's all men have ever done to me." She slid out of bed and pulled a pair of panties and a bra out of the bags he had unloaded from his car. She stood, pushed her shoulders back, and brushed past him toward the bathroom.

A thought struck him. "Can you get pregnant?"

She stopped and threw him a too jovial smile. "Don't worry. Us Fae know how to take care of those kinds of things."

The statement hammered him in the gut like a battering ram. Take care of? What the hell did that mean?

She headed for the bathroom, closed the door and the lock clicked, shaming him further. Did she really think she needed to lock the door to protect herself from him?

He played and replayed the last hour in his head, the pleasure, the pure release, the pain. Holding her, touching her, feeling her, had felt so right. The connection between them went deeper than any before.

The sense of utter betrayal. It couldn't have all been a lie though, could it? She had to have felt something. It wasn't all about just using him, was it?

The room slowly spun to a halt, but his limbs twitched. He wanted answers.

Neeman strode to the bathroom door and raised his hand. A small sound from the other side stopped his fist mid—strike. His gut clenched, and he lowered his hand. Beyond the sounds of water from the shower, her soft sobs tore through his heart like a silver—tipped dagger.

He shook his head. He was an asshole.

A few hours and several bottles of Savor later, Neeman lay on his bed trying to recover when his phone rang.

He contemplated not answering it, but his phone never rang for no reason.

"Neeman."

"It's William. I think you should grab a few trackers and come over." Neeman sat up too quick, and his head once again did an impression of a carousel. "What's up?"

"Danika's relatives are coming, and we need a show of solidarity."

"Absolutely. When do you need us?"

"As soon as you can get here."

"Will do. William?"

"Yes?"

"Does she know we're coming?"

The line went silent for a minute. "Does it matter?"

"Not at all."

Neeman got to his feet and made for the shower. Whether or not he was at his best didn't matter. Danika needed him, and the fate of Chicago could very well depend on him showing up.

CHAPTER TEN

S elene lay in bed till she could no longer stand it. Her conspicuously quiet mind reeled with images of Neeman and how hurt he'd been by what she'd done. In the past, she'd never stayed around long enough to find out how the men turned out. Seeing him like that had been more painful than she'd like to admit.

For all of his standoffish, boorish ways, Selene liked Neeman. Both honorable and loyal, he'd not done anything but try to keep her safe— even though she'd been... less than easy to get along with.

She blew out a heavy breath. She never used to be this way. Okay, she'd always kind of been like this, but that had been when she'd let her Demon side rule her actions. Her other half craved chaos, pleasure, and pain. Unlike Mason's other half, which craved destruction. She wondered why they'd turned out so different despite having the same father.

It had been her chaotic side that the elders had tried to control. She laid her palm across her stomach.

"Manifesto," she whispered. The air around her stomach shimmered with light and then peeled back, revealing the skin underneath.

Scars crisscrossed her skin like a preschooler's doodle board. Deep burgundy grooves coursed over her ribs and down her belly. White puckered scars from each piercing of the skin, each cut, each burn. She ran her trembling fingers over them, remembering each in turn and who had produced them. A face burned into her memory, the man who haunted her nightmares.

She took a deep breath, to calm her pounding heart. He didn't matter. He couldn't reach her anymore— not now that she and Mael had been reunited.

Footsteps pulled her from her memories.

"Obscuro." She waved her hand over her stomach.

She jumped from her bed and riffled through the bags. Pulling on a pair of black leggings, a blue couture T—shirt, and a pair of flats, she pried her door open. Neeman, Riley, and another tracker marched toward the elevator. Neeman looked over his shoulder, and she closed her door.

A minute passed.

"Dispareo." She waited until her image faded and then opened the door again and stepped into the hall. Rushing to the elevator, she moved to the side when the doors opened. Silly since she was already invisible.

She glanced inside then hopped into the empty elevator and rode up to the warehouse floor.

The doors opened, and she tiptoed out and waited. Riley turned and looked at the elevator.

"What's up?" asked Neeman.

"Nothing. Someone must have pushed the wrong button." Riley got into the SUV. The engine started. She sprinted for the vehicle and jumped for it. She planted her foot on the rear bumper and landed on all fours on the bars of the roof rack. The window rolled down and a Vampire she didn't recognize looked up.

"Why are you two so antsy?" Neeman barked.

The SUV backed out of the warehouse and Selene settled herself on the roof.

By the time the SUV pulled into the drive of a large estate, Selene's arms and legs burned from hanging on. At some point during the ride, a bug had hit her in the face. She wiped the splatter from her cheek and swallowed down her disgust. Cleaning toilets, bug guts, and prison. So much for her glamorous return to Earth.

Neeman pulled up to Coven House and Siad, the Coven House's head of security, opened the gate. The driveway already held several cars in addition to those owned by coven members.

Neeman still wasn't up to his normal strength, but that wasn't going to stop him from doing his duty. His thoughts turned to Selene. He hadn't told her he was leaving the compound. What did it matter, though? She wasn't his mate.

He cut off the engine and stepped from the car. He stopped at the faint scent of cinnamon and vanilla and glanced around.

"Are we waiting for something, boss?" asked Riley.

Neeman scanned the area once more and sniffed again, but the scent had left. He shook his head. Selene had gotten under his skin.

He headed to the entrance with the other trackers and met several of the house guards and William. "Are they here yet?"

"Not yet." William stuck out his hand. "Within the hour. Thank you for coming."

Neeman shook hands. "Chicago is our home, and Danika is our Lord. We'll always be here to protect those two first."

"As will we all," replied William. The young vampyr grew in strength and wisdom every day. "Come on. We better tell her I called you."

"You haven't told her yet?" Maybe William hadn't grown in wisdom as much as he'd thought.

The group entered the front hall. All around the splendor of Coven House hit him once more.

William turned. "We will be meeting in the atrium, but—"

"Neeman?" Danika and Mason descended the stairs. Even after several months, Neeman hadn't yet grown accustomed to her almost human coloring.

He bowed to her, as did the rest of the entourage.

"What are you doing here? We didn't have a meeting, did we?" She plucked at her red silk blouse.

She looked from William to Mason and back. Her amber eyes made his gut clench. He much preferred her blue ones.

"I heard you might need some help, so I thought we'd make sure everyone played nice."

"Played nice? That's one I've never heard you say before," she said. "I thank you for coming, but this is a private meeting and—"

"I asked him to come," said William.

Danika's brows furrowed. "Why didn't you consult me first?"

"Because you would've said no."

"Damn right I would have said no. There is no reason—"

"We need them," interjected Mason. "You're being pressured from every side. I need to keep a level head while they're here and I won't be able to do that if I am trying to watch everything at all times."

Danika ground her teeth together. She turned to her mate and stepped up to his enormous frame. "Who is the Lord of this coven? You? William? It is just this kind of thing that makes the Kings think they can push me around, telling me what to do, and who to let onto my lands."

"That's not fair," said Mason. "William and I only ever have your back. We called Neeman because he is family. Coven family. And he has a right to know what's going on if he's to do his job effectively."

Neeman couldn't see Danika's expression, but he had a pretty good idea what it looked like. He'd had her disapproving glares aimed in his direction all too often.

Danika didn't like being wrong, but she liked being perceived as weak even less. So, if having him there strengthened her, she'd allow it.

Mason set his hand on her waist and leaned in close. He whispered something so low that even Neeman's vampyr hearing couldn't pick it up. Danika replied, and after a second, Mason chuckled, and Danika's posture relaxed.

"Fine. Neeman can be here." She turned to him. "But you are here as coven family members, not trackers. Which means I don't want Coven War Five breaking out tonight. Are we understood?"

Neeman nodded.

"Come on," she said. "Let's have a drink before they get here."

The group headed into the kitchen. Neeman caught William's arm.

They hung back until the rest of the group moved out of earshot. "Do you have anything besides Savor?" he asked.

"We have blood slaves if—"

"No." Neeman waved his hand and licked his lips. His gut clenched. He'd never told anyone he didn't drink directly from the vein. Not even Danika. "Do you have anything in stock?"

"We have some in the cellar storage."

"I'll be back in a few."

William looked at him, quizzically for a moment, and then nodded. "Of course."

Neeman walked to the back stairs. At least they'd won the first battle. Danika agreed to have them there. Now to make sure no one killed each other at the meeting— including himself.

CHAPTER ELEVEN

S elene slid from the roof of the SUV and stretched. She
shouldn't have worn flats. Holding on for the fifteen—
minute ride had given her calves a harder workout than
an hour on the stair stepper. Guards milled about the estate
grounds and dogs ran the perimeter. She tiptoed to the bushes
below a large front window and peered inside. Neeman and the
others spoke to Mason and the vampyr William who'd met
them at the door. She caught a glimpse of the back of a thin, red
—headed woman. Mason laid his hand gently on the woman's
waist. *Danika.* Selene moved to try and get a better vantage
point to see what she looked like, but the group retreated to the
rear of the house. Neeman stopped to talk to William, and then
he headed to the back of the staircase and disappeared.

Inside, the beautiful interior rivaled the opulence of the
penthouses her mother used to live in. Antique European
furnishings gleamed from frequent polishing. A long, red
carpet ran to the door, covering beautiful marble floors.

Barking pulled her attention. The large guard dogs chased

two sedans up the driveway. She crouched behind the bushes as the cars stopped. The dogs barked until several Vampire guards reined them in.

The doors opened to the first vehicle and out stepped two identical men— surprisingly average with dark hair, dark eyes and expensive suits, followed by four other Vampires. The second vehicle emptied half a dozen Vampires onto the driveway. The group stared at the house guards for a moment before being showed to the door.

One of the twins spoke to the other. She recognized their language as Russian.

"We aren't even greeted by Danika. I told you coming here would be futile." The speaker nodded to the guard and threw a fake smiled.

The second twin looked around. *"See how few guards there are. This place is wide open for an attack."*

The hairs on Selene's neck stood on end. The guards made no move against the men, so she could only assume they didn't speak Russian.

"That's not why we're here, Alexi. We wait and see how things play out."

The group disappeared into the house. One of the guard dogs passed her then stopped and sniffed the ground. His head raised and sniffed the bushes. He growled and then began barking.

The guard holding the dog looked directly at her and then yanked the dog away. "Shut up. They're already inside."

Selene slipped backward and rounded the side of the house. The dog tracked her the entire way. She headed for the back of the property.

A large brick building stood behind the main house and next to it stood another recently added building. Inside, humans milled about. Some ate, some read, others watched television.

The front door of the human house opened, and three females dressed in all white walked toward the main house, carrying cleaning supplies.

As the humans opened the door to go in, a male Vampire and a heavily pregnant blonde female Vampire exited, followed closely by a human male in his early sixties, whose gaze darted back and forth.

"Ike, would you please get one of the blood slaves? I'm going to walk Sinya to the garden to sit for a few moments of fresh air," said the male Vampire.

Ike nodded and headed to the human house.

"Are you sure you feel up to working?" asked the male Vampire.

"Lance, honestly. I'm pregnant, not dying." Sinya laughed.

"I worry is all, my love." Lance kissed her hand.

"All I am doing tonight is talking to the humans to find out what they need and how training is going. The baby isn't due for another month. With Danika lessening my workload and giving it to William, I feel like I'm no use to anyone anymore."

Lance held her face in his hands. "You are more precious to us all than you know. Which is why Danika doesn't want to overburden you."

Ike returned from the barrack alongside a female human.

"Come," Lance called. "Let's dine in the gazebo under the stars." He took Sinya's arm, and the two walked into the garden, followed by Ike and the slave.

It fascinated Selene that the humans obeyed so willingly, allowing the Vampires to take their blood with no thought for their own wellbeing. They were no better than pets.

Neeman's words floated back to her. *"You're too pretty to*

clean toilets." Her skin prickled, and her stomach lurched. She couldn't imagine being bitten and sucked on day in and day out. Unless it was for someone, she cared about. Maybe she'd let someone she loved bite her.

Neeman, William, Riley, Stephos, and several house guards stood behind Danika's and Mason's chairs in the nighttime atrium of Coven House. In front of them stood an entourage of a dozen Russian Vampires, not one vampyr among them. The two men in front were Danika's second cousins, twins—Alexi and Eliander. The twins, over a hundred, had spent the last ten minutes trying to break the ice with Danika. They had yet to succeed.

"I see no reason for you to be here, is explanation enough," said Danika.

"Cousin, we come as an offering of solidarity. We only want to help strengthen you and your position in the States. In light of recent events in your area, we worry for you."

"And what events would those be?"

"The threats to you by Lord Garon and by the abundance of humans who need tending to."

"So, you have no problems with Mason as my mate then?" Her voice held surprise.

"Not at all, cousin," said Eliander. "We are more than happy to have a male such as Mason standing at your side. Demons have ever been a noble race, worthy of our respect and alliance."

Danika tapped her nails on her chair arm. "Don't you think

it's time you stop telling me what you think I want to hear and tell me what you really want?"

Neeman wondered how much longer she would go on with the farce of listening to them before throwing them out.

The brothers looked at each other.

"I don't understand," said Alexi. "We're here to help."

"Really?" said Danika. "Where were you when my parents were murdered? Why didn't you offer to help me then? And when my life was almost taken a year ago by my minion, why did you not come?"

"Because you had Chase," said Alexi. "But when we heard you'd been attacked by him as well, we knew we could no longer sit still."

Danika continued to tap her nails. She had always been adept at waiting and letting people sweat. Making them as uncomfortable as possible while she worked out what their angle was.

Minutes passed, and finally, she stopped tapping. "I'm sorry. I thank you for your offer, but I cannot agree."

"But cousin—"

She held up her hand. "Please stop calling me that. I do not know you. You are no more family to me than the Three Kings are."

The twins sniffed in unison.

"Then maybe we should take our request to join you directly to the Kings," said Eliander.

"From what I understand, you already have." Danika stood. "Do not try to intimidate me. I don't intimidate. And with that, this meeting is adjourned."

Mason rose from his seat, and Danika's took his arm.

Anger burned in the twins' eyes. Neeman reached for his gun as he waited for them to make a move.

After a tense moment, Eliander smiled. "Lord Danika, we'd like to remain in Chicago and to call on you again. In a less formal setting, perhaps? To have dinner?"

Danika inclined her head. "I give you leave to stay in Chicago for the next thirty days. In that time, having dinner would be acceptable. If you have any other questions or concerns, feel free to call upon William." Danika looked at William, and he moved to her side. "Please see our guests out."

William nodded. "Yes, M'lord." He walked to the group. "If you will follow me, gentlemen." The Russians bowed as a group to Danika and then followed William.

After they'd shut the outer door, she turned and met Neeman's eye. "I don't like it."

"Me neither," he said. "Do you believe they genuinely want to help?"

She shook her head. "I think they're more trouble to deal with."

"I think this is going to get uglier before it gets better." Mason stepped closer to Danika.

"We're here for you. Whatever you need," said Neeman.

Danika gave him a tight smile and nodded. "I'm counting on it."

Selene ran to the front of the house. The Russian visitors stormed out the front door.

"Stupid girl. She has no idea who she's dealing with."

"It's Chase's fault for trying to kill her. If he'd kept his wits about him, none of this would have happened."

"We never should have taken him in."

"It doesn't matter. We'll have to give her some incentive to want our help." The Vampire pulled out a phone. *"Time to set things in motion."*

A pit formed in Selene's stomach.

The vehicles pulled away, and a ripple raced through her. She looked down. *Damn.* Her spell was waning— stupid Earth plane. If there were more magic left for her to draw on, her magic would replenish itself, and her spells would last as long as she wanted.

She had to get to the compound. If Neeman found her... If *Mason* found her... They would never trust her. Running down the driveway, she slipped out the gate behind the sedans.

She ran down the beautifully manicured street toward the compound, passing the well cared for houses, none of which were half as nice as Coven House. Of course, the Vampires took the finest neighborhoods for themselves and let the vamps live in poverty.

Half a mile down the road, a shiny, ebony motorcycle caught her eye, and she slowed. A smile crept over her face.

"Sick."

She rushed to the bike and tipped it off its kickstand. She snorted, spotting the keys dangling from the ignition. The world really had changed.

"Their loss."

Placing her hand on the handlebar, she became completely visible again.

Time to go.

The bike roared to life between her legs, and she laughed. She revved the engine and stared down the road. With a full tank, she could get out of Chicago and then some. Maybe to New York. Possibly Virginia or Pennsylvania. She wondered if Las Vegas had survived. Or Hollywood. If she left now no one would even know she'd disappeared for an hour or more at least. She could take off. Disappear. Hide. The thought of leaving Mason tugged at her gut. But Mason didn't need her anymore. He had Danika. And if she left maybe the Fae would leave Danika be. They didn't have anyone else that could get close enough to either Mason or Danika besides Selene.

Selene revved the bike again. For the first time in a long time, she could be free. Free of her mother. Free of her father. Free of the Fae. Free to be herself.

"Hey! That's my bike!" A vampyr sped toward her.

Selene looked down the road. Time to go.

She pulled the bike into the warehouse and hid it in a dark corner behind various boxes of supplies, cursing herself for not having just kept going. She yanked the keys from the ignition and ran for the elevator; there was no telling when Neeman would return. She needed to make sure she was in her room when he arrived.

Her heart sank. Not that he'd check on her. After what she'd done, she wouldn't blame him if he never spoke to her again. Even so, she'd stayed. Not for him, she told herself. For Mason. She needed to tell him the truth about why she'd come. He needed to be warned. And Neeman as well.

"*Who cares about Neeman?*" Her inner voice chimed in for the first time in hours.

"I do." Her words surprised even her. She didn't know why she cared. The idea that his opinion mattered nagged at her like a small child tugging on her sleeve for attention. He wasn't her husband. Hell, he wasn't even her boyfriend. He was her captor, warden, and babysitter.

She plopped down on her bed, the words ringing false in her ears.

"If that's how you feel about him, why did you come back? Why didn't you keep on riding until you found humans?"

She grabbed her pillow, threw it over her face, and screamed.

Her inner voice laughed. *"That's what I thought."*

"Shut up! We aren't on speaking terms, remember?"

A rumbling sound from above drew Selene's upward. The ceiling shook, and the standing lamp in the corner crashed to the floor.

What the hell? Did they get earthquakes in Chicago?

The elevator rang in the hallway. She darted to her door and grabbed the knob as a hissing sound sent a shiver up her spine. Selene swallowed, closed her eyes, and breathed deep. She knew that sound. A million years could waste away, and she would still remember the sound of every monster.

Despite the magic Selene had invoked, her Demon broke from her cage and screamed like a banshee.

"We were too late."

When Neeman had picked up Rex and brought him back, Rex had sent a signal. And now the Demons had come for her.

Selene covered her ears with her hands as a wave of nausea hit her. A fine sheen of sweat blossomed on her skin as her inner beast clawed at her to be let loose.

Outside the door, shouts and gunfire bounced down the hallway, muffled by the closed door.

"Do something. Go out and fight."

"I can't," she cried.

"Then let me out."

"No!"

More gunfire rang out, and a roar shook the walls. She needed to get out of there. Where was Neeman? Her phone!

She rushed about the room throwing new clothes and shoes everywhere. She grabbed one of the new bags and slung it over her shoulder. Then she stuffed a pair of underwear in it, a hairbrush and found the phone under a pile of her new expensive yet non—practical clothing.

"What's wrong with you? Demons in the hallway and you're looking to comb your hair?"

"Shut up! I have to think!"

"Fight. It's the only way."

No! She should stay hidden and wait for Neeman to come. She swiped the phone to turn it on, found Neeman's number and dialed it. The phone beeped and turned off.

What?

She tried again, and again it beeped and turned off. She hit the phone on her hand.

"Why won't you work?"

A terrible shrieking bell went off in the hallway, and suddenly water poured down on her.

"Just what I needed. A shower."

The lights flickered and went out. A set of dim backup lights turned on. The acrid smell of smoke drifted under the door and panic settled in her chest. She couldn't sit and let the whole place burn around her while she drowned.

She grabbed the door handle and pulled the door wide. Smoke billowed into the room, making her cough. Down the hall, near the elevator, the walls and ceiling were alight. Three trackers engaged in a battle with two Demons. The giant, human looking Demons with eyes like blood and blue ooze dripping from their lips slashed and spit at the Vampires.

Everywhere their spit landed, the floor melted away. Ash Demons.

"Kill them."

She didn't want to get involved, she wanted out— but there was nowhere to go. One of the Vampires fell to the ground, a sizzling hole through his chest. They'd all die if she didn't do something.

Selene took a deep breath, dropped her bag, and slipped off her flats. She ran toward the Demons. Three rooms away, a massive shape jumped in her path and shoved her backward. She flew through the air and landed in a heap, sliding on the wet tile back to where she'd started.

The air whooshed out of her lungs as her head hit the ground with a thwack. Lights exploded into her vision, and she blinked rapidly trying to clear the stars. This wasn't the time to get caught blind. She wiped water droplets from her face and pushed her hair back.

"Ah, there you are, Princess. We've been looking for you." An incendiary Demon smiled and strode toward her, the water glistening off his blackened skin.

She sucked in huge gulps of air trying to get the tightness in her chest to dissipate. Not fully able to see, she leaned on the wall and rose. Her head pounded and a trickle of blood skimmed down her temple to her cheek.

"Let me out!"

The Demon advanced, his massive frame taking up the entire hallway.

She needed to act fast.

She cradled her arm and massaged her shoulder, her vision clearing. "Please. Just go. Leave me be."

He laughed and continued to advance. "You should savor this moment, Princess, because it shall be the last time you feel no pain in a long while. You ran away from your father, and he is not very happy about it." The ancient language slithered from his mouth like venom.

She backed away. "Please, don't hurt me."

He grabbed her by her right arm, and she cried out.

He snorted. "Stop mewling like a newborn babe. You are the daughter of a god. It disrespects his honor for you to act so low."

Selene straightened and centered her energy, dropping the facade. "Does it?"

She thrust her hand forward and called upon her inner Demon. Her baser self roared to life. Selene's nails lengthened to the size of pencils. She slammed her hand inside the Demon's chest cavity and grasped his oversized heart. He gasped and stumbled backward, but Selene held fast. His eyes widened, and blood poured from his mouth. His claws dug deep into the drywall, ripping it away as he hit the ground.

She jumped on top of him, his heart still in her fist. "Tell my father I'll see him soon as I'm ready."

The Demon coughed once, and then his eyes dimmed. She threw the heart on the floor and darted for the elevator. She bounded over the body of the dead Vampire and made for the first ash Demon.

"*Oblittero.*" She slid into the Demon and her hand connected with the Demon's chest before he could make a move. A pulse of heat traveled down her arm and out her palm. A hole scorched his chest, and his skin lit up from within.

The second Demon swung at her, but she ducked. He missed and hit the overhead light, showering the florescent bulb glass down on everyone.

She whirled in a circle and then slammed him in the center of his chest. "*Eradico.*"

She sprang at the two stunned Vampires and grabbed them by their shirts, pulling them behind her. "Run!" she yelled.

She scooped up her flats and bag as she passed.

The Vampires followed her as a high whistle permeated the air. They needed to get out of the hall.

"In here." She ducked into a room. The Vampires followed, and she slammed the door shut as a blast shook the entire compound. The door rattled with force, and she leaned on it, keeping it closed.

The ceiling cracked, and plaster collapsed in giant chunks.

"We need to get out of here," yelled one of the Vampires.

"The whole place is going to come down," said the other.

Selene nodded. If they stayed here, they died.

They stood in Neeman's room. One of the trackers flung the door open and disappeared into the hall.

"Make for the elevator."

Selene took a step and stopped. She looked at Neeman's closet and opened it; inside sat his wooden box. She pulled it out and set her hand on top. *"Minor."*

The box shook and shrunk to the size of a small jewelry box. She shoved it in her purse with her shoes.

The trackers ran back in. "The elevator's gone."

She rushed to the door. The fire had spread down the hall, approaching rapidly. A siren sounded in the hallway, and a red light flashed overhead.

"Come on," said one. "We'll take the emergency stairs the other way."

He slid out of the room, and she followed. All around, fire and debris hailed down from the ceilings.

A roar emanated from the floor above, and she shuddered. Only one thing made that sound.

Selene and the two Vampires hit the stairwell and had

ascended half a story when the door above burst inward and four Demons rushed down toward them.

"There she is," one of them yelled.

"Down, down, down." She tore down the stairs past the door they'd come through, to the last flight, and then stepped into a narrow gray hallway.

"Try the elevator. I'll hold them off." She placed her hand on the handlebar. *"Securus."* The bar glowed white—hot.

"The elevator's destroyed," one of the Vampires called.

Damn. They were trapped.

The Demons slammed into the stairwell door from the other side, making her jump. They tried the handle and swore in Draconic. She swallowed hard. She didn't have much magic left. Neeman had helped her, but she needed rest to refuel fully.

The gray metal door glowed, and the smell of burning metal tickled her nose.

"We have to get out of this hall."

"Down into the arena," one of the Vampires said.

She reached down and set her palm on the floor in front of the door.

"What are you doing?" a tracker called.

"Ignis Laqueium," she whispered.

"Damn! Move it, girl. That's gonna be one hell of a fire."

"I know. I know," she muttered.

She stood and ran to the Vampires. They closed the door to the small observation room behind them. On the arena floor stood a dozen people, weapons ready, scanning the upper area.

One of the Vampires banged on the door. "Open up! It's Kirt and Jonas."

The group looked at each other, but she couldn't hear what they said.

The Vampire banged on the door and yelled again. One of the vampyr on the floor broke from the pack and ran up the ramp. As he reached the door, an ear—splitting explosion blasted in the sidewall of the observation room. Time slowed as pieces of the cement blew inward like a high speed snow storm. Selene flew backward through the glass window. Gravity caught up to her, and she hit the arena below with a thud. Her vision blurred once more. Dust flew all around her, and she coughed and gagged, trying to suck in a breath.

A tremendous roar sounded above her, and her vision focused enough to see a gigantic brown beast with two dog—dragon like heads lumber onto the ramp that led down to the arena. *A hellian.* Her father's pet. The animal sniffed the air, trained its eyes on her, and then howled.

"Move, girl! Move, or let me take over!"

Pops of gunfire sounded around her as she stumbled to her feet. The hellian advanced and the ramp creaked and groaned under its tremendous weight. Bullets struck it everywhere, making it shake its head and roar— but didn't stop it.

Selene's mind whirled. She couldn't go back. She couldn't. The darkness, the Demons, the despair. Even as the daughter of Mephisto, she didn't want to be in that place. It made the Fae realm feel like a vacation to the Caribbean.

The gunfire slowed as one by one the Vampires, vampyr, and humans ran out of bullets. In the upper window, several faces appeared with pitch—black eyes.

They were surrounded.

"Do something," she shouted to her inner beast.

"You have to say my name."

"Seraphine!"

The voice cackled with laughter. *"Couldn't even last a whole day without me."*

145

Fire ignited within her. Starting in her belly, the inferno blazed and traveled up to her chest. Selene backed down, allowing Seraphine to take over but refusing to lose consciousness. Panic settled inside her as she lost control of her limbs and laughter that was not her own broke from her throat.

Her fingernails lengthened like sharp knives, and her teeth descended into her mouth. Her skin darkened and her eyesight sharpened. Selene looked on as Seraphine moved to the forefront.

"Back up," she told the others in a voice all too low and strange.

The hellian reached the bottom of the ramp and stepped off while the Demons above gnashed their teeth. The beast roared, and Seraphine lifted her head and answered its call.

"*Hellian of the other plane, I call thee and bid thee obey,*" she yelled in the ancient language.

The animal pawed the ground and growled, showing row upon row of razor—sharp teeth.

"*The hellian obeys no one but your father,*" a Demon yelled from above.

"*Then it shall die as a message to you all. I am Seraphine, daughter to Mephisto, Lord of Destruction, and I will be slave to no one.*"

She ran at the hellian. The animal charged at the same time. She leapt into the air and landed on the beast's back. The animal's two heads swung in different directions, both trying to get at her, but she dug the nails from one hand into its spine and held fast. With the other hand, she swiped at the right head. Deep wounds dripped blood onto the floor as the animal gnashed at her and spun in circles.

The beast made a wild attempt to bite her leg, and she slashed at its exposed throat. The hellian gurgled, and acid poured from its throat, hitting the ground with a sizzling, popping sound. The second head reared back and roared then it let forth a burst of fire from its gullet.

"Get down!" She slashed through the animal's throat, jumped from its back and ran for cover, but in the arena, there wasn't any.

NEEMAN'S PHONE BUZZED IN HIS POCKET AGAIN. THE FIRST CALL FROM Selene had dropped. The reception down in the compound wasn't great in some areas.

Then Riley's phone buzzed, and Stephos' as well. The hairs on Neeman's neck prickled.

"What's going on?" Danika asked.

"Neeman," he said, hitting his Bluetooth. He couldn't make out the words on the fuzzy, broken line. He looked to Riley and Stephos. They too couldn't understand.

Just then Mason lurched and gasped. His hands shook, and he grabbed his chair, his nails lengthening.

"Mason, what's wrong?" Danika moved to his side.

"Trouble," Mason panted. He locked eyes with Neeman. "You need to go. Get to the compound."

"How do you know that? What kind of trouble?" Danika looked around the group. "Someone better tell me what the hell is going on!"

Mason's skin darkened, and the bones in his face shifted violently.

Danika bent over Mason's large frame and spoke softly into his ear.

"Move out." Neeman motioned to Riley and Stephos. They

ran for the exit and stopped when the ground shook, and an explosion sounded somewhere north of Coven House.

Selene!

"What was that?" asked Danika.

"Go," Mason bellowed. "I'll follow."

Panic drove Neeman's instincts into overdrive.

He exited the back of the atrium at top speed, raced around Coven House through the garden, with Riley and Stephos in tow. Above the trees, a plume of smoke came from the direction of the compound.

He reached the driveway, pulled open the driver's side door, and hopped in. The other two slid in as well.

"What's going on, boss?" asked Riley.

"I don't know. But whatever it is, I bet it has something to do with Selene."

SELENE COUGHED AND SUCKED IN THE DUSTY AIR. SHE TRIED TO shimmy herself out from under the piece of fallen ceiling, to no avail. Her ankle screamed in pain as the cement stone crushed it. The pain traversed her leg, throbbing till she couldn't think straight. Her magic had all but been depleted.

The humans and trackers helped each other to their feet inside the destroyed arena. Echoes of the crumbling building reverberated around them. It wouldn't hold much longer. If they didn't get out, they'd be buried alive.

Her Demon self had retreated for the time being. Not very convenient as she could have used the extra strength. But her Demon had done enough for one night.

"He's dead, isn't he?"

"Yup." Killing the hellian had been a feat, but not thinking through the repercussions of what would happen afterward hadn't been the wisest decision.

Above, in the broken window of the observation room, the remaining Demons had disappeared.

She touched her leg and a bolt of pain shot up it. "Exsurdo."

The pain dulled to a minor ache. A pain removing spell had been the best spell she'd ever taught herself— especially in the Fae realm— though because she'd used up most of her power the strength of the spell wasn't as she'd hoped. Still, every little bit helped.

"We need to get out of here," said a Vampire sporting a large gash across his torso and leaning heavily on another Vampire.

"We have to search for survivors first." A second one coughed.

The ceiling shook.

"We have to go," said the first. "We'll take these to the surface and come back for the others."

"What about me?" she asked.

The group looked at her.

"We'll come back," said the first.

"Come back? I just saved your lives. You can't leave me here."

"Saved us?" said the first. "You're the one who caved this place in."

"If it wasn't for you," said a human. "These things wouldn't have even been here. They're looking for you."

"*That's gratitude for ya.*"

"Don't even go there," Selene retorted. "You have no idea who I am."

"No," said the human. "But I can guess."

Dread itched its way across her skin. "Don't leave me here," she said. "You won't like what happens if you do."

"And what's that?" asked the first. "You're trapped." He turned to the second Vampire. "Come on."

"No," said the second. "She saved us more than once. I'm not leaving her." The second Vampire walked over and looked at the fallen debris on her leg. He tried to lift it, but the cement shifted, and she cried out, so he stopped.

The rest of the group headed to a far wall of the arena. They pushed on a panel of the wall. It popped open, and they disappeared.

The remaining Vampire looked over the rock and tested it here and there, but couldn't make it budge.

"What's your name?" She tried to get her mind off the imminent doom coming her way.

"Jonas."

"I'm Selene."

He stopped pacing and sat next to her. He looked up at the ceiling, his eyes scanning the damage. "At least the sprinklers aren't going off in here."

"If they were, we could have a mud wrestling contest." She laughed, and he looked at her, perplexed.

"What are you doing here, anyway? Are you with Neeman?"

Was she with Neeman? Well... she'd been with Neeman, but that wasn't the same thing. "I'm—"

"Seraphine!"

The call came from far away. A hail of gunfire followed a roar.

Maelstrom!

"Uh... You should probably go now." Her eyes trained on the escape panel.

"No, it's not right—"

150

"Really. Go. It's fine. The guy coming for me sounds like he's not having such a good day and I can't guarantee your safety." She hadn't seen Maelstrom in a long time. And as protective older brothers went, he was the best... and worst.

"I won't." Jonas laid his arms over his knees.

She blew out a breath. "Okay, I'm going to tell you a secret. You know Mason?"

"Lord Danika's Mason?"

"Yeah, him."

He shrugged. "Everyone does."

"Have you seen what he turns into?"

Another cry of her name rang out, shaking the ceiling.

"Yeah. I was there when they found the humans in the warehouse."

"Okay, so he's my brother. And that's him. Not the Mason him, but the Maelstrom him."

Jonas's eyes widened.

"Go. Tell him where I am, and then run like hell."

"Seraphine!"

Jonas leaped to his feet and swallowed.

She waved him off. "You know what, I'll tell him. You go."

Jonas reluctantly headed for the door. Selene laid her head on the ground and centered herself. She reached deep within, to the place she hid her magic when she'd been with the Fae.

Centering what remained of her energy and let it flow from her, sending up a location signal. The floor above shook with a roar and then heavy footsteps pounded down the concealed hallway. She stared at the hole, waiting for him to burst through. Instead, a tall, tan—skinned man with long, white—blond hair stepped out. His piercing, aqua eyes made her heart thunder, and her whole frame shake. As odd as seeing him in a pair of jeans and white T—shirt was, it did nothing to squelch the terror that threatened to rip a scream from her vocal cords.

Seraphine roared. *"Let me have him!"*

Selene fought to yank her leg free, ignoring the increasing pain. The man walked to where she lay. Her Demon screeched, commanding to be let free.

He stopped next to her face and crouched beside her. Though panic coursed through her, she stayed entirely still.

"Hello, Selene." He brushed the hair from her face.

She couldn't bring herself to say his name. Not after what he'd done. The pain he'd inflicted.

"You were supposed to contact me." His eyes held restrained anger. "Do you not remember the reason for your mission?"

All at once, she was tied to the altar, and he stood with a Demon stick, marring her skin.

"I didn't know it was you," she said, surprised that the tremor stayed out of her voice. "How...how did you find me?"

He laughed. "My sweet, I've been aware of you every second since you arrived. Watching. Waiting. I thought this might be a good moment to remind you of your mission. Your job isn't to worry about the Vampires, humans, other Demons. Your job is to get Danika Chekov and lure Maelstrom into our world so he can be contained. With you and him gone, the Demons will go back to their plane, and we will seal the rift between our Fae world and this one, and we will be safe."

She stalled. "What if they don't leave?"

"Well, it won't matter, will it? Because we will be safe on our plane." He stroked her cheek.

"And what about me? What will you do with me?"

He smiled and her gut clenched.

"You will be mine again, as a reward for your service." He

152

leaned in and inhaled the scent of her hair. "Your mother told you what we intend to do if the plan fails, didn't she?"

She shook her head.

"Let's say, if you fail, there won't be a creature left on this plane to care."

They were going to kill everyone.

Maelstrom roared and called her name.

"I do hope you make the right choice, my sweet." And with that, he walked to the other end of the arena where the observation window hung, lifted himself into the air, and disappeared behind the broken glass.

"Selene!" Neeman's voice pulled her focus. He raced to her side and looked her over. "Are you all right?"

"My ankle's stuck."

He tried to lift the cement block. It shifted and then it dropped. He tried a second time, but could only lift it a couple of inches.

"Where's Mael?" she asked.

"He can't get in. The tunnel's too narrow. If he tries, he'll bring the whole place down."

She swallowed hard, hoping Maelstrom found the High Elder Fae. That was one death she'd pay money, buy a bag of popcorn and a soda to watch.

The ceiling shook, and several pieces of cement plummeted to the floor. "The structure isn't going to hold much longer," he said. "I'll go get help and come back."

He tried to stand, but she grabbed his shirt. "Don't. Don't go. Stay." She stared into his stern face. "Please."

"Selene, I can't lift it on my own. I'm too weak because—"

"Because of me." How ironic that taking from him would end her life.

"Give him what he needs."

No, no, no. No way!

"Then, we die."

She looked down at her dirty arms and lifted her wrist. She blew out a long breath.

"Take my blood. It will make you strong enough."

Neeman backed away a step. "No."

The overhanging observation room creaked, and the supports groaned and began to bow underneath it.

"Neeman there's no time to get help. Either drink from me or leave."

Neeman stared at her. She was trapped. He couldn't leave her. But he'd never drunk from someone before. He'd sworn he wouldn't.

If she'd asked him hours ago while having sex, he didn't think he would've been able to resist, but now...

"I— I don't drink from the vein."

Her brows furrowed, and she blinked several times. "Like, never ever? Or not random people?"

He planted his fists on his hips and blew out a long breath.

"Well," she said. "Then I guess I'm gonna die."

Neeman growled. Damn, she was frustrating! But he wasn't about to her to die, not on his account.

He knelt beside her. The observation area supports groaned and bent further. Okay, no time to waste. The bitterness of her pain floated off her like the stench of brimstone. Though she masked it well, the cement block pinning her to the floor wasn't a pillow. He had to do it or be crushed alongside her. This was the moment— time to choose.

Every day of his vampyr life he'd woken up thinking he'd end it all that day. And now he had his chance. It would be known as a tragic accident from when tried to save Selene. He'd be hailed a hero. The only people who would know the lie would be Selene and himself.

And even if he died, he still wouldn't be able to live with such cowardice.

Neeman swore and brushed the hair from her neck. Her pulse beat fast and strong, and her eyes stayed locked on him.

He licked his lips, and his mouth tingled in anticipation. He wrapped his arms around her torso, supporting her. The feel of her in his arms brought back the horrible memories from earlier in the evening.

He leaned in and sniffed her neck. Her pulse quickened, and his body quaked with need. He struck boldly and let his mouth fill with blood before he changed his mind. He didn't want to do it. He didn't want to. The first gulp slid down, warm and sweet, lingering on his taste buds. He filled his mouth again, and his thoughts faded except for the taste of her. Spicy and sweet the blood rolled over his tongue and down his throat in a mixture of pleasure and guilt.

She grabbed onto him and moaned his name, making him drink faster. Gulp after gulp, he took her blood into him. It surged through his veins and fortified his muscles. Every fiber of his body warmed and pulsed with life, and in that moment, he no longer felt like a vampyr. He felt human.

A crash sounded behind him.

"Neeman, we need to hurry."

Her words pulled him from the feelings of euphoria. He

licked her wound closed and gazed into her eyes. He wanted to kiss her. To feel her lips on his, her body under his body as they—

"Hey!" She pinched his arm, pulling him back to the present. "Seriously, we have to go."

He got to his feet in a flash, his movement quicker than ever. The energy that pulsed through his body was like nothing that he'd ever experienced drinking blood from a cup. His mind snapped and ran in a dozen different directions. His energy rivaled that of a fighter jet. Every muscle in his body flexed stronger than before. He hefted the cement block off her as if it weighed no more than a large couch.

She scrambled from underneath it, dragging her injured leg. He dropped the block again, shaking the ground.

"Can you stand?"

She scrambled to her feet but wasn't able to put weight on her leg. "I think my leg's asleep."

Without a thought, he whisked her into his arms.

The observation room gave a horrible screeching noise, and the whole structure groaned.

"Time to go." He turned and ran for the exit.

"Wait!" She pointed. "My purse."

Seriously? Neeman shook his head.

CHAPTER TWELVE

Selene's teeth chattered as she jostled in Neeman's arms. They reached the surface and ran onto the warehouse floor as the earth shifted beneath them. Her leg and ankle throbbed, the pain increasing as her spell faded, but she had no magic left to ease the suffering.

Outside the warehouse, an enormous roar exploded. Maelstrom. It had been decades since she'd seen her brother in his true form, but the beast called to her inner Demon, awakening her once more.

"Put me down." She nearly lurched out of Neeman's arms.

"No, not till we're out of here."

"Stop!" She pushed hard against him, and they almost toppled to the ground.

"Let me out. Let me see him."

"What the hell?" Neeman glared at her.

"Trust me. Put me down."

He set her on her feet, and she tested her ankle. A pain shot up her leg. Damn. It wasn't asleep. She limped to the door and looked out. The trackers huddled together in a far corner near the awaiting vehicles. Maelstrom stood in the center of the blacktop, his hand aflame, towering over the group.

"Maelstrom," she called.

He turned her direction, his eyes narrowed.

"*Mael. It's me,*" she said in Draconic.

"Seraphine?"

"*You heard my call.*" She hobbled forward, each step shooting fireworks up her leg.

Maelstrom took to the air and landed in front of her, making the ground crack. "*You're hurt.*"

"*I'm okay.*" She reached up and laid her hand on his arm. The fire from his palms extinguished.

"*Who did this? Who hurt you?*"

"*Father.*"

Maelstrom's eyes widened, and his hands caught fire once more.

"*He sent a hellian. They're looking for you. He's looking for us.*"

Maelstrom roared. "*I'll kill him.*"

"*No!*" She grabbed his arm. "*No, Maelstrom. Not today. We'll deal with him another day. Right now, you must calm down.*"

"*I must take care of you. Protect you.*"

She gave him a shaky smile. "*You have. You did. We are good. We are safe. Sleep.*"

She hummed the tune that their mothers had taught them. His eyes locked on hers, and he listened. Slowly his skin lightened, and he began to shrink.

The sounds of cars broke her concentration, and he roared in anger. Three vehicles sped down the road and straight onto the asphalt where they stood. Maelstrom grabbed her and crushed her against his chest.

"Mael, stop," she yelled.

Neeman ran forward, and Maelstrom roared at him as well. She held up her hand and Neeman backed off.

The car door opened, and Danika emerged. Behind her, William stepped out as well. The redhead looked over the scene and marched straight up to Maelstrom.

Her bright golden eyes took in Selene. So, this was Danika, Mason's mate. Her eyes glowed like Mason's and her skin... had turned almost human color.

"Maelstrom," Danika commanded. "Put the human down. Now."

"Danika," he said.

"Put her down," Danika commanded again.

"Mael, put me down," said Selene.

Maelstrom looked from Seraphine to Danika like a confused puppy. *"Sister,"* he said in Draconic.

"It's okay. I'm not going away again. You and me."

He set her on the ground, and she wobbled on one foot for a moment. Danika strode forward, giving Selene a look that could've flayed her on the spot.

Selene hobbled backward, and Neeman grabbed her by the arm, holding her up. Maelstrom looked at Neeman and roared.

Danika commanded his attention. Maelstrom picked her up gently, and she stroked his cheek.

"Hey," Danika said. "Did you do what you needed to?"

"Yes," said Maelstrom.

"Then it's time to go home."

"Home." Maelstrom locked eyes on Danika. His finger rubbed a spot on her chest.

Selene watched in rapt fascination as Danika did what only she had been able to do a handful of times. Danika soothed Maelstrom to sleep, whispering words of love and affection. Slowly Maelstrom shrunk, and his horns and fangs disappeared. His gigantic wings folded and morphed into his skin. Back in his human form, Mason grabbed onto Danika and held her close. Selene's chest squeezed, seeing her brother's utter adoration for his mate. She'd never seen him so happy before. The sight made her long to know that kind of love.

Danika pushed away from Mason and turned her eyes on Selene.

"Now. Who the hell are you?" She bared her fangs.

A SHIVER SHOT THROUGH NEEMAN, SEEING MASON IN HIS TRUE FORM once more. The last time Mason had been Maelstrom, he'd almost killed Neeman, along with most of the Tracking Squad. Danika strode to where Neeman propped up Seraphine.

"Danika, wait," called Mason.

Neeman put a protective arm around Selene's waist. She gave him a dubious look, but he shook his head. She needed to stay quiet.

"I asked who you are," said Danika.

"My name is Selene."

Mason came to a stop right behind Danika. "I can explain."

She whipped around to him. "You better."

"It's not safe here. Let's take everyone to Coven House, and we'll talk in private."

"She's not going into my house until you explain."

"It wasn't what it looked like," said Selene.

"She's my sister," Mason interjected.

Danika's eyes widened, and she looked between them.

"Maybe we should do what Mason suggests and take this somewhere private," offered Neeman. He scanned the other survivors who had begun eavesdropping. "Besides, the Demons who blew up the compound most likely weren't working alone. More will come."

Danika's brows knit together and then she pursed her lips. "Someone better tell me what the hell is going on behind my back."

"We will," said Mason. "I will. But we really should go."

"They're right," said William. "With the Russians in town, we should do this in private."

Danika growled. "Did you all forget who the Lord is here? Again?"

"I didn't," said Selene. "I know who you are."

Neeman pinched her side. She flinched and smacked him in the chest.

"Knock it off," he whispered.

Danika's gaze moved between them. She didn't say a word, but he read her expression without her voicing one syllable.

She turned on her heels and marched to her awaiting vehicle.

Selene beamed at Neeman. "I like her. She's feisty."

Mason stepped close to Selene. "You're my sister, and I love you, but I'll do anything to protect Danika, and in a fight, I'll take her side. So please, whatever you do, don't piss her off."

"I won't." The hurt in Selene's voice made Neeman's chest ache.

Mason hugged Selene and kissed her head. "I'm glad you're okay. It would've killed me to lose you again."

"As I said, I'm not going anywhere."

He let go and got in the car with Danika.

"Now," said William. "I'm William, Danika's second assistant. It's nice to meet you, Selene."

"It's nice to meet you as well." Her gaze stayed glued to Mason and Danika's car.

Neeman looked down at Selene, unable to believe she was the same woman he'd known for the last week. There was no vibrato to her voice, no seduction, no jibe, just the honest her.

She gave William a tight smile, and Neeman caught a glimpse behind her facade. A lonely, sad little girl peered out from behind the mask she put on for the rest of them— a girl who more than anything wanted her big brother.

She looked at Neeman. "Are you going to carry me heroically to your SUV or are you going to make me walk on this stupid broken foot?"

Neeman shook his head and snorted. And just like that, she disappeared again.

Neeman parked in the Coven House garage. Selene had spoken and flirted with William most of the way, making Neeman wonder how bad her foot truly hurt.

Riley and Stephos pulled the other two SUVs up the drive and parked by the garage as well. Danika and Mason were nowhere to be seen.

"I'll help the humans get settled in the barracks, and then I'll meet you inside," said William.

Neeman nodded. How had the Demons found the compound? And why would they go through so much trouble for one low—level Demon? They couldn't care that much about one of their kind, could they? Something didn't add up.

He rounded the car and pulled open Selene's door. Dirt, blood, and ash covered every inch of her, and scrapes ran up and down her arms. A large bruise purpled her cheekbone.

Blood caked her hand, and her hair looked like someone had tossed cinnamon in it.

Neeman offered her his hand.

"Aren't you going to carry me?" she asked.

"You're doing fine."

Her eyes met his. "Just because I can handle pain doesn't mean I'm not injured."

He wanted to punch something. Somehow in drinking from her, she'd gotten to him. Inside him. Under his skin. Like he couldn't see her clearly anymore because she'd threaded into his muscles, his skin, his brain.

The blood electrified his senses and energized his body. Physically he'd never felt better, but mentally he'd never been more mixed up.

She limped toward Coven House's back door. Jonas ran to her, wrapped his arm around her waist, helping her into the house. The sight made Neeman want to tear Jonas's limbs from their sockets and beat him with them.

He cursed under his breath. He wasn't the jealous type. What had happened to him? He still wasn't sure. All he knew was that he had to find out.

CHAPTER THIRTEEN

Selene limped into the kitchen of Coven House with her arm over Jonas's shoulder. The human servants and other human survivors stared at her as she passed.

Jonas deposited her on a couch in a small den. "Can I get you anything?"

More magic? "I think I'd like to sit for a moment."

She went to run her fingers through her hair to flatten it, but dried black blood caked her nails and hands. Instead, she opened her bag and pulled out her brush, yanking it through the strands.

"It's been a hell of a night. I've never seen anything like those guys before," Jonas mused.

Her body drooped with fatigue. Soreness settled into her muscles. The next day would be even worse unless she could perform a healing spell.

"Yeah, well, I've seen a lot of them. I was raised with them when I was younger." A clump of dirt fell from her hair and plopped onto her lap. Lovely.

"How did you survive?"

"By being the daughter of the Lord of Destruction. They didn't dare bug me with my father and Mason looking after me. That changed, though, when we ran here."

Neeman came through the door and scanned the room. His gaze landed on her, and she turned away. The trackers milled in the kitchen and other humans piled in from the barracks as well. Everyone had heard the explosion and were looking for answers.

"Where do we to stay now?" she asked Jonas.

He looked around. "I don't know."

She smiled and touched his arm. "Well, when we get where we're going, maybe you can help me hobble to my bed."

His eyes glittered, and he revealed his fangs.

She swallowed. She hadn't meant it like that.

"You should come with me." Neeman pulled her to her feet.

She winced as his fingers dug into a cut on her wrist. She needed to rest and recharge her depleted magic. He slid a strong arm around her waist and helped her away from the others.

"I told you not to talk to my trackers," he grumbled.

Couldn't she do anything, right? "I didn't mean it the way it came out. It wasn't an invitation."

His eyebrows raised. "Wasn't it?"

She threw his arm from her waist and wobbled on one leg. "I don't go around sleeping with just anyone."

He crossed his arms over his chest and cocked his head to the side.

"Okay, I don't anymore. And for the record, I've always been discerning when I pick a guy."

He shook his head.

William jogged down the stairs toward them. "You two

should go up. It's going to get crazy down here in a few minutes when the rest of the coven members come back for the morning. Danika will see you in her sitting room."

Neeman nodded. "Is Doc around?"

"Of course, are you injured?"

Neeman pointed to Selene. "Her ankle is hurting."

Selene's jaw dropped at his tone.

William looked between her and Neeman. "I apologize, of course, you are hurt. You're covered in scrapes and bruises. I'll send him right up. And I'm sure you would like to shower as well."

Neeman nodded, and William left for the kitchen.

"Come on." Neeman leaned in, but she pushed him away.

"I'm not going anywhere with you. I'm done."

He looked at her as if she were crazy. "What are you talking about?"

"You." She punched him in the chest. "I'm sick of you. Your bad attitude— acting like I'm such a pain in your ass. Such a burden. I'll do you a favor. I'm no longer your responsibility. I can take care of myself." She limped toward the front door, her ankle shooting pain up her leg. She hoped she wasn't leaving a trail of dirt in her wake— that would be too much humiliation to bear.

"Selene, stop."

She continued. She didn't have to put up with this.

"Seraphine."

Neeman's voice made her stop with her hand on the doorknob. He stood so close to her that his cold breath fell on her exposed shoulder. He'd never used her real name.

"I'm sorry."

She gave him her best 'get lost' glare.

He shoved his hands in his pockets and shifted from foot to foot. "I'm not good with this stuff."

She crossed her arms over her chest. "What stuff?"

"You. Females. Relationships."

"Is that what we're having? A relationship?"

"Not like that," he said. "I'm... I'm not good with people in general. I don't do personal." His eyes lit, pained but sincere.

What did she say? She'd never done relationships either.

"Selene, where are you going?" Mason called down the stairs. He walked toward her and Neeman backed up a pace. "What's going on?"

Great. Big brother to the rescue at the most inopportune time, as usual.

Selene smiled at him. "Nothing. I'm leaning here because I heard folks would be coming home soon and I figured I'd be considerate and open the door for them. Oh, and because my foot's broken."

"Broken?" He looked around. "Where's Doc?"

"I sent William for him."

"Let's get you a room so you can clean up and rest." He moved to help her.

"I'll take her," said Neeman. "Better that we don't get more people speculating about the two of you."

Mason stopped. "Good point."

Neeman scooped her into his arms and carried her up the stairs before she could protest.

She tried not to enjoy the feel of security she got from his embrace, his firm, hard muscles moving around her body, cocooning her from harm. He'd said he wasn't good at relationships, but did they even have a relationship?

"Up there." Mason pointed to a set of stairs up to the third floor.

"Mason." Neeman's voice held a warning. "You do know whose room that is—"

"I'll work it out," he said without turning around.

They headed around the landing and up a narrow staircase and down a small hallway to a large wooden door.

Mason took a key from the top of the door jamb and unlocked the door. The door creaked as it open, revealing a dark, musty room. They walked into a sitting room, and Neeman set her on a light blue couch.

Mason rubbed his neck. "I'll make sure Doc gets up here, and have food sent up as well. I'll tell Danika that it'll be a few minutes before we can meet, but when you're feeling up to it, come down."

Neeman nodded. Mason handed him the key and turned to leave.

"Mason?" she called.

He turned.

"Are you okay?"

He shook his head. "No. Not at all."

The stricken look on his face slugged her in the gut.

Mason closed the door. Neeman set the key on a glass top coffee table and glanced around. The stiff sofa sat facing a dead fireplace flanked by two matching plush chairs. Bookshelves mounted one entire wall and French doors that led to a bedroom in the corner.

She took off her purse and tossed it next to the key. "Whose room is this?"

Neeman looked at her, clenching and unclenching his fists. "It used to belong to a traitor."

"A traitor?"

"Danika's uncle, Chase, tried to kill her."

Something pricked in her memory, but she couldn't figure out what through the growing haze of pain.

Neeman took a seat in an overstuffed chair. "Why did you do it?"

"Do what?"

"Kill that Demon, Rex."

She picked at the black stains under her nails, flicking the dried blood to the plush carpet.

In light of what had happened, killing him to keep her whereabouts from her father was as dumb as if she'd sent up a beacon announcing herself.

She looked over his shoulder to the door, remembering every sensation, every thought as she'd pressed her hands into Rex's skin.

"Mason told you that he's my brother."

"I don't understand how that's possible because his mother died when he was young."

"His mother Pia and my mother Yelena were half—sisters. Pia's father, my grandfather, was Fae and her mother was a Demon. They didn't marry, and Pia's mother abandoned her. Her father lied to save his reputation and told everyone that Pia was half human, not half Demon. He married my grandmother, and they had Yelena, my mother."

"Different mothers but the same father?"

"Yes. Our mothers both have Fae in them. But the Fae only see those who have pure Fae blood as being worthy." Memories of being tied to the stone altar had her pressing her fingertips into her temples.

"Are you okay?"

She waved him off. "So, anyway, Mason's mom learned the truth about herself and ran away to find her Demon birth mother. My mother followed her to the Demon world. But once

my mother got there, Mason's father, my father, seduced her...
as he had Mason's mother. Mason is three—quarters Demon
and the heir to our father's throne. My mother is full Fae, so I
am only half Demon, half Fae." She paused to make sure he
understood.

"So, you and Mason are sibling cousins."

She smiled. "Basically."

She watched as he continued to process the information.

"Pia disappeared from the Demon world. My mother had
me open a rift so we could come here to find Pia and Mason,
but we were too late. Pia had already died. We followed
Mason's trail for years before finding him."

"So why did you kill Rex?"

She sucked in a breath. "Like Mason, I too have an inner
beast. She isn't as strong as his, but she's deadly. When we got
here, my mother caged Seraphine with a magic amulet. My Fae
side is strong, making me able to bind her in the Fae realm, but
it's harder here. So many things set her off. The sights, sounds,
smells. I'd forgotten about that. How strong she is. How hard it
is to keep her under control without the amulet."

"What about where you were before?"

"When my mother took me to the Fae world after the
outbreak, the Fae elders didn't want us. They said my mother
had been spoiled. They said I was 'Diabolus Enim Hypocritæ'.
The devil's spawn. Desperate to stay, she let the High Elder
have me. When I rejected him, he kept me for months anyway,
testing me. Torturing me. Saying it was to ensure that I could
keep my Demon half locked away."

"But you had the amulet."

She caught his gaze. "It was just an excuse."

"They hurt you." His voice held a hard edge.

"Here, Seraphine is stronger, and I am weaker. My mother

taught me about chi and how to use it, harness it, before she made me the amulet. I haven't had to worry about Seraphine in so long..."

"Stop talking about me like I didn't just save your life."

Oh, please. Don't even pretend you didn't do it to save your own tail.

"The amulet my mother made me didn't make it through the portal." She was silent for a minute. "Last night my skull pounded worse than it had in decades, and then I heard her. I had absorbed too much energy at the club. I needed to release the magic, or I risked her becoming too strong and taking over again."

"So that's why your eyes turn purple."

"Seraphine's eyes are purple, yes." She massaged her temples. "I only wanted to hurt Rex. I needed to release my magic to weaken her. But he started talking and telling me all the things he'd done to those vamp women. Even then, I walked away until he threatened to tell my father where Mason and I were. He said that if I was here, Mason had to be here." She stared off, unable to look at Neeman anymore. "I lost it." Tears leaked from her eyes. "But it was all for naught. He'd already told the others where I was."

"How?"

She swiped her cheeks with the hem of her shirt, trying not to get any Demon blood on her face.

"Demons of the same race have a connection. It gets weaker the farther apart they are. It's used for hunting purposes mostly. But if he concentrated hard enough and long enough, he could send them a signal."

"You did that with Mason."

She glanced at him. "How did you know that?"

"After the meeting, he doubled over in pain and told us to

get to the compound right before the explosion."

"That's enough sharing for one day."

She nodded and then yawned. "I think I'll close my eyes till the doctor gets here."

"Maybe we should prop that foot up." He crossed to her.

Fatigue crushed down on her. "Mmmhmmm." She closed her eyes and drifted off.

Neeman closed the door and met Doc in the hall. "She's sleeping."

"I heard the girl might have a broken foot."

"She does, but she's resting at the moment so it can wait."

Doc shook his head and stomped back down the stair muttering about respect, and listening, and why did he even bother.

The old Vampire made Neeman smile. Doc had patched him up more times than he cared to remember.

Neeman continued down the stairs and headed across the landing toward Danika's sitting room. The shouts that drifted through the crack in the door made him halt.

"You should have told me, Mason. You should've been honest with me about the Demon sighting," yelled Danika.

"I explained already. I wanted to make sure first. I didn't want to worry you with everything—"

"I can take the male chauvinistic crap from the Vampires in my Society, but not you. I need you on my side. I couldn't bear it if you didn't believe in me as well."

The voices lowered.

"You know that's not what I meant. You have a lot on your plate right now, and I wanted to help."

"I do have a lot going on, but I'm a Coven Lord. I always have a lot on my plate. It's my life. The way I want it."

"Okay. Okay." Mason's voice softened. "I'm sorry. I don't like people trying to push you around, and with Chase still out there, I know the stress you've been under."

The talking stopped for a moment, and then Mason said, "Come here. Let me help you feel better."

She laughed. "Stop. Don't do that when I'm so—" She sucked in a sharp breath and moaned.

"I love you, Danika. You are mine, and I'm yours. I will always protect you. Even if you get angry with me for it."

"I love you too."

Neeman turned away from the intimate moment, as embarrassment fluttered through him.

Neeman spent the next hour with William organizing the trackers into rooms. They took a new section of the barracks that no humans yet occupied. The human tracking students bunked in with the human slaves.

Word had spread about the Demons and the demolition of the compound. The Tracking Squad had lost close to half a dozen men in the compound demise, not including two human trackers. It had taken years to assemble such a good group. He didn't know how long it would take to gather another. The east coast, as well as the west coast squads both, remained under his control. If a coven war broke out, he'd need to call them to Chicago and possibly call in all the retired trackers as well. If he did that, he might be able to get fifty to a hundred trackers, each worth ten regular Vampires.

William shoved his phone in his pocket and rubbed his forehead as he walked in from the barracks.

"Something wrong?" Neeman asked.

William gave him a bland smile. "Slave troubles. Sorry... minion troubles."

"You have a minion?"

"No." William waved his hand. "Evan is being returned again."

"The one with blonde hair and a bad attitude? Didn't we recently drop her off to a businessman south of Chicago?"

"That would be her. Unfortunately, I'm going to need you to go pick her up once more."

"Doesn't this make the fifth time?"

"Sixth and I'm afraid if Danika has her way, that'll be her last." William ran his hands over his face.

"What will you do with her?"

William shrugged. "I have no clue. We've never had a human so hellbent on destroying us that they disrupt every house they go to by trying to rally the other humans into mutiny."

"That's the last thing we need right now, on top of everything else."

"Exactly."

"Let me make sure everyone is settled, and I'll go get her."

"It can wait." William waved his hand. "Let's figure these other problems out tonight. Tomorrow evening we can arrange her pick up."

Neeman nodded and headed to the third floor. Between Selene and Evan, Danika might go insane, having two women as stubborn as herself in Coven House.

CHAPTER FOURTEEN

"All righty, young lady, I'm going to need to examine your foot." Doc set down his bag on the coffee table.

The pain had intensified while she'd napped, and Selene had awoken with only enough magic to do a small pain relief spell. It wouldn't last long though. While sleeping, all her previous spells had dissolved away. In the Fae realm, it had been easier to hang onto magic, even while sleeping, due to magic being all around her. But here she had to suck magic out of everything like blood.

Neeman stood by the door, his arms crossed over his chest.

She tried to sit up.

"You don't need to move." Doc's eyes remained surprisingly sharp and alert squished into his doughy, wrinkled face. She wondered his age. He moved to her propped—up foot and examined it.

"It's significantly swollen. You've been walking on it; I take it?"

"I got some help moving around, but I didn't think it was broken," she lied.

Neeman looked at her and shook his head. Nice. That's what she got for trying to cover his ass?

"We should wrap it up and find you a pair of crutches. Unless..." He looked at her with a knowing gaze.

"I can heal it myself when my magic recharges."

He nodded. "Then I think the best thing you can do is take a bath, wash the abrasions, and then sleep. I can bandage you up after that if you wish."

"That won't be necessary, thank you." She'd had much worse.

Doc grabbed his things and looked at Neeman. "Should I call for a house slave? She's going to need help bathing."

"I'll make sure she has help."

Doc nodded. "I'll let Danika know she can't be moved before tomorrow. She needs to rest."

"Thanks." Neeman let the old Vampire out and then closed the door, laying his forehead against it.

"*Why does he keep offering to take care of us?*"

"You don't need to help me. I can bathe myself."

He turned to her, his face expressionless and his tone flat. "Not with that foot, you can't. You may not be able to feel it, but if you walk on it, you'll make it worse."

She rose from the couch. "Trust me, I've been through worse, and I'll heal it up fine when I'm recharged."

He moved to her side in a breath. His eyes flashed. "Don't be stubborn about this. You need help. If you don't want me, I can go get one of the female house slaves."

He'd offered to bathe her? To rub her naked body with a wet cloth? "I guess it wouldn't be too terrible to have you scrub my lady parts. You are going to give me a sponge bath, aren't you?"

A smile crossed his face, and he shook his head.

She gasped. "Oh my— did you just smile at me?"

The smile snapped away as quick as a flash of lightning. "Don't get used to it."

"Oh, I won't." She snorted. "I think that one almost broke your face."

He chuckled, and it warmed her inside. Again, he looked like the old photos she'd seen— especially the one from his surfer days. She imagined him with tan kissed skin. His hair textured from the saltwater, sand clinging to his dripping wet body.

She bit the inside of her cheek and looked away. Her gaze lit on the coffee table.

"By the way." She grabbed her purse, pulled out the small wooden box, and handed it to him.

He turned it over in his hand. "What's this?"

"I got it for you before we ran to the arena. I thought it might be... important."

He ran his thumb over the surface of the small box and recognition dawned on his face.

"I had to shrink it to be able to carry it, but I promise everything in there is fine, and when I am recharged enough, I'll make it bigger again."

He looked at her, his expression conflicted. "Thank you," he managed. "I... Thank you."

She shrugged, her cheeks heated, and she looked away. "It's no biggie."

He caressed her cheek, persuading her to look into his eyes.

"It's big for me."

Her chest tightened, and she licked her lips, unable to think of something to say. How did he do that to her? He made her weak with desire. Something her mother had taught her never to allow a man to do.

He set the box on the table and entwined his fingers in hers. "Let's get you in that bath and get you some fresh clothes."

"Oh!" She snapped her fingers, opened her purse, and pulled out the thong she'd shoved inside. "I have these."

He cocked an eyebrow. "You didn't happen to pack anything to go over those, did you?"

She shrugged. "I was in a hurry."

Neeman set her purse down and then carried her into an adjoining bedroom and from there to the ornate bathroom. A beautiful granite counter with blue blown glass bowls sat under a gilded mirror. On one end of the bathroom stood a large, slate, glass—enclosed shower with four shower-heads; on the other, a sizable sunken tub.

Neeman sat her on the toilet lid and turned on the water for the tub. She stared at his broad shoulders as he tested the temperature of the water. She wondered if they could both fit into the bathtub.

"I can find out for you."

Selene bit her cheek. How was it possible? The urges should have gone away after having sex with Neeman. But they hadn't. The urges to ride him once more had only gotten stronger.

Between the steam from the bath and the flush of heat in her body, Selene's temperature spiked.

She stripped off her shirt and bra and flung them to the floor. Modesty had never been one of her virtues. Neeman grabbed a towel and turned but dropped it and cleared his throat.

Selene laughed. "What? They're only breasts. You've seen mine before. I mean, they are pretty amazing, but you don't need to stare."

His eyes widened, and he continued staring. Then his features darkened. "How did you get those?"

A chill rushed through her. Her gaze dropped to her stomach. Her glamour magic had faded. Selene curled her hands around her middle and shut her eyes, slumping forward. Suddenly she didn't want a bath. She wanted to crawl into bed and never emerge.

NEEMAN STARED AT THE BURNS AND CRISSCROSS MARKS THAT RAN IN every direction from her stomach like tree roots.

He cracked his knuckles. Who could do something like that to her? Bile rose in his throat, and anger shook his limbs.

"Selene," he said, trying to keep the rage from his voice. "Who did that?"

"I think I'd like to lay down." Her voice came out so small he barely heard her.

He stepped closer, but she cringed away. He clenched his jaw several times. Taking a deep breath, he knelt by her, trying not to let her see his abject horror. He tried to look up into her face, but her dark hair hung loosely around her, shadowing her features.

"Selene."

"Don't." Her head whipped up, and she narrowed her gaze. The anger that rolled off her burned through him. "Don't you dare pity me." Shame and pain played over her features like a firework show.

"I don't." His arms yearned to hold her. He understood finally. Her need to toy with men, to feel sexy. They were a mirage to disguise the truth, like the spell she used to cover the scars.

He slid his hands over hers and tried to unwrap them from her stomach. She resisted, her eyes conflicted and flickering between green and purple.

"Please," he asked.

Finally, she allowed him to move her arms away. Some scars were white and fine like they'd been done with a thin blade, some jagged and thick. Long, short, older, newer. He ran his fingers over them one by one.

"You said they tried to teach you to control your inner Demon. Is this what you meant?"

"Yes," she whispered.

"How long did you endure this?" *Please say only minutes.*

"Days, months. These were the ones that stayed open too long and couldn't be healed with magic."

"There were more?" Anger almost choked him.

Her gaze dropped to her lap. "Many."

He wanted to tear down the walls to the Fae world and kill them all for what they'd done. How could anyone be so cruel? The thought almost suffocated him.

How many evils had he seen in this world alone? Why should other races be any different? The things that had been done to Vampires and vampyr by human doctors after the Awakening, to figure out what they were? The things Vampires had done to the vamps after the outbreak. All of it the same, the reasoning the same. They did it out of fear.

He massaged her neck. "Let's get you washed up and then figure out what we can do to heal that foot."

Her face held raw, pure emotion with eyes rounded wide like a beaten puppy. Her shoulders slumped, and she nodded.

He wanted nothing more than to carry her to the bed and cradle her.

He helped her up and turned her to lean on the counter. Mild pain echoed through his cheek as he chewed the inside of it. The sight of the curve of her spine, the flawless skin that flowed down to her firm round backside had his pants suddenly feeling a size too tight.

He took in a sharp breath and steadied himself before slipping his fingers in the waistband of her ripped and dirt—caked leggings and tugged them over her curvy hips. His arousal grew larger as he slid them off her shapely legs. She lifted herself with her arms as he slid them over her feet. Standing, he caught a full view of her black, lacy thong.

Memories of how good her blood had tasted rippled through him. He stared at the creamy expanse of her neck before turning away and pushing his fingers through his hair. The last thing she needed was him trying to get all over her while injured.

"Neeman?"

He stared at the ceiling. *Get a grip.*

"It's okay if this is too hard for you."

"Is that a joke?" He turned.

She stared at him over her shoulder, and her gaze dropped to his pants.

"It wasn't meant as one, but I guess it could be." She spun on her working foot and faced him.

Her perfectly supple breasts stared at him, begging to be touched. "What do you think is going to happen when you get me in the water?" she asked. "If it'll help, I can use the toilet first and ruin the moment for you."

"I'm good."

He stepped up to her and tried to look anywhere but at her

tempting body. He wiped his slick palms on his pants then hooked his fingers under her waistband and removed her underwear. Then, he swooped her up and placed her in the tub, propping up her broken foot on the edge with a towel.

Intimacy had never been his strong suit. Sex, yes, he was good at that. Taking a woman, bending her over, and getting down to business. Cuddly, emotional, connecting stuff, he'd never learned. Yet that sensitive, cuddly stuff was precisely what Selene needed.

He located a washcloth under the sink, rubbed soap on it, and dipped it in the water.

Selene closed her eyes and relaxed into the tub.

He wasn't sure what to do. "Uhm... Do you want to..."

She opened her eyelids. "You're supposed to be helping me."

"Okay." He cleared his throat and started at her shoulders, working the washcloth over her neck and collarbone. He pushed back her hair and wiped the smears and dirt from her face. The bruise on her cheek had stopped swelling, but the grayish—purple hue remained.

Dirt and blood dripped into the water, staining it brown. He grabbed the shampoo and lathered her hair. He massaged her scalp, and she slid down, dunking her head under the water and swishing it back and forth. When she finished, he drained the tub while refilling it at the same time, so she didn't catch a chill. He lifted her wrist and squeezed the washcloth over a cut to her upper arm and then proceeded to clean her other arm.

Selene snickered. "I think you can move on to other parts."

He swallowed back the boulder wedged in his throat. "Are you sure? You're in pain."

"My pain dulling spell helps."

Okay. Neeman swirled the towel lower over her firm breasts that bobbed under the surface of the water. Desire shot straight through him like a bullet, making his erection strain against his pants, begging to be let free.

Her ripe nubs puckered at the touch of the cloth. She moaned and turned her head to the side. He moved the towel lower and rubbed over her stomach. Then lower to her thighs. His gaze trained on her neck. The vein at her throat pulsed with life. Her blood pumped faster as he rubbed down one leg and up the other.

He reached her most sensitive spot and hesitated.

"Don't stop." Her voice came out husky and low.

He slid the washcloth between her legs and pressed it against her, making her moan again. He moved the cloth in slow circles. She reached out and grabbed the collar of his shirt.

"Neeman," she breathed.

He tried to hold back. To be gentle. To give her what she needed. But his body throbbed and pulsed with need. His teeth ached, wanting to bite into her peachy flesh.

He worked the cloth softly over her small nub, making her body jerk. She pulled him so close he stopped an inch from her lips. His erection pushed painfully against the side of the tub.

"Kiss me," she demanded.

He froze with fear. He didn't want to do this again. Didn't want to make love to her only to have it mean nothing and for her to suck him dry again. But he did want her. And last time... she'd refused to kiss him.

Leaning in, he pressed his lips firmly to hers. She wrapped her arm around his neck and yanked him closer. Water— soaked his T—shirt as her tongue swirled against his teeth, demanding access. He gave in to her. He continued working his fingers against her. She panted into his mouth, and he tasted her sweet breath. His head pulsed with wanting to bite her, to taste her blood again and feel the euphoria he had hours early.

She broke their kiss, nibbled down the side of his neck, and grabbed his T—shirt, trying to pull it off.

"I want you," she whispered.

Dropping the washcloth, he stripped off his shirt and helped her from the tub. Her slick body rubbed against his bare chest, and he fought back the rapidly building urge to take her right there on the bathroom floor.

Standing on her functioning foot, she turned to the bathroom counter. He planted his palms on either side of hers and moved her hair aside, nipping and sucking her neck. He battled for control of his desires. His veins burned for her blood. His body pulsed for her body. And his mind whirled with wanting her to be his.

The friction of their bodies had him close to losing control if he didn't get inside her again. Reaching around her, he squeezed her breast, making her arch against him. Her round rear rubbed against his erection, making him growl. She wrapped her arm around his neck as his other hand moved down between her legs once more. He teased and swirled her flesh between his thumb and forefinger. His fingers grew slick, and her musky scent hit him all the harder.

"Bite me," she moaned.

He grazed her throat with his fangs and dipped his fingers inside her.

She jolted. "Damn."

Neeman stopped. "Did I hurt you?"

She hopped on her foot. "No, it's just my foot. I got so caught up that I put my weight on it." She pressed his fingers inside her once more and kissed him long and deep. "Don't stop."

They should stop. She was injured, and though she said she wanted this, he didn't want to make her foot worse. She turned, and her hands went to his belt. She had it unbuckled and her hand down in his boxers before he could do anything. The feel of her soft slender fingers grasping him made him shudder. She stroked him tight and slow, and he rested his forehead on hers. He needed her. To take her right there on the counter in the bathroom. Neeman lifted her onto the cool tile and parted her thighs.

A knock on the outer door pulled his attention. He growled and his head whipped toward the door.

"Hello?" called a female voice.

"What?" he yelled.

"Uh... I was told to bring some clothing—"

"Leave it."

"Yes, sir."

He waited until the door closed and then turned to Selene. His gut clenched as he stared into her deep green eyes. The ends of her hair dripped, making her skin glisten. He wanted nothing more than to lap every last drop from her... but that wasn't what she needed. She needed to rest and heal.

He settled his hands on her waist and bowed his head until it rested on her shoulder.

"I should get you into bed," he said.

Her eyes glittered with mischief. "The bed might be a bit more comfortable."

Her willingness fed into his lust for her blood. He should take her blood and then take her. He forced his body to move away from her as every muscle resisted his command.

He picked up the towel from the floor and wrapped it around her. "Not tonight."

The encounter left him pent up, and the look on her face

told him she felt the same. His body ached for a release or sustenance. But more than that, he craved her. The admission left him shaken to the core. He'd resigned himself to never wanting another woman again... and yet every decision he'd made flew out the window when it came to her.

Leaving him in the one place, he'd promised himself he'd never be again– vulnerable.

THE THROBBING NEED INSIDE SELENE BLOOMED HOT ENOUGH TO HAVE her wanting to help herself achieve release on her own, something she had never done before. She'd read book after book about sex and the mind—blowing, fantastic release that was supposed to come along with it; but that she had never achieved. She'd been taught sex was for obtaining a male's chi. And with chi, you could do magic that wasn't possible on your own, like caging her inner Demon. There had been times when she had wanted more, craved more. But how did you ask a guy vomiting in the toilet to come in and service you?

The way Neeman had touched her stirred her... It made her believe that maybe he could be the one who would finally give her that release. But he didn't want her.

He wrapped her in a towel and carried her to the bed. Then he retrieved the clean clothing and helped her put them on. She wanted him to lie next to her. To hold her and touch her, the way he had in the bathtub. But he propped himself in the bedroom doorway, snapping and popping a fresh piece of gum. Every inch of his rigid posture gave the appearance of steel. Even so, his eyes sparkled like blue diamonds, belying his desire.

"I'll go get you something to eat and then you can rest."

She didn't want to be alone. All she'd been since she arrived was alone.

"What about me? I'm here."

"Are you going to stay here tonight?"

He jerked his thumb over his shoulder. "I'll sleep on the couch to make sure you don't need anything."

"Don't be ridiculous," she said. "That thing is barely big enough for me; there's no way you'll fit."

He shrugged. "I've had worse."

Why did everything have to be so hard with him? "Neeman, there is more than enough room for both of us in this bed. I promise to keep my hands to myself."

He stared at her for a moment and then headed out the door. "It's not your hands I'm worried about."

"Come on, we can be adults about this," she called.

He looked back at her, and the craving in his eyes hit her like a punch in the gut. "No. We can't."

CHAPTER FIFTEEN

S elene awoke the next evening to find a note from
Neeman. He'd run an errand for William and would
return later. He'd left her some fresh fruit and water.
She smiled. No one had taken care of her like that before – not
even Mason.

Recharged and refreshed, she sat up and spotted the neatly
folded blankets out on the couch in the sitting room.

"Neeman?"

No answer.

She shifted, and her foot shot with pain. Throwing back the
covers, she looked at the swollen, purplish—blue limb.

"Reparo."

She covered her mouth to stifle a cry as the bone knit back
together. The throbbing subsided after a moment, and she
breathed deeply. She fixed every scrape, every bruise, every cut
and then pulled up her shirt and ran her fingers over her stomach. Maybe because she was no longer in the Fae realm, her
magic would work. Her hand shook.

"Reparo," she whispered.

The air around her stomach shimmered, but nothing happened. A tear leaked from her eye.

"Stop getting your hopes up. Your scars are our battle wounds. They remind you of how strong we are. Why should you want to hide them?"

She'd never shown someone her scars before. Not that she'd had anyone to show besides her mother. But Neeman... He'd been gentle with her, concerned, angry even. He'd seen her as raw, her emotional shame laid bare, her heart flopping on the floor like a fish—and hadn't turned away.

"Obscondo."

The air twinkled again, and a veil fell over her skin, masking the scars. She stood and tested her weight. Her foot held.

The outer door opened. "Selene?" Mason called.

"In here."

Mason entered and looked her up and down. "Feeling better?"

"Right as a threshtal demon swimming in a pool of their own ooze."

His eyebrows smashed together. "Ooookaayyy. I need you to stay out of trouble tonight."

She crossed her arms over her chest. They'd barely had a chance to speak since she'd been back and that's what he had to say to her the first chance they had to be alone?

"Please," Mason said. "Today is visiting day, and I can't have anything go wrong. Word is already spreading about the compound explosion. We are claiming a gas leak, but that isn't going to hold forever."

"What's visiting day?"

"Prospective masters are coming to meet the humans."

She shook her head. "I thought the humans weren't slaves anymore."

"They aren't. They get a chance to pick their new... masters. Though they aren't masters anymore, they are more like mentors."

"How can you even say those words? You know as well as I do that this society isn't right."

"Don't, Selene. Don't start. You don't understand because you weren't here when it all went down. The fighting, the wars, the death. You can't even imagine. Danika is a good person. It's because of her and William that these humans haven't been turned over to the slave market. They're getting a choice in the matter of where they go. She's trying to help fix things."

They stared at each other for a long minute. He'd changed. Whether because of Danika, being mated, or because of what he'd been through, she didn't know.

"Okay." She held up her hands. "I'll be good."

His stance relaxed. "Thank you."

"Do you know where Neeman went?"

Mason chewed his lip for a minute. "You like him."

She shrugged. "He's all right."

He laughed. "Don't lie. I can see it on you."

"See what?" A flutter raced through her stomach like a rabbit on the run.

"Happiness."

She cocked an eyebrow. "You can see happiness? Is that a new power you gained in my absence?"

He crossed his arms over his chest, and his amber—colored eyes flashed with anger. "You know what I mean."

She didn't want to anger him. "So what? Maybe I do like him. He's handsome and strong. Why shouldn't I?"

He gave her an impassive look. "I didn't say you shouldn't."

"Then what?"

"Be careful." Mason's gaze grew serious.

She scoffed. "Don't worry, big brother. I won't get hurt."

"I'm not worried about you. You use men the way most people use tissue. But Neeman... He's different. He's been through a lot, and I don't want to see him get hurt. I don't know how he'll handle it."

"You do realize that you told him to help me out the other night. You're the one who asked him to crawl into bed with me."

"You were hurting and needed help. This is different. This is toying with someone's emotions, Selene. Not a stranger from a bar or a club, someone that is respected and loved in our family circle."

She'd never seen Mason be protective of anyone but her before. And this time he was protecting Neeman *from* her.

"You think I have no feelings, don't you?"

"Selene—"

Her inner Demon growled.

"Stop, Mason. I get it. You have a life here. *Family.* And that's great. I'm super happy for you. You finally have what we've always wanted. Both of us, together. You found it without me, and that's fine. I promise to behave while I'm here and at the earliest convenience I will leave you to your new family and make my own way, but please, whatever you do, don't treat me like I don't care. I know you see me as the annoying younger sister who you always had to get out of trouble, but I'm not that girl anymore. I can take care of myself."

Mason ran his hands through his hair. "I'm sorry, Selene. I don't mean to be like this, but you don't understand the strain, the pressure Danika is under. And what Danika is under, I'm under. This isn't the way I expected my life to turn out, but this is who I am now, and I have to protect it."

Oh, how she wished her mother had felt the same way when the Fae elders had come to their house to take her away. How would it be to have someone love you so much they were willing to risk everything they had, to make sure you were safe? She'd thought if she came back, that's how it would be with Mason.

A chasm opened wide inside her. And now she was here, back on Earth and as alone as she'd been in the Fae world.

She nodded. "I get it."

"I've said it a million times. It's just you and me, girl. Always has been. Always will be."

SELENE ATE AND THEN LAY DOWN AGAIN. WHEN A MYRIAD OF CARS pulled up outside, she walked to the window. Vampires of every shape and size poured into Coven House. Mason had told her they'd talk after visiting time ended, but Danika wanted to wait until Neeman returned for some reason. As if Selene couldn't be trusted to be without supervision or something.

Selene pulled a pale blue sweater over her cami and tugged on some jeans. She rubbed her palms on the material and purred. Man, she had missed denim. Walking barefoot to the upper landing, she gazed out at the people below. Vampires and humans milled about the foyer as if at an informal cocktail party. From her vantage point, she watched the strange sight. Some humans were outgoing, talkative, and friendly. Others watched everything without speaking unless spoken to.

The Vampires and vampyr held cards, presumably with information about different humans. It was like watching businessmen exchange contact info with a new client. But they weren't clients, they were people, humans, and these were their lives.

"Hello."

Selene turned to find a tall, black—haired Vampire with a stubbly goatee and sexy, messy hair standing nearby.

"Interesting party, isn't it?" His elegant voice stroked her smooth as a velvet cloak, and his bright hazel eyes took her in, alight with interest. He held a bottle of Savor synthetic blood.

"Party? Is that what this is? I thought it more like human prostitution."

He chuckled, and his smile shot through her. "I guess you could look at it that way."

She turned completely to face him. "Are you here to buy a human?"

"Oh, we aren't allowed to buy them anymore. Even so, no, I do not have one." He stepped forward, and his musky cologne floated to her. "Perhaps if I found the right one, I could be persuaded, though."

His dangerous bad boy air and handsome features were something that she would have loved to sample... if she'd met him a week or so prior. But now they didn't even send a tingle through her. "Isn't that why you're here? To find a human?"

"I came to see what the crop looked like this time."

He stepped closer to her and reached out, pulling on a lock of her hair. "I've not seen a human with hair the color of mine in a long time."

"I got lucky." She pushed her hair behind her ear, out of his reach. An unsettling vibe emanated from him, setting off her inner alarm. His sexy bad boy persona gave way to a more profound, more sinister air.

"Walk away."

"I'll be more than happy to brush it for you, daily." His smile showed brilliant pearly white teeth, but his eyes spoke of more disturbing ideas.

Selene swallowed. "I'm sorry. I think you misunderstood, I'm not a hum—" His handsome face loomed ever closer. "For sale," she added. "I'm...I'm not for sale."

"Aren't you?" He ran a firm hand down her arm.

"No. No, I'm not." She shied away from his unflinching gaze.

"Let me call to Mason."

"You know, I find that everything is for sale for the right price."

Her feeling of unease turned to anger.

"Let me have him. Let him try to brush my hair."

Selene slid sideways toward the staircase back to her room.

"And what do you think my price would be?" She smiled in an effort to ease the tension in her body.

"For you? I'd pay about anything." He set the bottle of Savor on a table and followed her step for step as she eased across the landing and closer to the stairs. Like a predator, he tracked her every movement. He smiled again, and his fangs dropped into his mouth.

Her heart galloped like a racehorse. How did she always get herself into these situations?

"Because you're you."

She plastered a fake smile on her lips. "And what exactly would you want me for?"

"Anything you wanted to do for me. Blood donor, lover, mate." His intense eyes bore into her.

She laughed, and her gaze darted to the people below again. She could scream for help, and a dozen or more men would be up the stairs in a moment. But she'd promised Mason she would be reasonable and not make a scene.

"Mate? For a Vampire? But I'm just a human."

"That could be changed." He snaked a finger down the side of her throat, and a chill made the hairs on her neck prickle. "With one bite and you could be a vampyr, worthy of being my mate."

She backed into the pillar at the edge of the staircase. There was no getting around it unless she deliberately turned and fled.

"And what if I didn't want to become a vampyr? What if I am happy being what I am?"

He loomed closer and planted a hand on the edge of the pillar, pinning her next to the banister.

"Then I'd be inclined to change your mind." He leaned in close to her ear. "I could teach you things that would take you to the heights of ecstasy. Teach you pleasures, such that you'd never want to leave the bedroom."

Memories of being tied to the altar made a fine sheen of sweat bloom all over her skin. Trapped, alone, scared.

He moved inches from her neck. "You smell so amazing. I've been trying this whole time to keep my fangs off of you. You don't mind if I taste you, do you?"

"I mind." Neeman rounded the pillar, grabbed the Vampire by the arm, pinned it behind his back, and shoved him into the wall.

"Oooh! Loverboy to the rescue again."

"Neeman, don't," she cried.

"Get off," the Vampire said.

Neeman pressed the Vampire's elbow upward, making the man cry out.

195

"What the hell do you think you are doing, Douglas?" Neeman demanded.

Douglas grunted and tried to twist away. "She's a slave, I only wanted to taste her," he said, his voice trembling with restraint.

Selene rushed to Neeman and pulled on his arm.

"Let him go," she whispered harshly. She looked around to make sure they hadn't drawn attention, but they stood so far back on the landing no one could see them.

Neeman flipped Douglas around and held him against the wall by his throat. "She's mine and don't let me ever catch you so much as looking at her again."

Douglas's eyes widened. "She never said anything. I thought she was for sale."

Neeman pulled Douglas close. "These humans are freed. They aren't for sale. They aren't here to be pawns in your sick little games. Not anymore. I suggest you take your worthless ass out of this house and not return."

"Only Lord Danika can banish me like that," he squeaked through his pinched airway.

Neeman's grip tightened on Douglas's throat. The look of menace in his eyes told Selene he was close to snapping.

"Neeman." She placed her hand on his arm and tried to keep her voice level. "Let him go."

Neeman's gaze flickered to her face for a moment.

"Please," she pleaded. "He's sorry. Aren't you sorry?" She looked at Douglas.

He nodded once.

"See. A misunderstanding."

"What's going on?" Danika ascended the stairs. "Neeman, let go of Douglas."

Neeman looked at Danika and let go. The Vampire's feet hit the ground, and he sucked in several large breaths.

"Does one of you want to tell me what the hell is happening?" She planted her hands on her hips.

"I was interested in this female." Douglas pointed in Selene's direction. "And Neeman came charging in like a bull-headed tracker and accused me of accosting her."

"Neeman?" Danika asked. "Is this true?"

Neeman grabbed Selene's hand.

Danika's gaze landed on Selene. "Did Douglas hurt you?"

"N— No. Not really," Selene stammered. She'd promised. No problems. She slid closer to Neeman.

"Not really? Douglas?"

"I was just playing—"

Danika moved to him so quick Selene didn't see her move. "Playing what?" Danika demanded. "Do you know who this girl is?"

Douglas' gaze scanned them all rapidly. "A... a human?"

"No," Danika said. "She is my husband's sister. And thereby, my sister."

"Wow! Did she just call us her sister?"

The thought made Selene smile. She'd never had a sister before... well a real sister.

"I... I had no idea. My apologies—"

"Don't apologize to me, apologize to Selene." Danika motioned to Selene and Douglas' gaze fell upon her.

"I... I apologize, Selene." He bowed to her.

"She's mine," Neeman said through gritted teeth.

"And to you as well, Neeman. I meant no disrespect to either of you," Douglas finished.

"Douglas, I suggest you retire for the night. At this time I don't think there are any humans present that will suit your particular needs."

Douglas' eyes narrowed, and he licked his lips and brushed himself off. "As you wish, my Lord." He bowed to Danika and headed for the staircase.

"Oh, and Douglas," Danika called.

He turned.

"Don't you ever come upstairs in my home again."

Douglas inclined his head and then strode away.

Danika turned and eyed Selene. "Are you all right?"

Selene nodded surprised how commanding a presence Danika held for someone so petite. She could see why Mason had chosen Danika.

"If you have decided to make her yours, Neeman, I suggest you mark her quickly so others will stay away. I don't need to tell you how tempting her blood is to everyone around us. If you don't, I can't guarantee things like this won't happen again."

Neeman nodded. "I understand."

"That is, if Selene wants that. The choice is hers, as it is with everyone else here."

"I would never force her." Neeman's voice came out like steel.

"That's not what I meant. I know you would never. I just want Selene to know that she has a choice. I'm sure being back here in this new world has to be very confusing for her." Danika looked at Selene again. "You are given all the same rights as anyone in our Society, though you are neither Vampire or human. As a member of my family you are under my protection."

Selene's chest squeezed. "Thank you."

"Oh please, mushy much?"

Shut up!

Danika nodded. "Good. Neeman, were you able to retrieve Evan?"

"William took her to Doc's office."

She stared between Neeman and Selene for a moment as if she wanted to say something. Instead, she turned and strode away.

When Neeman turned his gaze upon Selene, his eyes were icy. Again.

CHAPTER SIXTEEN

Neeman scowled as he dragged Selene up to the room. He couldn't leave her alone for even a minute without her getting into trouble. But finding Douglas, of all Vampires, ready to bite into her about made him lose all sense of reason.

He threw open the door, pulling her inside. She backed away from him into the couch.

"I didn't do anything." She stared at him; her arms wrapped around herself.

His anger pulsed through him.

"He was standing behind me when I came down from the room and started talking to me, and then he just... I don't know, got the wrong impression, I guess."

Neeman did not doubt that Douglas had been a frequent visitor of the blood club they'd raided and burned down several months back. Now the sadistic bastard would need to find new participants in the games he'd been known to play.

"He backed me against the pole and asked me for a taste. I

panicked. It was like when I was back with the Fae, and they had me in the woods and... and..."

Neeman crossed to her in one large stride. Her shining green eyes stared up at him. Every muscle in his body cried out for her.

He leaned in and kissed her soft on the mouth. "You're mine," he growled.

He swooped down again and kissed her. She returned his kiss with equal fervor. He grabbed the hem of her sweater and ripped it over her head while she pulled his T—shirt off and kissed his chest, running her warm hands over his stomach. His skin goosebumped at her touch, and his arousal strained against his fatigues. There would be no stopping this time. No interruptions. No holding back.

He grabbed her by the back of the head, drew her mouth to his and their tongues entwined. Unclasping her bra, she flung it to the floor and then undid the zipper of his pants. He cupped her freed breasts, and she gasped. His arousal pulsed as she pushed down his pants and then wrapped her fingers around it.

His skin grew tighter as she stroked him. Tingling began in his thighs and worked its way up to his core. The familiar sensations of pleasure made his head fog and his body slack. Pressure built in his groin as her nimble fingers worked faster and harder over him. At the last moment, he stopped her. This wasn't it. Wasn't how he wanted it. He wanted her.

He hefted her up, and she wrapped her legs around his waist before he carried her into the bedroom, her soft body pressing against his as she kissed down the side of his neck.

He laid her on the bed and stripped her of her pants and underwear. Starting at her toes, he kissed his way up her foot to her thighs. She reached down and locked her fingers in his hair, pulling him to up to her mouth. He pressed against her warmth and broke their kiss, sliding his tongue down her neck. Her nails dug into his shoulder blades, making his arousal ratchet even higher. He liked it rough, but this wasn't the time. He needed to go slow. To make her his.

He licked down her torso, paying special attention to each breast, eliciting moans of delight from her. He slid his hand to her most sensitive spot and rolled his thumb over it. She spasmed and arched at his touch.

He smiled.

SELENE SPLAYED ON THE BED, EXPOSED AND IN A STATE OF NEAR UTTER bliss. Neeman's expert hands and mouth molded her body like putty. He kneaded and suckled her to the heights of excitement, his cold flesh making her pebble with goosebumps.

"Take him," her inner Demon begged. *"Make him yours. Make him ours."*

The need to boost her magic and surrender to the pleasures of his touch conflicted inside her.

She pulled his mouth to hers, taking control of the situation. The magic. She needed the magic.

He broke the kiss and looked deep into her eyes.

"No." His voice came out firm, though his eyes remained gentle. He kissed her again and slid his fingers inside her, making her arch against him. "You are mine. Not the other way around."

Her brain fuzzed over as he brought her closer and closer to that edge of pleasure, she'd dreamed of crossing for so many years.

"Say it." He kissed down her neck.

She grabbed onto his powerful shoulders, trying to make her voice work.

"Don't. Don't give in. Take him."

"Say it." He trailed kisses down her chest and nipped at her breasts.

She'd never surrendered to a man before. Doing so now would give him a hold over her she wasn't sure she'd ever break.

He stopped moving. She tried to focus, but her body hummed with a thundering need and all she could think of was release. He brought both hands up and cradled her face. Looming above her, he stroked her hair. His eyes filled with so much compassion she didn't know if she could take it.

He indulged in a long, languorous kiss and then broke away. The thrumming slowed, and she got farther away from that bridge.

"Say it." His bright blue eyes begged her, and she broke inside.

"I'm yours," she whispered. He smiled and kissed her hard, entering her at the same time. She grabbed onto his hips as he thrust deep. She moaned at the feeling of complete surrender. He shifted his hips on top of hers and slid down. The sensation sent shockwaves through her. She kissed him harder, and again he thrust. A warm glow started in her breasts and rolled up to below her collarbone.

"Harder," she panted. Neeman obliged, and Selene found herself once again on the precipice of breaking apart. She willed her body to obey. Tried so hard to find release.

"Stop." He ran his hand over her cheek. "I'm in control, relax."

She didn't want to relax.

"I... I've never reached climax before," she said.

His gaze softened. "Like I said, relax. Let me take you there."

She forced her muscles to relax. He withdrew from her and kissed his way down her stomach, running his fingers down her legs. He bent her knees and pulled her to the edge of the bed while he knelt on the floor. His tongue flicked out and swirled her most intimate crevices. She grabbed his blond hair. Nothing in her life had prepared her for the soft sensations that now coursed through her.

"Neeman." She gasped.

He hooked his hands around her thighs and brought her closer. Minutes felt like hours at the pleasure he awakened in her. She pressed herself against him, wanting more and more.

"I need you."

He crawled next to her, lay on his back, and set her on top of him. "Go slow," he commanded.

She nodded, trying to keep her brain focusing. For the first time, having a man take charge didn't scare her— it thrilled her. She slid down on him and shuddered. He grabbed her hips and spread her thighs wide. Rocking back and forth, she reveled in the feel of their joined bodies.

She'd never made love to someone and concentrated so completely on her own body. She'd never had a lover who wanted her satisfaction more than his own. For all, she'd studied, and all she'd been taught about the art of sex, she'd turned into the pupil and he— her patient teacher.

Earthquakes of pleasure built as her speed increased and a shiver tickled up her spine. The inside of her thighs tingled as need built in her core. Every rock of her hips pulled her closer and closer to the edge. Warmth grew once more to heat almost unbearable and sent tendrils of pleasure down her breasts.

She moved faster, pressing her body down on his to gain

more friction. Her need intensified and she grabbed his shoulders for support. His arms worked feverishly, pushing and pulling her hips to gain even more traction. The demand built inside to the point of boiling over.

Neeman slipped one of his hands away and cupped her breast, pinching it, and her body exploded. Every muscle tightened as her neck whipped back, and her mouth dropped in a silent scream. Quicker and more intense than she could ever imagine, waves of ecstasy crashed through her.

Neeman hung on to her hips and continued to rock her through her climax. When she could no longer move, she sucked in a huge breath. The sensations began to fade, and she dropped onto his chest, panting.

No words in any language she knew could explain fully the experience she'd just been through. She had never let go so completely with another being. Never allowed a man to really be inside her. To see her without the façade she put on. No one but him.

For a moment she feared looking at him. What if he'd not liked what he'd seen in her? But curiosity got the better of her and peering up at him she couldn't miss the genuine smile planted on his face.

"Look how proud he is of himself."

"Bet you feel like a Viking now, don't you?"

He kissed her and pushed her into a sitting position. "Not yet."

Again, he rocked her. He hadn't even gotten there. He'd been so consumed with helping her.

"Sit up," she said.

He backed against the headboard. She leaned in and kissed him then shifted her hips back as far as she was able and slammed forward again.

He banged his head into the headboard, and his fingers dug deep into her hips. He moaned into her mouth. She broke the kiss and licked down his neck.

"When you get close," she whispered in his ear. "Bite me."

He stopped.

She thrust her hips forward again. "Bite me."

Their gazes locked as she increased in speed and friction. His face changed from fear to desire. His fingers dug deep into her skin, and his breathing came shallow and fast. She swept her hair over her shoulder and cocked her head to one side. Their bodies continued to move as his arms pumped faster.

She saw the chi energy building tight in his chest— the desire to consume it and strengthen her magic coiled inside her. The light of his chi grew hotter. She placed her hand on his chest, waiting for the right moment. Closer. Closer.

At the last second, she grabbed Neeman's face. "Bite me!" she demanded. "Bite me now."

He didn't hesitate. His fangs sunk deep into her throat, and he cried out, the sound muffled against her skin. The pull on her vein and friction of their bodies made her claw at him as everything dissolved, and she climaxed even harder the second time.

Her rapid breathing matched Neeman's. They sat, joined, holding, and kissing for several minutes. His bright blue eyes held a slightly purple tinge at the edges. She shivered at the sight.

He kissed across her collarbone and stopped.

"What's that?" He ran his finger over her collarbone. "I never noticed those before."

Selene looked down to find glowing runes flowing across her chest like a fiery tattoo.

Shit! Shit. Shit. Shit.

Those hadn't been there before. Her head pounded as panic settled in.

It wasn't possible. She'd never had the runes before.

Blood dribbled down her throat over the runes to her breast. She used the sheet to wipe off the blood and pressed it to the puncture wounds at her throat.

"Are you cold?"

"What?" She looked up at Neeman's soft smile. "You're shivering."

"No, I'm okay." Her hand shook, and she dropped the sheet from her neck, her eyes transfixed on the golden symbols.

"The hell you are. You know exactly what those runes are and what they mean."

"Let's get under the covers." He moved her to the side, and they both slid under the blanket.

He wrapped her in his arms, and she lay her still reeling head on his chest.

Her heart pounded. This couldn't be happening. He couldn't be the one. Her mother had told her that she would never find someone she was meant to be with. Being divided between herself and her inner Demon meant there would never be one who could satisfy them both.

"Mother was wrong about so many things."

"Are you all right?"

"Yeah." She cleared her throat and tried again. "Yeah, I'm great." She drew lazy circles around his right nipple, her brain working a million miles an hour. "What did Danika mean about 'marking' me?"

He ran a finger over her neck where he'd bitten her.

"She meant you needed to bite me?"

"That's part of it, yes. And you should probably call her Lord Danika."

She looked up at him. "What's the other part?" She needed to know. Did this marking have anything to do with her new runes?

His gaze lingered on her neck. "You need to ingest some of my blood as well."

"But isn't that how you bond a slave to you?"

"Yes."

"I'm not a slave. That won't work with me."

"True, but if you ingest my blood, every other Vampire and vampyr will smell it and know you belong to me."

"Is that what Danika did with Mason?"

Neeman's face darkened, and he worked his jaw as he stroked her throat. "He's had her blood, yes. But not many would dare mess with the slave of a Coven Lord, whether or not they are bonded. Even so, no one would dare have tried to bond your brother without his consent."

The hard edge to his voice told her she'd hit a nerve about something. "What's the deal with you and Danika?"

His gaze met hers. "There is no deal between *Lord* Danika and myself."

"Don't lie. I see it in the way you act when her name gets mentioned. And the way you act around Mason."

He stayed silent for a long time. "Lord Danika and I used to be lovers."

Her eye twitched, and she rubbed at it. It was unrealistic for her to be jealous. Neeman was good looking and smart. Of course, he had been with other women. How many men had she been with?

"For how long?" Her throat constricted.

"About five years."

Five years?

"You should shut up now. Stop being so nosy." For once, her Demon's advice was sound.

"How come you didn't marry?" she asked despite herself.

He stared at her, his fingers stopping. "She said no."

The answer chilled her to the core. She'd never opened herself up to a man. Never let one get close enough to have a third date, let alone close enough to ask her to marry.

"I told you to stop asking."

She coughed and tried to keep her tone light, though her heart felt like molten lead.

"Do you still love her?" She willed him to say no, but he stayed silent too long.

"So much for the stupid new runes."

"No," he said finally.

She nodded and set her head on his chest. She shouldn't have asked if she hadn't wanted to hear the answer. But she appreciated his attempt to lie and shield her from pain.

CHAPTER SEVENTEEN

An hour later, they were summoned downstairs. Jealousy still coursed through Selene, and every time she reminded herself, she was being stupid, her Demon half would set her off again.

Neeman cared for her, obviously, but she couldn't fight against the torch he still held for Danika. They'd been together for years, and he'd wanted to marry her. That wasn't going to change just because he'd decided he didn't want other Vampires messing with her, and they'd had a wonderful hour of passion.

They crossed the landing toward the hallway where Douglas had cornered her, and a chill ran through her. Below, the remaining Vampires headed out the door, stopping to speak to the beautiful, pregnant Vampire and her obvious mate before leaving.

Neeman turned down a dim hallway. Three lone doors stood on the left side. He got to the second to last and knocked. William beckoned them in. The scent of fresh paint and new drywall filled the air. The wall separating the sitting room from the bathroom was newer than the rest. She wondered what the place had been before becoming a sitting room.

"Please." Danika pointed to the chairs in front of a large wooden desk.

Neeman pulled one out for Selene. She looked up at him; his expression gave nothing away. Once again, they were back to him being in his head, and her feeling like a schoolgirl sent to the headmistress's office. Selene glanced around, trying to spot Mason.

"I want to apologize for my behavior yesterday." Danika's golden gaze stayed planted on Selene. "I'm afraid I wasn't much liked by other females growing up and so I have little tact when it comes to others. Even so, I am a Coven Lord and should try to act with some semblance of decorum. Not to mention we seem to find ourselves family now. I had no idea Mason even had a sister until yesterday."

"I accept your apology," said Selene. "I would have felt as you did if I had come to find my husband holding another woman."

Danika smiled, and it lightened her face. "I can only imagine how that would go over."

"Don't trust her. She wants something."

"So, Mason explained to me what's been going on with the Demons," Danika said. "I wasn't aware that they'd arrived. Can you tell us what happened at the compound?"

How much did she say? What should she say? Should she tell the truth? "Where is Mason?"

"Mason's attending to some other business."

A gnawing sensation settled in her gut, and she bit the inside of her cheek. "Why?"

Danika sat forward and smiled. "Can I be blunt?"

"Please do."

"Soon, I hope we can be the best of sisters. Maybe go shopping, have lunch, while texting each other every day. But this isn't that day. I don't know you. All I know is that Mason hid you from me. And he never hides things from me. So that leaves me to believe that there's something about you that he doesn't want me to know. But that isn't my concern at the moment. My concern is the Demons and what is going on in my city. So, if you could tell me what happened at the compound while Neeman was gone, it would be most helpful."

Selene wracked her mind to find a place to start. "What's texting?"

Danika growled in frustration, and her gaze traveled to Neeman.

"Selene," he said. "Tell Lord Danika what happened."

His respect for Danika and his taking her side galled Selene. She gripped the arm of her chair as her inner Demon gnashed her teeth.

"How dare she disrespect us! Where is Maelstrom, why does he let her treat us like this?"

"Shut up," Selene whispered, rubbing her head.

"Excuse me?" asked Danika.

Selene looked up. "I don't know what happened. One minute I was lying down, the next minute ash Demons crashed into the hallway, and a hellian chased me into the arena."

"How did they find you?"

"I assume Rex sent up a signal letting the other Demons know where he'd been taken. Like Mason accidentally did when he used his magic to take down the spell on the blood club."

"And how did the compound happen to collapse?" Danika leaned her elbows on her desk.

Okay, so that's the tricky part to explain.

"A hellian started to bring down the observation room and the ceiling. He charged me. I took him to the ground, and he misfired. The fire breath hit the ceiling, and the place started to fall."

Danika's eyes glittered with interest. "Did they say who sent them?"

"I—" She wasn't positive, but the Russians had phoned to put something in motion, and the attack had happened shortly after. She wasn't supposed to have heard them, but she couldn't let the coincidence go unsaid. "The Russians may be behind it."

"What?" Neeman turned to look at her.

"How do you know about them?" asked Danika.

She blew out a breath. So much for shopping and lunch with Danika. Things were about to get sticky.

"I followed Neeman here and hid outside that night. I heard them talking. They said something about putting a plan in motion and Chase—"

"Chase?" Danika jumped out of her chair in a flash.

Neeman hopped to his feet as well. Even William moved from his stoic position in the corner.

"Yeah. They said they shouldn't have helped him—"

Danika smacked her desk and swore. "I knew those bastards were up to no good." Her intense gaze raked Selene. "Did they say where Chase was?"

"They're overlooking the fact that we snuck on the grounds of Coven House, nice."

"No. They said they needed to contact Garon—"

"So, he's back in the game," said William.

"I don't think he was ever out," said Danika. Her gaze

shifted to Selene. "This is something we should talk about in private."

Neeman glared at Selene as well, but she determined not to squirm under the weight of their scrutiny.

Selene shrugged. "I can see where I'm not wanted. So, I'll go." She stood and turned toward the door, happy to be released without a fight.

She stepped into the hall, and a gentle hand fell on her arm. Neeman loomed close to her. Her gaze flicked to Danika, who watched them with interest.

"What?" Selene asked.

"You can't leave Coven House," Neeman said in a low voice.

She folded her arms. "Oh?"

His brows furrowed, and he removed his hand. "What's wrong with you?"

"Nothing, what's wrong with you?" she asked in her most childish voice.

"Why are you being like this?" His gaze darted to Danika and then back to Selene, making her blood heat with anger.

"What's the matter, am I embarrassing you by not being the compliant little slave?"

His mouth opened and closed several times as a mixture of anger and confusion played across his features.

She dropped her arms. Why was she acting like this? He'd made no commitment to her. They'd made love, that's all.

"I won't leave, okay?"

His dubious expression told her he wasn't convinced.

"You want me to pinky swear?"

She lifted her pinky, and he stared at it for a moment.

"Wow, does he not know what that means?"

"I'll be done here soon. And Selene?"

She rolled her eyes. "What?"

"We are going to talk about how you followed me here the other night."

She threw him a sardonic smile. "Can't wait." She closed the door in his face.

"Great! Can we go now?"

"No."

"Well, can we at least go to the barracks in the back and check out the hot humans?"

"No."

"You are no fun at all anymore."

Selene growled. Her panties were in a wad, and she knew it. Her irrational irritation had exploded beyond measure, and her inner Demon wasn't making things any easier.

SELENE STOMPED DOWN THE STAIRS AND INTO THE KITCHEN. THERE she made herself a huge plate full of party leftovers, from chicken tenders to mini eggrolls. Every food she could dream of had been packed into Tupperware and neatly lined up in the enormous refrigerator underneath an entire shelf full of bottles of Savor.

"I don't think you're supposed to be eating that."

Selene looked up to see a pretty blonde human staring at her from the back doorway. She put the lid on one of the Tupperware containers. "Why not? It's food. It's meant to be eaten."

"Not by us."

Selene stared at the girl with enormous, defiant sapphire eyes. "Oh." She nodded. "You mean, by slaves. I'm not a slave." She shoved the Tupperware into the fridge and closed it.

"Those marks on your neck say otherwise." The girl pointed.

Selene fought the urge to touch her neck. "Trust me. There's not a Vampire on Earth who could enslave me."

The blonde reached over and took one of Selene's eggrolls. "And why's that?"

Selene shrugged. "Because I don't want them to."

The female snorted. "If that were true, I'd not have been sold a dozen times."

"A dozen?" *Intriguing.* Selene studied the female as she chewed. "What makes you so special? I mean, I suppose you are pretty enough."

"It's the challenge, I think," said the girl. "They all think they can break me and make me submit to their will."

"But humans can choose their mentors now, right? Why do you keep going with them?"

The girl picked out another eggroll and crunched it. "Because I want to talk to the other slaves. To get them to see the truth."

"What truth?"

"That we don't have to live like this." She gestured around. "We can fight."

Selene spotted a tray of pastries. She walked to it and fingered through the assortment. Her hand hovered above a peanut butter cookie with nuts. Who the heck liked those gross things? She picked out a croissant and bit into it. The ham and cheese filling melted in her mouth. "And who's going to help them fight? Where will you go?"

The girl glanced around and then leaned across the counter and lowered her voice. "There's an enclave. The one I came from. It's large, huge even. They'll take us all in. They want to defeat the Vampires. Take back the world."

"They have weapons. Some even rumored to have a couple nukes hidden away."

Humans. Thought they owned everything. The last thing the world needed was human rebels with nuclear weapons. "And what makes you think that's a good thing."

The girl shook her head. "Why wouldn't it be?"

"Well, from what I see, this world is in the crapper, and the only thing holding it together are the Vampires. Without them, things would go back to the way they were after the Awakening. Chaos, wars, death."

The girl's eyes narrowed on Selene like a laser beam. "Better to have those things and be free than to die in comfort as a slave."

Selene shook her head. "And how many slaves agreed with you? In all those households you went to, how many said they'd return to the enclave?"

The girl frowned.

"Didn't think many would," Selene said. "No offense, but people don't want freedom. They want comfort. Everyone does. Given a choice between being a comfortable slave with safety and food and hot water, and going back to living in the mountains barely surviving, people are going to choose comfort every time."

"Dude, not me," said the girl. "Never me."

The girl still held the fiery passion of youth. She couldn't be more than twenty to twenty—five. Unfortunately, Selene was older. Much older.

"What's your name?" asked Selene.

"Evan."

"What did the Vampires do to you that was so horrible?"

The expression on Evan's face hardened. She closed her mouth and stepped away from the counter.

"I think you hit a nerve."

"What are you going to do now?" asked Selene. "Keep going house to house?"

Evan picked up a fork and flipped it between her fingers. "If I have to."

"I wouldn't count on it." Selene popped a piece of chicken in her mouth.

"What does that mean?"

"It means you were confined to your room, and you're not supposed to be out here," said a male voice from behind Selene.

Both turned to find William and Neeman entering the kitchen. Selene opened a soda and took a considerable swig as Neeman approached her.

Evan looked to William and groaned. "You're just going to keep me locked up?"

"Until Lord Danika decides what to do with you." He pointed toward the rear door.

"Dude, you can't keep me shut up forever. I'll get out." Evan tossed the fork in the air, and it rotated several times before she caught it and tossed it up again.

"I'm sure you will, but for now, please, let's go to your room." William opened the back door and waved her outside.

Evan looked between Selene and Neeman. She caught the fork and flipped it through the air. It landed sticking straight up in Selene's last eggroll.

"At least you get to be a slave to a cute one," Evan said.

Selene clenched her jaw. "As I said, I'm no one's slave."

Evan snorted again. "Sure, sis. You keep telling yourself that."

William pulled on Evan's arm, but she yanked it away. "Don't touch me, Vampire. You're cute, too, but not that cute."

William sighed. "How many times do I have to tell you that I'm a vampyr, not a Vampire."

"Okay, so you got bitten, not born, who cares? You still drink blood, don't you?"

William sighed and shook his head. "Come on."

Evan waved and headed out the door.

"What were you two talking about?" asked Neeman.

"Girl stuff." A piece of chicken spit from her mouth and landed on the counter.

"I don't want you talking to Evan."

She gave him a hard look, picked up a piece of chicken, and pointed it at him. "You know, you telling me not to talk to people is getting old."

"I don't care if you talk to any other female in this house, just don't talk to that one."

"Why? Afraid she might turn me to the dark side?"

"No." He shook his head. "I'm afraid you'll make her obsession with freeing humans worse."

Selene chewed quickly and then swallowed. "Me? What did I do?"

He cocked an eyebrow. "You need to ask?"

She advanced on him. "I'll have you know that though I don't agree with humans being slaves, I do understand it. I'm not an idiot. I can see what would happen if suddenly the humans were allowed to run amuck again, let alone rule this world. You guys may have screwed it up with the V2000 virus, but at least you're holding what little there is left together. The system isn't perfect, but at least it isn't total chaos."

"*I like chaos.*" Seraphine purred.

Neeman stared at her for a minute. "I don't know if I should be flattered or offended."

"I don't care which you are." She walked to the counter and stuffed more food in her mouth, not tasting any of it but chewing it hard enough to turn it to soup.

"Are you going to tell me what's bothering you?"

She took a long swig of soda before sucking in a breath and burping. "Nope."

He growled and grabbed her soda. "Come on." Then he picked up her plate and threw it in the trash with the drink. "Stop eating that crap. It'll kill you."

"Are you serious?" She trailed behind him, trying to keep up. "Where are we going?"

"Outside."

"Is there a barbecue out there, because I'm hungry."

"No. You're going to teach us how to fight Demons."

"Says who?"

"Lord Danika. Just like at the compound. You want to stay; you have to help out."

She shrugged. "Okay, then I'll go."

Neeman blocked her path and planted his feet on the ground. "No."

"But I don't want to help out. So, I have to leave." She moved around him.

"Why are you so stubborn? Why can't you do things without a fight for once?"

Selene stopped in her tracks. She glanced around at the finery of the house, and the High Elder's voice floated into her head. She couldn't leave. She had to stay close to Danika and Mason.

"Fine," she said finally. "Teach who?"

"Everyone."

Out back, trackers and house security gathered on the large lawn, assembled for her viewing pleasure. The sight of them in one large collective made her shake her head.

"What?" Neeman asked.

"How do you expect me to teach this many people to fight Demons? It took me years to learn how to deal with them all. I can't make them Demon destroyers in one night. This would take months of training. Years even."

Neeman eyed the group and then stepped closer and lowered his voice. "We don't have months. We have no idea when they could strike next."

"Well, I'm sorry, but I'm not going to be much help," she whispered. "Why can't Mason do this?"

"Because." Neeman's gaze darted away.

"Because, why?"

He licked his lips. "Because they are scared of Mason."

"And they aren't scared of me?" She snorted.

"They have no idea how scary we can be. Let's show them."

Neeman pulled on his hair by the roots and rubbed his face. "Okay, look; Don't teach them to fight, teach them the weaknesses."

She groaned. That alone would take days— and only if they were fast studies. She didn't want to do this. Why did she have to babysit the preschoolers? Her gaze traveled to Neeman again. If it meant she got a couple of hours without Neeman asking her what was wrong, she'd do it.

"Fine." She pointed at him. "But don't blame me if they all get killed."

She walked to the middle of the group and looked around. She could do this.

"Hey. I'm Selene, and I will be your instructor today in Demonology 101. First of all, you should know that you aren't as strong as a Demon. You aren't as fast as a Demon. You aren't even—"

"That's not helping," Neeman said.

She looked at him and scowled.

"Fine. The one thing you are most likely better at than a Demon is being smart. Demons tend to go on impulse. What they want, they go for, usually with no thought for the possible repercussions. For instance, let's say Neeman here is a quaser, Demon." She grabbed Neeman by the arm and led him to the middle of the group.

She walked around him and smirked. See how much he likes being part of the object lesson. "Quasers have long, tentacled arms with suction cups on them that are sticky as hell." She flopped his arms up and down. "But they aren't too bright." She flicked him in the back of the head.

Neeman glared at her while several people snickered. Selene smiled and continued. She rounded Neeman till she stood behind him.

"The way to bring down a quaser is right here." She dug her finger into the base of his spine. "You stab a quaser here, and he'll go down for the count."

"How many different kinds of Demons are there?" someone yelled.

"Hundreds."

Murmurs and groans mumbled from the peanut gallery.

"You're not helping," Neeman replied.

"Well, then maybe I should go."

"Do you want everyone to die?"

She shrugged. "What do I care? I don't know them."

"You know me."

Her stomach clenched at the look on his face.

"Look," he said. "You're obviously angry at me about something. And we can deal with that later, but right now you need to cut it out. This isn't you. I know you don't want everyone here to die. Put up this bitchy front all you want with me. But deep down, you care. My men told me how you saved them down there. You could have run, but you didn't. Stop making this so hard."

She pulled from his grip and sighed. "Fine. But I'm only doing this, so my conscience is clear."

A smile flickered on his lips. "Whatever you say."

NEEMAN WATCHED SELENE SPEND THE NEXT TWO HOURS TELLING THE group everything she could about different Demons and their weaknesses. She explained which ones to fight and which ones to run from. A dozen trackers and security members came into the middle to spar with her. As much as she would never admit it, she had teaching in her blood.

She was patient in a way Neeman wasn't. She took time to show them specific techniques or how to improve their defensive tactics. If they did something that wouldn't work, she told them what would.

She'd taught them to recognize fifteen of the most common Demons and the characteristics of over two dozen more. In the end, though he still wasn't sure they would win in a fight, they were more prepared than not.

It interested Neeman to see her put all attitude aside and just be herself. The her he was pretty sure few people had ever seen.

Mason came out to join them as they finished.

"She's good," he said. "Not like me. I don't have the aptitude for teaching. No patience."

"She's a natural," Neeman replied. "She'd make an amazing tracker."

Mason glanced at him sideways. "Maybe you should tell her that."

Neeman shrugged. "Maybe I should."

The group broke up, and several people thanked Selene. She waved them off, but the smile on her face rung genuine.

He walked up to meet her.

"So, did I pass, master?" she asked.

"You were great."

"They're still going to die."

"Not if you continued to teach them."

"What? Me?" She snorted. "No, thanks."

"I'm serious. You'd make a top notch tracker and a teacher. You should think about it."

She stared at him for a minute, and her eye twitched. She rubbed at it. "Yeah, well... I don't think I'm the right person for the job."

"I think you're the perfect person. And besides, what else do you have to do?"

She shrugged. "I don't know. Shopping, my nails, napping—"

"Be serious. You need something to do, and we need you."

She licked her lips. "You need me, huh?"

He swallowed and glanced around. There wasn't anyone in earshot, and yet this wasn't the place for a conversation of that magnitude.

"Never mind." She turned to go.

"Stop. Yes. We need you. All of us as a collective."

She rolled her eyes. "Whatever."

Neeman growled in frustration. Why couldn't things be easy with her? What she wanted him to say was as evident as what had set her off. The mention of Danika had sent a frostiness over Selene to rival that of a Chicago winter.

There was only one way to do this. He grabbed her hand and dragged her around the side of the house.

"Where are we going?" She trailed behind him.

"You'll see when we get there." He pulled her toward the car out front.

CHAPTER EIGHTEEN

Neeman drove downtown in silence. They'd made love, and it had been fantastic. He'd given her something that no man had before. And she'd given him something no woman ever had in return. The blood in his veins made him once again feel alive; connecting him to her in a way he'd never connected to another person.

But her discovery that he'd had a relationship with Danika threatened to ruin that. As hard as opening up was for him, he figured the best thing to do was try and help her understand.

He pulled his car into a vacant parking lot and stopped.

She looked out the window. "A parking lot? That's what you wanted to show me?"

"No, smart ass. It isn't." He tried to keep the irritation out of his voice, but man, she could be a pain sometimes. Though he'd begun understanding why she always had her defenses up.

He exited the car, and she followed. The cool night tickled his skin, but not uncomfortably. He walked to a one—story building with the glass front doors sitting wide open.

"What is this place?"

"You'll see." He continued through the empty entrance and down to a set of turnstiles. Dropping in a few pieces of change, he pushed the metal bar down with his hips and proceeded through. He turned to drop in a few more coins for Selene, but she jumped the turnstile instead.

"You're not supposed to do that."

She shrugged. "You gonna arrest me?"

He shoved the money back into his pocket. The approaching shriek of brakes against metal wheels shook the structure.

"Hurry." He laced her slender fingers in his and jogged toward the train that slowed out on the tracks.

She made for the open door of the train, but he shook his head.

"Up here." He showed her the ladder at the end of one of the cars, and she smirked. He hoisted her up, getting an ample view of her perfect backside, before following her onto the roof.

The train rolled forward, and they walked to the middle of the car and sat. Wind whipped her hair from side to side. She pulled a band out of her pocket and strapped her hair into a ponytail.

The smell of the crisp night air made Neeman relax. It had been months since he'd ridden the train. He closed his eyes and smiled as they moved down the tracks, closer to the city center. The familiar rhythm of the train lulled him into relaxation.

"So, what are we doing up here?" Selene scooted next to him.

"You wanted to know what I do for fun, so I'm showing you."

"You ride the top of an L train for fun?"

"I didn't become a vampyr by choice." He looked out at the

scenery, and his gut clenched. He'd never told anyone how he felt about being a vampyr. Never shared his experience of what had happened the night he'd been turned.

They passed an overgrown little league baseball field, and he stared at the rusted and falling down fencing. "When I'd finally come to terms with what I'd become, I joined the Tracking Squad. It was the only thing that made me feel like I might have a purpose in my new life."

"I get it. You're a man with a mission."

Neeman ran his hands through his hair. Why couldn't she shut up sometimes? "No. I'm not. That's the point. Ever since I became this, work is all I've had. Until Danika."

Selene glanced at him sideways. "You don't have to explain to me about her. It's cool."

"No, it's not cool. I saw how you got when you asked me if I loved her, and I'm trying to explain."

The sudden seriousness that came over Selene's features made him want to reach out and touch her.

"I'm listening."

"I didn't know anything else but the work. Picking up humans, tracking rogue vamps, protecting Danika's father at meetings. That was all I had until I met her. You asked if I love her. And in a way, I did. She was the first thing to ground me in the Society, to give me something other than just the job, and for that, I loved her. I hadn't been with anyone before her except for the occasional one—nighter. It's been that way ever since, as well."

They were coming close to their stop. If he didn't tell her everything, he didn't know that he'd ever work up the nerve again. "I'm not good at this."

"At talking? I've noticed."

"No. Yes. This." He gestured between them. "Talking, sharing. I haven't done it in over fifty years."

"Even with Danika?"

"Especially with Danika. Don't you get it yet? I hate what I am. I hate being a vampyr. Drinking from people, enslaving people, constantly craving sustenance. I hate it. How do you tell someone who was born this way that you hate that you're like them? That you'd rather still be human."

"I see."

"Do you? Do you know what it's like to worry every single day that you might kill someone? That you might turn them into someone like you and curse them with the same existence, you have? To know that you'll likely see the world end before your own life?"

She stared at him hard for a minute. "Yes. I know exactly what that's like, only more so because of my inner Demon. Were I to let her run free, I mean, really free, I can't even fathom the kind of chaos she would unleash."

He nodded. "Maybe you do understand, but Danika never would've. She loves being what she is. Ultimately, it was my inability to tell her I cared for her, or how I felt about what I am, that drove her away."

"Do you? Still, love her?" Selene stared at him, her eyes a mixture of hope and fear. It made his chest tighten.

"I love her as a friend. I will always care for her and her wellbeing. I'll always fear for her safety, especially as your brother's mate. But I'm not in love with her. I don't know that I ever really was."

Selene swallowed hard. "What do you feel for me?"

What did he feel for her? Her hair whipped loose from her ponytail, making him want to push it from her face. Even though it obscured her shining green eyes, she refused to look away.

"You? You make me feel...human again."

She laughed. "I'm not even human."

"Maybe not physically, but in spirit, you are the embodiment of humans. You're spontaneous and outspoken and spoiled and a pain in the—"

"Okay! I get your point." She looked at her hands.

He lifted her chin. "But you also care about others. You could've left my men to die and run for it, but you didn't. You saved them from a Demon. You could have told Evan she was right about Vampires and egged her on to go about trying to destroy the world, but you didn't. You're smarter than anyone gives you credit for and more loyal than just about anyone I've ever met. Besides, your brother."

"Most people call it being stubborn."

"Either way. The answer is, I don't know what I feel for you, but I know that I want to feel something for you, and that's more than I can say for any other person out there."

She pursed her lips and nodded. "I understand that. I've never had feelings for a guy before. I've used men to get what I want. Sex, money, power. My mother raised me that way. I've never even thought of opening my heart with a guy before you. My mother told me that doing that would be my ruination. That once I opened my heart to a man, I could never be fully in control of the situation anymore and that I always needed to be in control to get what I wanted. But now..." She sighed. "Somehow, you crawled right inside of me and rooted yourself in my breast. I can't seem to get you out of my head. Even though you're stubborn, and overbearing, and bossy, and won't let me drive your car—"

"That's a very expensive car."

"Even so... You've seen parts of me in these past weeks that I've never shown anyone. And you're still here."

"I'm still here."

He stroked her cheek. The brakes of the L screeched as they slowed to a stop. He wanted to kiss her. To run his fingers down the length of her body and feel her quake beneath him as he brought her to the heights of pleasure once more.

"I want to show you something else."

"More?"

They climbed to the edge of the train and descended the ladder. "Yeah, one more thing."

SELENE WALKED HAND IN HAND WITH NEEMAN THROUGH THE MOSTLY barren streets. Vamps moved here and there doing various jobs, but on a whole, the sounds of the city seemed muted by the death of so many humans. No one stared at her this time. No one called to her or chased her down. They moved out of the way, and some even bowed to Neeman.

They strolled past store after closed down store.

"It's sad," she said. "To see capitalism gone from America."

Neeman glanced at her. "Yes, it is. It's not completely gone, though. You're lucky you didn't have to watch its decline. Watching stores close or burn. Seeing vamps crying in the streets trying to understand what was happening to them. The smell of death that lingered for years. It was our job as trackers to keep the peace here in the Chicago territory."

"Did you have to kill people?"

His shoulders hunched, and he pulled his hand away, shoving them in his pockets. "Too many."

231

Compassion raced through her in a way she'd never experienced. The things he'd told her on the train seemed to be more than he'd shared with anyone before. It was childish to like the fact he hadn't shared those things with Danika, but she liked it just the same. All she'd heard about since her arrival was Lord Danika. From Neeman. From Mason. From the High Elder.

She glanced at Neeman and threaded her arm through his. She couldn't deny how much she liked the feel of having something of her own... someone of her own.

A bright marquee flashed up ahead. An old vamp sat inside a ticket booth reading an old magazine. Neeman pulled out his wallet as he approached.

"Afternoon, Neeman." The older man smiled, crinkling up his wrinkly face.

"Hey, Gus." Neeman slid the money under the gap in the glass.

Gus looked at Selene. "You finally got yourself a girl?"

Neeman chuckled. "Something like that."

Gus slid Neeman's change and his tickets through the gap. "Well, you treat her right. Good ones are hard to find." Gus winked at Selene, making her smile.

"I'll do my best," Neeman replied. "But this one's a handful."

"The ones that are worth it always are."

Neeman pulled open the door to the theater and held it for Selene.

Immediately a sense of nostalgia wafted over her. Inside the entrance of the theater stood an old fashioned candy counter and soda fountain. The aqua and red interior reminded her of when her mother used to take her out for a cream soda. Happy memories from before they'd found Mason flooded her. Memories she'd forgotten she even possessed.

"I figured you of anyone might get a kick out of this place."

Gus shuffled out of the ticket box and hustled his hunched body behind the soda counter. He threw on an apron and hat and smiled at them.

"Welcome, what can I get you?"

Happiness brightened Selene's thoughts. "A cream soda float."

"And for you, sir?" Gus looked at Neeman.

"A root beer float."

Gus nodded and set about getting out glasses and ice cream.

Neeman showed her over to the wall of candy dispensers, and together they picked out various old candies and put them into bags. They debated over whether licorice or licorice rope were the better candy and then discussed the old fashioned candies versus the newer sour candies. In the end, they bought some of about half the varieties in the store.

Gus handed them the floats, and Neeman ordered a bag of popcorn and paid.

Walking into the theater, butterflies fluttered in her stomach.

"Is this like a date or something?" she asked.

He glanced down at her. "Only if you promise not to argue about it."

She smiled. A date. A real date. She'd not been on one since... honestly, she couldn't remember ever having been on an actual date.

"Awww... That's so sweet."

"Piss off, Seraphine."

An old organ stood at the foot of a restored stage. A vamp sat at the organ, filling the theater with beautiful classic tones. Selene stopped and took in the beautiful red velvet curtains that hung around the stage and draped the walls. Ornate gilded busts adorned the wall, and a giant glimmering chandelier dangled above.

"Where do you want to sit?" Neeman asked.

"Well, since it's so packed in here, it's hard to choose. But I guess let's go dead center."

She headed to the middle of the theater and took the center seat. Neeman sat next to her, and they sipped their floats and munched on popcorn, listening to the music.

"How'd you find this place?"

"I've come here since the seventies. It had almost closed its doors by then, but I refused to let it go under."

She looked over at him. "You own this?"

He shrugged. "Gus owns it. I just... invested in it."

She shook her head.

"What?"

"The layers you possess know no bounds, Neeman."

"Like an onion."

"What?"

He laughed. "Shrek?"

She shrugged.

"Never mind. So tell me. What is the Fae plane like?"

She picked popcorn kernels out of the bag one by one and popped them into her mouth. What was the other plane like?

"Worse than hell."

"It's beautiful in its own way. There are no vehicles. The technology is more organic. There are no such things as fashion or fast food, or television or anything that makes Earth, Earth."

"So, what did you do there?" He sucked on his straw and gulped down the rest of his root beer.

"I meditated and gathered food, took walks, and sat. I did a lot of sitting."

"So, there aren't jobs there?"

"Oh, there are. I just wasn't allowed to have one. They were too afraid I'd go crazy and start killing everyone."

"Is your Demon like Mason's? Destruction and fire and all that?"

Selene swallowed.

"Yes," her inner Demon roared.

"Mine likes chaos. She thrives off energy and madness."

"So, she isn't into destroying us all?"

"No."

"Liar."

He raised an eyebrow

"To be honest, it's been so long since I've let her take over completely that I have no idea what she would do if I ever let her have full reign. Chaos, sex, fighting, jealousy, those have always been vices of choice, but she's been cooped up so long..."

"But it was her that I met the first night, wasn't it?"

"Yes. But not completely. She has been taking over my consciousness, but my form stays mine. She can't turn into her true form unless I let her."

"Mason can't control his Demon side that well."

"Yes, but I am more Fae than Demon."

The music at the organ stopped, and the curtains parted.

"I'm going to run to take our glasses back before the show starts," said Neeman.

Selene handed him her glass, and he headed toward the lobby. She watched him go, getting a nice view of his firm buttocks and broad shoulders.

"He's nice to look at, isn't he?"

Selene whipped around. Her Demon roared and clawed to be let out. She tried to keep her hands from shaking, staring into the aqua blue eyes of Lorcan. She'd almost forgotten about him and her mission since he'd left her for dead pinned under the fallen ceiling in the compound. He plucked several pieces of candy from her bag and stuck one in his mouth. The sight made her chest squeeze tight as the ties he'd used to bind her.

"He's okay." She faked nonchalance, taking a piece of candy back out of Lorcan's hand and munching it.

Lorcan's eyes bore into her. "You can't lie to me. I heard what you said on the train. For you, that was as much as saying you loved him."

She crushed a handful of popcorn between her fingers. "I never said that."

"The tension in your voice betrays you."

She swallowed and tried again. "What do you want, Lorcan? Why are you here?"

"Me? What are you doing here? I told you that you were supposed to contact me. You've been in Coven House for almost three days. When are you going to be delivering Danika?"

"It's not that easy—"

"It is that easy. You get her, you bring her, Maelstrom follows. We go home."

"I'm doing my—"

"It would be sad to see Neeman hurt because you couldn't fulfill your orders."

Selene refused to look away, but her body shook as her inner beast clawed at her stomach to be let out at the thought of Lorcan hurting Neeman.

"You would never obliterate this plane."

"Oh, you think so, do you?"

She chuckled. "You forget, I lived with you. You think I didn't know you were coming to this plane regularly? I smelled it on your sweat soaked, over sexed body every time you returned. You would never destroy the earth. You can't because then you wouldn't have anywhere to go to live out your sadistic fantasies. The ones that the others on the Council would banish you for."

Lorcan stared at her hard for a moment and then popped another candy in his mouth. "I have taken matters into my own hands. Things have been set in motion. You'll see your opportunity to strike and grab Danika soon enough. Just stay close to her and Maelstrom, and you will know when to make your move."

His gaze locked on hers again, and he brushed her hair behind her ear. "I know you think I hate you, but I don't. With that said, I won't hesitate to fulfill your mission if you won't and kill everyone you care about in the process— including your mother."

"My mother's father would never let that happen."

Lorcan sneered. "Who do you think suggested that I be the one to make sure you comply with his plan?"

Selene resisted the urge to pull away. Her mother's father had come up with the idea to kidnap Danika and imprison Mason? His grandson? She wished the news shocked her.

"I'll see you soon, and remember, to honor your family is to love your family."

"Hey! The movie's starting."

Selene whipped around to find Neeman coming back into the row. Her heart stopped, and then thundered. She looked back over her shoulder. Lorcan had vanished.

The seat next to her groaned as Neeman sat. "Are you all right?"

Tell him the truth. Tell him why she'd come and what Lorcan wanted her to do. Tell him he was in danger if she didn't betray her brother. *Tell him!* The words stuck in her throat like a lump of cookie dough.

"I'm fine." She sipped the new soda he'd brought.

"Are you sure? You look frightened. Was it the organ player? Did he do something?" Neeman scanned the theater.

"No. No," she said. "The boy didn't do anything." He stared at her hard, searching her face.

She threw him a smile and patted his arm. Then she turned to the movie screen. Out of the corner of her eye, she could see Neeman still looking at her. She hooked her arm in his and laid her head on his shoulder.

Her mind whirled. She didn't want Neeman hurt, but she couldn't do what Lorcan wanted her to. The Fae were wrong. Their plan to trap Mason would fail whether or not she helped. She believed Lorcan when he said he'd kill everyone she cared about, and that included Neeman. She couldn't let anything happen to Neeman... Or Mason. Question was, who did she care about more? If she had to choose, who would it be?

Her brother, or her lover?

CHAPTER NINETEEN

Selene spent the entire movie staring at the screen, but seeing nothing, Lorcan's words playing over and over in her head.

"Did you not enjoy it?" asked Neeman as they walked to the exit.

"I haven't seen a movie in so long. It was just like I remembered." She threw out the popcorn bag.

"Do you want anything before we go?"

"No, thanks." She patted her stomach. "I'm ready to burst."

He stared at her for a moment. "We should do this again. Gus is running a Star Wars marathon in a couple of weeks."

"Huh?"

He chuckled, and his smile slammed into her like being tackled by a hellion. Her knees wobbled, and her chest burned.

Neeman held the door open. She stopped, waiting for him to walk out ahead of her and then realized he held the door for her. It had been close to half a century since she'd experienced such gentlemanly kindness.

They waved to Gus back inside his little booth, and Neeman led her to an awaiting vehicle. He opened the back door for her, and she looked inside. Riley waved from the driver's seat.

"How did he know where to find us?"

"I called him while I was in the lobby." Neeman smiled again.

His countenance had changed. He seemed lighter, less stressed. It chafed her that she couldn't go anywhere or have even a moment of happiness without Lorcan trying to rip it away from her.

"How was the movie?" Riley asked as she slid in.

"Great."

Neeman hopped in his seat and threw Riley a hard look. "Drive."

All talking ceased as they made their way to Coven House— but that didn't bother Selene. Tangled up in her own web of thoughts and problems, she took solace in not having to carry on a conversation for a short time.

The more she relaxed into the leather seat, the more she realized how tense she'd been through the movie, and Selene found herself more tired than she could imagine. With everything she'd been through, she'd hardly taken a moment to really think. Watching the buildings whiz by, the rhythmical sounds of the road pulsing through her body lulled her into a hypnotic state.

Things had grown so much more complicated than she'd anticipated. If it was only the Earth being destroyed as he threatened, she might be able to carry that burden, but the torture of Neeman... Strangely that wasn't something she thought either she or her Demon would be able to handle.

When she'd lived in Chicago previously, it had been her, her mother, and Mason. No one else had mattered. She'd gotten soft. Possibly because of the loneliness, she'd been subjected to for the last two decades. But Neeman... He'd gotten inside of her soul somehow. He'd opened her up, made her feel, care. But the worst of it was— hope. Getting her to hope was the worst of what he'd done. He'd made her hope that there could be a chance for them. Hope she could start a new life. Hope she could finally find a family to belong to. But once again, the Fae were determined to ruin everything.

The car halted, and she opened her eyes, recognizing Coven House. Maybe if she ran, joined one of the human enclaves, and stayed away, they would leave Mason, Danika, and Neeman alone— knowing with her gone, they'd never get close enough to Danika to nab her. But how could she be sure? Lorcan wasn't an easy man to dissuade. If she ran, he'd hunt her to ends of the multiverse— but would that keep Neeman safe? Possibly. He wouldn't want to kill Neeman until she could witness it, up close and in technicolor. But she ran, and Lorcan ever found her... His punishment would know no bounds. To keep Neeman and Mason safe, it would be worth it, though. Her mother could fend for herself, the same way she'd left Selene to.

"Are you okay?" Riley's voice broke into her thoughts. He stared at her through the rearview mirror.

Neeman turned, and his eyes lit on her hand, which gripped the door handle. She swallowed and tried to force herself to smile, but couldn't make her cheeks work.

"Get out. Run. Leave. Keep them safe."

Ironic that Seraphine was the one who wanted to run away, and she wanted to stay and fight. She looked down at her hand. Her nails lengthened, and her head buzzed.

No. Not now.

She fought to keep her Demon down, but her vision

blurred, and she fading into the oblivion of sleep. The gate finished opening, and the car rolled up the driveway.

Selene bolted from the car before it had even stopped and made it to the house steps before Neeman caught her by the arm.

"What's going on?" His voice came out flat and emotionless, but his eyes probed for answers.

The words once more stuck in her throat. She wanted to tell him. To let him in, and have him tell her he'd keep her safe. That they'd figure it out together. All the loving words people who cared about each other said to help console and support each other in times of need. The words danced on her tongue, willing her to say them. To tell him the truth.

"*Let me out. Let me handle Lorcan. I'm the strong one,*" her inner Demon raged.

Selene's gut clenched as her inner Demon tried to pry her way out.

"*When I'm free, I'll protect Loverboy. I'll protect all of them!*"

"I'm tired," she managed. "It's been a long night." She could barely see him through the blurry haze of unconsciousness.

"Your eyes are turning purple again," he said. "Is Seraphine trying to get out? Why? What's going on?"

"Nothing. I'm just tired, and she can feel it."

"*Liar.*"

"You're lying. You're as pale as I am and have been since the theater. Something happened. Was it what I said on the train?"

"*Tell him. Then let me out so he and I can go destroy Lorcan together.*"

The door swung open, and gratitude flooded her for the interruption.

Mason stood in the doorway. For once, Neeman didn't pull

away. He moved closer to Selene, his body pressing against hers.

Mason looked between them. "Your phone is off."

Neeman removed his phone from his pocket. "We were at the movies."

Mason nodded. "Sherman's here."

"Let me out!"

"Who's Sherman?" Selene rubbed her temple, trying to stave off Seraphine's incessant screaming.

Neeman slipped his arm around her waist, and she was glad for the support as she almost lost control of Seraphine and passed out.

"What's he doing here? Are the others with him?" asked Neeman.

"You need to come in." Mason's gaze turned to her, and he looked her over. "What's happened?"

Selene only managed to shake her head.

Mason took a step closer and turned her face upward. Seraphine stared back at him.

"You will sleep," he commanded.

Seraphine chuckled. "Nice try, but you're not the one who can order me about, Mason."

"I'll take her upstairs and join you in a minute."

Mason didn't move.

"I can control it," Selene whispered. "I just need to rest."

He finally nodded and moved out of the doorway. Neeman slid his hand from her waist and ushered her toward the foyer. She pulled out of his reach.

"I'm not a child, Loverboy." Her voice wasn't her own, and she slapped her hand over her mouth. Seraphine had gained too much control. She cleared her throat several times.

Neeman's eyes turned to cold steel. "Sometimes, I'm not so sure."

"And what does that mean?" Seraphine spat. "You have no idea what's going on—"

Selene slammed her lips closed and regained control of her vocal cords, ending Seraphine's rant.

"It means..." He sighed and looked to Mason. Mason nodded and walked a few steps further into the house. "It means that I know something's going on with you though you won't tell me. When I got back from the movie lobby, you were terrified. Something or someone happened in there. Why won't you just tell me?"

"I—"

"Yes, tell him. Tell him everything. Why you came, what your plan is. You do have a plan, don't you?"

She took a deep, cleansing breath and closed her eyes, centering herself.

Go to sleep, she commanded her Demon. Seraphine grumbled but backed down.

When she opened her eyes again, her vision cleared, and the headache subsided. "I can't," she said.

"I'm not stupid, Selene. You may have convinced Mason about why you are here, but from what you've told me about your experiences in that other place, I know they wouldn't simply let you go. You're here because they want you here. They need something from you, and I can only assume it has to do with Mason."

She pressed her lips together in a tight line.

Neeman's eyes narrowed. "Fine. Don't tell me. But I won't help you if you aren't honest with me."

"I understand." Tears flooded her eyes, and she raced up

the stairs toward her room. Saving Neeman and the others was all she could do... even if it meant they hated her for it.

"There's one way to keep Loverboy safe."

Selene stopped with her hand on the knob to her bedroom door.

"One thing you could do to ensure he'd stay away. A way to push him away for good. If you push him away, Lorcan won't hurt him."

Selene's heart pounded. She bowed her head, and fat tears fell on the stairs below her. She didn't want to push Neeman away. She wanted to feel the safety of his arms. The touch of his lips on her skin. The taste of him lingering in her mouth.

"Let me out. I'll do it."

"No," she whispered. "I can do it." But she wasn't sure that was necessarily true.

Selene turned around and wiped the tears from her eyes. She'd do it to keep him safe. To get him to hate her. To keep him from looking for her— when she ran.

NEEMAN HELD BACK THE ANGER THREATENING TO SWALLOW HIM. HE'D opened up to Selene, and she'd begun shutting him out harder than ever. Obviously, he'd hit a chord with her about why she'd returned to Chicago. Should he say something to Mason? If Demons looking for her didn't make her flinch, he couldn't imagine what dangled over her head.

He stepped into the house. Coven members hung around the upper landing, whispering and looking down at him. The unsettling arrival of Sherman, one of the Three Kings of America, couldn't be a good omen. Sherman wasn't even the king over the Chicago area, which led Neeman to wonder why he'd come, and if the other Kings knew about his visit.

Neeman knocked on the door to the back study where Danika held her smaller meetings. William opened the door, his expression grave.

"Ah, there he is." Sherman stood. His tall, thin stature had inches on Neeman. The epitome of a New York banker, his dark suit and polished shoes screamed success.

Neeman shook Sherman's hand but looked to Danika. "Sorry to keep you waiting."

She gave a tight smile. "Have a seat."

Mason loomed behind Danika, ever the guardian protector.

"I'd prefer to stand if you don't mind," he said.

"It's fine," Sherman replied. "As I told Lord Danika, I've come to warn you all."

"What's happening?" asked Neeman.

"The High Council is coming. They heard about the bombing of the Tracking Squad training center, and they want to investigate."

"The High Council?"

The High Council lived in Romania and oversaw the entire Society from the Gothic Palace once rumored to belong to Dracula. Neeman found it pretentious, but that's how things were done in the Society. But if they were coming themselves... things we bad. Really. Bad.

"There has been mention of moving the trackers to a more secure location, from what I've heard," said Sherman.

"With all due respect," said Neeman. "That was the most secure location. The best minds in the world had created it."

"You misunderstand. They don't mean that the training center wasn't secure enough, they mean Coven House isn't secure enough."

"And what makes them think that?" asked Mason.

Sherman blew out a breath. "Let's be honest here. There's been more upheaval here in Chicago than in the entire Society in the last decade. Danika's parents, murdered. Danika almost murdered. Traitors in the midst, humans in an unsanctioned blood factory, underground blood market, rogues, Demons. Mason is the only reason the High Council hasn't forced Danika to step down as Lord. If it were anyone else, she'd be gone already."

Sherman's words rang true. Without the fear of Mason and what he might do, Danika would have been ousted a year prior.

"So, what do we do?" Danika asked.

Sherman's gaze moved to Neeman. "They're scared of what is coming. They've heard of the Demons returning. They want to make sure their security is assured."

"You mean they're cowards who want to hide behind my men's coattails." Neeman ground his teeth together, once again struck by the sheer selfishness of Vampires.

"And what about the rest of us?" asked William.

"I don't know," said Sherman. "I'm sure most of the Lords, their offspring, and mates will be secured if things get worse. Other than that, who knows what they'll do."

"Why are you telling us this?" asked Danika. "Shouldn't it be Melton here? He's the king of this area."

"Because, despite what my peers think, I believe that the four of you have done a better job at cleaning up the mess here in Chicago than most of the Lords in the US Territory could have. While I understand the real fear of what may be coming our way, I think the High Council is overreacting and not acting in the best interests of the entire Society."

"What do you mean?" asked William.

"They don't like the idea that there might be someone- or

something- out there stronger than they are. Especially Lucian. After all, it was he and his brothers who called for the eradication of the Demons from Earth decades ago. It's why he forced the Werewolves leave America and follow him to Europe, so he could control them, use them as protection from anything and everything. But also so he could keep his eye on them. Melton and Vinton do not agree that Lucian is overreacting. So, I decided to warn you myself. I must ask, though; is it true that other Demons have been seen here?"

"It is," said Mason.

"Then, can I assume that they are coming because of you?"

"Partly."

"What else do they want? Have you captured them? Questioned them?"

"We captured one," Neeman chimed in. "But it died."

Sherman looked at him. "Did it say what it wanted?"

Neeman walked a fine line. He didn't want to lie. Sherman risked a lot by coming and trying to save them all. That kind of honesty and loyalty were rare. But at the same time, he didn't want to involve Selene.

"He didn't tell me what he wanted," Neeman finally said.

Sherman looked at everyone in the group in turn. "What aren't you all telling me?"

They all stayed silent.

"I can't help you if you don't tell me what's going on," said Sherman. "If Demons are here, you need all the friends you can get. We all have to fight together if we want a chance of saving what's left of this planet."

"He might have spoken to someone else," said Neeman.

"Another tracker?"

"No." The weight of Mason's stare made the hairs on

Neeman's arms prickle. He didn't want to bring Selene into things. The fewer Vampires that knew about her, the better.

"Selene?" Mason asked.

Neeman nodded.

"A female?" asked Sherman.

"She's been... staying with me."

"If you think she knows why they are here, then we need to know," said Sherman. "Have you questioned her? Who is this woman? Is she a tracker?"

"No," said Neeman. "She isn't a tracker, she's... my guest."

Sherman raised his eyebrows.

"I'm not sure she will be very forthcoming," said Mason.

"Is she a vampyr?" Sherman asked.

Every ounce of Neeman wanted to protect her from Sherman. Even though he'd come as a friend, that could change in an instant. As a King of America, his rule was law.

"She isn't a vampyr," said Danika. "She's human."

"Even better. Then we'll make her tell us. Where is she?"

Neeman stared at Mason. Mason nodded slightly, and Neeman's gut clenched tight as a wet rope.

"I'll go get her." He prayed she would be cooperative.

Neeman stood outside the door to the bedroom. He wanted to grab Selene and run. He couldn't perceive a situation where a talk with Sherman would go well. In Neeman's limited interaction with Sherman, he'd gotten the impression that Sherman was a decent Vampire; but as a king, if he perceived Selene to be a threat, there could be no telling what would happen.

Neeman opened the door a crack and stopped at the sound

of giggling. Icicles shot through his body. He opened the door wider and stepped inside. Selene sat on the couch, straddling a house slave named Matthew.

Matthew squeezed her buttocks. Her head thrown back, she moaned as he kissed down her neck.

Anger coursed through Neeman at the sight and quicker than he could think, he jumped across the room, pushed Selene off Matthew's lap, and threw him to the floor.

"Neeman!" Selene screamed.

He lunged at Matthew, who scrambled away. Selene stepped between them, her eyes fearful.

"Neeman, stop!" She put her hand on his chest, but he tried to push past her.

Matthew got to his feet and held on to the fireplace mantel. "Neeman, I'm sorry. She didn't say anything. I didn't know she was yours."

"Get out," Neeman said through gritted teeth.

Matthew nodded and ran from the room.

Neeman's gaze turned on Selene, and he flung her hand away. "What the hell is wrong with you?"

"Lots of things."

"Do you have any idea what would happen to you if you'd drained him here?"

"I could've wiped his memory."

"Would you've? Would you have even thought about doing that before he went back to the barracks and told them all that you'd done something to him? And how had you planned on getting him out of here without anyone seeing him vomiting down the stairs?"

Confusion played across her features. "I... I didn't think about that."

He didn't say what he wanted to. Didn't tell her of the

excruciating pain that ripped through his heart at seeing her with Matthew. At realizing how little she cared about him. The impact of that knowledge threatened to crush him.

"That's the problem. You don't think, and now you're in trouble. Real trouble. Sherman, one of the Three Kings, is down there, and he wants to ask you about the shred Demon and why he was here."

She swallowed and blinked several times.

"Don't you get it? I can't protect you."

"I can protect myself."

Neeman planted his fists on his hips and stared at the floor. All his life as a vampyr, he'd been accused of not letting anyone in. Accused of not caring, of not sharing, of not opening up, and now he'd waded right into the mire of the same situation. Ironic.

"Okay, then. Let's go down there and explain to Sherman how you are Mason's half—sister who killed a Demon while in my care and how the Demons are here to get you and Mason. Meanwhile, the Fae have sent you here for another reason, which you won't tell me. Let's go do that."

She stared at him and bit her cheek. He wouldn't let her talk herself out of the hole she'd dug for herself— not this time.

"Neeman..." She reached for him, but he stepped out of range.

His chest squeezed as he realized that he'd been wrong about her. She wasn't his, and that sucked because his heart already belonged to her.

CHAPTER TWENTY

Something was definitely wrong with her. Something had been broken inside, or maybe it had never been right, to begin with. But those things had nothing to do with why she'd gone to the barracks and flirted with Matthew. Had nothing to do with why she'd brought him up to the room, knowing Neeman would find them sooner or later. That she'd done to shut him out, to push him away.

"To keep him safe."

Neeman strode from the room and stomped down the stairs. She followed, trying to form words that would make things okay between them, but was unable, again.

"If you crumble now, letting that cocky human grope us will all be for naught."

Selene let out a shuddering breath and nodded. She had to do was stay strong. It was the only way to throw off Lorcan.

They made their way past the prying eyes of the house members to a door she hadn't noticed earlier. A conference type room held an enormous wooden table surrounded by low leather chairs. Danika sat at the head with Mason standing behind. William sat at her left, and an older Vampire dressed in a dark suit sat to her right. He'd slicked back his white hair from his warm but calculating eyes.

"Have a seat." Sherman pointed to a chair opposite him.

She tried to catch Neeman's or Mason's eye, but both refused to look at her. She pulled out the chair and sat.

"I've been told you spoke to the Demon that Neeman caught," said Sherman.

"Tell him nothing."

"Maybe." She shrugged and crossed her arms over her breasts.

Sherman chuckled. "You have spirit. I like that. But this isn't the time or the place. What's your name?"

"Don't tell."

"Selene."

"Okay, Selene, so why were you talking to the Demon?"

She licked her lips. "I wanted to see what he was."

"Why were you with the Tracking Squad? Neeman said you were a guest there."

"I... stole a car to try and get out of town but stopped for a drink first. Neeman found me at a bar and took me to the compound to figure out what to do with me."

Sherman's gaze traversed her face. He inhaled, and his pupils dilated slightly. "Where did you come from?"

"Well, see, when a man and a woman—"

"Selene!" Danika's voice cut straight through her. But Sherman concealed a smile.

She needed to play the part of human militant. "Fine. I came from far away."

Sherman nodded. "What did the Demon say to you?"

She needed to get the conversation off the Demons. The

closer Sherman got to the Demons, the closer he got to her secret, and if he found out the Fae sent her, she didn't think his means of getting her to talk would be much different than Lorcan's.

"Nothing." She scratched at the surface of the wooden table. "Now, the Russians, on the other hand, they said something interesting."

Sherman sat forward and folded his hands on the table. "What do you mean?"

"I overheard them talking about helping Chase and going to Las Vegas."

Sherman looked to Danika. "You met with the Russians here, didn't you?"

"I did," Danika replied.

"How did you hear that?" he asked.

Every eye in the room landed on her. Exposing her ability to cloak herself wasn't a secret she was ready to spill yet.

Selene shrugged. "I have my ways."

The glint in Sherman's eyes had gone from amused to annoyed. He looked to Danika again. "I take it things didn't go well."

"They did not. I believe that they have been hiding Chase and are still in collusion with both Garon and Chase to take over," she said.

"Do you think they could have had something to do with the bombing of the training center?"

"It wasn't a bombing," said Neeman. "It was more Demons. They attacked right after the meeting went south."

"How many more?" asked Sherman.

"A dozen or so that we saw," replied Neeman.

"Why haven't they come back?"

"Mason took care of them," said Danika.

Sherman shook his head. "But if Mason is who they are after, now that he's been spotted, they'll come back."

"I killed them all," said Mason. "Another wave will come, but I bought us a bit of time before they figure out those are dead."

"Nice of Maelstrom to give us credit. I mean, we did most of the killing," Seraphine sneered.

"Do you know how they got through?"

"There has to be a portal, but we don't know where it is right now."

"It's a portal, how hard could it be to find?"

"Unless you know what you're looking for? Very hard," said Mason.

Sherman gazed at Selene. The intensity of it made her squirm. His aura radiated power and intelligence.

"It's too dangerous for you all here," Sherman finally said. "We need to find you a place to hide."

"I'm not going anywhere," said Danika. "I won't leave my coven or my company. And I refuse to run from Garon or my uncle."

"I'll be staying as well," said Mason.

"As will I," said Neeman.

"I'm afraid that might not be so easy. For you, especially Neeman," said Sherman. "The High Council will be here within the next day. They'll contact you to set up a meeting and will expect you all to be there. Neeman, you should prepare to move and have your guys moved as well."

"I won't go," said Neeman.

"You may feel that way now, but wait till you see them. They aren't the kind of Vampires that you say no to. Besides, I understand that you are loyal to Lord Danika, but your duty is to the Society as a whole, not just this area. You go where you are told to."

Sherman's phone rang, and he answered it.

Selene snuck a look at Neeman. He glanced at her, his face unreadable.

"I need to go," said Sherman. "Melton and Vinton are landing soon. They know I've been here. I lied and told them I came to pick up a new slave. I need to take someone with me." Sherman's gaze fell on Selene.

Her mouth dried like she'd eaten raw cranberries. She wanted to look to Neeman for help, but she didn't dare.

"We have plenty of humans here," said Danika. "But they've been given the option to pick their new masters. We had a meeting night a couple of days ago. It could take hours to go through everyone and find one willing to go with you."

"What about you?" Sherman asked Selene. "You don't belong to someone, I take it. Would you be willing? It would be a great favor."

"No." Neeman stepped forward.

A wave of relief washed through her.

Sherman looked up and locked eyes on Neeman.

"I'll go," Seraphine blurted.

Out of the corner of her eye, she saw Mason inch forward. Danika's gaze landed heavily upon her.

Dammit! Why did you do that?

"You wanted a way to keep him safe? Distance yourself from him."

She cleared her throat, and after a moment, she smiled. "I'll go if you'll give me a minute to collect my things."

"Of course," said Sherman.

"But I must make something clear first," she said. "There will be no sex, and no drinking of my blood."

"I understand. However, you may change your mind about that." Sherman winked at her.

Neeman stepped forward, and at the same moment, Danika stood. "Neeman, why don't you help Selene collect her things while we finish up."

Selene caught Neeman's face clearly for the first time since she announced she'd go with Sherman. His body stayed rigid as an iron pole. His eyes sparkled with a bright iciness. He said nothing but moved to the door to hold it for her.

Selene kept her head high as she strode from the room.

"Can you give me a moment, please?" Mason said. "I need to use the bathroom."

"Of course," Sherman replied.

Selene kept walking into the foyer and then up the stairs. Neeman's aura swarmed her, and her brother's ever looming presence hung just behind Neeman.

They all reached her bedroom, and she turned to face them. She wouldn't back down.

"What?" she said.

Mason crossed to her, his face a mixture of emotions. "This is a dangerous game you're playing."

"He's your friend, and he needs our help."

Mason's face darkened. "Don't lie to me. I know you're lying. Maelstrom even knows you're lying."

"It's not a big deal. He needed someone, and I'm not doing anything here. All I've done since I got back to this realm is hang out and wait for my fate. I can't do anything. No one knows what I am. I'm not allowed to go out by myself." She looked to Neeman. "I'm not allowed to talk to anyone. Not even the humans here in this house who think I'm one of them. I have more degrees than any human left on this earth, and I've been reduced to toilet duty so far and teaching toddlers. So, I might as well be useful. Besides, he's going to be meeting with the other Kings. Maybe I can find out something that will help."

"He won't take you with him to the meeting," said Mason.

"He will because he needs me as an alibi. I may only be there for show, but I know how to stay hidden and get around on my own. You don't need to worry about me. I can take care of myself... Okay, so maybe I haven't been such a good job of that so far, but I promise to be careful and stay in control. If I have any problems, I'll send a signal. Or call Neeman on my cellphone. I can do that now."

Mason stared at her for a long time and then turned to Neeman. "I don't like it."

Neeman's jaw worked hard, but his eyes held something different. Pain. "Neither do I. But what choice do we have? She's made up her mind."

Mason pulled her into a tight embrace. "You keep your eyes open and your mouth shut. Do you hear me?"

"Easy peasy."

He pushed her to arm's length and gave her a dubious look. *"I would die if anything happened to you, baby sister,"* he said in the old language.

"And I for you," she replied.

Mason kissed her on the head and then strode to the door. "I'll wait for you downstairs."

She nodded, and he closed the door behind himself.

"Oh." She snapped her fingers and moved to the table where Neeman's box sat. She placed her palm on it. *"Dilato."*

The wooden box grew until it was the right size again.

"Didn't want to forget to do that, in case..." She trailed off. She didn't want to say, in case they didn't see each other again.

But she was leaving with a Vampire. There would be no one to protect her from what was to come, except for herself.

"You still have me."

Neeman stepped up until their bodies almost touched. "Why did you tell him, yes?"

She licked her lips. The cool feel of his skin near hers made her blood pump. His hard chest pressed so close it chilled her through her shirt. His solid arms, near enough to crush her. She wanted to feel him. To touch him. To taste him. One last time.

"Because he asked," she replied.

Neeman raised his finger and stroked her cheek. "Why do you do this to me? You've gotten in my head, and keep spinning me around like a vinyl record. Have you been playing me this whole time? Manipulating me? Using me?"

She wanted to shout to him that she hadn't. That she wasn't using him. That she felt the same way and wanted to stay with him.

"I never used you, Neeman. You've known who I am from the beginning. I never hid myself from you."

He grabbed her by the hair at the base of her neck and yanked her to him. Her body pulsed with excitement, and her breathing hitched. He bent in close so that his fresh breath tickled her neck.

"You're lying again. I hear the pounding of your heart and the rush of blood through your veins. I smell your arousal at this very moment." He locked eyes with her. "What I don't understand is why you are lying."

"I'm not." Her voice came out strangled.

"Then look me in the eye and tell me. Tell me you have no feelings for me and that you aren't pushing me away on purpose."

She swallowed hard. "Neeman, I don't have feelings for you, and I'm not pushing you away."

He pursed his lips and nodded. "Okay, then. Go." He backed up and bowed. "Your Vampire King awaits you."

She located her purse and sweater, grabbed them both, and headed for the door.

"Don't look back. Don't look back. If you look back, you'll blow it."

She kept her shoulder square and her eyes ahead.

"Is that all you have, my dear?" Sherman stood at the front door.

She nodded. She had to admit Sherman wasn't unattractive. But she preferred Neeman's hard body and brooding scowl to Sherman's sophistication and grace.

A man walked forward, took her purse, and carried it outside for her. Sherman smiled and ushered her out the door. She looked over her shoulder at Mason, who held hands with Danika. Neeman was nowhere to be seen.

The man who'd taken her purse held the door to a sedan open. Sherman slid inside, and she followed. Anxiety swirled in her stomach like a vortex as the door to the vehicle closed. She peered out the window, praying to see Neeman once before they pulled away.

She reminded herself that she'd volunteered for this.

"And besides, I'm the most powerful being on this planet next to Maelstrom, so if anything goes south, you can always let me free."

Selene hoped that wouldn't be necessary.

"How long have you been out of your enclave?"

She turned. "I'm sorry."

"Your enclave. How long have you been gone from it?"

260

"Uh..." She scratched her head and tried to come up with a lie. What was the point? "A couple of weeks."

Sherman nodded. He gave her a gentle smile. "Were you looking for supplies?"

She returned his smile and then turned back to the window. "Something like that."

They pulled away, and her heart sank as the front door to Coven House shut without one last chance to see Neeman.

He laughed. "You aren't much of a talker now that we're alone."

"Sorry." She rubbed her brow. "All of that vibrato was just for show. I'm used to keeping to myself."

"Pretty girl like you? That's hard to believe."

His expression and tone seemed playful, but she wasn't sure how to answer. She rode in his domain now. With no Mason to keep her safe, and no Neeman to keep her in line, she was sure to blow it.

"You have beautiful eyes," he said. "I haven't seen green eyes like yours in years."

"Thanks."

She turned to the window. "Where are we going?"

"I'm staying in a hotel downtown. My counterparts will assume that I've bought you as a blood slave, so I'm sorry to say that we will need to stay in the same room."

"In the same bed?"

"If you wish it." He smiled broadly.

She sighed. This would only work if she was honest with him. Funny that she was able, to be honest with him and not with Neeman, or even her brother.

"Look, your highness—"

"Sherman."

"Sherman. I'm not sure what to say. You hold the fate of

several people I care about in your hands. You were kind enough to invite me to come with you instead of ordering me, and I was smart enough to comply, though I find I did not have to. You seem to be rather decent, and though I did go through a daddy phase, you really aren't my type. So please know, while I'm flattered by your flirting, I'm not interested. I'm sorry."

He inclined his head. "I understand. But know that if you ever change your mind, you would be welcome in my home and bed. Your scent is most enticing."

"You do me a great honor."

"Well," he said, with a glint in his eye. "Now that we have that out of the way, what do you want to do tonight? I have to go to a dinner meeting, but after, we have time to do anything you wish."

Was he offering to take her out?

"When was the last time you had a gourmet meal?"

"I... I don't remember."

"Wonderful. Then we'll get you a dress and some shoes and go to eat at The Marciano. You do like French cuisine, don't you?"

She hadn't had French food in so long she didn't remember the taste. "Anything but snails."

"Wonderful."

She chewed the inside of her cheek. "Why do I feel like you're buttering me up for something?"

He laughed. "Because I am. I have a final favor to ask."

CHAPTER TWENTY ONE

Good to his word, Sherman had taken her to an expensive dress shop and bought her whatever she wanted. For the first time in her life, she hadn't been extravagant. Her melancholy about Neeman left her, not even wanting to shop. But she'd promised Sherman to help him out, and so she'd gotten dressed up and gone with him to dinner, accompanied by the two other Kings, Melton and Vinton. Sherman's temperament told her that he hadn't wanted to eat with the other kings.

She'd done what he'd asked though. She'd played the game her mother had taught her and had been the perfect escort. She'd laughed at his jokes. Smiled and been pleasant and had even touched his arm on two occasions, everything to convince the other Kings that she was his human blood minion. She'd even convinced them of her sincerity by telling them what staying at Coven House had been like, and how she'd decided to choose Sherman as her master.

Toward dawn, they headed to Sherman's hotel. Her body

sagged with fatigue. She rubbed her temples and let the tingling sensation run through her body.

"Did you enjoy yourself tonight?" Sherman asked.

"The food was lovely, but the company stuffy."

He chuckled.

"Present company excluded, of course." She smiled.

"Of course."

Sherman's smooth air made her comfortable. She could see how being his minion would have its perks. He was handsome, sophisticated, rich...

Selene removed one of her heels and rubbed her foot.

They reached a brightly lit hotel, and Sherman ushered her inside. They walked arm in arm through the beautifully crafted lobby, every eye on Sherman. She imagined movie stars must have felt much the same as she did as everyone bowed to Sherman or moved out of his way and gawked.

It surprised her that so many vampyr and Vampires still traveled and stayed in hotels, but when you lived indefinitely, you had time to do those kinds of things.

Back upstairs, Sherman opened the door, and she marched to the bedroom and plopped on the bed, kicking off her shoes. She sighed and flexed her toes. It had been a long time since she'd worn heels for more than a couple of hours.

"I'm going to shower and prepare for dawn."

"I'll get ready out here. I don't have much to sleep in."

"I could send down for something if you want."

"Don't bother." She waved him off. "I usually sleep with very little on."

A sly smile crept over his face.

"Don't even think about it."

He raised his hands. "My dear, I wouldn't dare." He walked into the bathroom and closed the door. When the water began to run, she stood and stripped off her dress, draping it over the arm of a chair. She pulled off her hose and laid them on top. Then she rummaged in her bag for her cami, slipped it on, and put her hair up in a ponytail.

She slid under the crisp sheets of the bed to be flooded with memories of lying in Neeman's arms. She'd been able to push him from her thoughts for a good part of the evening. But now alone, she ached to be near him, and her conspicuously silent inner Demon mewled to be near him as well.

The tenderness of his touch. The feel of his hard body on hers. The look in his eyes as she'd told him she didn't care. It made her gut clench.

"Remember why we're doing this," said her Demon.

"I am. Every second. I am."

"Selene? Selene?"

"Neeman!" She jolted awake and scanned the dimly lit room, trying to orient herself. Sherman sat on the edge of the bed in a pair of dark blue silk pajamas.

"Are you all right?" he asked.

She rubbed her eyes, trying to rid herself of the horrible nightmare. The scent of the stone altar still filled her nose.

"You cried out in your sleep."

"I apologize." She pushed her bangs from her face. "I do that a lot, I'm afraid."

Sherman looked her over. She reached for the sheets and clutched them tight in her hands.

"You called for Neeman."

"Did I?" She chuckled. "That's strange."

It wasn't, though. She'd dreamed that Lorcan had Neeman tied to the altar and was torturing him.

Sherman's gaze lit on her neck, and he reached out and turned her head to the side.

His brows knit, and his lips drew into a grim line. "He's marked you." She jerked her head away and removed her hair from its ponytail. "Why didn't you say something?" Sherman pressed.

She shrugged. "It doesn't mean anything."

Sherman raised an eyebrow. "Marking is reserved for only those that share the most intimate bond of mates. Were I or any Vampire or vampyr to touch you now, he could call for retribution."

"But Vampires and vampyr bite blood slaves all the time without any repercussions."

"True, but we don't leave a mark. We lick the wound, so it leaves no trace."

Neeman hadn't told her that. "Well, I wouldn't worry about it. It was left accidentally in the heat of passion, that's all."

The dubious expression Sherman gave her made her shiver.

"We had some fun is all. I mean, you've met him, right? He isn't one to let people in. I'm sure it was just an oversight."

"Neeman isn't known for wearing his heart on his sleeve, that's true."

"See. And I'm not the only one he pushed away. I hear Lord Danika had a hard time with it as well."

Sherman raised an eyebrow. "Did you now?"

"What?"

He patted her leg. "Thou doth protest too much."

Busted. "Do you think if there were anything between us, he would've let me leave?"

"He obviously didn't want you to. I saw his reaction when you said you'd go with me."

"But in the end, he let me. Does that sound like someone who intentionally marked me?"

"What it sounds like and what it looks like are two different things. Either way, you should be careful. There are those in my Society who would rather kill you and dispose of the body than have Neeman find out what they did. Even if he didn't mean to mark you."

"But he's a vampyr. Why would Vampires care what he thinks?"

"Because Neeman and his squad have saved more Vampires than anyone else in our Society. Just because he's a vampyr doesn't mean he's considered a lesser."

"Isn't that rare?"

"Extremely. But he's owed favors by most of the Vampires in the world, including myself. He's a good man. If you were looking for one, you couldn't do much better."

She bit her tongue to keep from saying anything.

"Now," said Sherman. "Do you want to tell me what you're doing here?"

"What do you mean?"

"Please, Selene. I'm four hundred years old. Your eyes took on a purple tinge tonight at times, and your scent is so strong that I'm surprised the other Kings didn't mention it. But they are much younger than I am. I've seen your kind before. I know you aren't human."

Neeman lay in the bed that smelled like Selene and tried to keep himself from exploding with thoughts of what she and Sherman might be doing. He'd watched the night before, as

Sherman had escorted her like a queen, from Coven House. Neeman held no ill will toward Sherman. He'd been through a lot.

Several years prior, Neeman had helped Sherman track down his escaped breeding slave. The female had bolted before her due date, and Neeman had found both mother and child dead twenty miles away in a wooded area. The mother had strangled the child with its cord and then killed herself with a knife. It had devastated Sherman.

Neeman wracked his brain, trying to piece together what Selene was doing in Chicago. What wasn't she telling him?

She'd been sent by the Fae to do something, but who knew what. The scars on her stomach were a testimony to how far the Fae would go to get what they wanted. Or to get rid of what they perceived to be a threat.

Neeman bolted upright. What they perceived as a threat. Mason.

Selene was his sister and the only one equal in power. The only one he trusted enough to let in and let get close. But Selene loved Mason.

She wouldn't really do something to him, would she? With her, there was no telling.

Neeman rushed out of his room and down to the landing. He made his way to Danika's room and banged on the door. There was no answer.

"Mason? Danika?" He banged again.

The door next to Danika's opened, and William stepped out. "They aren't here."

"Where are they?"

"They went to the office for the evening. They should be back soon."

"I need to speak to Mason."

William's brows knit together. "Is something wrong?"

Neeman snorted. "When is something not wrong anymore?"

William nodded. "Too true. Is there anything I can help with?"

"No." He needed to calm down. He had no real proof. He could be wrong. "It can wait, I guess."

"Will you walk with me a minute? I need to head to the barracks, and I want to ask your opinion of Evan."

Neeman didn't want to talk about Evan. He wanted to figure out what the hell was going on with Selene. But maybe talking with William would help him clear his head. His obsession with Selene teetered on the unbearable.

"What about her?"

"I thought that you might be able to give her something to do."

They headed into the kitchen, and Neeman noticed the three roast chickens with vegetables and dinner rolls sitting out. Danika had been stress cooking again.

"Honestly, William, I've had enough of babysitting the brats for one century."

William stopped by the refrigerator to grab a bottle of Savor. He handed one to Neeman as well.

He chuckled. "I understand, it's just..." He looked at his bottle and turned it over in his hands. "It wasn't so long ago that I lived in an enclave trying to survive, cursing the Vampires for what they'd done to all of us. I understand why she wants to fight, to kick back against those who she sees as having destroyed the world. I don't want to see her life wasted by sitting around in a solitary room and rotting." William opened his bottle and took a drink.

"Then free her."

William covered his mouth as he almost spit out his Savor. He swallowed and then coughed several times. "Excuse me?"

Neeman shrugged. "Let her go. She isn't doing anyone any good here, and she doesn't want to be here. With the game changes, Danika has made pertaining to humans; you are correct. There is nothing else to do with her. But if you let her go... Then she's not your problem."

William stared at Neeman and said nothing for a minute. Neeman had seen that same expression many times. William wasn't prepared to let her go.

"Well," said Neeman. "I guess you could always take her for yourself."

"What?"

"Take her as your slave. Or minion, I guess is what they are now."

"I... I... I couldn't. I'm still a fledgling."

"No one cares about that, and I'm sure there are more than a few Vampires who would be happy you did. Besides, it's obvious you care for her, and if you want to ensure she doesn't end up somewhere that is going to get her beaten, turned, or worse, then I suggest you do something about it. Because no one else will."

William chewed the inside of his cheek.

For the first time, he wished he could turn Selene and make her bend to his will. The thought made him curse himself. What was he becoming? How could he even consider doing that to another person? The thing he hated most about himself.

"Something to think about." Neeman drained his bottle of Savor and put it in the trash. "I should check on my men and patrol if there's nothing else going on tonight."

"Sounds like a good idea."

Neeman headed for the back door. "Sherman hasn't

checked in, has he? We haven't heard any more about the Kings or the meeting with the High Council?"

"Not yet. I'm sure we will before dawn, though."

Neeman nodded, but the knot in his gut twisted like a hangman's noose.

He checked on his men, who were pent up and ready for a fight. Being so close to humans for a prolonged period wasn't helping. He rounded up his men and broke them into groups, sending them out to patrol for Demons.

The human tracking trainees were told to stay with the other humans. He didn't need to waste any more lives out there.

Neeman paired up with Riley and headed out to see what remained of their previous home. The complex had mostly caved in, leaving a giant hole.

"Looks like we won't be going down there any time soon," said Riley.

"Looks like. Come on. Let's check out the other side of the warehouse."

They walked around the exterior of the crumbling building and entered on the north side. They crawled over debris and came to a section that still stood. A yellow glint caught Neeman's eye.

"No way," said Riley.

Neeman shook his head in disbelief. His baby sat in the corner, the yellow paint only slightly smattered with dust.

"You are one lucky SOB, boss."

Neeman had to agree. "There's no way to get her out."

"If we took out a section of that wall, we could."

"That would take some finagling. Not something the two of us could do. She'll have to wait till things settle down. Come on, let's see if we can get the weapons."

Reluctantly, Neeman backed away from his car and hopped over downed shelves to the spot where they stored the heavy weaponry. Smashed crates of weapons had been strewn between cinder blocks and crushed shelving units.

Neeman and Riley gathered what they could and piled the equipment into the SUV. It wasn't even close to what they'd need if there were a real fight, but it was a start. He'd been smart enough to make sure their weapons weren't all stored in one place, but the most extensive cache had been at the compound.

After getting into the SUV, they started north to patrol. Barely anyone lived north of the pier anymore. Vamps tended to live near their jobs, and most of the society members preferred to be close to their own kind. Even so, no neighborhood could go unchecked.

They spent the night patrolling the area, and then Neeman and Riley returned to Coven House. They'd spoken very little, and despite his best efforts not to, Neeman had checked his phone a dozen times to see if Selene had called.

She hadn't.

He played and replayed their time together on top of the L. The feelings he'd shared. It was possible he'd scared her off, but something nagged at him that she'd pushed him away on purpose. A thought hit him and made his gut clench. Maybe because she wouldn't be staying. Perhaps she had to return to the Fae plane after she did whatever she'd been sent to do. Possibly because they had her mother.

He needed to talk to Mason. If she wouldn't talk to him, maybe she'd tell Mason the truth.

They pulled up to Coven House about an hour before dawn. William stood outside the entrance waiting for them.

"We have a problem," he said, approaching Neeman.

"Surprise, surprise." Neeman slammed his door.

"A couple of the trackers approached me. They want to feed."

Neeman shrugged. "And?"

"Well, it would be up to you, of course, but I suggested maybe they should go out to feed. Most of the humans here are spoken for."

"What did Danika say?"

"I haven't talked to her yet, because I didn't know what you usually do for blood."

What Neeman usually did and what his trackers did were two different things.

"A couple of them have girls in town they can go to. The others will need to be fed. There's a service I can call, but it's too late now. They'll have to wait till tomorrow."

"And there's one other thing. I overheard the trackers mention they want a service for their dead brethren."

Neeman rubbed his forehead. He'd been so wound up with Selene, that he hadn't even thought about his fallen men.

"There should be. I'll make arrangements with Doc to have their bodies readied for the service."

William nodded.

"We'll hold the burial tomorrow at the pier where the rest of our trackers are buried if Danika hasn't heard anything yet about the High Council."

"I don't know. She and Mason should be back shortly."

Neeman made for the group standing by the garage. His

squad seemed to be shrinking every day. And if they couldn't get the Demon problem under control, soon, they'd all be gone. For the first time in decades, he thought about the fact that his life could come to an end.

For the first time in a long time, the thought conflicted him.

CHAPTER TWENTY TWO

S elene spent most of the second day tossing and turning in the hotel bed while Sherman slept in the other room. The blackout curtains and roll—down steel window covers were enough that not a peep of light shown through. Even so, her dream left her shaken.

The feelings she'd been fighting before, she could no longer deny. The dream had proven it. She cared for Neeman. A lot. More than she should. More than she had for another man in her long life. Keeping him safe from Lorcan was no longer something she could be wishy—washy about. She would do it no matter the cost. After all, wasn't that what Mason had told her he'd do for Danika?

She ran her fingers over her collarbone, where the runes sat silently, awaiting the opportunity to awaken.

"He loves us. Loves us both."

He'd proven he wanted to be with her. No matter what. He knew what she was, and he hadn't run. He'd tried to bring her closer, to let her in, to care for her. Maybe when it was all over, they could be together. If she did what Lorcan wanted her to... Probably not. More likely than not, when Neeman realized the purpose of her mission, he'd want nothing to do with her. Nausea gripped her, and she rolled over in bed. She'd have to cross that bridge when she got to it.

AROUND TWO IN THE AFTERNOON, SHE TOOK HER PHONE FROM HER purse. She plugged it in like Neeman had told her to and moved from screen to screen until she landed on his phone number.

Her finger hovered over the call button, and minutes ticked by as she contemplated whether or not she should phone him. The desire to hear his voice threatened to overwhelm her.

Finally, as her phone dimmed, she pushed the button, bringing it back to life and the call connected.

"Don't be stupid."

After the third ring, she hung up and threw it on the bed. What was she doing? She'd just promised she'd keep him safe. What had she been planning to say?

Suddenly, her phone buzzed, making her jump.

She pushed the on button. "Hello?"

"You called?"

The sound of his voice soothed her like a refreshing wave of water over her fevered mind.

"How did you know?"

"Your name popped up on my phone when it rang."

"I didn't know phones could do that."

"So, did you need something?"

He didn't sound mad, but his tone wasn't inviting either. She swallowed, wanting to tell him she missed him. To apologize and tell him she did care— maybe even lo—

"Don't go soft now."

She squeezed her eyes shut, searching for something to say.

"Hello?"

"Yeah, I'm here. I just wanted to check to make sure the phone still worked. You know, in case I have a problem. I didn't think you'd be awake. Did I wake you?"

"I'm usually not awake, but I'm preparing for a memorial service for my fallen trackers."

"Oh. I'm sorry about that."

"Sorry about the attack?"

"Well, yes. And I'm sorry for your fallen comrades." She wanted to keep him on the phone. It was selfish to take him away from what he needed to be doing, but she'd been cooped up in the room for so long... "Were you able to retrieve all of the bodies?"

"There are still a couple unaccounted for."

"Well, I know one is in the hallway by the elevator on the floor I stayed on. He died before I could help."

He was silent for a moment. "Thank you. When we're able to get down there and start digging things out, we'll take a look."

Why did she have to make things so awkward? "Are you going to rebuild?"

"Probably not there. I went by, and it's pretty much demolished," he said.

"I'm sorry."

He snapped his gum. "You keep saying that."

She hadn't seen him chew gum in days.

"Well, I feel bad. The Demons were there because of me and Mason."

"When are you coming back?"

His question caught her off guard. She opened her mouth

but couldn't think of how to answer.

"Selene, I know you're trying to push me away, but you need help. What happens if your other self gets out of control? Who are you going to get chi from, Sherman?"

"Is that what you're afraid of? That I'm going to sleep with someone else?"

He sighed, and his voice somber. "No. I'm afraid for you. When they find out what you are—"

"I lived in this world since long before Vampires came out of the closet and started ruling things. I've had interactions with your kind before. I can handle myself."

"I'm sure you're right. Well, you have my number."

Her heart sank. This wasn't how she wanted it. She didn't want to leave it like this with him.

"Why did you let me leave?" she blurted.

"Excuse me?"

"You let me go. You didn't say anything to Sherman about marking me. You didn't even say anything to me about it. He said it's significant. Yet, you didn't try to stop me."

"I did try. Look, Selene, I'm not sure what you want from me. You made it clear you had no feelings for me. I'm not the kind of guy who goes chasing after a woman who doesn't want him. If you wanted to stay, I assumed you'd stay."

She swallowed. "You're right. I'll let you go so you can get back to your planning."

"Selene—"

"I don't want to wake Sherman."

"Wait—"

"I'll see ya, Neeman." She hung up fast enough that she didn't have to hear him backpedal. He was right, of course. It had been her choice to leave. She dropped the phone and threw her hands over her face. She had to keep it together.

"And you need to remember why we left."

Hearing Seraphine refer to them as "we" sounded strange. They'd never been "we" before, but everything had changed, and not just between the two of them. She'd changed.

Neeman had opened her up, and now she couldn't figure out how to stuff all her feelings and emotions back behind the walls she'd built around herself for years. She needed to hold the shredded pieces of her sanity together. At least until she finished her mission— then she could deal with everything else.

SELENE DRIFTED IN AND OUT OF SLEEP FOR MOST OF THE AFTERNOON. By seven, Sherman arose and took a shower. She sat in the bed, unsure of what she was supposed to do, and still weighed down by her conversation with Neeman. Sherman had guessed she wasn't human, but he'd called her a celestial— which was about as far from her true nature as calling a dog a cat. Nonetheless, she didn't correct him.

"I need to get my messages and make a few calls, and then I'll need to meet with the other kings again and see if the Salvatoris have arrived. Why don't you shower, and I'll have some clothes brought up for you to choose from?"

She'd obtained more clothing since she'd been back than even she'd thought possible. Sad that she kept losing it all.

"I can do that."

"Wonderful." He smiled and closed the double doors, leaving her to herself.

The shutters opened for the evening, and she got out of bed and opened the blackout curtains, revealing the city. It bustled with a cornucopia of life. Several tall buildings stood black and vacant against the skyline, but many smaller buildings lit up lively with vamps working. She looked north and wondered where Neeman might be and what he was doing at that moment. Was he thinking about her?

"Stop being stupid. You made a choice. Suck it up, princess. This fair maiden longing makes me want to rip out someone's heart and eat it."

"Shut up," she whispered.

Turning from the window, she walked to the bathroom. Her gut told her it wouldn't be long. Whatever Lorcan planned, it would happen soon. If only she could find a way out of the mission and keep Neeman and Mason safe.

Neeman worked on his remarks for the funerals, but couldn't concentrate. All night he'd hoped she'd call and when she had, he wished she hadn't. She exasperated him till the point that he couldn't think of anything but her. She'd pushed him away, and what? Expected him to chase her? How messed up was that?

He wished he had stood up to Sherman. Told Sherman that she was his, and he wasn't letting her go. But he'd been a coward, afraid of his feelings. And now it might be too late.

There was a knock on his door. He set down the pad of paper he'd been writing on and ran his fingers through his hair.

"Come in."

Mason opened the door and crossed, sitting in a large arm chair. "Sherman called. Lucian and the High Council have arrived. Danika told Sherman about the ceremony tonight for the fallen trackers."

Neeman nodded.

"The bodies have been prepared and are ready to be laid to rest. The families of the four trackers have arrived. Danika would like to start about ten."

"I'll get everyone prepared."

Mason stared at the table where Neeman's wooden box sat. "Have you heard from her?"

Neeman licked his lips. "She called a couple of hours ago."

Mason met his eye. "Is she okay?"

"Same, Selene."

Mason cracked his knuckles.

"She knows how to take care of herself," said Neeman.

Mason snorted. "That's what I'm afraid of. She always thinks she can handle herself, and she doesn't need anyone's help."

"Do you know why she's here?"

Mason stared at him for a moment. "I know she isn't telling me why she's here."

"So, you don't believe they let her go either?"

"I've dealt with the Fae. They are meticulous, if anything. They shut all the entrances to the Fae plane when they left, and so I'm not entirely sure how they opened a portal up, to begin with. But to answer your question, no. I don't think they would let her come back here."

"Do you think you're the reason she's back?"

Mason nodded. "It's very well possible, which is why I've kept my distance. I love my sister, and it has killed me to stay away, but I have to keep Danika safe as well as my sister. I can't chance the Fae or anyone else trying to use them as pawns to get to me. I can't protect them both at the same time, so I've kept Danika close and left Selene in your care. There isn't anyone else here that I trust more to keep Selene safe from the Demons and the Fae."

"They tortured her. She hides the scars with magic, but I saw them."

Mason's expression sagged, and a rumble escaped his chest. "The Fae aren't too different from the Demons in that regard. They'll do anything to protect their way of life. I've thought about it a lot since she's been back, and I'm surprised my aunt took her there at all. Fae prize purity of their race above all else. Her mother had to have known what would happen to Selene there."

"What kind of mother would take her daughter to a place where they wouldn't accept her but actually want to hurt her?"

"My Aunt Yelena was never one to think much of Selene or anyone else for that matter. She's always put herself first."

Neeman shook his head. That explained a lot. When you grew up with a selfish mother, it stood to reason you'd turn out similar. But Selene wasn't the same. He'd seen her kindness. She'd let him in, and he'd seen behind the superficial walls she used to keep people out. Selene was a passionate woman, strong and utterly amazing— he just wished she let people see that.

"The real question is, what are they holding over her? What do they have that's forcing her to do their bidding?" said Mason.

"Her mother?"

"That's possible. For as selfish as Yelena is, Selene always sought her mother's approval for everything."

"If only she'd tell us, we could protect her."

"Possibly not," said Mason. "Fae have powers beyond the security measures that even we have in place."

"Like what?"

Mason shrugged. "Opening locks. Spells that can be cast on

people without even touching them. Influencing people. The elders can even cloak themselves."

"Cloak?"

"Diminish their appearances, so they disappear, which is what I suppose Selene did so she could sneak onto Coven House grounds the night the Russians came. I didn't mention it before because I didn't want to freak anyone out," said Mason.

Neeman's stomach soured, and his brain worked overtime.

"What?"

"The movie theater," said Neeman. "I left for a few minutes, and when I got back, Selene had gone white as paper. Her whole demeanor changed. As if someone had gotten to her. She's been pushing me away since then."

Mason steepled his fingers. "If she was sent here for a reason, it makes sense she wouldn't have come alone. They would have someone to make sure she fulfilled her duty."

"Another Fae?"

"Undoubtedly. And not just anyone. Someone who could handle her. Someone she'd be afraid of. And Seraphine is strong enough that I've never seen her truly afraid of anyone but our father."

"As strong as you?"

"Not quite. She's only half Demon. I haven't seen her, Seraphine, in ages. But Seraphine was no cowering kitten when we lived in the Demon realm."

Neeman stared at the table in silence. More than ever, he was worried about Selene being out there with Sherman. Hell, with anyone but him. Not that anything qualified him to take care of her, but for some reason knowing that a Fae skulked after her...

"You care for her," said Mason.

Neeman looked up. He couldn't deny it. His feelings for her were a surprise to even himself.

"I don't like her being out there with Sherman."

"Me neither," said Mason. "But there was no way to say no without him thinking something was up."

"How do we get her back?"

"I assume she will come home when Sherman leaves."

Neeman's heart squeezed. "And if she doesn't?"

Mason's brows furrowed. "Let's cross that bridge when we get to it."

Neeman nodded.

"You'd be good for her," said Mason. "She needs a strong hand. Someone who can keep her focused."

It was weird talking to Mason. He and Mason had barely said anything to each other since Mason had mated Danika. Not that they'd been bros before, but they'd at least had mutual respect.

"I've never apologized for what happened with Danika," Mason continued.

"There's no need. She's a big girl. She made her choice."

"Still. I knew you had feelings for her, and I didn't respect that."

"Things turned out the way fate designed. I see now that Danika and I were never right for each other. I could never give her what you do."

"Maybe you could be what Selene needs," said Mason. "Heaven knows you could give Seraphine a workout if the two of you ever sparred."

"Maybe."

Mason chuckled. "Well, I think we've done enough touchy feely stuff for one year."

"Absolutely." Neeman stood. Mason followed suit.

"I'll let you get ready for the ceremony." Mason headed for the door and stopped. He turned and met Neeman's gaze. "I know that you and Selene haven't known each other long, but I've seen a change in her since she's been in your keeping. I've never seen her care for anyone but me before. You should know that if you two did end up together, I'd be proud to call you brother."

Neeman's chest tightened. "You, too."

Mason left without another word.

Neeman stared at the door for a long time. He needed to get Selene back. Not only for her safety but his sanity as well.

SELENE DECIDED TO NOT GO OVERBOARD. SHE PICKED OUT A BLACK dress, a nice pair of slacks and blouse, a pair of jeans and a couple T—shirts, half a dozen pairs of underwear, a pair of pajamas, some sensible pumps, and pantyhose. She then asked for a small suitcase. She was sick of having to leave everything behind because she didn't have something to keep them in.

She slipped into the black crepe dress, which hugged her curves and ended conservatively below her knee. She wanted to throw on her jeans and T—shirt, but she and Sherman were going somewhere important.

Sherman had been nothing but a gentleman to her since she'd arrived. His cultured air and extensive knowledge of art and history made him easy to be with and fun to talk to. He was the kind of man her mother would've thrown her at and insisted she pursue him for his security. But for all the niceties that Sherman possessed, her heart ached for Neeman.

Even her inner Demon missed Neeman's hard body and icy stare.

"Are you about ready?" Sherman entered the room.

"I think so."

He handed over a red velvet box.

She opened the lid with a crack. Inside lay a beautiful emerald necklace and matching earrings.

"I... I can't accept these." She snapped the lid shut and held it out to him.

"I insist. You're helping me out of a tight spot, and you deserve to have something for it."

"You've already given me clothes, food, an incredible hotel room."

"And now these. Take them. They match your eyes so nicely. Besides, I have one more favor to ask of you."

"What's that?"

"I'm having a meeting later tonight, and I need you to stay here while I attend."

"Is the meeting with Lord Danika?"

He paused. "It is, and you going would be more than a bad idea. The High Council members are even older than I am. They'd figure out what you are in a heartbeat, and there is nothing anyone could do to protect you from them."

A shiver of dread raced like icicles through her veins. The rumors surrounding the High Council were legendary. In all of her time on Earth, she'd never seen one, nor had she ever wanted to.

"Why don't I help you put on your necklace and then we can go."

"Sure." Selene turned and lifted her hair. Sherman removed the necklace and placed it around her throat.

His cold fingers lingered on the side of her neck right where her pulse throbbed.

"Let me get these earrings on." She slipped from his grasp and walked into the bathroom before he could get any unwanted ideas.

SELENE SAT NEXT TO SHERMAN IN HIS EXECUTIVE SEDAN, HER HANDS clutched in her lap. They pulled in behind the long line of limousines, executive cars, and SUVs.

Sherman's driver opened the door and helped Selene out. She waited for Sherman, her eyes on the large crowd that had gathered at the gravesite north of the demolished tracker compound.

"Wow," said Sherman. "It really is destroyed. Such a waste."

"Be glad you weren't in there when it started coming down."

He looked at her. "You were?"

"Caught under a piece of the ceiling in the arena, to be exact."

His brows furrowed. "How did you get out?"

"Neeman."

Sherman smirked and nodded.

They walked toward the ceremony, and she hung a step behind to keep up the appearance of being his slave. All eyes followed her and Sherman, and for the first time, she didn't like being the object of people's attention. Even the prying eyes and wagging tongues made Seraphine uncomfortable.

Sherman moved to the front of the crowd, and Selene waited in the rear.

These weren't her people.

Danika stood before the gathered crowd, speaking of the bravery of the Tracking Squad. After several minutes, she turned the lectern over to Neeman.

Selene sucked in a breath at the sight of him. She'd not seen him in anything but his tracker outfit, but tonight he wore a dark three—piece suit that hugged his chest and arms and tailored nicely to his waist. He flipped through several note-cards, looked up, and scanned the crowd. His gaze landed on her, and his shoulders relaxed. She smiled. She couldn't concentrate on any of his words as their eyes stayed locked on each other.

"He's doing well." Lorcan's voice sent a chill down her limbs.

She refused to turn. "It's a solemn ceremony. I'm not sure 'doing well' is the way to describe what he is doing."

"True. He isn't the reason I came anyway. Well, not entirely. The opportunity I spoke of is tonight. There will be a meeting. Maelstrom will be distracted. When he is, grab Danika and bring her to your old apartment. I'll take it from there."

"Are you going to hurt her?"

"Not that it is any of your concern, but no. And we won't hurt Maelstrom either, once you tell him where she's been taken. Then you and I will bring them back triumphantly, and you will sit at my side as my wife."

Anger bloomed in her stomach, and she clenched her fists. "I'm never going back with you."

"Let me have him."

"I'm sorry to hear that. I had hoped that we could let bygones be bygones." He stroked her hair from her neck.

She shrugged his hand off and bit the inside of her cheek to keep from unleashing her disgust on him. "Not bloody likely."

"Then, think of it this way," said Lorcan. "You and Neeman will be free."

"Free to what? Defend against the Demons alone?"

"When Mason's gone, the Demons will return to their own plane."

"How can you be so sure?"

He patted her shoulder. "I can't."

An idea shot through her mind like a bullet. Her heartbeat quickened as adrenaline flooded her. She closed her eyes and breathed in deep and slow. She couldn't give Lorcan one inkling that she might have a plan of her own.

"So, I bring her to the apartment, and you'll go home and shut the rift for good?"

"Yes."

She turned to face him. His piercing eyes bore into her, but she refused to lose her nerve.

"Do I have your word as High Elder of the Fae? If I bring Danika to the apartment, you will leave the Earth realm?"

His eyes narrowed, and he tensed. "You think I would give you my word so easily?"

"Fine. Don't. I'll tell Mason what you plan to do, and he'll rip a hole in the universe so big that every Demon my father has will flood into your precious sanctuary and tear it apart."

"You wouldn't dare."

"You beat and tortured me. I've lost just about everything I am because of you. I have nothing left. So, you can either promise me or suffer the wrath of my brother and father."

The thin tightrope line she walked threatened to snap with one small breeze. If he wanted, he could pull her through a rift before anyone knew what had happened. She couldn't spend another hour tied to that stone altar.

"How dare you threaten me."

She clasped her hands behind her back to keep him from seeing her shake. "What will it be?"

"Let it be recorded. You have my word." A wisp of light flew from his mouth and snaked into the sky. A whisper echoed on the wind, carrying his word into the record books.

She nodded and faced forward again, hugging herself.

"Do your job well, Selene." Lorcan's fingers brushed her cheek. "Your family is counting on you."

"Not my family."

He inhaled, and then his lips grazed her neck. "Gods above, how I've missed you in my bed," he whispered. He ran his palm down her arm.

"I suggest you remove that hand before I break it," she said through clenched teeth.

Lorcan chuckled. "Willful as always. I miss that most about having you tied to the altar. Our sessions always left me so... pent up."

Selene whipped around, but he'd gone. She clamped her lips together, refusing to cry. Her blood pumped hard, making her head throb.

"You should have let me kill him."

"Right, because what we need is to be hunted by Fae and Demons."

She scanned the area, but Lorcan had vanished. Her sights stopped on two identical men standing with a light—haired, vulture—like man, wearing a long dark coat, behind a cluster of trees, apart from the group.

The Russians she'd overheard at Coven House days before. They'd said they were going to Las Vegas but hadn't. A chill ran through her. She glanced at Neeman. She didn't want to cause a scene, but something wasn't right.

The three men walked toward the street.

"Follow them," said her inner Demon.

Neeman finished speaking and stepped down. She should tell Neeman about the men, but there wasn't time.

He walked to the first coffin with Danika. Together, they threw dirt on top, and the casket lowered into the Earth. A woman followed them, clutching onto a man.

Selene watched the Russians get farther away. She didn't want to leave Neeman, and she'd accompanied Sherman. She couldn't just leave.

The men disappeared around the corner of the crumbling compound. Dammit.

The families gathered in a group to cry, hug, and lend support to each other. Selene turned from the scene and walked toward the compound where the men were getting into their car. She hurried as fast as her heels and tight dress allowed, but she was unable to catch up before the sedan disappeared.

"I could follow them. I'm fast enough."

"Shut up." Her hand rested on the wall of the compound. Memories of being trapped under the falling stone caused her gut to clench. "This is what you did the last time I let you out."

"I saved your life."

"You almost got us killed."

She stared at the spot where the car had been. She might still be able to catch up if she ran now, but doing so would cause even more problems. Lorcan had told her that tonight was the night. She needed to stick close to Danika, not follow the Russians. Whatever they were up to wasn't her immediate problem.

She ran her fingers over the compound, following the wall around the side to a hole in the cinder blocks.

"Hey!" A strong hand wrapped around her arm. "What are you doing?" Neeman's icy gaze met hers.

Her body tingled, being near him.

"Keep him safe."

"I wanted to see what was left," she said.

"The rest of that place could crumble at any minute." His eyes held concern.

She hadn't thought about that. "Your speech was nice."

He cocked an eyebrow. "Nice?"

"Okay. It was... I don't know. What do you want me to say? It was nice. You did great. You look amazing in that suit. You seemed to help those families."

The corner of his mouth curved up. "I look amazing?"

She blinked.

"Typical male."

"Well... you always look good, but in a suit, you look..."

"Amazing?" He stepped closer, and she backed into the cold stone.

He lifted a finger and ran it under the edge of her necklace. His expression hardened. "Nice."

"Thank you." Why couldn't her voice and her head work together? She needed to tell him something, but she suddenly couldn't remember what.

"Sherman must have spent a pretty penny on it. Earrings too." His stare bore into her.

"Probably."

"What did you give him in return?"

She clutched her purse. "Are you accusing me of something?"

"I'm simply asking."

"Would you be upset if I gave him something in return?"

Neeman stepped so that he almost touched her, his eyes bright under the street lamps.

"I don't think upset begins to describe what I would be."

Words failed her. The nearness of his body made her inner Demon purr.

"Neeman..."

"What?"

"I told you—"

"That you have no feelings for me? Yes, I remember. But I've been thinking."

"That's not good." He was smart. If he'd figured out what she planned to do...

"Let me out. I can take care of Loverboy. You're too weak. You'll tell him. But I won't. I'll keep him safe from Lorcan."

"I think you're scared. I think someone here is manipulating you. Maybe they threatened you. Maybe the Fae have your mom. I don't know. What I know is I won't let anything happen to you. I won't let them hurt you. I can protect you."

Selene bit her lip as her knees shook. He couldn't protect her. She was the one who had to protect him.

"Not you. Me. I can protect him."

He reached out, wrapped his large hand around her neck, and squeezed, massaging it with his fingers. He pressed into her, and his musky scent enveloped her. She'd never had someone so willing to help her. She'd been fending for herself for so long just hearing him say those words made her want to say yes. Fear and excitement swirled in her veins.

"Kiss me," he demanded.

"No."

Her desires collided with Seraphine's. For the first time, Seraphine was the level—headed one, and she was the one being ruled by her emotions.

"We can't be together," she said, more for herself than for him. She couldn't give in.

"Why?" His eyes probed her for the truth as his hand caressed her neck, reminding her of the pleasure he'd brought her previously.

"I don't care about you." The lies clung to her mouth.

"You're lying."

"Let me out."

"What do you want from me?" she cried. A headache clustered and stormed her mind.

He leaned in closer, his lips an inch from hers. His tight body swathed in the designer suit rubbed up against her, making the chiffon of her dress brush against her nipples.

"I want you." He looked her dead in the eye, and her resolve almost broke.

"I can't." A tear leaked from her eye.

"Why? Tell me the truth."

The headache doubled as Seraphine clawed her way toward the surface. Selene fought to keep control of herself, to the point that her limbs shook.

"Why can't you tell me? Why are you here? Who is your contact?" The pain multiplied till she couldn't concentrate.

"He's watching me. He'll hurt you."

"Who?"

"Don't tell him."

"Lorcan," she blurted. Tears streamed down her cheeks, itching her skin. "He's here. He's everywhere. He saw me with you, and he figured it out. He told me if I don't do what he sent me here to do, he'll take you and torture you the way he did me."

Neeman blinked several times. "This Lorcan is the one who hurt you?"

She let out a shuddered breath. Seraphine was right; she was weak.

"I have to do what he wants. You're strong, but no one should endure what I have. Go, Neeman. Leave me to my fate. I'm nothing but trouble like you said before."

"I don't care what he threatened. Let him come for me." He swooped in and kissed her hard. His arm snaked around her waist, and he pulled her close. Her mind fuzzed over, and she kissed him, giving him all that she had.

She couldn't stand it if anything happened to him. Despite what she said... she loved him. He'd seen her at her worst, and she'd done her worst to him, and he still stayed. Her Demon roared to life within her. She broke the kiss and pushed away, clutching her chest.

"What is it? What's wrong?"

She bent at the waist and sucked in large breaths. "It's Seraphine. She wants out."

Selene stared at her pumps, trying to keep from blacking out. Now was not the time. This couldn't be happening.

"You've ruined it all by telling him. Lorcan will see. I am the only one who can save us all now."

"What can I do?" Neeman pleaded.

"I need Mason," she gasped.

She tried to concentrate on the sound of Neeman's shoes, hitting the pavement.

"Not now. Not your turn," she said.

Her nails lengthened, and her fangs filled her mouth.

"No. No. No." She turned and dug her nails into the cement wall.

"Selene!"

She turned her head.

Mason walked quickly toward her, with Neeman in tow. "You need to stop her."

A wave of pain rippled through her. "I can't. I don't have my amulet. You do it. You can command her not to rise. I know you can."

"You're strong enough," said Mason.

The skin on her forehead split at her hairline. It wasn't possible. Seraphine wasn't allowed to manifest fully without her permission.

Seraphine cackled. *"Move over."*

"Mason. Do something," she cried.

Mason locked eyes on Neeman and then looked back at her. "No. You are the daughter of a god. You need to do this yourself."

"What?" She shuddered and small horns pressed out of her skull through the split skin.

"Do it," he commanded in the ancient tongue. *"Control her. Contain her."*

"I can't!" she screamed.

Neeman stepped up to her and grabbed her wrists, twisting her, so she faced him. His eyes met hers.

A wave of desire coursed through her so strong she almost climaxed.

What the hell?

"Let her out." His voice was gentle yet firm.

"No, Neeman."

"I want her. I want to see her."

Panic overtook Selene, and then, everything began to dim.

NEEMAN GRABBED SELENE AS SHE WENT LIMP. HE COULD DO THIS. HE knew he could. No matter what happened.

"We need to get her out of here," said Mason.

"I'll get her to the car." Neeman slipped his arm under her legs and lifted her. The touch of her supple body in his arms once more made his soul feel complete.

"You can take me wherever you want, Lover." It was Selene's voice, but the husky, silky tone was someone altogether different.

The same amethyst gaze he'd seen the first time he met her stared back at him. Fangs protruded from her mouth. The sight both excited and terrified him.

"So, where are we going?" she asked. "Or do you want to take me here against the wall, in front of everyone?"

"Seraphine!"

She turned and looked at Mason.

"Awww... It's the human non—equivalent of my brother. You should let Mael out. We could have so much fun." She giggled.

Mason took a step closer, and his eyes glowed like embers. "You need to sleep now and let Selene out."

"You can't order me around, Mason. I've been caged too long. And I have no intention of going to sleep so soon. I have a job to do. One that my lesser half is too weak to do herself." She ran a long fingernail down Neeman's cheek. "Besides. I want to spend some time with my Loverboy."

"Why don't we get you to Coven House, and we can spend time together there?" Neeman asked.

All of Selene's features had accentuated. Her cheekbones more prominent, her lips a darker shade of ruby. Her eyes shone like faceted jewels. She exuded sexuality in a primal way that called to him.

Her eyes narrowed, and she snickered. "Oh, sweetie, it's not going to be that easy. I need to go out. Not back to the one place where you can tie me down and shove a needle in my arm till I fall asleep, and my lesser half wakes up in my place."

"Actually, I want to spend time with you." He wished it wasn't the truth, but he did. He wanted to take her anywhere he could and bend her over and—

A sly smile spread over her face, making her fangs even more prominent. She leaned in and sniffed his neck before snaking out her tongue and licking up the side. She purred.

"I see that you do. I promise you, Lover, one night with me, and you'd never want her again."

Neeman bent his head close to her; every inch of his body anticipated the pleasure that could be experienced at her hands. "Prove it." He kissed her hard.

She licked across his teeth, then ran her tongue over the roof of his mouth. Her scent intensified, and he ached to bite her. He set her on her feet, and her hand cupped him between his legs, making him groan.

"Seraphine, stop behaving like that in public." Mason rushed forward and grabbed her by the arm.

Neeman tried to control his mounting lust, but the effect she had on him grew too strong for him to deny. Seraphine spun and planted her palm in Mason's chest.

Mason sailed through the air and landed hard on the ground several feet away.

"Seraphine!" Neeman reached for her, but she rounded on him and held out her palm. The gleam in her eyes made him stop in his tracks.

"I like you, Neeman, but I'm not her, and I'm not above hurting you." Seraphine's smile fell, and the purple color to her eyes diminished. She looked around, bewildered. "Mason! Help me," she yelled. Then she convulsed, and when her eyes opened, they grew purple again.

"Oh, that was new. She doesn't like me threatening you. But it doesn't matter. After I fully transform, she won't be able to get out again until I say so."

Mason flipped back to his feet. He advanced on Seraphine, speaking in a language Neeman didn't understand. His eyes burned golden, and his deep voice resonated like a bass drum.

Mason's fangs descended.

Seraphine's eyes widened, and she backed up.

Just as Mason reached out to grab her, she yelled, *"Obscuro."* And disappeared.

Mason roared and rushed forward, swinging wildly, but she was no longer there.

Danika raced around the building. Mason turned to her, and his shoulders slumped. "Are there more Demons?"

"No." Neeman stepped forward. "Yes and no."

"What does that mean?" She stepped to Mason, and he enveloped her in his arms.

"It's Selene," he said. "She's lost control, and her Demon, Seraphine, has taken over."

"What's she going to do? Where did she go?" Danika looked between the two men.

"I don't know," said Mason. "It depends on whether Selene can regain control. If she can't..."

"If she can't, what?" asked Danika.

"Then, the chaos that will ensue in the next twenty—four hours could be catastrophic."

"We need to find her."

"She disappeared," Neeman answered. "She could be anywhere."

"Lord Danika?" At the sound of Sherman's voice, they all turned. "The High Council is awaiting us."

"We're coming." She straightened her skirt.

Sherman turned to Neeman. "Have you seen Selene, by chance?"

"I think I saw her get in a car." Neeman wasn't sure why he lied, other than to protect Selene's identity.

Sherman nodded. "Very well. We should go too."

Neeman nodded and followed the group to the cars. He had no interest in going anywhere except to find Selene, but right now, he had a job to do.

CHAPTER TWENTY THREE

"*Stop!*" Selene yelled.

Seraphine laughed.

Selene witnessed everything Seraphine did and felt every pound of the pavement under her feet, but she wasn't in control. She could do little more than sit back and watch as Seraphine ran through the darkened streets toward the downtown area.

"*Where are we going?*" she asked.

"To find Lorcan."

"*Don't be stupid. You can't find him unless he wants to be found. You used my magic. How did you do that?*"

"Oh, baby girl. While you've been getting your kink on, I've been paying attention to the changes inside us. Like right now. You can see and feel everything I do. We're closer than ever now, you and I."

"*You used my magic. Any Demon on this plane will have felt it. They'll be looking for us.*"

"Let them find us. I can take them all, like before."

Fear shook Selene to the core. Her lungs burned as she continued toward the lights of downtown. She reached deep inside and practiced the things Mason had tried to teach her. She located her center. The spark of magic deep inside that was her, Selene. She followed the thread that wove through her body. Her arms, her legs, every part of her.

Concentrating, she pulled on the magic like pulling on the reins of a horse. Nothing happened.

"Nice try, sister, but you'll never be more powerful than me."

Selene cursed and tried again. She let her mind wander over every inch of her body, feeling the muscles and joints in turn. The magic pumped through her veins. Again, she pulled, and this time her body stopped.

"What the hell?" Seraphine said.

"*As you said, we're closer than ever. Guess you aren't the only one who can climb back out when she wants to,*" said Selene.

"Don't bother. I've always been stronger."

"*I know you think I'm stupid, but you have to trust me. I know what I'm doing. If you kill Lorcan, the entire Fae nation will come after us. We have to do things my way.*"

"No. He dies."

Selene let the thoughts and feelings of her Demon half wash over her. "*You don't want to kill Lorcan because of Neeman. You want to kill him because he tried to kill you.*"

Seraphine chuckled. "Wow, you're smarter than I gave you credit for."

"*It was all a lie? You don't care about Neeman?*"

"He doesn't care about me. He just wants you back."

"*That's not true. He wants you as well.*" Selene hated to admit it, but she'd seen the look in Neeman's eye when he'd told her Demon he wanted to spend time with her. He'd meant it. The curiosity in his gaze made Selene jealous beyond belief. She wouldn't let anyone endanger him, even herself. She reached out and made her arm jerk.

"What are you doing?" Seraphine laughed.

"*Taking my body back,*" Selene replied. She forced herself up through her veins into her limbs.

"Stop it. You're going to hurt yourself."

"*Never. I'll never stop. This is my body, my life, not yours.*"

Her inner Demon never had learned to shut Selene down.

"And what about me? When you unleash me, it's my body. I'm part of you. A part you may not like or want, but I'm here just the same. You can't get rid of me."

Selene pulled on the magic inside her. She had a job to do. She couldn't fail. If she did, Neeman would die. "*Watch me.*"

There was a loud crack several blocks away. Seraphine turned and sniffed the air.

Demons.

"*We better come to an agreement quick,*" said Selene. "*Or we're both dead.*"

Seraphine growled.

NEEMAN PULLED UP TO DANIKA'S OFFICE BUILDING AND STOPPED THE SUV.

"Our job is to protect Lord Danika." Neeman turned to Riley and Stephos. "No matter what happens in there, with me, or anyone else, you keep her safe."

"Are you expecting trouble?" asked Riley.

"Let's say it wouldn't surprise me."

He tried to focus his thoughts on the issues at hand, but his mind kept straying to Selene and where she might be. Who knew what Seraphine had already gotten them into.

"Are we going, boss?" asked Riley.

Neeman blew out a breath. "Yeah." He opened his door. Riley and Stephos followed suit and walked with Mason, Danika, and Sherman to the entrance of the building.

A second group of trackers jogged up and met them as Neeman scanned for signs of trouble.

"You three check the perimeter and stay by the front exit. No one comes in without my or Lord Danika's say so. Everyone keep their phones on and text every five minutes, so I know we're good."

"Yes, boss," they said. Then the three headed out.

He turned to Stephos and Riley. "You two will take the ground floor elevator. Stay there with the other guard and monitor the lobby."

The men nodded. Together they entered the building. Neeman waited till Danika, Mason, and Sherman got into the elevator before joining them. The doors closed, and the elevator pulled them up to the conference room.

"When we get in there, be polite, but give nothing away," said Sherman. "There's no telling what kind of mood the Venerable King Lucian could be in."

The doors opened. Tension clouded the hallway.

"I'll go first," said Sherman.

The wooden conference room doors stood ajar. Sherman pushed them open and stepped inside. Danika took Mason's hand and followed Sherman. Neeman brought up the rear.

Everyone stopped. Electricity charged the air.

"What the hell?" Danika yelled.

"Easy," said Sherman.

Neeman stepped into the room. At the other end of the

conference table sat Chase, the Russians, Lord Garon, and the other two kings, Vinton and Melton.

"Good Evening, Lord Danika. Sherman, Neeman," said Melton. "Would you be so kind as to join us?"

Neeman's muscles twitched with the need to wring Chase's neck for what he'd done to Danika, as well as her parents and everyone else.

"What the hell he is doing here," said Danika, pointing to Chase.

"He's here at our behest," said Vinton. "We've come to negotiate."

Neeman's gut tightened. Something wasn't right. Where was the High Council?

"You lied to me," Danika hissed at Sherman.

"I didn't know, I swear." He held up his hands. "Nika, if you'd have a seat—"

Mason rushed Chase and lifted him by the throat. Danika raced to Mason's side. Neeman reached down and undid the buckle on his gun holster.

"Stop," she ordered.

"He tried to kill you. I promised I'd make him pay for it."

"If you kill him, then they have reason to go to war," Danika pressed. "It's what they want."

"Let them come." Mason's deep voice resonated in the bass tones that belonged to his Demon half, Maelstrom.

Neeman moved to Mason's side. "She's right. You have to let him go. If we start a war with the other covens, it will be like the Outbreak all over again."

Mason continued to squeeze Chase, whose color drained as he stared at Mason, impassive. Up close, Chase appeared to have aged dramatically in the past six months. His suit wasn't designer, and his skin had a milky pallor accentuated by deep purple circles under his eyes.

Mason threw him to the ground.

"I think you'd better explain what's going on." Sherman looked from Melton to Vinton.

"Let's do try to be civil," said Melton. "Have a seat."

Chase got to his feet and then sat in his chair. Neeman, Mason, and Danika retreated to the other end of the conference table with Sherman.

"There. Now, the reason we are here," Vinton gestured to everyone on his end, "is that we knew you weren't exactly on board with our feelings, Sherman, about the slaves and having Lord Danika removed, so we decided to take matters into our own hands."

"What have you done?" asked Sherman. "Aligning yourself with Garon and Chase? After what they did? They enslaved the humans, tried to kill Lord Danika. They'll turn on you in a heartbeat."

Melton shrugged. "She left us no choice. We weren't going to get through to her about what to do with the new humans."

"We're creating a scenario that will ensure Danika's removed and someone more fitting is put in her place," said Vinton.

"What are you talking about," asked Danika. "Where's the Venerable King Lucian? Where's the High Council?"

"Back in their palace, I'm afraid," said Vinton. "But don't worry. We're going to give them a reason to come."

"What do you want?" Neeman tracked the group at the end of the table and noticed Lord Garon and the Russians stayed conspicuously silent.

"Well, we can do this easy, where Danika steps down and is allowed to own her blood company while Chase runs it—"

"Never going to happen," said Mason.

"Or, we can do it the ugly way, where we enforce a hostile takeover," said Vinton.

"We tried to unite with you, cousin," said Alexi. "But your stubborn streak goes beyond what even we Russians are capable of."

"You are not my cousins," said Danika. "My family sits on this side of the table."

Chase's expression saddened, making Neeman wonder if he was now just a pawn in someone else's game.

"I think you underestimate our ability to protect our own," said Mason.

"Oh no," said Melton. "We don't. Which is why we brought help."

As if on cue, an explosion sounded from down below, and the rumble shook the building. Neeman raced to the window. A horde of Demons burst from a building across the street and stormed the building. Mason roared, and his form enlarged.

"You aligned yourself with Demons, so did we," said Garon.

Chase stepped forward. "I warned you, Danika. I told you there'd be repercussions."

Mason's frame touched the ceiling, and his wings ripped from his back. Melton and Vinton shied away from the table as flames engulfed him.

Neeman needed to keep Danika safe. That was the job.

He pulled his gun and shot one of the twins straight through the head. The Russian gasped and fell to the ground. His brother cried out and dropped down beside him, causing Neeman to miss his head, and hit the glass window instead.

Mason grabbed Chase by the throat and hurled him into the window. Chase's head cracked against the glass and crumpled to the ground in a heap. Mason flew at Chase, picked him up again, and hurled them both through the window. Out in the night sky, Chase clawed at Mason's talons, crying out for help. Mason pulled him in close and said something Neeman couldn't hear and then opened his hand. Chase disappeared from view as his screams followed him to the cement below. Mason roared into the night.

Garon ran at Danika, but she got to him first and punched him in the face before tackling him to the ground.

Melton made a run for the door, but Neeman brought him to his knees as Sherman battled Vinton.

"I'll see you hanged for this," Melton screamed.

Neeman punched him in the face. "You can try."

There were several popping noises, and Neeman looked up to see four tall, thin men in flowing robes standing in the doorway. Who the hell were they?

One of the men spotted Danika and pointed. A pit grew in Neeman's gut.

Melton locked a leg over Neeman and flipped him to the floor, planting his heel in Neeman's chest.

Winded, Neeman sputtered and landed an elbow to Melton's windpipe. Danika screamed as one of the new men grabbed her around the waist.

Another one took her place battling with Garon. Two mysterious men dragged the screaming Danika into the front office.

Dammit. "Danika!" Neeman sprung up and chased after them, leaving Melton to run for the elevator. Neeman looked back only once before following the men in the opposite direction toward the stairs.

They pulled open the door as Danika fought against the men. The door flew inward, and a group of Demons poured in. Front and center stood Seraphine. Her dark gray skin shone with a sheen of sweat encompassing her amethyst eyes that twinkled in the soft glow of light that emanated from her fingertips.

"Hello, Loverboy." She smiled, and her thin tail swished back and forth near her feet.

"Get him," yelled Melton.

SERAPHINE STARED PAST THE VAMPIRE TO THE TWO FAE HOLDING Danika. They took one look at her and ran in the other direction.

Neeman stepped closer to her. She needed to get him out of the way.

"He's mine," she yelled. "Fan out, kill the rest."

She ran at Neeman, taking him to the floor. The other three Demons took off into the conference room as the fat Vampire Lord headed toward the elevator.

"You can't do this." Neeman rolled her underneath him and pinned her to the ground. "I won't let you ruin Selene."

She didn't want to hurt him, but she had a job to do. "It's me. It's Selene," she lied.

He pressed her into the carpet and dropped his weight on top of her. "It's not possible. You don't even look human."

Seraphine hooked her legs around his waist and flipped him on his side. Twisting his arm with her hand, she pinned it behind him. He struggled against her hold, but she kept him down.

"Stop. I don't want to hurt you."

"Trust me. You won't." He flipped onto his back and yanked his arm from her grasp. He wrapped his arm around her waist and pitched her sideways. Suddenly they rolled across the floor, locked in a battle of arms and legs.

"Convince him to let us go. You have to pretend to be me," Selene said.

"I had to look like Seraphine to get in with the Demons," she whispered. "They found me, and I didn't have a choice. If I hadn't, they would've taken me back to my plane or killed me."

His gaze met hers, and he searched her face. He stopped struggling, but his body remained wound tight.

"What are you going to do?" he asked.

She relaxed, and so did he. She leaned in close and kissed him.

"Save your life." Seraphine punched him in the jaw, knocking him out.

"Hey!" Selene fumed. *"That wasn't part of the plan."*

"Improv, little sister."

Seraphine hopped to her feet and dragged him to the corner of the office, hiding him under a desk. She stared at him for a split second and grumbled at the remorse that coursed through her.

"Forgive me, Lover," she whispered.

Seraphine stood, her eyes trained on the conference room. Inside, two Demons fought Vampires and Fae alike. Danika had managed to get out of the Fae's arms and fought them off alongside a Demon.

Stupid Vampires hadn't realized, they couldn't make deals with Demons. Demons were never out for anyone but themselves.

"All right," she said. "Time to get some payback."

She raced into the room at a speed faster than she'd moved before. She located the first Fae and pressed her palms onto his back. *"Ignus!"*

Light shot from her fingertips up his spine and over his shoulders. He turned, his mouth hung open, and his eyes wide. He tried to breathe, but smoke poured out of his mouth instead. His body glowed from under the skin, then he darkened and fell to the ground, gasping for air, his body burning from the inside out.

"Nice," Seraphine purred. "Who's next?"

Two Fae battled with the Russian and another Vampire as well as a Demon. The Fae caught the Demon with a death spell, and the Demon crumpled to the ground.

Her gaze locked on the handsome surfer looking Vampire who had Sherman on the floor and slashed at him left and right.

Seraphine tackled the younger Vampire Lord, catching him by surprise.

"Let's see how you like it." She struck out with her nails and ripped into his throat. The Vampire's eyes widened in surprise as dark, thick blood seeped from the wound into the carpet. She leaned in close to him and planted her palm in the middle of his chest. *"Ignus."*

Again, glowing veins snaked out from under her finger, up his face and down his chest. His eyes bulged, and then his skin turned to the color of ash, and he stopped moving.

Jumping from the dead Vampire, she headed for Sherman.

"No!" Selene yelled. *"Not him!"*

Seraphine growled and surveyed the scene. The light—haired Vampire now fought a kocar Demon. The Russian fought a pince Demon, and Danika fended off a quaser.

"Danika. We need Danika to save Neeman," said Selene.

"Going somewhere, Selene?"

Seraphine spun to find a Fae behind her.

"Did you think Lorcan wouldn't send backup? From the

looks of you, I'd say he was right. He'll be more than pleased when I tell him I killed your Demon half for good, in battle."

"I wouldn't be so sure about that," said Seraphine. "Your precious High Elder and I used to have plenty of fun between the sheets. Not that you'd know what that was like, as I'm sure you've never even been with a woman before."

The Fae's eyes flashed. Before he could pronounce a spell, Seraphine kicked him in the chest and sent him flying across the room. He crashed into the wall and fell in a heap. He leapt to his feet, and Seraphine ran at him, planting her talons in his ribcage.

He stumbled, and his eyes widened.

"Guess you won't get that chance to be with a woman now. Tell Lorcan hello for me when you reach my father's under-world." She reached up, grabbed his rapidly beating heart, and ripped it from his chest.

Leaving the Fae to die, she dropped the heart and surveyed the scene.

Seraphine jumped the conference table, knocking a pyramid of Savor bottles to the floor, and ran at the quaser. His long tentacles swung wildly, knocked a large portrait from the wall, and wrapped around Danika. Seraphine thrust her hands forward, and her long nails slid easily into the quaser's spine. His limbs shook, and he gasped for breath.

"Sorry," Seraphine said. "That one's mine."

The quaser locked eyes on her. *"Traitor."* Blood bubbled out of his mouth.

She smiled. "Yup."

She squeezed his spine until it crushed in her hand, and then the quaser's eyes went blank, and he fell to the ground.

Seraphine grabbed Danika by the arm. "I'll get you out of here."

Danika pulled away. "I need to get to Mason."

"He's outside." Seraphine grabbed her arm again.

"Gentle," said Selene. *"She doesn't trust us."*

Seraphine tried to smile. "You can stay here if you wish, but I don't recommend it. Either way, I'm outta here."

"All right," said Danika.

Together the women ran from the room to the elevator. The door opened, and they took it down to the lobby.

"Where's Neeman," asked Danika.

"I... I don't know." Seraphine refused to look her in the eye.

Where they were going, Neeman couldn't follow. If he did, Lorcan would kill him for sure. This was the only way to keep Loverboy safe.

The doors opened, and Seraphine stepped out and looked around. "Come on."

They ran toward the exit. Behind the receptionist's desk, a slurping sound emanated.

Seraphine bounded over the desk to find a quaser Demon hunched over a dead female vamp on the floor. Without a sound, Seraphine planted her palm on the Demon's back. *"Torque."*

He let out an ear—piercing screech, and then his spine twisted in a full rotation, and he dropped.

She hopped over the desk and continued to the door with Danika.

They hadn't been outside for a split second before a giant fireball hurled over their heads and bowled into a Demon running toward them. The Demon burst into flames.

Danika stopped short and looked down at the broken body of a dead Vampire on the ground. The old Vampire with long, white hair stared off, his eyes blank. Danika walked up to him and regarded him for a moment before kicking him, and spitting in his face. "See you in hell, you murdering bastard."

"I like her!" said Seraphine.

Maelstrom swooped around to the front of the building and landed on the cement. The sight of him in his true form made Seraphine quake with joy. It had been a century or more since she'd seen him. The idea of taking this plane and making it their domain ran through her mind.

"Danika!" Maelstrom scooped Danika into his arms.

Seraphine's heart crumbled at the sight. Danika was his life now. Not even Maelstrom would hurt her. This was his home, and he'd do anything to protect it. Loneliness caught her in the chest and sent its icy agony through her heart.

She had no home.

His gaze lit on Seraphine. "Sister."

She wanted to smile, to run to him and... And what? They were no longer children. The world she'd been praying for had dissolved long ago.

"Get her to safety," commanded Maelstrom.

Seraphine nodded. "I know a place."

A slasher Demon jumped on Maelstrom's back and bit into his neck. He stumbled and set Danika down, then grabbed the slasher by the arm and flung him through the window into the lobby.

"Go!" he yelled.

Two more Demons headed right for them.

"Come on." Seraphine grabbed Danika's arm and propelled her toward the awaiting SUV.

Danika stumbled out of her heels, hitched up her skirt, and ran at the vehicle. Seraphine rounded the driver's side and jumped in. No key.

"*My turn,*" said Selene.

"No, I'm stronger," said Seraphine.

"What?" asked Danika.

"If Lorcan sees you, he'll kill us all on sight," Selene pleaded.

"Not if I kill him first."

"Who are you talking to?" asked Danika.

"I have a plan. You have to trust me," said Selene. *"Don't make me take the body by force again."*

Seraphine wavered but then relented. Selene took a deep breath and cried out as her body morphed back into its human form. Her horns and tail retracted, as did her teeth. She gripped the steering wheel until her knuckles grew bloodless. She held her breath and tried to stave off the agony of the change. After a moment, she took in a deep breath.

"Man, I haven't done that while conscious in a long time." She panted and set her hand on the ignition. *"Illuminationes."*

"What the hell was that?" asked Danika.

Selene smiled. "Just me arguing with myself."

The vehicle roared to life.

"Where are we going?" Danika asked.

Selene threw the SUV in reverse and peeled out. She sped down the deserted streets toward the area she knew all too well. Pain trickled through her limbs like a waterfall. Seraphine still hovered close to the surface, refusing to sleep. For once, Selene didn't mind.

"You said you knew a safe place," said Danika.

"I'm taking you to my old apartment."

"How do you know it's still there?"

"I've been there. The wards on the building held in our absence."

They rounded a corner too fast, and Danika grabbed the door to hang on.

"Do you have a phone?" Danika asked.

"No."

"I need to get the word out." They rounded another corner.

"Word to who? The Kings? I think they already know." Selene snorted. She sped down the road, came to an intersection, and shot through it. At the end of the block, she slowed and rolled into an underground parking structure. She pulled the SUV into a spot and shut it off.

"Hurry." She hopped out of the driver's seat.

"We should go back," Danika said.

"Maelstrom told me to take you somewhere safe, so that's what I'm doing."

They ran to the elevator. Once inside, Selene closed her eyes and took a deep breath.

"All right, girlie, don't screw this up," said Seraphine.

"I know what I'm doing," she tried to convince herself again.

CHAPTER TWENTY FOUR

Neeman sat up and hit his head on something hard. His groggy state gave way as pain jolted him to the present, and the sounds of battle caught his attention.

Selene.

He rolled out from under the desk, trying to remember how he'd gotten there. What had happened rushed back to him, and he made for the conference room. Sherman lay on the floor, barely alive. One of the twins and Garon battled a Demon side by side.

"Help us," the remaining twin yelled.

The Demon rounded on Neeman. He recognized it from the description Seraphine had given him. The weakness lay on the right side of the Demon's torso, where his heart beat.

For Neeman, the kill would've been easy. Instead, he looked between Garon and the twin.

"No."

Neeman bent and hefted Sherman over his shoulder and

headed out of the room, ignoring Garon and the Russian's threats and curses.

He carried Sherman to the elevator and set him on the floor inside. Instead of going to the lobby, he headed up to the top floor.

"Where are you taking me?"

"Chase's old office is upstairs. It is lightproof, and you can hide out there till we get this sorted. There's a stock of Savor in a fridge. Stay inside, and I'll send help when I can."

Sherman nodded— his breathing labored. Neeman eyed him. "Are you going to make it?"

"I need blood, but I went through worse during the Outbreak."

The doors opened, and Neeman lugged Sherman to the office and set him down on the couch.

"Keep your phone on, and I'll call when I can."

Sherman coughed, and blood dribbled out of his mouth. "Go," he said. "Find Selene."

Neeman didn't bother arguing. He sprinted to the elevator and headed down to the lobby. He pushed his hands through his hair, and his muscles twitched with anticipation of a fight.

Seraphine had knocked him out. He'd been stupid to think it was Selene in there. He had to find her. Who knew what kind of trouble they were in.

A tremor shook the building as the elevator reached the lobby. He ran out to find it a disaster. A huge hole had been blown through the front window of the building. Glass scattered the floor, and the receptionist's desk lay on the wrong side of the lobby. Two Demons lay dead on the floor along with the receptionist.

Outside his trackers fought alongside Maelstrom against a group of a half dozen Demons. He couldn't help the smile that broke his lips as he ran out to join the battle. Despite Maelstrom throwing fireballs, three of the Demons continued to attack as if unaffected. Neeman ran to the first assailant, pulling his gun, and aimed for the Demon's back. He hit the Demon in the spine, and the creature fell to the ground, flopping its upper half. He grabbed the Demon's head, wrenching it around, breaking its neck.

Maelstrom grabbed the second Demon and ripped its head off, spewing oily blood through the air. The third Demon turned and ran the opposite direction. Neeman aimed and caught the creature in the leg. Maelstrom flew to the Demon and finished him off.

To his right, Riley and Stephos fought a slasher Demon. "He has to be stabbed in the head!" Neeman yelled.

Riley jumped on the Demon, knocking him to the ground as Stephos pulled his knife and stabbed the beast in the temple.

The remaining Demon had one of the trackers on the ground, feasting on his blood. Neeman ran at the Demon, unloading his entire clip into it. The Demon stumbled and fell to his knees. Neeman jumped on him, knocking the monster onto its back. Row upon row of razor—sharp teeth snapped at Neeman. He wrapped his hands around the beast's throat and strained to crush it. The creature clawed at Neeman's arms, but he took no notice. After a minute, the Demon stopped moving, and Neeman stumbled to his feet. Blood dripped from his arms in long rivulets.

His ears rang from the gunfire, and he looked around, winded, at the Demon bodies strewn on the ground.

Maelstrom paced in a circle and roared, making the hair stick up on Neeman's neck.

Riley and Stephos met him as he walked toward Maelstrom. "The others are dead," said Riley.

Neeman nodded. "Go up to the conference room and see if there's anyone still alive. If there is, arrest them and bring them down. No matter who they are."

The two headed into the building. Maelstrom rose into the air and then landed again, making the ground shake.

Neeman blew out a huge breath and picked up his gun, releasing the empty clip and shoving a full one in. He loaded the chamber and stuck the gun in his waistband.

Maelstrom's gaze landed on Neeman, and he pointed. "You. Where is Danika?"

"I don't know," Neeman replied.

Maelstrom roared again and then stared at Neeman. "You know, Seraphine."

"Yes."

"Seraphine took Danika."

A chill ran through Neeman. "I'm sure they're fine. Seraphine will protect her."

Maelstrom's facial bones shifted into human form. He shrunk in size, and his enormous black wings melded into Mason's back. His skin lightened, and his horns retracted. Mason stumbled to Neeman.

"Seraphine better protect her. Or I'll kill her with my bare hands."

Neeman ground his teeth together, biting back his desire to threaten Mason for saying the words. But he knew better than to engage Mason while he tried to control himself.

"Do you have any idea where they might have gone?"

Mason nodded. "I think I do."

Selene walked down the hall to the door of her old apartment. She tried to keep her jitters at bay, but it wasn't easy. Silence permeated the air. All of the other apartments in the luxury building were empty. Her bare feet slid over the plush, loopy weave of the carpet. Only half the sconces on the walls were still lit.

She stopped at her door and lay her hand on the knob. *"Recludo."*

The door swung inward with a click.

"Why can you do that, and Mason can't?" asked Danika.

Selene shrugged. "He can. He just doesn't. I did spend a thousand years training in magic though while he spent time at our father's side learning how to torture people." She paused and looked at Danika. "Sorry."

Selene stepped inside and turned on the light. Everything remained as she'd left it. She peered inside for Lorcan but didn't see him.

"You need something to wear besides that suit. It can't be comfortable."

Danika looked around.

"My mother and I used to live here." Selene walked into her room and grabbed a pair of jeans and a T—shirt, and tossed them to Danika.

Danika held them at arm's length. "I haven't worn jeans in close to thirty years."

Selene took the clothes and pointed out the door. "My mom's room is down the hall. You might like her style better."

"Do you have a phone so we can call Neeman?"

"No," Selene lied. She stripped off her black dress and hose and tugged on the jeans and T—shirt.

Danika crossed to her and gave Selene a tight smile. "Thank you for helping me and getting me to safety."

"No problem. Maybe I can get some goodwill out of it."

"From Neeman?"

"From me."

Danika spun around at the sound of the male voice and sucked in a breath.

"Hello, Selene. You did well." Lorcan looked her up and down.

Selene tried to keep her composure. She pulled on the T—shirt and headed to the closet for some shoes.

"You didn't think I'd do it, though. I ran into a few of your lackeys at the office."

He shrugged. "Didn't think you had it in you. Did any of them make it?"

"Not that I saw."

"What going on?" asked Danika.

Lorcan's brows knit together. "Selene, didn't tell you?"

Selene sat on the bed and slipped on her flats.

Danika whipped around to Selene. "Tell me what?"

"Why she's here," replied Lorcan. "We let her come back to Earth to get you."

"Me?" Danika stepped back so she could see them both. "What do you want with me?"

"Nothing, actually," said Lorcan. "It's Maelstrom we want. You are just a means of getting him."

Danika turned her fiery gaze on Selene. Selene swallowed hard and looked away.

"Keep cool. Give nothing away."

"Maelstrom's too powerful to be left on this plane," continued Lorcan. "We'd assumed he'd gone back with the others when the rifts closed, but then a tear appeared in the fabric of our world. A tear he caused when he used his Fae magic to unbind the building concealing the blood den your uncle built."

"How did you know that?" asked Danika.

Lorcan shrugged. "Because I'm the one who created the spell."

"On one of your trips here," said Selene.

Lorcan laughed. "I've always traveled between the planes. I've done it for centuries. Who do you think helped the humans in the first war against the Demons? And all the advances in medicine in this realm, do you think humans discovered those?"

"What do you plan to do with me?" Danika asked.

"Take you to my realm and keep you there until Maelstrom follows. Once he's there, we can capture and contain him. Seal the rift between this world and mine, thereby keeping my realm safe."

"And what about this world?" asked Danika. "You're going to let Demons destroy it?"

Lorcan shrugged. "Maybe it will be destroyed, and maybe it won't. Either way, it doesn't matter to me. The rift has been opened to the Demon world, and with no one to close it, more and more Demons will pour into this world, sad as it is from what you Vampires have done to it."

"Us?"

"Of course, you. If you'd kept your mouths shut, none of this would've happened. But no, you had to come out of the darkness, thereby assuring the destruction of this world. For highly intelligent creatures, you Vampires are immensely stupid." He held up his hands. "But it's no matter to me anymore. Now I worry about the end of my race. And the only way to make certain that doesn't happen is taking the one

Demon who is capable of reopening the rift to my world and trapping him where I can keep an eye on him."

Danika looked at Selene. "How can you let him do this? To your own brother? We trusted you."

"Oh, don't be too hard on Selene. She's never been one of strong will. She, like all Demons, has a weakness. And once you find it, it isn't too hard to get her to do what you want." He patted Selene on the shoulder. "For Selene, it was Neeman. Isn't that right?"

Danika looked between them.

"Lorcan threatened to take Neeman to the Fae realm and torture him if I didn't bring you here. Like he used to do to me."

"Then what do you think he's going to do to Mason?"

"The same thing." Selene stood and moved in front of Danika. "Which is why he's going home without you."

Lorcan turned his gaze on her. "Excuse me?"

"You heard me," Selene said. "You're going to leave this plane and go back to the Fae realm without Danika and Mason."

He laughed. "And what makes you think I am going to do that?"

"Because you promised."

His brow furrowed. "I did no such thing."

"Oh, but you did. You gave me your word that if I brought her here, you'd leave for the Fae realm, and no harm would come to us now, or in the future."

His eyes narrowed, and his body tensed. She knew the wheels were working in his head, searching for a loophole, a way out.

"Let me help you," she said. "Would you like me to open a door?"

She centered her energy. Together, she and Seraphine

reached into the fabric of the world. She saw beyond the wall, beyond the building, beyond Chicago. She saw the world, the material it was made from, and everything in between. She pressed her palm to the wall and a shimmering crack appeared. The draw on her magic physical pulled on her body, sucking her close to unconsciousness the wider it got.

"How..." Lorcan's voice faltered.

She removed her hand and opened her eyes. "You've always underestimated me. All those years of torture, you thought you'd beaten my Demon into submission. You didn't. You made us stronger. And then you sent us here, where instead of tearing us apart, you brought us closer to working in unison than we ever have in the past. All this time you've been afraid of Mason and what he might do, but what you didn't count on was me. I'm the one you have to worry about. Because I'm the one who wants you dead."

The anger that emanated from him made his limbs shake.

"We can't hold it much longer," said Seraphine.

Her legs wobbled from the pull on her magic. She was running out of time. A large bang on the outer door made her jump.

"Selene! Danika!" Mason.

"You should go before my brother breaks that door down," said Selene. "I won't hold this thing open much longer, and I don't suppose you're able to create a portal quite as quickly as I am."

Mason banged on the door again.

Lorcan looked toward the outer door. When he turned back, lightning flashed through his eyes. The exterior door shook as someone rammed into it from the hallway.

"I will not forget this betrayal, Selene. You have disgraced your mother. She will pay for your treachery. Think about that as you languish here in this plane of debauchery."

"My mother abandoned me the moment we stepped into the Fae realm. I'm just following her example."

The outer door cracked under Mason's weight. Lorcan moved to Selene and leaned in close.

"I will never give up trying to make you who you should be. Nothing I have done was to harm you, but make you better. To separate you from your evil half and make you mine."

A white—hot pain seared through her belly, and Seraphine screamed. The outer door burst open with a crack. Selene fell to her knees, as Lorcan stepped through the closing portal and disappeared. She tried to suck in a breath, but the familiar agony in her stomach made it hard. She looked down to find the black handle of Lorcan's Demon stick protruding from her belly.

Her head rang with Seraphine's screams. She tried to grab the stick to remove it, but it burned her palms.

Danika rushed to her side and grabbed the stick, yanking it from Selene's belly and tossing it away. Selene shuddered as blood poured from her wound. Danika laid her gently on her back.

"Mason!" she cried. "Mason, help!" Danika pressed her palms over the wound.

Selene's vision dimmed. Inwardly she searched for Seraphine, who had curled into a ball, barely moving.

"Seraphine?" Selene called. "Stay with me."

Mason and Neeman ran into the room.

"She's been stabbed with that stick," said Danika. "What do we do?"

Mason picked up the stick and dropped it immediately.

"Demon stick." He knelt by Selene's side and picked up her head. "Selene, can you hear me?"

She blinked, and metallic tasting blood gurgled in her throat. "Seraphine... She's dying."

Neeman joined the group. "What do we do? What happens if her other half dies?"

"I don't know," said Mason.

"We have to save her. She's part of me. She is me. If she goes, I go."

Never before had Selene felt so much compassion for that side of herself, but it finally dawned on her. Seraphine had kept her alive in the Fae realm. Seraphine had strengthened her, protected her. She needed Seraphine. Without her, what was she? Who was she?

"Give her blood," said Danika.

Selene shook her head. She'd never fed on blood before. The thought of it made her cringe.

"It strengthened you, Mason. Maybe it will help Seraphine." Danika stared at the group. "She can have mine. She saved my life more than once tonight."

"No," said Neeman. He locked eyes with Selene. "It should be me."

She knew what it meant. If she drank from him, they would be joined. From the state of her runes, if they did this, there would be no turning back.

"Neeman—"

"I know," he said.

She stared at him, fear coursing through her.

"You need to hurry," said Danika. "This bleeding isn't slowing and she and I haven't even gotten a chance to go shopping yet."

Selene chuckled. "Seraphine loves to shop."

Neeman bit into his wrist and held it to her lips. She resisted swallowing as the blood flowed into her mouth. They needed to talk about it. He needed to truly understand what could happen. But there wasn't time. The liquid filled her mouth too quickly, and she had no choice but to swallow.

Seraphine gasped, and Selene lurched off the floor, grabbing Neeman's wrist with both hands, pulling it to her.

FEAR TWISTED IN NEEMAN LIKE A COILED SNAKE. A MIXTURE OF possibly losing Selene, or being bonded to her forever. He had no idea which scared him more. But there was no time to think. What ever happened, happened.

The sensation of her sucking from his vein was both purely visceral and completely satisfying.

Her eyes opened, green orbs tinged amethyst. Desire stirred him deep within. He lifted the hem of her shirt. Her wound began sealing shut.

Holding her close, he stroked her hair. Mason and Danika left without a word, closing the door behind them.

He allowed Selene to drink from him for another minute, and then he pulled his wrist away and licked the wound shut.

He stared into her eyes, not sure who peered back at him. She sucked in a sharp breath and then runes he'd not noticed before glowed beneath her shirt. The golden color pulled him in, like threads connected them. He wanted to kiss her, to feel her, to make love to her. Though she'd drunk from him, he'd been filled in a way that completed him somehow. As if this was what he'd waited for. She was who he'd been meant for.

"Thank you for healing me." She met his gaze, and the

runes faded once more. "I know how hard that must have been for you."

"I don't know that you do," he replied.

She pushed herself up and wrapped her arms around her knees, drawing them up to her chest.

"Who was that man?" he asked.

"Lorcan."

"The one who tortured you."

She stared at him, unblinkingly. "I'm sorry Seraphine lied to you back at the office and pretended to be me. It was the only way we knew how to keep you safe." She reached out and ran her fingers down the slashes on one of his arms.

"We?" He'd never heard her speak about her inner Demon as a "we" before.

She blew out a breath. "You and I have a lot to talk about. But right now, we need to make sure the rest of the Demons are gone."

Hearing her so logical threw him for a loop. Her voice so calm. Her face, passive. Even her body remained completely still. He wanted, no, needed to talk to her. To find out what had happened between her and Seraphine. But there wasn't time. He and Mason had taken off so quick, who knew what was happening to the rest of the city.

He got to his feet and helped her up as well. They stood for a minute holding each other.

"As soon as we're sure everything is fine, we will have a conversation," he said.

She bit the inside of her cheek and nodded. "I don't think I could get away from you now if I tried."

Her peaceful expression made him wonder what meaning her words held.

He opened the door and stepped into the front room.

Danika spoke rapidly into her phone, and Mason walked over and hugged Selene.

He pushed her to arm's length and opened his mouth.

"I know you're mad at me," she said. "I don't blame you. I lied to you. To all of you. But I tried doing the right thing."

Mason closed his mouth and pulled her into a hug again. "I'm glad you're okay, baby sister."

Danika ended her call and strode over. "William is at the office with Siad and the house security. We should get over there. There are dead Demons all over, and vamps are starting to gather in the area. We need to contain this."

"What about Garon and the Kings and the Russians?" asked Neeman.

She shook her head. "Alexi is dead. Vinton is dead. Garon and Eliander are missing. Chase is also dead." She blew out a breath. "This is a huge mess. On top of all that, Sinya has gone into labor."

"The baby's early," said Neeman.

"Yes. Doc is with them now." Danika pinched the bridge of her nose.

Mason gathered her in his arms.

"War is coming," said Mason. "This was only the beginning. Someone has made a deal with the Demons. More will come. Many more."

"This is bigger than a coven war. Vampires will be divided between siding with the Demons and fighting against them," said Danika.

"We need to get on top of this. Send a message to the High Council. Call all the trackers in," said Mason.

"I'll call everyone I know," said Neeman.

"We'll need them on our side if we are to survive."

"First thing's first," said Danika. "Let's clean up the mess.

Tomorrow we'll start strategizing. Garon, Melton, and Eliander are on the run if they're still alive. It will take them a couple of days to regroup."

"There's something you're all missing," said Selene. "The portal to the Demon Realm. If we can find it, and close it, we may be able to finish this thing before it starts."

Danika stared at her. "Can you do that?"

"I'll need to heal first, but I believe I can."

Everyone nodded in agreement.

"Let's move," said Danika. "I want my uncle's sorry remains scraped off my office steps as soon as possible."

CHAPTER TWENTY FIVE

The mood between Selene and Neeman grew tense as they helped carry the bodies of the Demons to the SUVs and stacked them in the back. Neeman had called every tracker from Coven House to come help. The dwindling numbers punched her in the gut.

Less than a dozen trackers remained in Chicago— and that included the humans who had been trained. As much as she hated to suggest it, she'd mentioned to Neeman that he might want to ask the human trackers if they wanted to become vampyr. The look he'd given her made the tension between them skyrocket to a new level.

Mason picked up the dead Vampire with the long white hair. Chase, Danika's uncle. Danika had insisted that Chase be put in the dumpster instead of taken with them and given a proper burial. Even Selene found that unusually cruel, but she understood how Danika felt.

Selene looked on as Mason dumped the body inside and lit

it on fire. She wished she could gain the satisfaction of watching Lorcan's body burn. But his time would come.

"We should get you to Coven House to rest." Neeman threw two tentacles into the SUV.

"What about up there?" She pointed to the broken window on the side of the building.

"It's already done. Alexi's body is in the other SUV, as is Vinton's."

"And Sherman?"

"He'll live. His driver picked him up an hour ago."

She nodded. "Things are going to get ugly here, aren't they?"

He wiped his palms on his pants. "Yes. But not today." He slammed the trunk closed.

Selene's body sagged. Seraphine hadn't spoken to her since the Demon stick incident. But she knew Seraphine was still in there. She felt her, deep inside her cage, curled in a ball. It worried Selene. Maybe Neeman was right. Perhaps rest would help.

She trudged up the stairs of Coven House to the second floor landing. All around, coven members stared and whispered. News in the Vampire society traveled faster than among mean teenagers in high school. Several of the house slaves had gathered in the entryway as well, their eyes frightened, and their voices animated. She supposed she should feel the same way. After all, it was about as bad as the world could get.

Beings that were stronger, faster, and all around deadlier than any they'd met were about to flood in and destroy everything or take it captive.

Neeman placed his hand on her lower back and guided her up to their room. Their room, what a strange thought.

"Neeman?"

They stopped and turned. William walked across the landing. "Danika would like to meet—"

"Not now."

William's brows furrowed, and he licked his lips. "I... well..."

"Not now, William. Tell Danika I'll be down later."

William's gaze shifted between the two of them, and he nodded and headed toward the other side of the house.

Neeman looked at her, and she swallowed. His grim expression tied a knot in her stomach.

"After you," he said.

She continued up to the room. As the door closed behind them, the silence of the suite threatened to suffocate her.

"Why don't you go lie down?" Neeman said.

"Are you going to lie with me?" *Why had she asked that?*

"I don't think that's such a good idea," he said.

She sighed. Her nerves jittered like a twenties style dance. She'd never be able to sleep. She walked to the couch and sat, crossing her arms and her legs.

"Don't do this," he said. "Get some rest. I'll stay out here, and we can talk later."

"I don't want to talk later."

She stared at his box on the table— the one she'd saved from the collapse.

"Why do you have to be like this?" he asked. "Why can't you just do as I say, for once?"

"Because I'm not good at taking orders."

"Oh yeah? Really? You've been letting someone order you around since you got here." He threw himself into the overstuffed chair to her left.

And so, it began.

She nodded and stared at her hands. "Lorcan is the High Elder of the Fae."

"The one who tortured you. And your ex—lover."

She caught his gaze. The only way they would get through this was, to tell the truth.

"We had sex. But he was never my lover."

"So, what were you sent here to do?"

She hung her head in her hands and stared at her feet. Bloodstained her shoes, and she rubbed them together in an effort to remove some of the spots.

"I was sent here to kidnap Danika and take her to Lorcan."

"Why?"

She looked up. "Because the Fae are afraid of what Mason can do. They wanted to take Danika to their realm where Mason would follow and then trap him there."

Neeman sat forward, resting his hands on his knees. "But what made them think they could contain him? He's the strongest being I've ever seen."

"He is, but the magic of the Fae rivals that of even Demons. As a unit, they can combine their power. There are few things more formidable than a collective of Fae." She shifted in her seat. "I meant what I said before. Seraphine knocked you out to save you. We had to get Danika to Lorcan to get him to fulfill the promise he made. I knew that you'd try to stop me. But if we didn't take her..."

"What?"

"If we hadn't, then he would've taken you to the Fae realm instead. On top of that, he wouldn't have stopped coming until he had her. What we did ensured he wouldn't be able to harm any of us, ever again."

"Why me?" he asked.

She stared at him. "Come on, Neeman, I know you aren't that dumb."

"Tell me." His eyes lit with intensity.

She took in his features: his fine Roman nose, his strong jawline, and lush lips, which split slightly in the middle. His handsome face sported a gash above his left eye, and the deep shadows under his eyes told her he hadn't been sleeping. His blond hair stuck up haphazardly attesting to the fact that he'd not been well since she'd left with Sherman.

For the first time in hours, Seraphine sat up and took notice. *"Tell him."*

He wanted to make her say it. In a way, she understood. Just a day ago, she'd rejected him. He wasn't going to be made a fool again.

He moved from his chair to sit on the table in front of her, making her pulse quicken. He leaned in so that their hands almost touched.

"Tell me," he said again.

"Tell you what?" Her insides squirmed like a bowl full of caterpillars.

"Tell me why he thought taking me would hold such sway over you." He wasn't going to give her an inch.

"Okay fine." She threw up her hands. "Do you want to hear that I have feelings for you? That you're right, and I lied when I said I didn't have feelings? To tell you I'd do about anything to keep you safe, including sending my brother's mate off to be locked up by a sadistic son of a bitch? Because that's all true. And I'd do it again a thousand times to keep you safe."

"Why?"

"Because I love you. I've never been in love before, and I'm not entirely sure I like the feeling, but I do. I love you. Is that what you want to hear me say?"

He grabbed her by the back of the neck and pulled her face close to his. "Yes." He lingered an inch from her lips, making Seraphine roar to life.

She lurched forward and pressed her lips to his.

His grip on her neck tightened, bringing her closer. She touched the stubble on his cheek and ran her fingers through his hair. His tongue probed and explored her mouth, and his fangs grazed her bottom lip. She licked his fangs and pressed her tongue against one of them. A shudder rippled through him. He stood, pulling her to her feet, scooped her into his arms, and headed for the bedroom.

Her chest warmed, and she wanted nothing more than to be in his arms.

Seraphine fought for control, but Selene kept her at bay.

He laid her on the bed, and the hard planes and contours of his body dropped down on her, making her quake with desire.

Seraphine begged for freedom.

"What's wrong?"

"Nothing," Selene panted. "It's just... Seraphine wants out."

He stared at her for a long hard minute. "Let her out."

"What?" That wasn't part of the plan.

"Let her out. I want to see her."

Panic echoed through Selene. Maybe it would be all right. Maybe Seraphine would behave.

"She won't hurt me," he said. "She saved me, remember?"

He dipped down and kissed her long and slow, making her temperature rise. He kissed down the side of her neck, grabbed her hands, and pinned them above her head.

Truthfully, most everything Seraphine had done in the last twenty—four hours had been to protect Neeman.

"Let her out." He trailed kisses down the front of her shirt and nipped at her buds through the thin fabric.

Selene moaned. Neeman settled the weight of his hips on hers and rubbed his long, hard length against her core. The seam of her jeans rolled against her most sensitive spot, heating her further.

"Seraphine," he crooned. "Where are you?"

Selene's mind floated on a cloud of bliss, and her resolve slipped. Before she regained control, Seraphine tore out of her cage.

"HELLO, LOVER." SELENE'S EYES TURNED PURPLE, AND SERAPHINE shone through. She smiled at him and stroked Neeman's hair with her long slender fingers.

Relief settled in his chest. He hadn't even been sure she still lived. "You're still in there."

"Of course, Lover. You don't think you could get rid of me that easy, did you?"

"Who said I wanted you to go anywhere?"

Her smile faltered, and her brows furrowed. "Don't you?"

"You are part of Selene. Of course, I wouldn't."

She tried to scoot out from underneath him. "I don't understand."

"Don't you? You're the one I met in the club that first night, aren't you?"

"Yes."

"And you're the one who saved Selene from the Demons."

"Guilty as charged."

"Then why would I want you to go anywhere?" He swooped down and kissed her hard. "I love you. Both of you."

Her body stiffened, but he refused to back down. The only way to have Selene was to have them both. He kissed her harder, and her body softened against him. She grabbed onto him, digging her fingernails into his back. The sensation sent a ripple of pleasure down to his toes. He lifted her T—shirt and ran his hands over her soft flesh. She moaned into his mouth, and her double fangs descended.

"Neeman." She broke their kiss and looked into his eyes. "I want you."

He didn't need to be asked twice, and this time, he didn't need to be gentle. He ripped her shirt over her head as she reached for his belt buckle and undid his pants. Grabbing his mouth with hers, she bit his lip, making him come closer to losing control. Tearing at her jeans, he broke the zipper.

She shimmied out of them and pulled down his boxer briefs as he slid off her panties and she unclasped her bra. The sight of her sprawled before him had him shaking with need. Her perfect body lay ready and waiting.

He started at her toes and kissed up the inside of her foot. Licking her ankle, he slid his tongue to the backside of her knee, making her shudder.

"Neeman," she moaned. "I don't need the niceties. I'm happy to have you fast and rough."

He continued up the inside of her thigh and over her hip. She fisted her hands in his hair as he swirled his tongue over her belly button and kissed her flat stomach.

"Show me," he said.

"Anything."

He looked up and met her eyes. "Show me the real you."

Her fingers slacked. "What?"

He propped himself on one elbow. "Show me the real you. I want to see you."

Seraphine's eyes flickered from purple to green and back again. "I can't," she said.

"I want you," he said. "As you are. No spells, no lies, no walls. Just you. Both of you."

Her expression shifted several times as if having an inward battle. Then her eyes turned green once more. She stared at him and placed one of her hands over her abdomen.

"Manifesto."

The skin shimmered and revealed not only the old scars but also the new one from Lorcan.

Neeman leaned in and reverently kissed over her stomach and up to her newest scar. Her body trembled beneath his lips.

He kissed up her torso to her breasts, swirling his tongue up over her sensitive peaks, making her arch against him. Spreading her thighs with his, he kissed up the side of her throat and met her gaze. Her eyes continued to flicker from green to purple.

"Take me," she whispered.

Neeman entered her in a hard, precise thrust. Selene cried out and grabbed on to him. Her warmth wrapped around him, cocooning, squeezing, and massaging him closer to climax. Neeman swooped down and kissed her as he thrust inside her again. Her breathing hitched with every thrust of his hips.

Tingling built in his legs and burned up the backs of his thighs, pooling in his groin. The feel and smell of her body connected to his was almost more than he could take.

Selene broke their kiss and took his face in her hands. Her eyes bright, her fangs long in her mouth. "Bite me."

He kissed her again, their teeth, tongues, and lips mingling, scraping, and swirling together like their bodies.

He pulled away and struck, sinking his fangs deep into her throat. The taste of her warm, sweet blood rushed through him and pulled him to the brink. Their bodies merged faster and harder. She dug her fingers into his hips, forcing him deeper inside her. He moaned and drank from her as she guided his hips. The build inside him tightened until it finally snapped and broke loose. He disengaged his fangs and roared as he came.

Her fangs pierced his neck, and her body shuddered and pulsed around him. She drew from him, moaning against his neck. His climax reached a crescendo and then tapered off. She stiffened around him, her fingernails digging deep into his shoulder blades, then sighed, disengaging her fangs.

Warmth radiated from her chest and spread over him until her skin grew so hot he had to pull away. Her body lurched beneath him. He rolled off her as she arched off the bed and sucked in a harsh breath.

The runes on her chest glowed brighter and brighter. Fear held him tight in its grasp.

"Selene? Seraphine?"

A humming sound emanated from within her. Neeman grabbed her by the shoulders. "Selene? Can you hear me? Selene?"

She stayed in her arched position, mouth open, eyes staring at the ceiling.

He jumped from the bed and ran his fingers through his hair. "Selene!" he yelled.

Her body sagged, and she bounced back onto the bed.

He dashed to her side. "Selene? Seraphine?"

Her eyes reopened slowly. Emerald green outside, amethyst in the middle.

"I'm here." She smiled.

But which one was it? Which one?

She raised her hand and touched his chest. He looked down. Just below his collarbone above his left pec sat a glowing rune that matched hers.

He searched her face, trying to understand.

"Thank you," she whispered. "You did this for us."

"What?" he asked. "What did I do?"

"You brought us together."

"I... I DON'T UNDERSTAND." NEEMAN'S FACE GREW PALER THAN USUAL, and fear etched his features. His eyes no longer remained ice blue, but now held a most alluring light violet tinge. Selene reached up and laid her hand on his face.

"We're one now, no longer separate."

His brows furrowed. "How? Why?"

"Because," she said. "You loved us both."

"So, Seraphine?"

"She's here. She's just... It's hard to explain. Our thoughts are joined now, and we're connected in a way that makes us no longer want to fight."

"But, you can still change your form?"

"We can. But it's not like she will be in the driver's seat and me in the back. We're both in control. Together."

He blinked several times. His brows furrowed.

"I don't understand it all myself yet. It will take time for us to discover what it means. But she and I are now one. We're just me. And I am one with you." She touched his rune.

He stared at the tattoo, which glowed like molten gold against his pale chest.

"You know what this means now, don't you?" she asked.

"What?"

She pulled him into a kiss and then bit his lip playfully. "You're mine. No one else's. Not now, not ever."

Neeman's genuine smile warmed her all over. "I think I'm okay with that."

CHAPTER TWENTY SIX

Neeman and Selene stayed in bed for hours. They made love several times and spent the moments in between talking. For the first time, Selene knew where she belonged. In his arms, with the two of them together, the pain of her past washed away.

The time passed too quickly, and they soon had to come back to the reality of their situation. They dressed and headed down to collaborate with Danika, Mason, and William.

"We need to find the portal, that is the first and foremost plan of attack," said Danika.

"I can handle that." Selene looked between Mason and Danika.

"I'll go, too," said Neeman.

"No," said Danika. "We need you to call all the trackers. Mason can go with her."

Neeman glanced at Selene and took her hand in his.

"I'll be fine," she said.

No longer having Seraphine chattering away in the background, narrating all of her actions left Selene's head oddly quiet. Instead, it was more like impressions. Something would suddenly come over her, and Selene would have the impulse to do something crazy or spontaneous and totally out of character. Instead of being two separate people in the same body, they were more like conjoined twins. Seraphine no longer needed to be caged either, remaining content to feel through Selene.

"All right," said Danika. "We also need a game plan in case the Demons return."

"They will," said Mason. "Now that they've located both Seraphine and me, they won't stop until they have us."

"Till they have this world," said Selene. "They only want us to lead the way."

"We're no match for them," said William. "There aren't enough of us. Even with you and Mason, there have to be thousands of Demons."

"More," said Selene. "Which is why we have to close the portal."

"What about the humans?" asked William.

"What about them?" said Danika.

"They can help. We can find out which ones have military experience."

Mason shook his head. "There aren't enough of them."

"True, but if this comes down to a war, we're going to need all the help we can get," said William. "I have heard rumors that there may be a huge enclave with nuclear weapons as well as advanced technology."

"How's that possible?" asked Danika. "We still haven't been able to get into those military bunkers."

"At this point, it's only a rumor, but I have a feeling there's one person who knows for sure. And if we can convince her, we may be able to convince them all."

Danika stared at William for a moment. "No."

"Danika, with all due respect, if there are humans out there with nukes, we need to reach out. They could be crucial. Not just in fighting the Demons, but for our survival as well."

"She's nothing but a problem, William."

"Then let her be my problem."

Danika sighed and rubbed her temples. Several tense minutes went by. Finally, she waved her hand. "Fine. But I don't want any trouble from Evan, or I swear, she won't be given another chance."

William nodded. "I understand."

"I know no one wants to think of this," said Selene. "But, you might consider asking if there are any humans who'd like to be turned."

"No," said Neeman.

"They'd be stronger and faster. I know you Vampires like to keep the blood pure, but this could very well mean the difference between humans living and dying. It's an option they should be given."

No one spoke. Being a vampyr wasn't the end of the world. Though she knew Neeman disagreed with her, they needed to consider the option for the upcoming war.

Danika looked at them in turn. "What we do or don't do in the next few days could mean the difference between our existence and our extinction. Is there anything else?"

"One thing," said Neeman. He squeezed Selene's hand. "When you get a free minute, I'd like to take Selene as my mate."

Danika smiled and nodded. "We will make it an affair worth celebrating."

"Thank you," Selene said. "But I think a small intimate ceremony would be more to my liking."

"Are you sure?" asked Mason. "That's unlike you."

Selene looked at Neeman. He gave her the winning smile she'd become so accustomed to in the past hours.

"Yes," she said. "We're sure."

Danika nodded. "Then, let's finish up what we need to do tonight, and tomorrow we will stand in the light of the moon, and you two shall be mated."

MASON AND SELENE HAD TRACKED THE PORTAL TO THE SOUTH SIDE OF town, but they'd been unable to pinpoint precisely where the rift occurred. A tear in the fabric of the world wasn't easily found. Their magic had drawn them to a general area, but after hours of searching, they'd come up empty.

Mason met with Neeman to organize a patrol to stand guard in a one mile radius until the portal could be located.

Over the following evening, a dozen new trackers arrived at Coven House, and two dozen more were expected to arrive within the next two days. Word of the attacks spread like rapid fire. Danika's phone had been ringing so much that Selene had even helped answer calls and take messages. The consensus was the same. Fear had blanketed the Society in a cloud of darkness.

Danika had sent word to the High Council, but she had yet to hear back from them, leaving them to prepare and wait.

Selene looked in the mirror at her green—purple eyes. Never in her wildest dreams had she thought she could be made whole. But Neeman had done that for her.

She fiddled with the cream silk, which draped over her shoulder.

"You look lovely, my dear," said Sherman.

Selene smiled. The Vampire King had returned to help out, after healing.

"Thank you," she replied.

"I must tell you. Had I known what you truly were, I would have had a harder time letting you go."

She laughed. "Oh trust me, as soon as you'd met my other half, you would have begged Neeman to take me back."

He snapped his fingers. "I almost forgot. You left this at the hotel." Sherman pulled her suitcase from behind the door and set it on her bed.

"Thank you. I began to think I'd never wear the same outfit more than once."

Sherman looked at his watch. "We should go down."

She nodded, her gut clenching. She stepped to Sherman and took his arm. Together they proceeded down to the landing where Mason stood in a pair of pinstriped suit pants, a white shirt, and a black vest. He looked dashing and uncomfortable.

Sherman handed her off to Mason and then bowed and headed down to the atrium.

"You look beautiful," Mason said.

Selene looked down at her long, fitted, cream silk gown and promised herself for the millionth time that she would not trip and embarrass herself, as well as Neeman.

She flipped her veil, almost as long as her dress, over her head and covered her face. "I bet you never thought you'd see this day."

"No, I didn't."

"Me neither."

He held out his arm for her to take.

"You clean up pretty good yourself, bro."

"That's all Danika's doing."

"Amazing how this new race is trying to better this world," she said as they descended the stairs.

"I hope we don't end up destroying it."

She squeezed his arm. "Me, too."

Mason stopped at the bottom of the stairs and she fanned her train out behind herself. *Don't trip. Don't trip. Don't trip.*

"Do you love him?"

She looked up. "What?"

"I want to make sure you love him."

She ran her fingers across her collarbone. "Come on, Mason. I have these beautiful runes now because of him, what do you think that means?"

"I think it means he loves you."

She tried to keep her voice level. "Yes, Mason. I love him."

"Good," he said. "Because above all else, I want you to be happy."

Her heart squeezed. "I am happy. For the first time... I am truly happy."

"Then let's go get you hitched." He kissed her on the forehead. "Oh, and Maelstrom wants you to know that if he breaks your heart, we're going to kill him."

She laughed. *Brothers.*

SELENE STOOD IN THE MIDDLE OF THE ATRIUM, HER HANDS IN Neeman's. Once again, he wore a dark suit, which made her knees feel like gelatin. He'd slicked back his hair and trimmed his scruff into a sexy goatee.

Sherman presided over the ceremony as the rest of the

coven looked on. Danika, William, and Mason stood alongside the blond Vampire pair who proudly held their beautiful new bundle of joy.

For a moment, Selene wished her mother were there. But the feeling left her as quickly as it had come. Being there with Neeman and Mason, Danika, and William, she realized she'd finally found what she'd been searching for her whole life. Family. And she'd be damned if she'd let anyone take that away from her.

"You are now mated as husband and wife," pronounced Sherman. "You may kiss your bride."

Happiness she'd never felt burst through her, and Selene jumped into Neeman's arms, tackling him with her lips. All around, chuckles and applause rang out. Neeman laughed, and when they broke apart, she saw a sight that warmed her entire being. He smiled at her so broadly it revealed a dimple on his left cheek.

He pulled her close. "You're mine," he whispered.

"For until your blood runs dry," she replied.

The End

VENGEANCE OF THE DEMONS

USA TODAY BESTSELLING AUTHOR

REBEKAH R. GANIERE

FALLEN
ANGEL
PRESS

CHAPTER ONE

William took another deep draw from Sue's neck as his body shook with the strain of holding back. The soft throaty moans she uttered along with how deep her nails scored his skin told him that she was almost there herself.

Her thick, rich blood slid down his throat and tingled his limbs with energy.

"William." She panted his name the same way she had every time she climaxed. Over the last year of using Sue for a blood servant, he'd explored every last fantasy he'd spent his life dreaming of but never fulfilling.

Her breathing quickened and her nails dug deeper into his skin as she sucked in a sharp breath. He rocked himself through his climax then licked her neck wound shut and rolled away.

She laughed. "Wow, that was a quick one."

"Sorry. It's been a while." In truth he'd been envisioning her as someone else and that had gotten him excited in ways he'd not expected

She lifted his hand, kissing it. "I'm not complaining."

He sat up and wrapped his watch around his wrist. A nice watch was something he'd always wanted but never would have been able to afford before becoming a vampyr. His father had had a nice watch. No where near as nice as William's, but he'd always told William that an expensive watch was the true testament of a man's status.

"Nice watch. Nice Shoes. Nice Car," his father always used to say... It was one of the only things he still remembered about his father.

Behind him, Sue slipped out of bed and pulled on her clothes. "Have you given any thought to what I said before?"

A gnawing sledge-hammer pounded his gut. "I've told you. I'm a fledgling. I'm not old enough to have a human of my own yet."

"William, you practically run this coven next to Danika and Mason. You could do whatever the hell you want."

Her words may be sound, but that didn't change the fact that she would never be the one he wanted.

"We have fun. That's all it can be." He turned to her. "If that isn't what you want, I completely understand and respect that. You are welcome to find a different member of the society to spend time with."

She stared at him for a moment and then sighed and shook her head. She climbed back onto the bed and leaned over to him. Her mousy brown hair hung haphazardly around her face, a testament to their recent intimacies.

"You know what your problem is?"

He shook his head. "Tell me."

"You're too nice. I've never met a guy who as nice as you before. Not pureblooded Vampire, or a bitten vampyr. Not even those mutated vamps or stupid human men are as nice as you.

You'd think that with the vamps and humans being lowest on the totem pole that they'd be the nicest people ever. But nope. It's you."

"I hope that whomever you end up with, they are much nicer than I," he replied.

If she even had a clue that every time for the past two months they had been together, he'd been envisioning her as someone else... No. He wasn't as nice as she thought.

He pulled on his slacks and sweater, ran his fingers through his hair, and stepped into his loafers.

"Come on. I'll walk you to the barracks."

She nodded and moved to the door. He held it for her, and they both headed into the hallway. They proceeded onto the landing and down the stairs to the grand foyer.

Selene and Neeman stood talking to Sinya and Lance. Selene cooed over Sinya's new baby. Seeing Lance wearing a baby carrier, and Neeman with a smile on his face were only the newest of strange sights changing his world. Most were for the better.

Selene caught William's eye and walked over. "Hey."

William motioned for Sue to continue into the kitchen area. "Evening, Selene."

She lowered her voice. "We still haven't found the rift, but we're getting closer."

"Good." If they didn't find the rift soon, all hell was going to break loose on Chicago- literally. The demon attacks were taking their toll, and it was only a matter of time before a vamp saw something and the news spread. They'd quarantined the area surrounding a park they suspected was the location of the rift. For now.

"Have there been any demon sightings tonight?" he asked.

She shook her head.

"Let me get Sue back to the barracks, and then we can all sit down and debrief before sun up."

Selene nodded and walked back to Neeman, slipping her hand in his back pocket.

William joined Sue in the kitchen and ushered her to the back door. They'd just stepped out into the fresh night air when his ribcage squeezed.

A strong, blonde-haired beauty with peachy skin and eyes like aquamarines strolled out of the barracks. She spotted William and Sue.

"Well, well, what have we here?" asked Evan.

"Good evening, Evan." Just looking at her made his throat dry like instant paint. His skin prickled and he tried to keep his hands steady as his desire spiked.

"Midnight snack at the local concession stand?" asked Evan.

"Shut up. You're just jealous." Sue walked past Evan.

"Jealous? That you let a bloodsucker drain you and have his way with you? I think not, bloodwhore."

"Stuck-up redneck. If you hate it here so much, do us all a favor and leave. Nothing's keeping you. Lord Danika said any of us that wanted to leave could." Sue pointed to the gate.

"That's enough." William strode forward. "Sue, please go inside. I need to have a word with Evan."

Sue rolled her eyes and stormed into the barracks.

Evan put on a falsely jovial smile. "Oh yippee, is it time for my 'be a good girl' speech again from the big powerful Vampire? I swear, William, you're like a broken record."

"How many times do I have to tell you I'm not a pure-blooded Vampire? I was bitten. That makes me a vampyr. Meaning I used to be human." He grabbed her by the arm. "Come on."

"Dude, let go of me." She ripped from his grasp. "What? Did you mix me up with Sue? See, I'm the pretty blonde and she's the plain brunette."

William clenched his jaw several times. "You shouldn't talk about her that way."

"Why, because she's your Lovermuffin? Vampyr."

"No, because she's a nice person."

"Oooooh, right. The world's just full of nice people now, isn't it?"

This wasn't going the way he had planned. He'd rehearsed this. He only wanted to have a civil conversation with her about helping them out. But he'd have better luck talking a tornado out of spinning than he would talking to her. Evan reminded him of a hurricane. All bluster and noise, leaving destruction in her wake. Why had he told everyone that her helping would be a good idea?

He blew out a heavy breath. Her blue eyes raked him up and down.

"I need to speak to you. Can we please go up to your room?"

"Are you joking? No way. I'm not like your blood buddy, Sue."

"Fine, then we can go to my room."

"Are you out of your gourd? Dude, I wouldn't be caught dead being seen walking into your bedroom."

Her contagious anger had William taking a deep breath to keep from exploding on her. "What's wrong with you? Why are you so mean all the time?"

Her jaw dropped. "Me? I'm not the one holding people here against their will."

"No one is a prisoner here. You know that. But if we let you go, you'd be picked up by slavers for sure."

She shrugged. "I can handle myself. I got places I can go."

He chuckled. "You think you can, but you have no idea."

"And I bet you're so tough. How many slavers have you killed in your fine silk sweater and shiny, expensive loafers?"

The memory of plunging a knife deep into the neck of a slaver who'd injured Mason raced through his mind. It had been a recurring nightmare of his over the last year.

"One," he said quietly. "Just one."

She snorted and crossed her arms over her chest. "Yeah, I bet."

"The night that we were captured. I killed him because he tried to to kill my friends."

She laughed again and then stared at him for a minute. "You're serious."

"It's not something I'm proud of, and it's harder than you think. So that's why you're better here. Even if you don't want to be."

"You're damn right I don't want to be here. You bloodsuckers think you know everything and that you're so much better than us humans."

"No, they don't."

"They?" Her eyebrows knit together. "You're one of them. Or haven't you noticed?"

Yes, technically he was a member of the Vampire Society, but he still saw himself as human in some ways. It wasn't easy to identify as something for over twenty years and then overnight be told you were no longer that person.

"Please, Evan. I need to speak to you. And we need to go somewhere that no one will overhear. The bedrooms in the barracks are cement blocks. They're practically soundproof."

She stared at him for a moment and then her posture relaxed. "Fine. But you better not try anything."

"I would never think of it." Well, he'd surely think of it, but he wouldn't act on it.

He followed Evan toward the front of the barracks. When he'd been human, she was the kind of girl who wouldn't have given him a second glance. The hot ones never wanted the geeks, no matter what the movies used to portray. Even so, he knew that deep down she put up a big show because inwardly she was scared. He couldn't blame her. They all were.

She threw open the door while looking straight ahead. A group of guys were in the kitchen making popcorn. They stopped when she walked in, but she ignored them and headed up the stairs. The humans stared at William and nodded but didn't speak.

One of the things William actually appreciated about being a vampyr was the respect. As a human, he'd never been respected, not even very well liked. No matter how hard he'd tried. At least if people didn't like him now, they still had to respect him and that was good enough for the time being.

He'd headed for the stairs when he heard whispers from the kitchen.

"Lord Danika really turned that guy?" asked one.

"Do you think he wanted to be turned?" asked another.

"I heard he saved her life and in return she made him a vampyr as some sort of honor," said another.

"What a traitor to humankind. To want to sell out and be one of them."

"Shut up. You'd do it too if someone offered, Matthew."

He continued up the stairs, and clenched his fists. A traitor? Was that how humans saw him? As a traitor to his kind? Little did they know that his turning had been an accident. All he'd done was try to save Danika's life by taking a bullet for her. In return, she'd tried to heal him with her blood.

He shook his head and sighed. He'd been wrong. Humans still didn't respect him.

He reached the upstairs hallway and walked down to the open door. Evan sat back on her bed, picked up a pencil, and flipped it through her fingers.

He closed the door quietly.

"I need your help," he said without pretense.

"What?" Suspicion clouded her voice. "What kind of help?"

"Can I trust you to keep something quiet?"

She put on a pageant queen smile. "Of course you can, because we're BFFs."

"I'm serious."

"So am I. Can we braid each other's hair and paint nails too while we—"

"Will you shut up?" William hated losing his temper.

Her mouth snapped closed and she stared at him for a moment. William pinched the bridge of his nose and blew out a breath. Why did he think this would be easy? In all the time he'd known her, she'd not made one single thing easy.

"Okay, what?" Her voice no longer held the mocking tone it had a moment before.

Their gazes met. After he told her, there was no going back. If he brought her into the circle of trust...

"Seriously, either tell me or let me get something to eat."

"You know Mason, Lord Danika's mate?"

She sat forward. "Dude, is it me or is that guy enormous?"

"He seriously is the biggest guy I've ever met." They laughed together for a moment, and in that instant William really saw Evan. But in a flash the girl vanished.

She began flipping the pencil again. "Okay, what about him?"

"You know he's not human, right?"

"He's a Vampire?" Her eyes widened. "That explains a lot."

"No, no. He's not a Vampire or a vampyr. He's something else."

Her eyebrows drew together. "Something else?"

"He's a demon."

She snorted. "A demon. Like, angels and demons and heaven and hell?"

"I'm not joking."

Her smile fell and she leapt to her feet, dropping the pencil to the ground. "You're serious?"

"Yes. And Selene is his half-sister."

"So, she's a demon as well?"

"Half demon, half fae."

She grabbed her hair with both hands and pulled on it. "There are fairy people as well?"

The tension in the air thickened. He wasn't doing it right. The worry and horror that now etched her features threatened to explode.

"Okay, why don't you sit down?" he offered.

"I'm fine. I can handle it. Just tell me. Are there tortoise ninjas too? Because if a talking tortoise sporting nunchucks walks in here—"

"A month or so back, before you returned to us, there was an explosion." William shoved his hands in his pockets.

"At the tracker compound, I heard."

"A group of demons caused it."

She closed her eyes and rubbed at them for a moment. He observed her quietly, waiting to gauge her reaction.

"Where did they come from?" she asked. "Have they always been here?"

At least she didn't explode. "No. The point is— and this is the point that I need you to promise to keep to yourself— there are more coming, and we can't fend them off alone. We need help. We want you to take us to the humans."

"Are you out of your friggin' mind? No. No way." She stared at him as if he'd sprouted a set of horns.

"We're out of options. We're sending emissaries out to all the covens to try and get them to side with us, but who knows if they will. And I overheard you saying to Selene that you knew of an enclave that had weapons—"

"Nope." She shook her head. "For all I know you're trying to get in there so you can get more slaves."

"Humans aren't slaves here anymore. You know that."

"Come on, William, I'm not an idiot. You bloodsuckers are going to run out of blood some time. You're going to run out of humans unless you allow us to have families. But if you do that, then you won't have a free-for-all blood-buffet at your beck and call. Do you really think Sue would come running back to you every time you snapped your fingers after she drives carpool and picks up her husband's dry cleaning?"

"This isn't about blood."

"You say that, but how do I know?"

"I'm not lying to you."

"All bloodsuckers lie. It's what you're good at."

He moved to her in a blur of speed. "I don't." Anger and frustration gripped him tight making it hard to breathe. "You can accuse me of many things— and you'd probably be right— but being disingenuous isn't one of them."

She blinked rapidly, and, in their close proximity, her eyes changed. Heat wafted off her skin as did the scent of lust. For as much as she professed to hate him, her body chemistry said something else entirely.

She laid her hand on his chest and the warmth of her

fingers spread through his sweater. His gut tightened and for a moment he thought she might kiss him.

He'd dreamt of the taste of her lush petal lips more times than he cared to remember.

"You say you don't lie, but you told me outside that you wouldn't try anything. Yet here you are inches from me." She pushed him away and stepped back herself. "I see the way you look at me. Watch me. You think I'm naïve? I know what you really want and you'll never get it. And that, William, is not a lie."

He should have known better than to think she'd want to help— even if it meant helping herself.

"You know what? Forget it. But believe me when I say if you utter a word of this to anyone, Danika will kill you." He left without another word.

She couldn't be trusted. As much as he wanted to believe there was good in her, she wasn't the one.

He jogged down to the first floor. The human men had gathered around a television to watch a movie. They eyed him as he passed.

His entire life he'd wanted to be included in a group the way they were. Sitting around watching a movie. Throwing jabs at each other. He'd never known that kind of camaraderie as a human. But now, because of Danika, he'd found a place he belonged. In the vampire society.

"Did you get her to put out?" asked one of them. "That one's a ball buster."

William stopped. He turned to the group. Matthew stared at him with a smirk on his face.

"If I were you, Matthew, I'd keep my comments to myself. I know for a fact that there are two males in Coven House who'd like any excuse to rip you limb from limb because of what you've done with their mates. Do you really want to add a third to the list?"

Matthew's smirk fell as his eyes did. The other guys snickered. As William pushed out into the yard, the men burst into laughter, jibing Matthew.

William stormed into the garden. For the first time it struck him just how much he'd changed. How much he'd grown. How much he'd advanced.

He was no longer human. And he was fine with that.

TO READ MORE GO TO YOUR
NEAREST RETAILER!

Dear Reader,

Thank you for taking the time to read *Rise of the Fae*. I love writing this series. It's been a lot of fun writing a series about a dystopian world told from the Vampires and now the Fae's point of view. It's fun writing so many different creatures.

If you enjoyed the book, please take a moment to leave a review on your favorite retailer. Your reviews make all the difference to an author and the success of books.
Feel free to take a moment and email me and let me know what you liked about the book or who your favorite character was and why. I love hearing from readers. It makes writing so much more fun when I hear from my readers.
VampWereZombie@Gmail.com

To find out more about me and my Upcoming Releases, Please Join my Street Team for Swag and Freebies.

I also love connecting with readers! Stalk me everywhere!
I look forward to hearing from you!
Rebekah R. Ganiere - BOOKS WITH A BITE

USA Today Bestselling Author

Rebekah R. Ganiere

Fairelle Series

Red the Were Hunter - Book One

Yanti's Choice - Free Fairelle Short Story

Snow the Vampire Slayer - Book Two

Jamen's Yuletide Bride - Book Three

Zelle and the Tower - Book Four

Cinder the Fae - Book Five

Belle and the Beast - Book Six

Gerall's Festivus Bride - Book Seven

Jak the Giant Healer - Book Eight

Olivia and the Giant - Book Nine (Coming Soon)

Eric's Wayward Bride - Book Ten (Coming Soon)

Wolf River

PROMISED at the Moon

CURSED by the Moon

RECLAIMED from the Moon

TAMED under the Moon

UNLEASHED with the Moon

FATED despite the Moon

FOUND because of the Moon (Coming Soon)

The Society Series

Reign of the Vampires

Rise of the Fae

Vengeance of the Demons

The Otherworlder Series

Kidnapped at Christmas

Vigilante at Valentine

Massacre at Mardi Gras

Hoodwinked at Halloween

Nightmare at New Years (Coming 2023)

Speed Dating with the Denizens of the Underworld

Thor

Loki

Fenrir

Tyr (2024)

Odin (2024)

Dead Awakenings

Kissed by the Reaper

Dracula's Bride

Rekindling Christmas

Christmas Lodge

Newsletter

To claim your Two FREE Books and find out more about
Rebekah R. Ganiere and her other Upcoming Releases
You can Go Here:
www.RebekahGaniere.com/Newsletter

www.ingramcontent.com/pod-product-compliance
Lightning Source LLC
Chambersburg PA
CBHW020515260626
47156CB00006B/2019